# CLUTCH OF PHANTOMS

CLARE LAYTON, having done a variety of jobs, is now a full-time writer living in London. This is her first novel of psychological suspense, but she also writes crime novels as Natasha Cooper. She is a past Chairman of the Crime Writers Association.

# POISONED PEN PRESS MYSTERIES
*published by ibooks, inc.:*

*At Risk*
by Kit Ehrman

*Beat Until Stiff*
by Claire M. Johnson

*Flash Flood*
by Susan Slater

*Clutch of Phantoms*
by Clare Layton

<u>COMING JANUARY 2004</u>
*False Images*
by Catherine Dunbar

# CLUTCH OF PHANTOMS

## CLARE LAYTON

**ibooks**
new york
**www.ibooks.net**

DISTRIBUTED BY SIMON & SCHUSTER, INC.

A Publication of ibooks, inc.

An ibooks, inc. Book

ibooks, inc.
24 West 25th Street
New York, NY 10010

The ibooks World Wide Web Site Address is:
http://www.ibooks.net

The Poisoned Pen Press World Wide Web Site Address is:
http://www.poisonedpenpress.com

ISBN 0-7434-7965-3
First ibooks, inc. printing December 2003
10 9 8 7 6 5 4 3 2 1

Printed in the U.S.A.

*For Mary Carter*

# Author's Note

Many people gave me advice, information and support as I was writing this novel. Among them are Mary Carter, Mary Corran, Tom Corran, Sarah Molloy, Hugh and Judith Robinson, and Susan Watt. I am grateful to them all. *Criminal Women*, edited by Pat Carlen, (Polity Press, 1985) provided invaluable insights into the lives of women in prison in the 1970s and 1980s.

This is, however, a work of fiction. None of the characters in it bears any relation to any real person, and, while Wast Water is, of course, real, the village of Esk-foot, along with all its inhabitants and visitors, is a product of my imagination.

—Clare Layton

# CLUTCH OF PHANTOMS
## An Introduction by Barbara Peters

My friend Daphne Wright is a real woman of mystery. Not in the sense of hiding secrets or sinister acts, but because she so loves the form of the crime novel—any novel, really—and has explored it under several identities: Kate Hatfield, Clare Layton. Natasha Cooper. I know many of you enjoyed her Willow King mysteries written as Natasha Cooper. Willow King is a severe civil servant with a secret double life as glamorous romantic novelist, Cressida Woodruffe. They allowed Daphne "to take a frivolously irreverent look at various institutions that affect life in Britain, and to challenge the lazy habits of those who make judgements about people on the basis of their appearance alone." When the duality of King's life came to a natural conclusion, a new character from the series, London lawyer Trish Maguire, stepped up and took the lead in a new set of novels that are more or less whodunnits with an ensemble cast.

Daphne, a longtime Londoner, was born in Berkshire into a large family and after leaving school made a career in publishing before taking up her own pen. She has a wealth of family and personal experiences to draw upon which she does to advantage in this edgy update of the British village mystery less concerned with whodunnit than with what happened, why, and what are the consequences?

It's no longer Miss Marple grilling the housemaids or the vicar coming to tea and spilling the parish beans. No, it's a darker, more modern tale, one that posits a dilemma that was, in a different way, explored some fifteen years ago by P.D. James in *Innocent Blood*. What is the family, more specifically, the child (or grandchild) of a convicted killer to do, what does he or she experience, when the convict is let out of gaol and back into ordinary life? Can it ever be an ordinary life, or is it one forever bent out of true, both the killer's and the child's?

You could look to a Laura Lippman novel, *Every Secret Thing*, that published in October 2003, where the Baltimore author explores the act committed by two young children that results in the death, the murder, of a baby, and what happens to those two young killers when they emerge from prison into adult life. Can they ever explain either the crime or its aftermath? Can they tell their stories? Will anyone want to hear them, will someone listen if they find the words? And even so, can such a sin as theirs ever be forgiven?

So, our story opens upon a tough young woman, Cass Evesham, one able to hold her own in stockbroking, take the piss from her male colleagues, make it in the City. But she's bummed by the cancellation of a holiday—and a lover. Comes a greater shock: her grandmother, Livia Claughton, a woman Cass had believed to be dead, is alive! More astonishingly, she turns out to be a celebrated murderess, a woman who's being doing twenty-five for her crime. And now she's coming out.

Moved into a safe house under an assumed name, Livia takes up the threads of a life forever warped by a crime, and by her punishment—one, perhaps, endured for a different deed than the one for which she was convicted, the murder of her husband, Cass' grandfather, and his lover. Can she tell anyone her story? Does she want to? Will Cass want to hear it? She has after all grown up with the lie that her grandparents were dead, killed in an accident.

All manner of questions and situations soon arise, fuelled by gossip and innuendo. Can Cass accept a new reality, survive snubs and harassment at work, not to mention the loss of clients. In Britain "respectability" is still God, the conventions (on the surface) need to be observed. It's a cruel society to anyone caught out, swift to snub and to punish. And it isn't just about the image, it's about questions like was Livia insane to do the deed? Mad with rage? Is such a gene, such a temperament, inherited? How can Cass think about children of her own, passing this flaw on? What kind of person, in fact, might she herself be?

And Livia, what's it like for her after years of isolation, protection, really, to be back in the public eye, even in so small a place? Can she keep her head, and courage, up? Can she keep silent or must she speak out? Will she accept help however kindly, or maliciously, it's meant?

To the isolated village where Livia and Cass dwell comes a third woman, Julia Gainsborough. Julia is an actress, daughter of the dead diva. Julia's career needs a jolt. She's starring in a cycle of revenge plays and here is the very publicity opportunity she needs. It's like a gift. Or is it?

What baggage is Julia carrying, what story has she grown up with? A mother who was a mistress, a role that got her killed?

And who else might have an agenda in all this? Aye, there's a rub....

*Clutch of Phantoms* offers you a smart, suspenseful read. In its glowing review, *Publishers Weekly* concluded: "Layton's insightful and provocative portrait of Livia's existence in prison and the life she leads after her release as she and Cass try to reconnect will engage and touch the reader. While this may not appeal to fans of traditional mysteries, memorable characters and an engrossing plot make this a first-rate psychological thriller." I think that any reader who enjoys the British style, the nuances of English life, and good writing, will devour "Clare Layton's" first novel.


—Barbara Peters
Senior Editor,
Poisoned Pen Press

# Chapter 1

'If you screw me on this one, Cass, you're dead.'

Cass did not react. Gary, even more irritated by her cool than usual, banged his head on the edge of his desk. Still she refused to look away from her screen.

'Let's hope the earth moves for you both, then,' Sam said from the other side of the row of desks. He was momentarily between phone calls and thoroughly enjoying the prospect of Cass's disaster and what it would do to her team leader. Gary muttered an unintelligible insult and gave him the finger.

Cass ignored their antics. All her attention was on the Reuters' screen in front of her. Her heart was thudding, and she could feel the sweat trickling down her back and arms under her shirt. But her face was calm and her breathing even; there was a small, confident smile lifting the corners of her lips.

Neither of the men had any idea of the willpower she need-ed to keep the smile in place as she controlled her fear, riding it, refusing to let it beat her. She was aware of Gary's anger and Sam's *Schadenfreude*, just as she was of the phones ringing and the voices that flung mockery like snowballs from desk to desk, but she was blocking them out.

Silence spread as news of her deal rippled through the room; then the voices started again. Jokes spluttered like sparklers all around her. The insults were riper than ever, and the laughter more manic. Even Sam thought he might last the day without stuffing something up his nose.

It was the biggest gamble Cass had yet taken, writing 15 million put options, at ten pence per option, on sterling dropping against the Deutschmark when the Chancellor made his announcement about the Euro.

Each option was for a thousand pound's worth of sterling, entitling the client to sell at 2.90 and buy back at 2.65, so that he had the chance to make a profit of nearly £150 million at a cost of only one and a half. If the client turned out to be wrong about which way the Chancellor was going to jump—as Cass believed he must be—he stood to lose his one and a half million. But if he were proved right, the bank would have to write a cheque for his profit, and Cass would have thrown away her future. She'd be out of Stogumber's without any right of appeal, and she'd never get another job like it.

She couldn't think about the future now. All she could do was watch her screen and keep her fear under control and out of sight.

'Cass,' said Gary, moving up behind her to look at her screen instead of his own, as though that could make it any better.

She did not answer, surprised he was letting himself sound nervous. It was bad for morale—and for his reputation. Letters appeared across the top of her screen: 'Chancellor's announcement expected 11:05.'

Gary's eyes flicked upwards so that he could see the clocks high on the wall above the rows of dealers' screens, finding the one that showed UK time. There was still a whole minute to go. Cass's gaze had not wavered. He could feel the heat of her body from where he stood, but for once he couldn't find the words to mock her for it.

When her client had phoned to say what he wanted, she had asked him to wait and swung round on her chair to check with Gary that the team was prepared to write options at that level. She'd had to ask him; he was the team leader and she was still on probation. Not for the first time, he cursed the system. It wasn't only her career she was risking; it was a fair chunk of the team's profits and probably the whole of his bonus, if not his job.

He'd have stopped her if he could, but only yesterday Michael Betteridge had told him to give her more freedom to deal. It was make or break time, he'd said, and the directors needed to know which before they took their gamble on her. But she was on Gary's team and her losses would be his responsibility. He loathed her for that even more than he loathed her for her cleverness and her legs and her exasperating aura of success.

Cass wished he would move away, but she couldn't spare the energy to say so. There were only seconds to go. Her hands were lying relaxed on her short black skirt, but inside her smile her teeth were clamped on a small piece of lip. Her eyes lost their focus just as the words at the top of the screen began to change. She blinked, once, twice, brushing fluid over her dry eyeballs. And then she saw it:

'No intention of taking Britain into Euro in first phase, says Chancellor.'

Gary put his hands on her shoulders to hold her down in her chair as they waited for the currencies to move. Sterling was still at 2.90 against the Deutschmark as the Chancellor's announcement appeared.

Cass wasn't sure if the trembling of the numbers on the screen was real or something happening to her eyes. Her teeth were still clamped together with part of her inside lip between them. She could not feel the pain. The figures flashed and moved upwards. And then upwards again. Gary's tight fat fingers dug deeper into her shoulders, through the pale-pink shirt that was plastered against her back. At 2.98 the figures stopped moving—and held. When they'd stayed rock steady for long enough to confirm that Cass had won, she let her teeth unclamp and felt the blood flooding back into the pinched flesh.

Gary's hands left her shoulders to punch the air as he yelled out her triumph, but she sat almost still, just allowing her muscles to relax and her lungs to expand. Her back straightened into its normal shape. Her breathing quickened slightly and she licked her lips.

'Shit, Cass, you bloody did it,' said Gary, wanting a more visible reaction.

'I know, but it's all in a day's work,' she said, her voice not even quivering, although she felt as though there was a washing-machine drum in her gut, churning and screaming on its ball bearings.

'You're a fucking psychopath, you know,' he said admiringly. 'Aren't you even a little relieved?'

'Relieved?' Cass shook her head. 'No. Why? I knew we'd be OK.'

As she slowly came down, she began to feel again, to notice the wetness of her back and the pain in her lip, to hear the excited buzz all round her, and to feel the ache of adrenaline withdrawal in her taut legs and hands. At last she let herself push the flyaway dark hair out of her eyes. She smiled.

'One great step for womankind,' said red-headed Sally, from the other side of the bank of screens. She was the nearest thing Cass had to a friend on the dealing floor. 'That was really cool.'

Cass grinned at her, then turned to look up at Gary. Foreshortened, his neck and chin looked even fatter than usual, and his eyes piggier. There were black hairs poking out of his nostrils.

'See?' was all she said, and even that was redundant. She knew he had seen what she—or any other woman—could do. They weren't wimps or girlies, and they wouldn't crack. There was relief in his expression, but disappointment, too. He'd taken against her from the start and had done his damnedest to scare her off with his sexist jokes and his savage criticism. But his bonus depended on her performance, so he had had to hold on to the cruellest of his impulses.

Cass had occasionally wondered whether that was why she'd been put in his team. Not that the directors would have cared about his attitude if they hadn't been slapped with a huge sex-discrimination suit from one of her predecessors.

'Not bad for a girl,' Gary said, trying to sound as casual as she, then adding, 'I suppose.'

A door at the far end of the dealing room opened and Michael Betteridge yelled: 'Cass! Get in here.'

She pushed her chair back, knowing it would ram into Gary's fat gut if he didn't move quickly enough.

'Fuck it, Cass,' he said. 'There was no need for that. I let you do it. I supported you.'

'Didn't realize you were so close, Gary. Sorry. Got to go. Michael's waiting.' She was flinging the black jacket of her suit around her shoulders. The phone rang. Tempted to leave it unanswered, she knew her client might want something more. She tucked the receiver under her chin and thrust her right arm into the jacket sleeve.

'Cass Evesham.'

'Cass, I…'

'Alan.' Her lips curved into a far sweeter smile. She took hold of the receiver again and held it comfortably against her ear, thinking he must have a spy at Stogumber's to have got on to the news so fast. 'How did you…?'

'Cass, not now. There isn't time, but I must see you. I…'

'You're going to see me tonight and all day every day for the next two weeks.' There would be hot sun and crisp sea and time to bask alone together without any risk of calls from work for either of them or demands from his ex-wife to pick up the children or write ever bigger cheques to pay for her uncontrollable greed. Cass couldn't wait; nor could Alan by the sound of it. 'What's the rush?'

'I'll explain when I see you. I've booked a table at the Blue Print Café for one o'clock.'

Cass had loved the Blue Print Café ever since their first lunch there and wished she could say yes.

'Al, I can't. Not today. There's just too much on. Can't it wait a few more hours—till this evening?'

'No. Be there. Don't be late.'

Even more than the Blue Print Café, she loved the urgency of his need. She loved him, too, cynical and hardened—and occasionally a little rough—though he was. Perhaps even because of that. The contrast between his outward spikiness and the depths of vulnerability she knew it concealed really got to her. She would have done anything for him.

'OK,' she said, longing to be in a place where she could tell him how much she cared.

'Cass!' yelled Michael. 'Where the hell are you?'

'Got to go, Alan.' She put down the receiver and slid her other arm into the jacket, buttoning it as she walked down the length of the dealing room.

As she went, noticing that her right kneecap still wobbled from the slackening tension, she heard her friends' and enemies' voices, deliberately audible despite the whispers:

'That was a grade-A killing.'

'Beginner's luck.'

'Sexy isn't she? Look at those legs. No wonder she got the job.'

'Pity about the tits though. Raisins on a pastry board if you ask me.'

'Seen them, have you?'

'Not yet, worst luck.'

Cass paid no attention. It was the sort of thing they all said every day. She rarely let it worry her, any more than they let jokes about big swinging dicks bother them. Today she'd taken a risk as big as any of theirs, and won. Nothing, not even skiing the sheerest, iciest black run had ever given her anything like the same high.

'Hey, Cass, you did great,' called a voice she did not recognize. She turned and smiled generally at the line of animated twenty-something clones in striped shirtsleeves, not knowing which of them had said it.

With the accolade ringing in her ears, she moved into the director's grey office and shut out the frenzy. There was silence now, and a calm that was no more real than her outward coolness.

'Have a seat, Cass.'

'Thank you, Michael.' She sat down, remembering not to tuck one long leg under her bum, and smiled confidently.

'I thought I ought to tell you that we've decided to cut your probation short.'

Sadist, she thought, watching a flicker of pleasure in eyes that were almost as dark as her own. He smoothed his already pristine hair back from his high forehead and exuded all the sleek satisfaction of one who has scoured every rust-like patch of weakness from his public persona.

'And confirm your job.'

'Great, Michael. Thank you.' Cass hoped her voice sounded gracious as well as grateful. Then, just in case it had sounded too grateful, she added: 'Salary?'

When he told her, she couldn't stop her eyes widening momentarily and wished she'd had more self control.

'Yes, I thought you might be pleased.' He looked amused. 'It should make for a good holiday. Going somewhere nice?'

'The Seychelles. We wanted somewhere that would still be hot.'

'Yes, it's a tricky time of year, October, but we couldn't let you go any sooner. Had to be sure of you, you see.' Michael's smile loosened a little and for a moment seemed more real. 'And now we are. You did well this morning, Cass. Confirmed what I've been telling the other directors ever since I picked you out: you've got a real killer instinct and a nice icy nerve.'

Cass just nodded; she'd already thanked him and she didn't want to gush.

'I've a feeling this is the beginning of something good. You could go all the way.'

'I bet you say that to all the girls,' she said, laughing at him.

'Aren't you supposed to call yourselves "wimmin" or something even more liberated?' he asked, sharing the joke with an air of equality that was new.

'You know what I mean.' She looked him in the eye. 'Are we talking main board director or what?'

'I don't see why not.'

She laughed again. 'But Stogumber's has never promoted any women beyond subsidiary board level.'

'I could say there's always a first time,' Michael started and then shrugged.

'But?'

'But I won't. Such a cliché, Cass. I've often wondered: why did you choose us? I know you had other offers from banks that have shown themselves much more woman-friendly.'

Hoping she looked as sleek and killer-confident as he, and not nearly as mischievous as she felt, she said languorously: 'Impossible challenges turn me on. Hadn't you heard?'

'Isn't that what they call sexual harassment, Cass?'

'Not unless I've been sexually harassed every day since I arrived,' she said tartly, remembering her second interview and the answer she'd given when one of Michael's co-directors had asked her how she would stand up to 'the joshing rough and tumble' of the trading floor. She'd told them that she always gave as good as she got and wouldn't faint at being called a tart or sue if someone tried to feel her up.

But she hadn't realized then how much she would come to detest it from people like Gary.

'It's time I had a turn, Michael.'

'Determined to have the last word, aren't you? OK. Just this once—as a reward for a good piece of work. But don't forget, it's only one piece of work. You've got to do it over and over again every day for years. Think you can hack that?'

'I think I might like it.' Cass licked her lips seductively as she stood up, laughed at his mock-furious expression and aligned her chair neatly with his big desk.

❧

She was five minutes late getting to the cool white restaurant with its low ceilings, excited clattering noise and spectacular view, and she still tingled from the morning's charge. Her job had been confirmed; she was about to start earning a vastly increased salary; and Alan couldn't wait even a few hours to see her. There was nothing else she wanted in the world.

He was sitting at one of the tables against the wall with his back to the room, and so she took a minute more to gaze at him and prolong the anticipation. At thirty-seven, he was ten years older than she, and a partner in one of the biggest of the City solicitors' practices.

He had a fascinating face, thin but lively because he was nearly always laughing. Someone had broken his nose years earlier so that it had a most endearing bend in it, and his light-brown hair was infinitely strokable. Cass's stomach lurched as reminiscent pleasure slid through her mind.

Still unaware of her, Alan lifted his tall glass of iced fizzy water and she saw the smooth, palely tanned skin of his long sexy hands and couldn't help thinking of the first time he'd taken her to bed. As he drank, she watched the movement of the liquid down through his throat and wondered how she would survive the whole of lunch without touching him.

That was the worst of restaurants without long tablecloths: you couldn't slip a foot out of your shoe and slide it between his sock and trouser leg, trying to pretend that your breath wasn't catching in your throat and your insides liquefying.

A waiter came to ask her if she had a reservation. She blinked and then nodded to Alan's table and walked towards it, waiting for the moment when he would turn and see her and his face light up as it always did.

He sensed her presence at last, and looked over his shoulder, frowning. He beckoned impatiently.

'Hi, darling,' she said as she sat down, dumping her shoulder bag on the floor and pushing her cheek forward for him to kiss.

He didn't see it, already signalling for the waiter to take their order.

'I can't stay long, Cass,' he said, sounding unlike himself.

'Nor me.' She had pulled back and was staring at him. It sounded as though the news about her job would have to take second place to whatever it was he had to say. 'What's so urgent that it couldn't wait until we go away?'

'We're not going.'

'What?'

'Mel's decided that she doesn't want you around any longer and so unfortunately I've got to pull the plug on our little jolly. Pity, but there it is.'

'Mel?' Cass's eyebrows were clenched across the top of her nose. 'D'you mean your wife?'

'Precisely,' he said, as though talking to a thick foreigner. 'She's put her foot down, so I think the best thing would be for me to pay you back for your share of the holiday and we call it quits. OK?'

'So that you can take her instead of me?' Cass was struggling to work out exactly what he was telling her as her head swam and her ears began to ring.

'That's right. Sorry if it's disappointing. But you'll be OK. You'll be able to fix up another trip easily enough. There'll be plenty of cancellations at this time of year. And you can take that bossy friend of yours. Sophie.'

'But, Alan, I don't understand.' Cass pushed her hair out of her eyes and looked at him, searching his face for clues. 'When did she come back? And why?'

'She never went. You didn't really think she had, did you?' Alan was amused, and his usual cynical grin had turned into something else, something that made her feel very young and not in the least successful. She looked away.

'You told me she had. Alan, you told me she'd abandoned you in the cruellest possible way, and taken your children, *and* pretty much driven you to the brink. What the hell's going on?'

'Oh, Cassie, Cassie, you're not telling me you took all that nonsense seriously, are you?' Alan finished writing her name on his cheque and took a sip of water. 'That was just to give you an excuse to give in to seduction, to make it all seem pretty and civilized. It's what we do in the big grown-up world.'

'But…'

'Now, don't pretend to be devastated. I know you through and through, Cass, and I'm well aware of just how tough you are.'

In that case you don't know me at all, she thought. I *love* you. And I believed every lying word you said to me.

'Two grand, wasn't it?' he asked cheerfully. 'Your share of the holiday.'

'Two thousand, three hundred and sixty-four pounds and seventy-five pence, actually,' she said, determined not to let him see how much she hurt. She stared at the bubbles rising in her Badoit and bursting as they reached the surface. In an effort to stop herself crying, she added crossly: 'Although I think you ought to add a hefty percentage to make up for the inconvenience. A travel agent would double the whole cost.'

She bent down for her bag and stood up with it dangling from her left hand. There was no point sitting for another hour or more, looking at food she'd never be able to eat.

'Ten per cent do you?' Alan asked, glancing up. He looked evil. 'Cheap at the price really for six months' fun. A decent hooker would've been much more.'

Cass wasn't aware that her right hand had moved until the back of it crunched into the side of his head with the full weight of her body behind it. Alan swayed in his chair, swearing, and grabbed for a handhold. There was nothing. Cass couldn't move. She watched him overbalance and crash into the next table as glasses broke around him and cutlery rained down.

All conversation in the room stopped. The atmosphere felt almost viscous with shock. Cass looked at Alan's tumbled body in its beautiful suit, aware that one or two of the lunchers were laughing, although most were dumbstruck with embarrassment. A sensation of crawling dampness on her hand forced her to look at it. There was blood on her diamond ring and sliding across her unbroken skin. Her lips parted as she understood, and she made herself look at Alan, who was picking himself up off the floor. His features were heavy with fury and there was a wet red line just below his cheekbone.

He put up a hand to feel his cheek and then looked at his splayed fingers in astonishment, exactly like someone in a film. He raised his eyes. Cass flinched.

As waiters rushed forward to help, Alan waved them away and shook the broken glass off his suit.

'What the fuck d'you think you're doing?' he hissed, grabbing a napkin and holding it to his cheek.

Still shocked at herself, but more furious with him, Cass was trembling. She knew she had to get out of the restaurant fast. Wiping the blood off her hand with a napkin, she grabbed his chequebook and ripped out the one he'd just written.

'So you *are* a bitch. I didn't believe them.'

She shook her head, too afraid of breaking down to answer back. As she stalked out through the restaurant, she tried to look as though she was still whole and nothing to do with the humiliating scene they had made between them. Some of the other lunchers were beginning to talk again; everyone tried to pretend that nothing had happened as she passed. She hoped no one she knew was there, but it was becoming hard to see anything very clearly, just a blur of white walls, stainless steel, black clothes and pinkish faces.

Not until she was well away from the restaurant and out of sight of everyone did she give way, leaning back against a handy wall, shutting her eyes and letting the tears seep out.

'Bastard,' she muttered, because it was so much safer to be angry than hurt.

Once she had started crying, she couldn't stop. Coughing, blotting her eyes and nose with a Kleenex, ordering herself to dry up, she knew she couldn't go straight back to the office. You didn't cry at Stogumber's if you wanted to succeed. And she did. She was a professional and she had a career to build. Just at the moment, that was all she had. Somehow she would have to pretend that nothing had happened and hang on until the end of the day. Then she could go back to the flat and be as weedy as she wanted for the next two weeks. There'd be no one to see her there. But until then she had to be tough Cass, hard Cass, clever Cass, *killer* Cass.

Taking a quick look at her face in the mirror she kept in her pocket to adjust her lenses, she saw that her eyes were like scarlet footballs and her make-up streaked and blotchy, like the paint on a cheap wooden toy that had been left out in the rain. She went into the nearest restaurant, where she knew the loos were between the front door and the bar.

Luckily there was no one else there. She ran a basin full of cold water, took out her lenses and laid her sore, hot face in it, keeping her hair well out of the way. Then she washed off all the old make-up, replaced it and dealt with her hair.

The whites of her eyes were less fiery now, and so far the lids hadn't had time to swell. She stuffed four sugar-free peppermints in her mouth, which would have to do for lunch, and went back to work.

❧

The only thing that salvaged Cass's pride was that she managed to join in all the jokes and not tell anyone what had happened, but it did nothing to help when she eventually got home with the enviously barbed good wishes for her holiday ringing in her ears. Banging the door behind her to make sure the locks had clicked, she let herself go.

The phone rang ten minutes later. Half hoping it was going to be Alan, wanting to tell her he'd made an idiotic mistake and couldn't live without her, she stopped kicking the sofa, blew her nose and picked up the receiver.

'Cass? Hi, it's Sophie.'

'Hi,' Cass said, hoping she sounded normal.

'Just phoning to say: have a great time in the Seychelles. God! I envy you. And see you when you're back.'

'Great. Thanks, Soph.'

'You sound a bit down. You OK?'

'I'm all over the place,' Cass said, suddenly remembering the morning's news. 'I can't take it in. They've cut short my probation and confirmed my job.'

'But that's amazing, Cass! You are brilliant.'

'Isn't it great?' She thought she must sound dreary beyond belief, but she couldn't say anything else. She'd make it right with Sophie later, when she could talk about what Alan had done. If she said anything now, Sophie would be sympathetic, and Cass wasn't feeling tough enough to take that from anyone. Even Sophie.

It was lucky, she thought as she said goodbye and went to shower, that there was no one around who was likely to be kind—or ask questions—for the next two weeks. Either would be unbearable. Her father was dead and her mother had moved to the States to marry again years ago. All her friends were expecting her to be away. She wouldn't have to talk to anyone until she'd got herself together again.

Turning on the shower and putting her face up to the water, Cass knew she'd be OK soon. A bit of time would give her back her proper tough self. That was all she needed: a bit of time. She could hack this, just as she could hack anything life threw at her. She always had.

# Chapter 2

A harsh burst of light flashed in Livia's face as she stepped out of the great door. It wasn't the sun; at six-thirty on a cold Saturday in October, that was only a faint promise. This was the result of at least fifty cameras pinning her down.

Why? she thought. Why now, after all this time?

Glad of the wig, beret and sunglasses she had never thought she would actually need, she tried to ignore the shouted questions, searching for a familiar face in the crowd.

'Livia, I'm here,' said a young man in indigo jeans and a Guernsey, pushing his way towards her past the few police officers who were trying to hold back the mob of journalists. For a second she did not know who he was. More cameras flashed.

I'll look hunted, she thought. But that's probably what they want.

At last she remembered the young man's name and put out both her hands, saying: 'James. Thank you for coming.'

He touched her hands for a moment and then relieved her of the plastic bag she was carrying, urging her towards the mass of people.

'How does it feel, Livia?' asked one complete stranger. He was dressed in skin-tight jeans and had greasy curls surrounding a thin face with a mean-looking mouth and avid eyes.

She blinked behind her glasses and looked away.

'Over here, Livia. Mrs Claughton, this way,' shouted another man above the general babble.

'What would you say to Julia Gainsborough?' One shrill female voice broke through to Livia, and she paused. She couldn't help it. James's hand tightened around her wrist, pulling her to follow him.

'I'm sorry about all this,' he muttered as he dragged her in the direction of a gleaming dark-blue car. 'I thought we'd convinced them that there wouldn't be anything to see until eleven, but someone's been leaky. I suppose I should've expected it, but I'm not used to this sort of thing. Thank God for the police.'

Livia did not answer. She was too busy trying to hide her horror of the questions and her fear of the shouting crowd that heaved and sweated behind the frighteningly few police officers.

'Julia thinks this should never have been allowed to happen,' the shrill voice went on. 'What d'you say to that?'

Livia's lips were clamped shut. There was a lot she would have liked to say, but not to this audience.

'Don't let them scare you. I'll get you through all right.' James's hand had moved higher up Livia's thin arm and his voice was tense. There would be bruises later. 'Don't say anything now. You can talk to them another day, if you want.'

'God forbid!' Livia had to run awkwardly to keep up with James, who was not only thirty years younger, but also a good foot taller.

'Livia! Livia! Tell us your side of the story. Now's your chance. You won't get another one.'

'Hey, Livia! This way. Julia can't do anything to you. Not now. Tell us what you think of her.'

'What are you going to do now, Livia? Where are you going to live? How are you going to live? Will you ever feel safe?'

'How does it feel to know Julia Gainsborough hates you?'

James pushed Livia unceremoniously into the passenger seat of his car, thanked the nearest police officer, slammed both doors and then revved the engine. Livia could feel almost as much aggression inside the car as out. She wondered if he loathed her as much as the journalists—and Julia—did.

The press were all round the car as it nosed forward. Even the police couldn't stop them banging on the windows, yelling questions and forming up into a phalanx in front of the bonnet. Livia covered her dark glasses with one thin, brown-spotted hand and stared down at her knees. She felt the car moving slowly forward and hoped James knew what he was doing. She flinched as a fist crashed on to the window beside her, and a muffled voice went on and on about Julia, but still Livia would not look up. She'd had no idea how much they still hated her.

The car began to pick up speed. Luckily there were no jolts or bumps; James obviously hadn't driven over any of them.

'There,' he said at last. 'We're through. You can look up.'

They were moving quite fast through the suburbs now, but traffic and idling pedestrians held them up at crossings. Only when they reached the motorway could James put his foot down. Livia watched the needle on the speedometer swing over past eighty, but when she risked a glance over her shoulder, she could see a long trail of chasing motorbikes and cars behind them.

'Why are they so interested?' she asked, her voice sticking in her throat. 'It was all so long ago.'

'We're not absolutely certain,' said James, looking at the road ahead or the mirror, never at her. 'Someone's been stirring them up. Presumably Julia Gainsborough, but we're not yet sure what she thinks she'll get out of it. It can't be just revenge. At least we don't think so. We're looking into it and we'll do whatever we can to stop them—get an injunction if we can. My father's taken it on as the one great challenge of his retirement.'

'Oh,' said Livia, who had more faith in his father than in anyone else. 'I ought to have been afraid of Julia, but I wasn't. She must be in her thirties now.'

'That's right. As I say, we'll do what we can, but it may be a question of gritting your teeth until they get bored,' said James. 'We think the house is still safe, so we mustn't lead them straight there. If I can't shake them off soon, we're going to switch to Plan B.'

Livia thought he was beginning to sound gleeful, almost excited. She wanted to know more about Julia and what she was like now, but she couldn't ask.

'It's important that you understand exactly what we're going to do. Are you listening, Livia?'

'I may be old,' she said in her hoarse voice, 'but I haven't lost my marbles. I'm listening.'

'OK.'

Glancing at his face, she thought he looked taken aback, which pleased her.

'So here's what we do.'

A few weeks ago his plans would have seemed idiotically melodramatic, but now they sounded sensible, admirable even. Livia started gearing herself up to do as he asked as soon as she saw the signs for the turn off the motorway, and hoped her old joints would cooperate. They didn't always.

She thought he was leaving it too late as he went batting along straight ahead at nearly ninety, but she had been well trained in passenger etiquette years before, so she said nothing; she did not even twitch her brake foot when, at the very last minute and without signalling, he wrenched the car over into the slip road, crossing the widest part of the pyjama stripes and missing the crash barrier by inches.

Livia admired his guts, but she wished her heart wouldn't bang so violently. She was not sure her ribs were still strong enough to contain it and pressed her right hand against her chest.

They had lost the first two of the chasing cars, but there were plenty of motorbikes still buzzing around them like insects, greedy for blood to suck. Slinging the car round corners far too fast, James drove into the centre of the ugly great city, cursing pedestrians and red traffic lights with savage violence.

At last he pulled up at the entrance to a multistorey carpark, just as a small tatty red car of a make Livia did not recognize slid in behind them.

'She's going to make a mess of getting her ticket and drop things that'll take ages to pick up,' he said with a satisfied smile at the sight of the press piling up behind the small red car.

The rider on the leading bike was trying to manoeuvre his heavy machine up on to the small pavement beside the car. The sound of horns punctuated his angry shouts and the voices of the drivers.

'She'll keep the cars stuck for ages, but they'll all send people in on foot, so we can't waste time.'

A yellow-and-black barrier clunked down behind them as they plunged into concrete gloom. James drove up a steep curving ramp towards the upper levels. He did not hit anything, but Livia heard metal scraping on concrete as they grazed one pillar. A bike's engine roared on the level below and there was the sound of skidding rubber. At least one of the hunters had got through.

'Are you ready? Robin's car should be round the next corner. I won't stop because I don't want them to hear the engine changing, but I'll go as slowly as I can to let you out safely. Don't shut the door. I'll deal with it. Move as quickly as you can. OK? Ready, Livia? Any minute now. Ready? There he is.'

The Rover slowed down as it approached a paint-splattered estate car with its hatchback up and the nearside back door open. A lanky young man with a shock of red hair and filthy overalls was lounging beside it, a bundle of paint-splattered dustsheets in one hand and an unlit cigarette in the other. His car radio was blaring out heavy-metal music. Livia did not think anyone would be able to hear anything over it.

'OK. Go. Go. Go.'

Livia tumbled obediently out of the car, hoping she would not slip and wrench an ankle, and flung herself through the open door of the estate car and onto the floor, gasping as her ribs crunched over the hump in the middle, bending her stiff knees so that she could drag her feet in after her. Luckily her shoes stayed on. She did not even see the young man move, but she felt heavy clothes falling on her and smelled dust, paint and something much worse as her head was jammed into the rough carpet. Even through the music that was so loud she could feel it thudding through her bones, she heard an idling engine and then a panting male voice call out: 'Have you seen a big blue Rover, mate?'

A nearer, younger voice with a Birmingham accent answered: 'The one with the blonde in the big black hat? Yeah. Went on up.'

'Blonde? Nah, black-haired woman. The bloke was blond.'

'Not in the Rover. And that's the only car that's been this way. Long blonde hair the woman had. And a hat. Bloke was fair, too, what I could see of him past her.'

'Shit. Must have changed her wig. OK. Cheers, mate.'

The hatchback crunched down as the motorcycle engine revved. Livia felt something else soft flung in on top of her and then heard the passenger door shut. A moment later the car began to move. The music was still crashing horribly. She should not have minded noise after the way she had had to live for nearly a quarter of a century, but she did. The filthy air made her choke and the grittiness of the rough carpet pressed into her cheek. But she did not move or speak, just lay there with the agonisingly hard hump under her ribs and the enveloping, painty cloths over her.

She knew they must be approaching the pay kiosk of the car-park because she could hear the shouts of the journalists through the music as the car slowed to a halt. There was a horn, too, sharp and peremptory from behind them. At last the car moved again and she felt it turn hard right.

Much later, it stopped. Then the cloths were pulled away and she smelled real air again.

'I think we've done it,' said the driver, who was leaning over to smile at her, one hand still on the steering wheel. 'By the way, I'm Robin Ludlow.' He no longer sounded like a Brummie workman. 'One of James's articled clerks.'

'How do you do,' said Livia politely from the floor. She shook his hand as well as she could and then pushed herself upright, suppressing a groan at the pain in her bruised ribs.

'Aren't you coming to sit in the front?'

'Are you sure it's safe? I don't want to waste all that effort,' said Livia, picking grit out of her grey eyebrows.

'No. I think we're OK. Four cars left the multistorey at the same time as us and all of them looked more likely to have you inside. But just in case anyone does spot us, there's a red wig under the seat, and a pair of old-lady specs. I'd put them on if I were you. Then you'll look like my old gran. At least that's the theory.'

'Sounds good to me.' Livia moved stiffly on the floor of the car so that she could pull off the black wig that had been covering her own soft short white hair. The replacement was an incredible dark-red confection that had been permed into a serpentine helmet. She added winged, black-rimmed spectacles and did not think anyone could have recognized her.

The young man opened the door for her and helped her up. As her rasping knee joints sent sharp pains shooting up and down her legs, she wondered whether James had any idea of what a seventy-five-year-old woman's body was like. Robin saw she was having difficulty and steadied her. Leaning on his arm, she looked around.

They were in the middle of the country. It had been so long since Livia had had a proper chance to see the English landscape in the autumn, that for a moment she just stood there, looking and breathing in the clear, cold air.

The sky was astonishingly blue, much deeper than she had expected, and the trees were a glorious mixture of golds and reddish-browns, not as spectacular as the New England Fall she still remembered, but much gentler.

'We'd better get going,' Robin said kindly after a while. 'James's instructions were quite clear. We're not to waste time because we've got to dump the car in the next town and go on by train to Manchester. Then I hand you over there to another colleague who's waiting with a hired car. He'll take you on up to the house, and James's father will be in touch as soon as it's safe.'

'It all sounds very complicated, and elaborate.'

'Had to be with the press on your tail like this.'

'Yes. Right,' she said, still appalled by the interest she had aroused. 'What's happening to James? He didn't tell me how he was going to get rid of them.'

Robin laughed. 'He's been having a wild time planning all this. I think he thinks he's in the SAS or something. He's really going for it now.'

'How?'

'D'you remember his father's secretary?'

'I think so. Wasn't she called Helen?'

'Hazel. She's always been one of your fans and she asked if she could help, even though she retired when Mr Bayley did. She's being your understudy in James's car at this moment. She was waiting in a green Mazda on the next level up at the car-park, wearing a long blonde wig with a big black felt hat in her hands. James was going to dump his car and leap into the driving seat of hers; then, as they got to the barrier, she was going to cram the hat on her head and start fiddling with her dark glasses and looking nervous. He's going to go like a bat out of hell back towards London and whip on to the M25 and lead them round for as long as it takes them to get bored or twig that they've been diddled. Here we are. We've made good time and I've already got the tickets. D'you want a cup of coffee? We've got nearly twenty minutes before the train.'

'Yes, I think we deserve some coffee,' said Livia, still breathless and wondering whether her heart would ever beat normally again. 'And even a bun too. You're all being quite extraordinarily good to me. I am so grateful.'

'No need. You're a client. We're paid to do whatever's necessary. But it's been great fun,' said the young man with a friendly grin. 'Much better than work.'

❧

For the first time that morning, Livia laughed aloud, revealing a sense of wicked delight that surprised Robin. She seemed far too old for anything like that. But then she had been pretty spry leaping in and out of cars, and not made any of the fuss he'd assumed he'd have to put up with. He was bothered because he hadn't expected to have any liking or admiration for her, given what she'd done, but in fact he felt quite a lot of both.

# Chapter 3

They were laughing at her, hordes of them, and pointing at her. She couldn't understand why until she realized she was naked and facing them all, quite alone in the rain. Alan was there with the rest, fully clothed and egging them on. A bell started to ring in her ear, as loud as a fire alarm. The people dissolved into a pinkish-red pool in the road. Alan was the last to go, leaving behind a sneer like the Cheshire cat's smile. And then it stopped raining and she wasn't naked after all.

Cass was sweating and trembling as she woke inside the tight cocoon of her duvet to hear the phone ringing. Her brain felt sodden. All she'd ever been to Alan was a free hooker. And she'd loved him. How could she?

As she turned over and pushed her face into the pillow, she remembered him slumped forwards on to her quivering body, mumbling incoherently about how much she meant to him. Could it have been pretence? All of it?

Eventually the noise of the phone became too irritating to bear and she rolled over to reach for the receiver.

'Jocasta Evesham?' said a completely unknown male voice.

'Yes,' she said, pulling out the vowel sound into a wary question. No one except her father had ever called her anything but Cass, or occasionally Cassie, and he'd been dead for nearly ten years.

'This is Jake Frensham from the *Daily Mercury*. Have you got any comment on your grandmother's release?'

'What?' Cass pushed the hair out of her eyes and felt them wet with tears she hadn't realized were there. She must have been crying in her sleep. She coughed to make her voice clearer. 'What are you talking about? My grandmother lives in Scotland; she hasn't been released from anywhere.'

'Not your father's mother,' the unknown man said impatiently. 'Your mother's mother. She's just got out. You must know that.'

'Sorry, you've got the wrong person. It's nothing to do with me,' said Cass with relief.

She put down the phone and propped herself up against the blue headboard, determined to get all the sludgy remnants of the dream out of her head before she got up. It might feel as though Alan had stripped her naked in public, but he hadn't. The dream had nothing to do with reality. The phone rang again.

'Cass Evesham?' said a different voice.

'Yes?' she replied, thinking with some sympathy of the namesake she'd never known she had. 'Who is this?'

'George Jenkins of the *Post*. I've been trying to get in touch with your mother, but I'm having trouble with her address. Can you give me a phone number for her?'

'No,' said Cass at once. Then curiosity got the better of discretion. 'What on earth do you want her for?'

He laughed. 'Considering her mother's just out of prison after twenty-four years, I'd've thought that was obvious. What are your views on the Harpy's release?'

'I don't know what you're talking about,' said Cass, before she took a moment to rub her dry, furry tongue against her upper lip. It felt like a piece of dirty old carpet. 'You've got the wrong Cass Evesham.'

'Oh, no,' he said, with a nasty laugh. 'No chance. You're the Harpy's granddaughter all right. We've had you on file for years. You and your mother, Rosamund.'

Cass brushed her left arm across her face, and felt the swelling in her sore eyelids.

'You're the only one of your generation and you work at Stogumber's, of all places. That's quite a laugh, I must say. Of all the fuddy-duddy firms to have taken in the Harpy's granddaughter! How are they going to take it when they've worked out who you are?'

Cass couldn't speak, but she couldn't put down the phone either. The laugh came again, this time with a hint of pity in it.

'You did know your grandmother, Livia Claughton, killed your grandfather, didn't you? And Flora Gainsborough with him.'

Cass said nothing. She had no idea what she ought to say. The whole one-sided conversation was surreal.

'Didn't you?' The voice had sharpened in interest. 'Sorry if I've given you a shock. How does it feel to discover it like this? What did you think had happened to your grandparents?'

Cass did put down the phone then, knowing it was madness; nothing excited journalists as much as a slammed door or a refusal to comment. But she couldn't help it. Her mother's parents had been killed in their car by a jackknifing lorry when she was three. It had happened in front of her mother, making her miscarry, and burdening her ever since with a load of neurotic fears that had made life hell for her and everyone around her.

Shaking her head to get the madness out, Cass shoved back the blue-and-white checked duvet and turned on the radio. It might tell her what was going on. She had known vaguely about the Harpy, of course; no one who could read or hear would have been entirely unaware of her, or of the judge who had given her the nickname by asking his jury to consider whether even a jealous harpy would have done whatever it was she'd been charged with. But the idea that she could be a relative was ludicrous.

'Home Truths' was being broadcast on on Radio 4, so Cass twiddled the tuning knob, searching for news. As she scanned through music, French, discussion and pop programmes, she remembered that she'd had no time last week to cancel the papers. Feeling as though the floor were made of jelly that might split at any moment, she abandoned the radio and went out to look. She saw the heavy black headline as soon as she picked up the news section: 'Outcry As Harpy Gets Parole At Last.'

Cass leaned against the wall for extra support and stared at the photographs of two women under the screaming words. One did not interest her much. The other was an intense, dark-haired woman, whose face was sickeningly familiar. Cass let her gaze drift upwards to the big mirror she'd hung to add light and width to the poky hall. Her black eyes widened beneath her fringe. How could she not have seen the likeness every time there were reports of the Harpy being put back on suicide watch after she'd been refused parole again?

Cass's face was years younger, of course, and without the lines that dragged at the corners of the Harpy's mouth and radiated from her black eyes. But the dangerous-looking cheek-bones and the vulnerable lips were exactly the same. And when she pushed back her fringe, the whole structure of their faces was identical, too. No wonder her mother had always banged on about how much a fringe suited her.

She let the hair flop back, just brushing the top of her eyebrows and completely changing the shape of her face. It was weird that it could make so much difference, but it did. She lifted it again, shuddered and let it drop.

'It's a genetic freak,' she told her reflection. 'It must be.'

The phone began to ring again. She left it, still staring at her face in the mirror. Could anyone, even a woman as riddled with anxiety as Rosamund, have left her only daughter ignorant of something like this?

And what about her father? Even when he had known he was dying, he'd said nothing about the Harpy. Cass thought of their last few talks before the pain and the weakness had made it so hard for him to remember who she was. He'd talked then about all sorts of things, and he'd begged her over and over again to look after her mother, whatever happened. Cass had been a few weeks short of her seventeenth birthday. Wouldn't the need to warn her that her grandmother was a killer have been urgent enough to distract him for a moment from his lifetime's task of protecting Rosamund?

The phone was still ringing. Cass swore. She wondered who else had her ex-directory phone number—and details of her ancestry—and whether she had ever had any privacy at all.

Alan. Her teeth crunched against each other. Could *he* have found out about this murderous grandmother of hers? Could it have been the knowledge of the Harpy's impending release that had made him dump her? He was a lawyer, after all; some friend in the law who knew of his affair with Cass could have warned him.

Breakfast, she thought, as she picked up the receiver, only to crash it down again immediately, before switching on the answering machine.

Her yellow-and-blue kitchen, which Sophie had designed to be as much as possible like Monet's at Giverny, was lavishly equipped for the kind of cooking Cass almost never did. Saucepans and sieves of every size and description hung from a rack over the cooker, and there were tools to deal with every possible ingredient, but there wasn't much to eat.

Luckily there was coffee and, miraculously, the milk was still fresh enough for cappuccino. Alan had given her the espresso machine for her birthday, and the sound of steam exploding through the milk brought back memories of what she had believed to be the perfect day. She felt her sore eyes seeping again and looked up at the ceiling, ordering herself to forget. He'd gone. He'd dumped her. And he wasn't coming back. She must sort herself out and get on with her life, or she'd turn into a mess like her mother.

Whatever else happened to her, it wouldn't be that. A bit of control was all she needed; control and something to eat.

An opened packet of 'Extra-crunchy' muesli looked promising, but the contents proved to have the consistency of old socks. Cass chucked it in the bin. She had a vague memory of stuffing a half-eaten Snickers bar in her pocket when she had been eating in the street and run into someone she knew. When she found it in the pocket of her overcoat, there was a fair amount of fluff and bits of old Kleenex sticking to the chocolate, but once she'd picked them off, it was fine.

With the sweetness coating her tastebuds, she sat at the tiny table by the kitchen window to read about the woman who might or might not be her grandmother.

The telephone kept ringing, but Cass let the machine answer, half-listening to the amplified voices of the journalists who left their names and numbers. Some of them offered money for her story; others just assumed that she must be longing to tell them all about her feelings. Cass ignored the lot.

According to the paper, the Harpy had once been a promising young architect in her husband's practice, but she had never achieved her potential. She had given up work as soon as she had a child, and had thereafter lived off the proceeds of her husband's labours. Unlike her, he had done well, so well that he had acquired the opera singer Flora Gainsborough as a client and gone on to win—presumably with her help—the most prestigious architectural competition of the decade: for an opera house in Southampton. Because of the murders and the resulting scandal, the project had been abandoned.

Flora Gainsborough—Cass tried to remember whether there had ever been any suggestion of a family connection with the diva. If the paper was right, the murder hadn't happened until Cass was three, and yet Flora Gainsborough's name meant no more to her than a CD's sleeve notes. She gulped some coffee and hardly noticed that she'd burned her throat.

The Harpy glowered out of the newspaper, while Gainsborough smiled seductively at her side. At the end of the caption was a note: '*Interview page 21*'. Cass opened the paper and shook the pages to flatten them.

I try not to hate her, but I can't help it.
I was seven when she killed my mother.

*Actress Julia Gainsborough on love,*
*loss, and the fear of revenge.*

Interview by Jennifer Ambro

Julia Gainsborough greets me in a bare, empty room at the top of the converted laundry in South London where she has lived for the past five years. The decoration is not so much minimalist as non-existent. The floor is of bare, unvarnished boards; the walls, off-white painted brick; the huge windows, covered in plain white blinds.

Gainsborough explains the lack of comfort, saying she needs to keep her surroundings plain to give herself room for all the clamorous emotions of her life and work.

But there is nothing harsh or cold about the woman herself. She is instantly welcoming, offering a bewildering choice of drinks, food, music, light and anything else that might make me comfortable. We settle for candlelight, which she says gives her the illusion of peace, a quiet Gregorian chant, and cups of hibiscus tea.

The china is as fragile as the atmosphere. Neither of us knows how to begin to talk about her mother. I decide to allow Gainsborough to choose when to begin and ask instead about her work.

With the help of an Arts Council grant, she has set up The Big Deal Theatre Company. She tells me that the company consists of eight actors, each of whom will alternate between major and supporting roles in a cycle of classic revenge plays.

And there we are, smack in the middle of the untouchable subject. When I ask about the choice of plays, and the timing of her decision to stage them, Gainsborough says painfully that she has reached a point in her life when she had either to explore the emotions left by her mother's death or suppress them for ever, accepting the damage they were doing to her.

With real courage, she has taken the first course, and it is clear from the words she chooses and the changes in her remarkable voice, that it has been far from easy. 'I try not to hate her,' she tells me, 'but I can't help it. I was seven when she killed my mother. How could I forgive her?'

I ask Julia if she has any of her mother's records. For a moment I think she's going to say no, but then in one graceful movement, she rises from the floor, where we've been sitting, and changes the CD. The distant chilly purity of the monks' singing is followed by silence and then, after a moment, by the richness and passion of Flora Gainsborough's agonizing Tosca.

We both listen, gripped by the music, until Julia can bear it no longer and stops the CD player. I still have pages of questions to ask, but one has been amply answered: if Julia Gainsborough can harness the pain she has shown this evening when she plays Sophocles' Electra in ten days' time, her performance will be a powerful one—and heartbreaking.

Before I leave, she tries once more to make me understand what Livia Claughton took from her, saying, with the kind of sadness that cuts right through you, 'You see, I've been lonely all my life.'

Cass let the newspaper drop, aware that the telephone was ringing again. It seemed irrelevant, no longer even an irritant. She felt as though she had spent her life sleepwalking across a filament of a bridge, unaware of the beasts that howled and ate each other in the chasm below.

# Chapter 4

The sun was well up as Livia's third escort drove her away from Manchester, and so bright that she wished she had not given the dark glasses back to Robin with the two wigs.

It did not last long. Ahead of them, as they passed the turn for Lancaster, loomed great rain clouds that looked like unpolished pewter baffles sullenly refusing to reflect any light.

'We turn off soon and then it could be as much as another hour and a half,' Simon Grantly said into the silence. 'There's a service station coming up. Would you like to stop?'

He's thinking about my aged bladder, Livia said to herself, touched that he should have bothered. 'I'd rather get on.'

They hit the rain almost as soon as they left the motorway, and eventually reached Wast Water in the middle of a cataclysmic downpour. Livia thought it was probably a good thing; otherwise the view might have been more than she could take. Even in the greyness and the rain, looking down from the hills over the lake was almost too much for her.

The trees were heavy with water, wide silver puddles lay on the slate path up to the rented farmhouse, and drips from the distorted gutters slid slowly down the slick stone walls.

It's as though the whole world is weeping, she thought, then corrected herself: no, it isn't; it's washing away the past. There's nothing left of it now. Nothing except Gordon. And he's the one good bit.

Simon had unlocked the front door and was calling her. The house was small and built of dark blue-grey stone. As Livia had asked, there was no garden to weigh her with responsibilities and backache; just the rough grass and the sheep coming right up to the small terrace, where on good days she would probably sit and watch the lake in the sun.

'James suggested I tell them in the village that you've been abroad for a long time and not very well,' Simon said when he had shown her round the house. He sounded a little tentative; perhaps he was embarrassed. 'I hope that was all right. They're good people down there; they won't bother you.'

'I hope not.'

'I've opened accounts for you at the Post Office, which is also the only source of food in the village, and the local taxi in case you want to go further afield for better shopping. Or for anything else. Now the doctor's number is with all the others you'll need beside the computer. I think I've got everything here that was on James's list. Can you see any gaps?'

Only Gordon, thought Livia. She tried to stop herself wanting him, concentrating instead on the house itself. It was an extraordinary place, full of light, even on this miserable day. There were full-length mirrors opposite and between each of the windows. Misshapen glass drops hung from bare black twigs in a heavy silver vase. There weren't any proper curtains, just squares of strange net-like fabric with sparkling strips woven into the mesh.

'It's perfect. How did James and Gordon know to make everything see-through like this?' Livia had been wanting to say Gordon's name aloud for a long time and be allowed to talk about him.

Simon did not encourage her. Instead he looked around the long room and shivered.

'This is how it was when we signed the tenancy agreement for you. Wet-looking. The owner's an artist, I understand, who's gone to the States for a year. I'd have thought you might want more colour after where you've…'

Livia saw him blush. She decided she wasn't going to help him.

'Has Gordon left any message?'

Simon shook his head. Before she had time to register the sharp hurt, he said: 'But he should be here within the hour, so he probably thought there wasn't any point.'

'Right.' A little warmth spread inside her, and she began to smile.

'Are you going to be all right up here on your own until he comes, Mrs Claughton? It's pretty isolated.'

'Lord, yes,' she said, wanting him gone so that she had time to get ready. 'Now, you probably need to set off. Or would you like some tea first—or the bathroom?'

'That, yes, thank you. But no tea.'

When he came downstairs again, still buckling his belt, he opened his mouth to ask a question, but Livia cut him short.

'I will be all right,' she assured him, not wanting to hear any of the obvious things about the first day of the rest of her life. At last he left her to it.

By the time she had stopped staring at the grey wet barrier between her front door and the hills, her hair was heavy with rainwater and she could feel the coldness of it dripping down her back and clasping her knees through the harsh wet denim of her jeans.

Oh, the luxury of all that space, she thought as she turned to go.

She considered leaving the door open, but that seemed exaggerated, mawkish even. Besides, it was very cold. Shutting the door and hearing it click felt so extraordinary that she unlatched it and went through the whole process several times.

Upstairs, she took off her wet clothes, dropping them where they fell, and had a hot scented bath. Afterwards, wrapped in warm towels of cloudy softness, she looked at herself in one of the mirrors, noticing all the marks of her seventy-five years: the few bristles that sprouted from her chin like the whiskers on a raspberry, the brown spots on the thin skin of her knobbly hands. She stretched them, then bent the fingers up, clenching them, thankful that she had no real pain today.

She wished she didn't look so ancient and shrivelled, but Gordon had watched her grow old, so he shouldn't be too shocked. Wherever the Prison Service had sent her, he had faithfully come every four weeks for almost a quarter of a century, staying away only once, in the month when his wife died. And even then he had written every week.

It had been extraordinary, the friendship they had built up with those letters. Sometimes she thought Gordon was the only person she had ever truly known or been known by. The only subject on which neither of them had ever written— or talked—was Henry and what had happened to him and Flora.

Livia dragged herself away from the mirror. Gordon would soon be here, and there were things to be done. It was so long since she had offered hospitality to anyone that she couldn't remember how to set about it. She ran through the possibilities in her mind, worrying about them all.

There was the fire to be lit for one thing, and some kind of food to be prepared. She'd start with the fire. That couldn't be too difficult, even for her.

A new white dressing gown was hanging ready on the back of the door, made of the same thick, soft towelling that smelled of expensive shops and the kind of absolute cleanliness she hadn't known for so long. She substituted it for the bathtowel and took the smaller towel from her head to comb out her damp hair.

The fire turned out to be easy, even though she was so out of practice, and the room soon began to smell lovely. Yellow light from the flames shot in dazzling bursts from mirror to mirror. She stood and watched, feeling the warmth and the freedom, and listening to the crackle. Now for food, she thought, encouraged.

Five minutes later, she was panicking in the middle of the kitchen, surrounded by raw food and cooked, frozen, tinned and freeze-dried. She opened the fridge again and told herself it was idiotic to be frightened of the piles of boxes and packets. At the front of the bottom shelf was a green plastic tray, covered with Clingfilm and a label telling her that the contents were lemon grass, best used by a date at the beginning of the following week.

The grass, whatever it was, looked like stiff spring onions and had very little smell when she poked a finger through the thin covering and sniffed, but it seemed to have cost a small fortune. She stood with the tray in her hand and the open fridge humming furiously.

Trying to think sensibly about the sort of food she might want to eat, she suddenly saw an afternoon in Paris, years ago, when the sun was so bright that the pale pavements of Montmartre had frilled at the edges and the dazzle had made her head ache. She and Henry had been sitting at a thin green iron table outside a restaurant, talking happily for once.

There had been a bottle of cold, sharp, white wine between them, and baguettes, and a whole downy white cheese. Livia could not quite remember what sort of cheese, probably not camembert or brie because they wouldn't still have had that soft white bloom when they were ripe enough to eat. Odd, the things she could remember and the others she could not— or would not. The look of the cheese was astonishingly clear in her mind, and the taste; the smell too; but not its name.

Once again she could feel the resistance against the knife as she pressed it into the thick skin and then the yielding yellow softness, which spilled out of the cut, freeing the rich, enticingly corrupt scent.

Shuddering, she abandoned the kitchen and the food she had meant to cook and went upstairs to find something to wear. She knew there would be something because she had asked Gordon to order a few basic clothes for her, even marking the kind of thing she wanted from a mail-order catalogue one of her friends had sent in to the prison after her own release.

When she opened the wardrobe, Livia felt a hot rush of fury that shocked her. Instead of the plain trousers, skirt, jacket and sweaters she had requested, there were rows of shimmering, luxurious silks and wools: jackets, dresses, skirts, even peignoirs for God's sake! She pulled out drawers in the two matching mahogany chests and saw that they too were full. The labels in most of the clothes were strange to her, but the feel of the fabrics, of cashmere, silk, pure crunchy linen, and richly smooth velvet, carried the same message as the expensive food that clogged every space in the kitchen.

Livia shook her damp head, trying to see the extravagance of generosity as Gordon must have seen it, a way of welcoming her back into freedom, giving her everything she could only have dreamed of in the bleak discomfort of prison. But she wasn't strong enough. She felt smothered, bludgeoned.

There was a pair of grey flannel bags on a hanger in front of her. She pulled those down and then found underwear, which was labelled 'La Perla', and socks and a black polo neck. It was cashmere. But at least it was plain.

By the time she was dressed, her hair was nearly dry. She brushed it again and was staring at the make-up that was laid out for her on the dressing table when she heard a car.

She took time to let the sensations that burst into her brain subside again. The car door slammed and wet footsteps squelched up the path, then stopped. Livia leaned sideways to look out of the window.

Gordon was there, looking up, water streaming down his face, plastering the fine grey hair over his head. But he was smiling the same smile that had blazed through all the dingy visitors' rooms. It was all right. She was glad to see him.

'You look like Juliet,' he called, 'sitting there in your lighted window, waiting.'

'We're about sixty years too late for that, Gordon.'

He laughed.

'I'll come down. There's a fire lit.'

'I can tell.'

She was puzzled and watched him laugh again, pointing towards the roof.

'The smoke, Livia. The smoke.'

Seconds later she had the door open. 'Come on in out of the wet, you idiot,' she said, reaching for the bag in his hand. 'Take your coat off and sit in front of the fire. You'll soon dry off.'

He dumped the bag, an old, cracked leather grip, in the porch and reached for her. Livia wasn't sure what to do as his arms closed around her thin back. She wasn't ready for this. His arms felt hard, tight: confining. Wrong. She made herself stay where she was and felt his hand on her head. Her neck seized up. She stopped breathing.

'What is it?' he asked with the sort of tenderness she'd dreamed of all through the lonely years.

She shook her head, withdrawing from him.

'I don't know. Would you like a drink?'

'Why not? I'll get them.'

She watched him walk to a cupboard in the wall near the fireplace. She hadn't noticed the half-concealed door. It was her house and yet he knew more about it than she did. He couldn't help that. And it shouldn't matter. She hated herself because it did.

'It's Campari, isn't it, Livia?' he said, turning with a large tumbler filled with what looked like cough mixture.

She couldn't speak. Memories of the taste filled her mouth. She hadn't thought of it in years: sickly and bitter and redolent of feelings she never wanted to have again. She shook her head. Her voice wouldn't work.

'I thought that's what you liked,' he said crossly, as though she was being deliberately tiresome, like a capricious child. But he hadn't asked before he had bought it for her. He turned back to the cupboard. 'But there's everything else here. What do you want?'

She didn't know. Gordon glanced at her again over his shoulder. He still looked hurt. It wasn't his fault. It wasn't.

Half the time she hadn't a clue how she felt either. Pushing her lips into a smile and creasing up her eyes, to practise for when he turned for another look, she said: 'Sherry. I think.'

'Oh, right. I didn't think you drank…Sorry. Silly of me. What sort? I got them to lay in fino, amontillado, oloroso, palo cortado, and even some moscatel.'

'Lovely. I'll have that. The last one.'

'The moscatel?' He sounded disapproving. When he turned to face her, his mouth looked as though he'd just bitten into something rotten. 'It's really better after dinner—or else very cold. Are you sure, Livia?'

'Yes,' she said through her teeth. The only thing she was sure of now was that no one else, ever again, was going to tell her what to do or what she wanted. Even if this moska-whatever tasted like washing-up water she'd get it down.

Gordon's face stiffened in shock. Livia knew why. She couldn't look at him. After everything they'd shared, she couldn't bear to see fear in his eyes.

'Here,' he said more gently. Perhaps he had understood. She looked back at him and saw only apology and anxiety. Her lips softened. 'If it's too sweet, let me know. I'll get you something else, Livia.'

It was too sweet, but now pride was involved. She watched him pour himself a whisky and soda and then turn towards the kitchen. A few moments later, he was back with a tray of small bowls. When he put it down, she saw olives, and crisps, and little biscuits. He looked up at her, worried, like a baby not sure whether it was going to get a smack or a smile. She would have wept if she'd been the weeping type.

As it was, she set about banishing the doubt from his eyes and the hurt twist from his mouth, dredging up funny stories, sad stories, anything to stop him asking her what the matter was.

# Chapter 5

The sweat was running freely down Cass's back and her muscles were pulling painfully, as they shortened and then relaxed in the rhythm she'd kept up for nearly half an hour, but her heart and lungs were still steady. Ben, who ran the gym, was keeping an eye on her. She could see he was worried, but she was working well within herself and the disciplined movement was helping to control the mess in her mind.

She had tried turning out her cupboards, black-bagging old clothes and everything Alan had given her, even the espresso machine, but that hadn't worked. She had gone on until the job was finished because she never left anything half done, but none of the sorting and chucking had helped. Only the half-pleasurable ache in her muscles could stop her thoughts churning.

If it had been just Alan, she could have coped. But to absorb what he had done at the same time as the news that she had a murderer for a grandmother was too much. Alan had lied to her all the time he'd said he loved her, but he hadn't been the first. No wonder she'd been such a sucker.

'Cass. Hey! Cass.'

She looked up, shaking sweat out of her eyes, to see Ben waving at her.

'You're doing too much. Cool it.'

Gradually she let the rhythm slow and felt the full shriek-ing in her arms and legs that she'd been ignoring as she rowed.

'Come on. Do your cool-down stretches,' he said. 'What's got into you? You're usually the most level-headed of the freaks who use this place.'

Cass tried to laugh and staggered as she climbed off the rowing machine. Ben's hand felt hard under her elbow. He led her to the mats in front of the full-length mirrors and accompanied her in the slow stretches he had taught her when she had first started coming here.

'So,' he said, when he was satisfied that she wasn't at risk of injury or lactic-acid burn. 'What's up with you, then?'

Cass shook her head, smiling. 'Nothing you need worry about. I was just angry.'

'I seen you angry before; it's not like this.'

She felt her eyes flash and wished they hadn't. After all, Ben was right: she had often come here to work off her frustration at Gary's taunts or her clients' refusing to do what she told them, and Ben had watched, monitored and only occasionally interfered with what she did to her body. Just as well. She knew how much it could take. No one else had the right to comment.

'Hey, it's no problem,' he said, backing away, hands raised in surrender. 'You don't have to tell me anything you don't want.'

'Right. Sorry.'

'Look.' Ben was pointing at the mirror in front of her. Cass looked. 'You're one sexy lady,' he said, 'and you got a great body. Don't risk it. You should know better. You're not stupid like them other freaks.'

Cass looked with dispassionate approval at her taut torso, square shoulders and long, smooth thighs. They'd get beefy if she went on rowing for too many years, but so far they were still OK, and it was the best exercise she'd yet tried.

'Yeah,' said Ben. 'Not bad. You look like you should have an Uzi over your shoulder and grenades hanging off your belt like grapes. But loosen up, Cass, and don't damage yourself.'

'I'll try.' She was laughing at his unexpectedly vivid imagination as she went to shower. An Uzi and grenades were just what she'd need if the journalists didn't let her alone.

Later, dressed in sagging khaki combat trousers and a short, tight, black sweater, she drove back towards her flat, stopping off at the local library to get herself a temporary ticket and look in the catalogue for books about her grandfather and Flora Gainsborough.

If her heritage were to be public property, she wanted to find out exactly what it was before she had to answer questions. She had checked her birth certificate before she left the flat that morning and seen at once that the journalists were right. There she was, unmistakably, the daughter of 'Rosamund Evesham, formerly Claughton'.

Cass still couldn't think why she'd never looked before. Or why no one had ever talked about her mother's maiden name. Except that they'd obviously been trying to keep it from her. Bastards, the lot of them.

The library wasn't a bad one, but it didn't offer much except a poorly illustrated book about the post-war reconstruction of British towns, which had several references to her grandfather in the index, and a general book about opera divas with a chapter on Flora Gainsborough.

Cass felt as near embarrassment as she ever got, presenting the books to the young librarian, but he showed no interest in them or her. He looked as bored as someone who had to stick cherries on cakes all day as he scanned the books with a light pen and pushed them to the far side of the counter.

Leaving the building, Cass had to suppress the urge to look behind her. The paranoia was scary. She'd have to find a way to control it before it turned her into a clone of her mother. She felt a draught against her skin, looked quickly down and saw that her trousers had slid down to reveal the top of her scarlet knickers. She hoicked them up before anyone had a chance to notice.

Half-way home, it struck her that she needed food. Long before she'd filled her trolley in the nearest Sainsbury's she was bored with the whole outing, but she stuck with it and bought enough to keep her fed through months of siege.

She saw a small group of people hanging about outside her building when she turned into the road. The way they readied themselves at the sight of the car told her who they must be and what they wanted. Without speeding up, she drove smoothly into the first left turning and looped round the block. No one followed. Although there was no access around the building itself, there was a yard at the back, connected by a narrow alley to a quite different street.

Cass drove slowly past the mouth of the alley, peering down it. There didn't seem to be anyone lurking there. She parked and lugged all her heavy bags of shopping from the car, between the huge smelly Wheelie bins, to the black-painted metal door. It carried no identifying marks or bells.

Occasionally one of the residents would bolt the back door from the inside as the building's insurers required, but most of the time they forgot. Cass felt the door give under her key and breathed more easily. It wouldn't be long before the journalists worked out that there must be somewhere for the flat-owners to put out their rubbish and found their way to the alley, but for the moment it provided inconspicuous access.

Once all the food was stowed in the kitchen, she made herself some tea. With a mug in one hand and the book about divas tucked under the other arm, she stood over her answering machine listening to the messages in case there were any that mattered.

All the callers were from the media. The sheer number of them would have convinced her that she was the Harpy's granddaughter if she'd still had any real doubt. But she hadn't.

It wasn't just the birth certificate that had convinced her. She was slowly letting herself understand how the news made sense of all sorts of memories, which she had never realized were weird until now. Looking back, she saw that she'd grown up with a sense of something awful that could never be mentioned, something that was too dangerous, too destructive. She'd never questioned the feeling, or even thought about it much. It was part of her life, like the importance of protecting her mother against the nameless threats that tormented her.

Cass tried to stave off the retrospective rage. There was no point feeling it now, and it was dangerous. But there were times when she couldn't stop her teeth grinding or her hands balling into fists.

She cleared the tape, without answering any of the messages, and took the book and the tea to the sofa. Emerging at the end of the chapter to find that the liquid in her mug was scummy and cold, Cass was puzzled.

Flora Gainsborough had had battalions of admirers. The photographs confirmed her luscious beauty, and the eulogies described her voice as superb, 'full of affecting sensibility', whatever that meant, as well as 'unmatched musicality'. And yet she seemed to have used everyone who came anywhere near her and had never had a single unselfish thought for anyone.

As soon as she had gained something of a reputation at Covent Garden and was beginning to earn a reasonable amount, she had ditched her husband, who had done a lot to help her get that far. Dragging their year-old daughter with her to Los Angeles, Flora had then enticed a famous film producer away from his wife, into her bed, through the divorce courts, and subsequently into a registry office, or whatever they had for weddings in LA. As a wedding present he had cast her as the lead in his next big movie.

The film had had an extraordinary success when it was released at the end of the sixties. Even Cass had seen reruns on Saturday afternoon television and been moved by it. Flora had proved she could act as well as sing, but neither the success nor the money the film brought her had stopped her wanting more. The director's next big film with her in it had flopped spectacularly and she was on the first flight home, five years after she'd left.

Back in London, according to the book, Flora had revealed her longstanding distaste for the shallowness of the movie world and her discovery of the importance of staying true to your gifts and your roots. The author's quotations from the galaxy of British writers and critics who had welcomed her back made it sound as though she had been a cross between Winston Churchill and Florence Nightingale, returning to the country of her birth to save it from the barbarian hordes who were threatening to rape all the women and roast the babies.

'Cow!' Cass muttered, assuming her grandfather had joined the long queue of Flora's passionate admirers.

She was surprised to find herself nearly ready to sympathize with her murderous grandmother, and thought she'd better find out a bit more before she got herself in too deep. There would be news on television in five minutes.

After the first lead-in about the upcoming world economic crisis, her own face, aged by fifty years, appeared on the screen, before fading into footage of a slight figure emerging from a fortress-like doorway to face dozens of flashing cameras. The newsreader's unctuous voice sharpened as he read from the autocue:

> 'Livia Claughton, who murdered her husband and the opera singer Flora Gainsborough twenty-five years ago, was released from prison this morning. Her current whereabouts are unknown and her family are refusing to make any statements. A spokesman for her solicitor has said that she deeply regrets the pain her action caused and that she needs to be alone to come to terms with it in whatever time remains to her. She was seventy-five two months ago.'

'And you don't think she deserves to have more than two minutes,' Cass muttered at the unresponsive face of the harmless newsreader. She turned off the television and wondered what to do next.

❧

By Sunday afternoon Cass was almost screaming with frustration. Some of the journalists were still hanging about outside, the phone had never stopped ringing and all the papers had been stuffed with her grandmother's story. She had drafted several furious e-mails to her mother, asking why she had been lied to all her life, but none of them had been fit to send.

She was back at her screen, having another go soon after seven, when she heard a new voice being broadcast from the answering machine, a quite different one from any of the journalists': much older, more tentative and not at all demanding. She listened more closely.

'Miss Evesham, I do hope you will forgive the intrusion of my ringing you like this. My name is Gordon Bayley. I used to be your grandmother's solicitor. Now that I'm retired, we're just friends.'

So the Harpy has friends, has she? Cass thought, pleased to hear it.

'I am very concerned for her. We had hoped to get her away without any publicity yesterday, but we failed. I can understand why you have chosen not to answer your telephone, but I should very much like to speak to you when you feel up to it.' There was a pause, and then the voice dictated a phone number.

Since it was Sunday, Cass had no way of checking his bona fides, but there didn't seem much point. If he were a journalist, he'd ask questions, which she wouldn't answer. If he weren't, he might be useful. She phoned him.

He soon convinced her that he was exactly who he'd said he was, and he sounded sad but not surprised that Cass had known nothing about her grandmother.

'I wish Rosamund could have seen her way to being less unforgiving,' he said. 'I can understand it, but it was cruel.

You know, she's never answered a single one of Livia's letters and she's refused all the money Livia's ever tried to give her.'

'Money? How does she have any money to give? She's been in prison for a quarter of a century.' Cass thought of all the times Rosamund had done without something she had obviously wanted, and the efforts she had made to ensure that Cass had as much as her schoolfriends.

'Prison has nothing to do with it,' Gordon Bayley said irritably. He hesitated, then added with a deliberation Cass didn't entirely understand: 'There's quite a lot of money, you know. Your grandfather put everything in Livia's name when they married, in case he should ever face a professional negligence claim his insurers refused to pay.'

'Smart move.'

'Yes. This way, even if he lost his practice, he would never lose the money or the house.'

'Unless his wife left him,' Cass said drily, 'and took it all with her.'

'I don't suppose that possibility would ever have occurred to Henry Claughton. Or to Livia, come to that.'

'Oh.'

There was a pause, as though he were waiting for Cass to ask why not, but she wasn't ready for that. Eventually he went on: 'But it did mean that there was no question of her having profited from her crime. It was hers anyway.'

Cass's sympathies began to move towards Rosamund. What must it be like to know that your mother had killed your father and then waltzed off with all his money?

'There's so much you need to know,' Gordon Bayley was saying. 'I've been wondering: would you let me give you some dinner tonight so that I can begin to tell you some of it?'

'I'm not sure...'

'I realize you must be very busy.'

'Well, not really, as it happens,' Cass said, facing the twelve empty days that stretched ahead of her before she could go back to work.

Work, she thought as her stomach lurched. I'll have to warn them. But what the hell do I say?

'Why not, Mr Bayley? Yes. Yes, thank you.'

'I'd ask you to the Garrick except that it's not open on Sundays. Is there somewhere you would particularly like to go?'

Cass thought of the restaurants she liked and shuddered. They would probably be full of people she knew, even on a Sunday.

'Why don't you choose, Mr Bayley? Somewhere quiet, where we can talk without being overheard—or recognized.'

'Do you like fish? There's an excellent fish restaurant I know well near Leicester Square. It's highly civilized and no one will disturb us there. Hold on for a moment and I'll give you the precise address.'

❧

The man who got to his feet as the waiter escorted Cass to his table an hour later was obviously in his seventies, but with his quirky face, good colour, and barely receding hairline he looked pretty well-preserved. It wasn't until she was close enough to shake hands that Cass could see the deep lines that ran between his nose and chin and the broken veins that made his face so pink. He also looked exhausted, but he set about entertaining her in style.

Cass felt as though she was in some expensive, beautifully upholstered antique car that moved in a stately fashion without any effort on her part. In such company, sitting in the dark-panelled room staffed with middle-aged waiters dressed in short white jackets over their black trousers, she felt impelled to order food to match and asked for potted shrimps and grilled Dover sole.

Gordon Bayley applauded her choice and asked whether she would prefer to drink white burgundy or something from the Loire. When everything had been ordered and the wine displayed, opened, tasted and poured with considerable ceremony, and they were alone again, he asked Cass about her work.

The last things she wanted to talk about now were puts and calls and currency fluctuations. She had an urge to tell him to get on with what they'd come for. But she knew he was doing his best and she tried to match it. As she ate the last of her brown buttery shrimps, she put down her knife and fork and, ignoring his last question, said:

'What's she like? My grandmother I mean.'

He looked across the candle, his face unreadable. After a moment he swallowed his mouthful and said simply: 'You.'

'No. I don't mean her face. I know I've inherited that. I'm not blind. I meant her character.'

'The answer's the same,' he said with a quizzical, slightly unhappy smile. He poured more Chablis into her glass. 'You have her brains, her courage, a lot of her humour, and I'm inclined to think that you might also have some of her largeness of spirit.'

And her violence? Cass asked silently, trying to keep her face politely attentive. Gordon Bayley seemed to think she ought to feel complimented by the comparison.

'Have you seen her since she got out?' she asked abruptly. He nodded. 'Where is she?'

'In the north,' he said, too sophisticated to whisper, but careful not to be overheard. 'In fact I stayed with her last night.'

'No wonder you look so tired.'

He nodded. 'It is a fairly long drive, and I didn't sleep too well while I was there.'

Cass drank some of the cold, sharp wine to give herself a thinking space. The ground had turned to jelly again.

'May I ask why you didn't stay longer?' she said, trying to smile. 'You can't have gone all that way meaning to come back so soon.'

'It was difficult.' A dark line appeared between his eyebrows as he frowned.

'Why?'

He looked at her as though he suspected her of prurience. She watched him gravely. Something in her face must have reassured him because his own softened.

'I still don't know. All I'm sure of is that I was annoying her.'

In that case, I'm not surprised you got yourself out of danger at the first opportunity, thought Cass. She felt as though invisible hands were squeezing the flesh against her cheekbones.

'And so that's why I've thrust myself on you like this.'

'Me?'

'Yes. She needs someone with her.' His voice was brisk. Cass wondered whether it was because he was used to giving orders that were never questioned. Or maybe he was just embarrassed.

'I'm sending her a dog, a puppy, but that's just for companionship. It won't help her get to grips with life in the outside world. She has no idea yet how little she knows or how difficult it's going to be. She needs help, human help, and you're the only kind I can imagine being acceptable to her now.'

Cass didn't answer. She couldn't. When she'd got her breath back, she picked up her glass and drank. Putting the glass back exactly where its weight had dented the tablecloth, she said: 'And what about me? What makes you think I'm prepared to have anything to do with a woman who might kill me?'

'Oh, don't be ridiculous!' he said, dropping his fork on his plate with enough force to break it. Cass raised her eyebrows.

'Wasn't that why you left? Didn't you think she was dangerous?'

'No, it bloody well wasn't.' She wondered whether he'd ever been in the army. 'I got out because I was making her unhappy. I see you're all Rosamund's, in spite of your looks. I shouldn't have troubled you.'

Cass seemed to be making a habit of walking out of restaurants, angry and unhappy, and leaving even angrier men behind. This time she waited long enough to thank him for dinner. He told her stiffly, clearly lying, that it had been a pleasure and then added that, if she changed her mind about her grandmother, she had only to ring him and he'd make the arrangements for her.

# Chapter 6

At nine o'clock on Monday morning at the small branch office of the Probation Service in Whitehaven, Colin Whyle was psyching himself up for his first meeting with the Harpy. She was going to be the first really high-profile client in his sole charge, and he was determined to make a success of her.

He had read the file over and over again, trying to put himself in her place so that he could understand what drove her and how she was likely to react to freedom. He knew her psychiatric reports by heart, and he had poured over the bleak conclusions of her various unsuccessful parole hearings. Until now, her uncontrollable temper and refusal to accept full responsibility for her crimes had been thought to make her too dangerous to release.

Colin had had several talks with the two governors who had known her best. One loathed her still, while the other confessed to a certain respect—which she admitted she herself didn't entirely understand—and even some affection. That had come partly, the governor had explained to Colin over the phone, from watching the patience Livia had shown when she was teaching a group of illiterate inmates to read, and partly from the way she tended to rush to the defence of the latest victim whenever the wing bullies really got going.

That had given Colin the clue he needed. Now, after discussions with the local police and the relevant social workers, he had decided to match up Livia, who could teach and needed an occupation, with another client, an eleven-year-old boy, who had exhausted the patience of everyone who had so far tried to help him. But Colin's boss was being difficult.

'Now, Meg,' he said, smiling kindly, as though he knew she couldn't help it, 'I know lifers out on licence aren't supposed to work with children, but this is different. Livia has no friends up here, no...'

'Then why the *hell* did she choose to come?' Meg asked, not caring how unsympathetic she sounded.

They had more than enough problems of their own without adding an impossibly difficult client, who already appeared to be exercising an exasperating fascination over Colin. They did that, some of these notorious lifers whose crimes took on a perverse kind of glamour over the years. But she wouldn't have thought Colin was the type to succumb. If she'd realized he was so susceptible, she'd have made sure the Harpy's case had been taken by someone else, even if it had meant recruiting a new officer and getting Colin shifted to another district. Too late now, though. They'd have to make the best of it.

Colin was snuffling in protest. For the fiftieth time, Meg thought he looked exactly like a hedgehog, with his upturned nose and his innocently bright eyes peering out of a face that was almost overwhelmed by long, prickle-coloured hair, moustache and beard.

'Because she used to come here for holidays as a child with her mother's mother,' he said with the kind of patience that set Meg's teeth on edge. 'Her life was bearable then. It sounds as though it was almost the only time she was ever happy.'

'Well, I wish her wretched grandmother had taken her to Bognor then. She's going to be appallingly isolated up here, you know, and bored. I doubt if she'll have the resources to deal with either. You do realize she's a serious suicide risk, don't you, Colin?'

'Not all the psychiatrists agree with that.' He was pouting, which made Meg want to stick pins into him.

'Shrinks never do agree. But take it from me: the risk is real.' She sighed and reached for the file. 'Hasn't she got any family?'

'Not a lot. Her husband's relations won't have anything to do with her,' Colin said, keeping his hands firmly on his file.

'Hardly surprising since she killed him,' Meg said, giving up the attempt to get hold of it. 'What about her own side?'

'There's a widowed daughter, now living in the States under her second husband's name, and a granddaughter in London. The rest are dead—or unrecorded.'

A faint perkiness tweaked Meg's lips. 'A granddaughter? Good. How old?'

'Twenty-seven.'

'Better and better. And what sort of person is she? Do we know?'

'Single. Successful. City hotshot.' Colin was riffling through his file. 'Yes, here we are. She hasn't had any contact with her grandmother since the crime, or any of her grandfather's family. She was three when it happened.'

'Damn. She's not going to be much good. So what about friends? Who's supporting the client? You did tell me, but I've forgotten.'

'Her ex-solicitor, now retired. Gordon Bayley. He's the one who's organized the house and has power of attorney over her money. There's a fair amount of that, I gather.'

Meg didn't like that one little bit, which surprised Colin. As far as he was concerned, the fewer people who made calls on the Social Services' budget, the better. It was stretched to tearing point as it was.

'Meg, this is the right solution, at least to begin with. Believe me. It may not be perfect, but it tackles two of our major problems. And someone has to deal with Bobby.'

Meg stared at him. She felt cross enough to stop a charging warthog in its tracks and hoped it showed.

'Have you thought about the publicity?' she said when Colin didn't react.

He shrugged.

'Think what a good story it'll make: "Probation Service offers up delinquent eleven-year-old to the Harpy". "Another classic cock-up in Social Services".'

'Why should the press get to know anything about it?'

Meg sighed. Could he be quite as terrifyingly innocent as he pretended?

'They always do. You know that. And if Bobby comes to some kind of harm—even if it's nothing to do with her— we'll be blamed.'

The very thought of the potential scandal made Meg feel ill. There wasn't anything the media liked better than crucifying probation officers or social workers whose misjudgement of their clients' capabilities led to death or violence. Meg did not want her own, so-far unblemished, record smirched. Retirement was only seven years off. She wanted to get there with her reputation and her pension intact.

'Look, Meg, with Bobby's record and her age, any harm is much more likely to come to her,' Colin said, as though that made it any better. 'Look at what he's done: arson, theft, possession of cannabis, joyriding, carrying a knife to school, wounding a teacher…'

'Another very good reason not to go down such a dangerous road. Colin, be reasonable: do you think it's sensible to send a thug like that for lessons with a physically fragile woman in her seventies?'

'Yes.'

His obstinacy had surprised her in the days before she had become acquainted with the ruthless mind that lived in his squashy body.

'What about his foster parents?' she asked, in a last-ditch attempt to avoid taking the lunatic risk. 'How will they take it?'

'They'll be dead grateful to anyone who can do anything with him, and there's no need for them to know who Livia is. She's going to be "Mrs Davidson" up here. Anyway, since Bobby's last exclusion, there's no school to take him. They're at their wits' end. All I need is your approval, Meg, and then I can get going.'

Colin looked at the enormous bright-green plastic dinosaur watch he wore on his pudgy wrist, perhaps as a joke, or perhaps because he had never noticed how silly it looked.

'And I ought to start now, if I'm not to be late for her. It's a good forty-minute drive. She's expecting me.'

'You'll need her agreement, too. What makes you think she'll take Bobby on?'

Colin tucked the file under his arm, as though he knew he'd won at last. He looked like a happy baby after a feed, ready for a burp, but not in pain yet.

'If you had an only daughter who'd deserted you, wouldn't you have been dreaming of a son? And if you had a record of violence—and probably an unshakeable belief that it was you who'd been the real victim—wouldn't you be tempted to save a boy like Bobby? I've got an angelic photograph to show her.'

Meg could never decide whether to admire or detest Colin's manipulative tendencies.

'I suppose if you can get her to agree,' she said at last, 'then who am I to object? And if you're really prepared to drive the forty-mile round trip twice a day.'

He smirked infuriatingly, but Meg kept her temper.

'Colin?'

He nodded, scratching his beard with a sound like a file rubbing against rusty metal.

'Don't forget that she's been inside for nearly twenty-five years. She's going to be completely discombobulated. She won't have any patience. She won't know how to take responsibility for herself, still less for anyone else; she'll be lonely, incompetent and very, very angry. If you do this thing, you're going to have to keep an incredibly close eye on her.'

He shrugged again. Meg tried to make him understand.

'She'll be right on the edge in any case, and if she topples over, you'll have to be there to catch her—her, or whoever her new victim is. OK?'

'Sure. But, Meg, I honestly think she and Bobby are bright enough to see what they'll each get out of this, and value it.'

Meg felt exhausted just listening to his ludicrous optimism. She gave in. 'Well, watch them both, Colin. OK? And whatever you do, don't give Bobby any idea that Livia has anything beyond the basic pension. Let him think that she's poor as poor. We do *not* want him digging his thieving little fingers into her purse and setting off that temper of hers. OK?'

'Yes. That's a good point, Meg.' Colin took out the idiotic little silver propelling pencil he carried everywhere with him and solemnly wrote her instructions on the inside cover of the file. She wished she knew whether he was taking the piss or merely a little mad.

She watched him go, feeling sorrier for the Harpy than she should have. Anyone faced with Colin had her profound sympathy. Now she came to think of it, he was more like a jellyfish than a hedgehog. He didn't so much roll up into a defensive prickly ball as float away as you tried to grasp him, only to leave stinging tendrils wafting at you through the waves.

❧

Livia was planning a long late breakfast in her dressing gown, listening to the radio. Since Gordon had left, she had learned to use the espresso machine and revelled in the strong, fragrant coffee it produced. She planned to drink this morning's cupful with a reheated croissant from the freezer.

The microwave still worried her, although there had been one at her last—open—prison, but she had discovered that the ordinary oven was fine for dealing with frozen bread.

She wished Gordon were still here. She knew why he'd gone. And she'd been relieved when it had happened. But she missed him. And she was angry with him. All he'd had to do to make it work was show her that he knew he was on her territory. But he hadn't. Not once. He'd behaved as though both she and the house were his property.

For a while, she'd thought they might be able to get it right because they both wanted to, so much. She knew that. But they hadn't been able to do it.

Even as she had been squashing down her fury below a smiling surface that first evening, she had caught him watching her in a way that sent icy little trickles through all the warmth she was trying to feel.

He had been weighing her up, watching for danger signs, monitoring her, assessing her. She'd felt as though the man she'd loved for years, the one who'd talked with such heart-breaking honesty about his wife and their difficulties and then wept after her death, had disappeared behind this headmasterly mask. And then, on top of that, he'd invaded every part of the house with his wretched generosity. There wasn't one bit of it that felt like hers now. He'd been every-where and left his mark.

Oh, how bloody ungrateful she was! She ought to have been touched that he'd taken so much trouble and bought her so many presents. No, she *was* touched. But she felt invaded, too. And when she'd tried to explain that, she'd made a hash of it and hurt him even more. Hurt him. Oh, hell!

The voices started to echo from the past. She put her hands over her ears, but they didn't stop.

'Livia, you must try to understand.'

Mama's tired face and thready voice were sad enough to make her feel very bad, but Papa's roaring was worse, and today he'd spanked her again. It wasn't fair. Mama ought to stop him, not be cross with her. It wasn't her fault. She hadn't done anything wrong. Her governess said so.

'Papa can't help it, Livia. We have to make everything right for him. I've told you so often. I wish you would try to remember and do what he tells you quickly and quietly, even when you don't want to or don't understand, and without making such a fuss. He hates that, and it makes him...'

'Cross,' Livia said, because Mama seemed to have forgotten the word. 'I know. And I do try. But it's different things that make him cross every day. So I never know what he wants. So I can't do it.'

Livia's bottom lip was sticking out so far that she could see it below the tip of her nose. Looking down at it made her eyes hurt, but she got quite interested in what she could make them do and the way her lip was there sometimes and sometimes not, depending on how much she squeezed her eyeballs together. She stuck out her tongue for an experiment. That was better; she could see that clearly even when she wasn't squeezing her eyes. She pushed it to one side and then the other, noticing the point in the middle where looking at it did hurt her eyes again. Someone was shouting at her. She looked up just in time to see Mama's thin hands reaching towards her shoulders.

'Olivia!'

'Yes, Mama?'

'You must listen to me.' The hands were gripping her shoulders now. It was funny how hard fingers that thin and trembly could feel when they started shaking you. Funny, but frightening too.

'Livia. Listen to me.'

'I am listening, Mama.' She pulled her tongue right back inside her mouth. Her lips were wet and she wiped them on the back of her hand and then dried it on her frock. Mama's hands tightened. Livia looked up and smiled to show that she was listening.

'Papa had to make a terrible sacrifice in the war. Do you understand me, Livia? Are you listening?'

'Of course. All his friends died and his head was hurt. That's why he's like this. It's not his fault that he shouts and gets so cross. It's because of his hurt head and losing all his friends. We have to understand. Isn't it only the littlest thing we can do for him now, after everything he did for us and all the other little children of England?'

Livia was rather proud that she could remember exactly what Mama had said last time and then repeat it all so quickly. She expected to be highly commended, like her governess did when she got her sums right.

But something seemed to have gone wrong today. Mama wasn't pleased. She was still looking thready and sad.

'I listened, Mama,' Livia said, earnestly pointing it out in case she hadn't realized. 'I did.'

Mama sighed like the bellows when the maids were blowing up the fire in the morning.

'Oh, Livia, what is to become of us all?'

'I don't know, Mama.'

And she didn't. She couldn't work it out. Only this morning she'd thought Papa would be pleased with her for getting all her sums right because three days ago he'd been angry that she'd only got eight out of ten. But he wasn't. He'd shouted and told her to get back to the schoolroom. She'd waited, about to ask why he was different today and he'd glared at her and asked why he was landed with such a burden. Livia, who always tried to give people what they wanted and tell them what they wanted to know, had had to admit this time that she didn't know and was sorry. And that had just made it worse. He'd roared and spanked her. And now Mama was cross again, when it was his fault. It wasn't fair.

Livia saw tears spilling down over Mama's powdery face. That was probably her fault too. Everything else always was. The last time Mama had cried like that, Papa had shouted: 'Look what you've done to your mother. Why can't you behave decently for once in your life? When I think of the men who gave their lives for nasty little girls like you, I could vomit.'

Mama took her lace hanky out of her dress. It smelled of the rose-geranium leaves she kept in the satin sachet Livia had made for her last birthday. That had been wrong too. Papa had thought that at her age she ought to have been able to sew a straight seam instead of producing a monstrous cotterbag. Livia had liked the sachet and she didn't think it was a monstrous cotterbag at all. She could see her lower lip again and this time it was trembling like Mama's hands.

'If you could just try to be quieter, not argue with him so much, Livia, he wouldn't be so cross. Try to be the sweet gentle daughter he longs for.'

Livia shook her head and tried to make Mama understand. 'But I'm not sweet, Mama. I'm a horrible, argumentative, unladylike, ugly, dirty, uncontrollable little slattern and I shouldn't ever have been born. That's what he said today.'

Livia quite wanted Mama to hug her then and tell her she wasn't any of those things, and that it was a good thing she'd been born, but all she did was cry even more.

❧

Livia took her hands off the frozen croissant. It was sixty-eight years since that dogged frightened child had faced the swooping, incomprehensible fury that could appear out of a clear sky and lead to shouting and vicious slaps and being locked in her bedroom for sins she hadn't known she was committing, broken rules she hadn't known existed.

Now she understood that the rules had changed daily with her father's moods, and that none of it had been his fault— still less hers—but she could remember the desperate anxiety she'd hidden so carefully as she tried to work out what it was that made her quite such an unacceptable child.

Her hands were freezing. She held them under the hot tap and felt the warmth painfully return.

All she had known at the time was that her birth had been a disaster for him. How she'd hated those friends of his who'd given their lives for her! Their names had been a litany of reproach, and for years her nightmares had been coloured by the rats that had eaten their bodies because of her, the water-filled shell holes that had drowned them because she was so bad, and the gangrene that had made the doctors cut off their legs, and the mustard gas that had blinded them. She knew all the smells of the trenches as well as the sights, and about how the stench of well-fed children's bodies could disgust a man.

Determined to forget, she concentrated on her breakfast. When the oven was hot enough, she slid in the metal baking tray with the croissants and then found butter and sharp morello cherry jam. Even in the old days she had never seen the point of the Swiss black cherry jam that Henry had always liked so much. It was far too sweet for her and cloying, and it gave none of the necessary contrast with the other tastes. But then Henry had never liked contrast, in his work or anywhere else. His taste was for sameness and safety. That's why his buildings had always bored Livia, and probably why they had appealed to so many other people.

She poured her first cup of coffee, revelling in the shuddering strength of it, and the flavour. Her concentration on the taste of food and drink was one of the few methods she had discovered of keeping herself on the right side of desperation.

Sleep had been difficult since she'd got out, determined to wean herself off the pills that had been handed out like sweeties in all the prisons she'd ever known. But it was not only the tiredness that was making her feel so awful. It was being so bloody lonely. She felt tears seeping out of her eyes and lifted her coffee cup. Her lips were trembling so much that coffee dribbled down her chin.

So, she was still disgusting. Still she couldn't even eat and drink tidily. When her face was clean and dry, she got half the coffee down her throat and ate some of the croissant, choking a little, but managing to swallow.

For years she had longed to be allowed to be free of other people and listen to quietness. Now she hated the solitude and was frightened by silence. All she wanted was warmth and comfort and other people, but Gordon had already fled, driven away.

Sometimes she talked to herself, to make sure that her voice still worked, and she felt as though she was talking to a stranger. It seemed that she would have to get to know herself all over again, as well as learn what to do with things like lemon grass and how to behave in a civilized fashion with a man she had loved for years.

On top of everything else, now she was going to have to talk to her probation officer. He would ask her how she was getting on and what she intended to do with the rest of her life, and she didn't know.

She was still brushing her hair when he knocked at the door, and so she opened the bedroom window to call out that she would be down in a minute. This was how she'd greeted Gordon; she should have made certain she was ready this time and been downstairs when the probation officer arrived.

What looked like a fistful of hedgerow tipped back to reveal a sweetly smiling face surrounded by whiskers. Their owner looked gentle and easy to manage. Perhaps she'd be able to control the session after all and make sure he didn't ask any unanswerable questions.

'Mrs Davidson?' he said when she opened the door.

For a second Livia frowned. The name seemed as unlike her as everything else, but it was the one she and Gordon had chosen together and so it was worth something for that alone. She pulled the door open wider and stepped aside.

'Come on in. You must be Mr Whyle.'

'Colin.'

'Colin, then. Would you like some coffee?'

He accepted and complimented her on the house, behaving with so little bossiness that she warmed a little more and fetched a tin of chocolate biscuits.

'You have a wonderful view,' he said as he put one in his mouth. Still chewing, he went on: 'Was that chance, or did you know this particular house when you arranged to live here?'

'No,' she said, looking past his soft body down the gentle greeny-brown slope to the flat, metallic sheet of the lake. For once it was glistening in sunlight and absolutely still. As they watched a sudden gust of wind blew across it, lifting ripples in an almost perfect curve that sharpened into an arrowhead as it shot across the water. The wind died as quickly as it had come and the lake slowly stilled again. The pale brownish hills at the far end rose in rank after rank against the brilliant sky. There was not a building to be seen.

'I've got a problem, Mrs Davidson,' Colin said, when they had politely agreed with each other about the pleasures of looking out at uninterrupted space. 'And I hope you can help me.'

'I'll try,' she said drily, already aware that he was devious.

'There's a child living down in the village—Eskfoot—a very difficult, very unhappy child, who needs a teacher.'

'No,' said Livia. She watched disappointment oozing over the few bits of his face that were not covered with hair, but she would not let herself be moved. 'No, Colin. I've got much too much to do dealing with my own problems. I'm finished with teaching difficult people. I have to be free of all that now. I'm sorry.'

'He's the fifth son of a violent father and a seriously inadequate mother.'

Livia turned away.

'He was beaten by his father, bullied by his brothers, neglected by his mother, underfed, undereducated, under-stimulated, and brutalized. He's been in trouble almost since he could walk. No school will take him since he burnt the last one down. And, although his current foster parents are doing their very best, they are almost at the end of their tether and talking of giving up.'

Livia could feel all her muscles hardening in resistance. She said nothing. It did not seem to worry Colin, who beamed at her as though she had agreed with every word he had said, and fished in his scruffy briefcase for a photograph. It was a snapshot, in colour, of a small boy standing in front of an ugly, graffiti-scrawled concrete wall. He was dressed in over-large jeans and a red blouson jacket with unlaced, dirty trainers on his feet. His hair was smoothly glossy and his face was the most beautiful Livia had ever seen in any child, alive or on paper.

'After his last spate of crimes when he was still living with his mother, the tabloids took to calling him Hell Brat. You've probably seen some of what they wrote about him.'

Livia felt her skin hardening, as though it was covered in plaster of Paris. But she didn't look away from the photograph.

The boy's face was delicately modelled, with a pointed chin and large, wide-open blue eyes beneath a straight fringe of dark-blond hair. Both it and his skin had the perfect smoothness for which any woman would have given a year's housekeeping—or wages if she had them. There was bravado in his stance, but his hesitant smile was heartbreaking. Livia pushed the print away.

'No.'

'Mrs Davidson, Bobby needs more than anything to be taught to read. Once he's got that, he has a chance. He's eleven and he can't even reliably remember how to decode The Cat Sat on the Mat. If he doesn't learn now there will be no hope for him. He'll be in a young offenders' institution as soon as he's old enough and on to adult prison a few years later. He'll be released time and again, only to reoffend.'

'I can't.'

'With his looks and the charm he has whenever he wants to use it, he'll find a girlfriend easily enough while he's out, and he'll get her pregnant. One day, through ignorance or malice or self-preservation, she'll touch one of his infinite number of raw nerves and he'll beat her up. If she survives to give birth and he's out long enough to see the child, he'll likely damage it—emotionally if not physically, but probably both. And the whole cycle will start again.'

Livia got up abruptly, seizing the mug of coffee, which Colin had not yet finished, and murmuring that she would get him some more.

When she returned with clean, full mugs for both of them, he continued as though she had never left the table: 'You might be able to change his whole life, Mrs Davidson.

Wouldn't something as important as that be worth an hour or two of your time each day?'

He looked away from her, glancing this way and that about the long room with its delicate ornaments and sophisticated silvery colours; then he looked back at her. She knew just what his expression meant: what on earth else have you got to do?

There were other things he could have said, too, things like: Don't you owe Society this much? Wouldn't saving a child's future make up for some of the damage you've done?

Livia knew she had to refuse. She did not have the strength to control any eleven-year-old boy physically, and it could take weeks to establish strong enough emotional links with him to prevent him from going on the rampage if he chose to. And she was so tired. She couldn't do it. She'd done enough, paid enough.

'When do you want to bring him?'

'What about this afternoon?' Energy had miraculously been restored to Colin's eyes and even his flaccid muscles seemed firmer, but his smile was still gentle and regretful. Livia felt a deep mistrust and an even deeper admiration for him. 'Then you can meet him and we can sort out the best time for regular lessons.'

'I'll need books.'

'Oh, I know. I've brought some.' He scuffled in his brief-case and brought out a bundle of books written for very young children.

Livia looked at the selection of large, thin, brightly-coloured paperbacks and felt discouraged before she had even begun. They were all about ducks or teddy bears.

'If he's eleven and an experienced arsonist, these are hardly going to catch his attention, still less encourage him to make an effort to learn.'

'No, I do realize that, but they were the best I could do at short notice. I've ordered more from a specialist shop. The budget will just about stretch to that.'

❧

Bobby was just as unimpressed as Livia when he first saw the books spread out on the table. He kicked the leg and told her they were crap.

'I know,' she said, glaring at Colin to make sure he did not intervene to chastise Bobby or try to protect her. 'But Colin's getting us some more. In the meantime, I thought you could tell me a story and I could write it down so that we can read it together.'

'I c'n write.'

'Great. We can do it together.' Among all the things with which Gordon had stocked the house were plenty of pads of unruled paper and felt-tip pens of all sizes and colours. Livia had not been sure whether Gordon expected her to indulge in some personal art therapy to exorcise her supposed demons or merely to reproduce the landscape, but they were going to come in useful for Bobby. 'Now tell me.'

'It's stupid,' he said, predictably enough. His face was closed in, tightly gripped between his eyes and very sulky.

Livia wished she knew more about small boys. She had met plenty of women in prison who could have given birth to a child like Bobby, and she had learned how to deal with their truculence as well as their cringing passivity, but he was different. She was sure that either mockery or anger would ruin any hope of opening communications with him, but she did not know what might help instead.

'What d'you like doing in your free time?' she asked.

'Thievin',' he said with an encouraging gleam of malicious humour.

'OK,' she said casually, having to hide her amusement at his surprise. 'Then let's write a story about a thief. How old is he?'

'It's like, stupid.'

'Humour me, Bobby. I like stories about people I've never met. Let's make your thief, what? Twelve?'

'Nah. Nine.'

'OK,' she said, writing a large red nine at the top of a sheet of paper and then spelling it out underneath, sounding the letters out as she wrote them, but not even trying to make him repeat them. She did not look at him again until she had finished, then she asked: 'Has he got a name?'

Bobby kicked the table leg again. She was glad for the sake of the owner that he was wearing trainers rather than heavy boots.

'All right. Then, I think I'm going to call him Jake.'

''S a crap name.' He got up and wandered about the room, picking up the shining objects, sneering at them and putting them down.

Livia schooled herself not to warn him about taking care or make a fuss if something broke. Nothing did.

'OK,' she said after a while, looking forward to the day when he allowed his vocabulary to increase a little. 'You choose a name for him.'

'You c'n call him Dare, 'cos he'd dare anything, like.'

Bobby squatted down in front of the fire, poking the thin kindling sticks into the flames for a minute or two, until, bored again, he slouched back to the table and started fiddling with the felt-tips and scribbling on one of the pristine sheets of paper.

By the end of an hour, they had established very little about Dare, except that he was small and tough and very clever and could do anything he wanted. But the effort of concentrating on not upsetting Bobby or getting angry with him had taken so much out of Livia that she greeted Colin's interruption with relief. Bobby was less pleased and swore vilely when he was told it was time to go.

'But I'll bring you back in the morning,' Colin said, 'if Mrs Davidson will have you.'

Bobby's face tightened still further until Livia said: 'Oh, yes, I'd like to see you again. What time will you get here, Colin?'

'Would ten be too early? That would suit my appointments. I could pick Bobby up in the village, drop him off here for a couple of hours—if that would be all right with you—and pick him up again on my way past and get him home for lunchtime.'

'That sounds fine,' said Livia, surprised that Colin's clients were so conveniently placed.

She smiled at Bobby and thanked him for coming to see her. For an instant, surprise relaxed his face into something like the attractiveness she had seen in his photograph, but then the sullen frown closed it up again.

The house felt even emptier when they had gone, and there were at least four hours until Livia could sensibly start cooking her dinner. When she tried the radio, there was nothing she wanted to hear, and all the television channels seemed to be showing either children's programmes or sport. The sound of a car pulling up outside made her think she would happily welcome anyone, even one of the journalists who had made her emergence from prison such a nightmare. She opened the door even before the visitor could knock.

The man walking up the path was a total stranger. He carried a wicker animal basket with a large brown envelope tied to the handle.

'Mrs Olivia Davidson?'

'Yes.'

'I've got a special delivery. Here.' He handed her the basket and took a clipboard from under his arm, asking for a signature.

Back inside the house, with the heavy basket dangling from her left hand, Livia listened to the dwindling sound of the van's engine and tried not to feel desolate. It was her fault that Gordon had gone and her fault that he hadn't brought the promised dog in person. But that didn't help. She ached to have him back.

Oh, God! Why couldn't she get hold of her emotions? She felt as if she was being flung first one way and then another, never given time to get her balance or be ordinary. She put the basket down in front of the fire and heard a whimper. Ignoring it, she opened the envelope.

All she could see at first was a batch of vaccination certificates and a note of the animal's pedigree. That made her bite her lip. Gordon had sent her a blue roan cocker spaniel puppy, the last animal she would have expected him to choose. She riffled through the papers until, at the back, she found one with his writing on it:

> My dear Livia,
>
>      Here is Cuthbert of Warmington III. I'd originally planned to bring him with me when I came on Saturday, but then I thought you might need more time to settle in first and left him in the kennels for another few days. He's Val's direct descendant.

Val, she thought, once more closing her eyes against memories. For years it had been a source of shame that for her first few months in Holloway all she could think about was Val's death. She ought to have concentrated on what she had done to Henry and poor Flora Gainsborough, but she could not. The only death she had managed to mourn was Val's: killed because she was an inconvenience after years of uncomplaining, faithful friendship.

There was a louder whimper from the basket and at last Livia unbuckled the fence-like front. As her hand was licked by a small warm tongue she knew she was lost. She picked the absurdly named puppy out of the basket and held him wriggling on her knee. As she stroked his head, gently pulling on his long ears and letting her fingers find the perfect tickling spot under his chin, she let him get used to her smell and her voice.

After a while his body stopped trembling. When he began to show an interest in his surroundings, she set him on his feet and took him to see the kitchen, where she opened one of the tins of puppy food Gordon had naturally provided along with everything else.

It was only much later that she had time to read the rest of Gordon's letter.

> I hope you come to like him. I have had his grandfather for several years now and found him an entrancing character, mad like all the spaniels I've ever known, but endearing. Cuthbert has had all the injections he needs for the moment, as you'll see from the certificates. If you don't take to him, let me know and I'll sort it out.

Livia looked up from the letter to see the puppy trying to find out what was making such intriguing crackles in the wastepaper basket. As she watched, he tipped it over and danced backwards, barking shrilly, as the bundles of white paper she had thrown away during Bobby's lesson leaped out of the basket to attack him. Bravely deciding that he was quicker and stronger than any of them, Cuthbert started to fight back, kicking them away and then flinging himself in pursuit, snapping and nipping.

It took him some while to admit their pathetic demise, but then with an almost visible shrug of disdain, he abandoned them and moved on to see what else might be waiting to entertain him behind one of the bookshelves. Livia was smiling when she went back to Gordon's letter.

> I am sorry that I got everything so wrong while I was with you. I'd wanted to make your return to life perfect and all I did was upset you. I'm sorry, Livia, even though I still don't understand quite where I went so badly awry.
>
> When you feel like company, will you tell me? Unless I've transgressed too seriously for that. I'd like to come back as soon as you'll have me. But the last thing I want to do is get in your hair or make your days more difficult than they inevitably must be. While things are settling down, I hope Cuthbert will be an easier companion than I was. I think of you all the time.
>
> Love, Gordon

'Oh, Gordon,' she said aloud. 'Why are you only like this on paper? Why is it so different in the flesh? So hard?'

When the telephone rang she felt as though her thoughts must have reached out to him.

'Hello, Gordon?'

'Is this Livia Claughton?' The voice was young and female. Livia agreed before she remembered her disguise.

'To whom am I speaking?'

'My name is Cass Evesham. I'm…'

'Cass? How wonderful!' Livia's breathing was quick and light. She felt weightless. 'How are you?'

'I'm not quite sure. This has all been…I don't know how you'll take this, but I should rather like us to meet. It's been a… I didn't know I still had a maternal grandmother. I wondered if I could come up to the Lake District. I'd like to see you.'

'Me, too. Cass, I'd love it. Can you come and stay?' Livia remembered how difficult it had been with Gordon and quickly added: 'For a day or two?'

'Could I? I've never been to your bit of Cumbria, but it looks a bit far to be able to get up and back comfortably within a day.'

It wasn't until later that Livia even considered the possibility that a journalist might be using her granddaughter's name to disarm her. Now, she simply agreed.

'How's Rosamund?' she asked before Cass could go.

'I've no idea. Didn't you know she'd moved to the States?'

'Well, yes, but she surely writes to you?'

'Not often.' Cass's voice sounded warmer. 'She…she wanted to start life again without encumbrances, I think, when she remarried. You'd heard that my father died? Ten years ago.'

'Yes. I'm sorry. He was a good man.' Livia was filled with such anger at Rosamund that she was surprised her voice worked properly. 'So you've been alone all this time?'

'From the family point of view, I suppose so. Although my mother writes occasionally,' Cass said in a soothing voice, apparently trying to reassure Livia. 'Christmas and birthdays usually bring letters of some sort. But please don't be so concerned. It's fine; not a problem.'

It is for *me*, thought Livia, struggling to control herself. Bloody Ros. She always was selfish.

# Chapter 7

'If you don't like Cuthbert, you oughter call him Flap,' said Bobby, looking at the puppy in disfavour as it leaped around his trainers, sniffing their intriguing scents and attempting to chew the long dirty laces. 'Fuck off. Filthy animal. Look at the way them ears flap when he jumps.'

'Flap,' said Livia in springing delight. 'That's perfect, Bobby. Thank you. Now, would you like something to drink before we get going on Dare's story?'

'What you got then?'

Thinking that there would be plenty of time to talk about manners and grammar later, and still distracted by the prospect of Cass's arrival, Livia offered him milk, Coke, apple juice, water or tea.

'No beer?'

'No,' she said calmly, not sure if Bobby was testing her shockability or genuinely in the habit of drinking alcohol first thing in the morning—or indeed at any time.

'Coke then.'

She fetched a glass and can and put them on the table beside the large sheet on which she had written the start of Dare's story. Bobby pulled off the tab with panache and tipped some Coke straight down his throat, ignoring the glass. He looked as though he was waiting for a protest but Livia did not comment; instead she invited him to read what she had written the previous day. As an aid, she had listed the whole alphabet across the top of the large sheet.

Mumbling, muttering 'crap' and 'stupid', and swearing when he could not work out what the words were, Bobby laboriously sounded out the simple sentences. He broke off whenever he made a mistake and roamed about the room, picking things up and rejecting them or aiming vicious kicks at the furniture.

After a while, when he could sit at the table for as long as five minutes at a time. Livia led him on to discuss the ways in which Dare might get into a flat, where he knew there was money and a compu'er. At times Bobby forgot to be truculent, and they were soon in the middle of a spirited argument about the pros and cons of climbing a drainpipe, which might pull away from the wall, and picking the front-door lock, which might be too difficult without the proper tools. They were distracted by a sudden splattering sound.

'Oh, Flap,' said Livia, seeing a spreading puddle exasperatingly close to one of the piles of old newspaper she had left for that very purpose all over the house.

'I'll kick him for you,' said Bobby leaping off his chair and making Flap whine and cower away from his feet.

'No, no, no, no,' Livia said firmly, trying not to shout. 'Honestly, Bobby, that'll only frighten him. It won't teach him anything.'

'Don't you want him hurt then?'

'No. There are other ways to teach him. Watch.'

She picked up the frightened animal and could feel the pumping of his heart and the trembling of the muscles just beneath his furry skin. She set him gently on the nearest newspaper pile, speaking firmly about the purpose of it and the importance of peeing nowhere else.

'He won't understand nothing of that. Dogs don't know English, y'know.' Bobby sounded enormously superior.

'In the end he will come to understand. It'll take time, but that doesn't matter. Nothing matters at the moment except not frightening him.' Livia risked a quick look at Bobby and saw doubt in his sharp blue eyes.

'You can't teach people or animals anything by making them afraid of you. It just makes them difficult and aggressive or breaks their spirit so they're no good to anyone. There's a floor cloth in a bucket under the sink in the kitchen. Could you fill the bucket with water for me and bring it and the cloth so that I can mop up?'

To her surprise, he made no protest and soon brought her the bright red plastic bucket three-quarters full of hot water. The cloth was neatly draped over the side. For a moment she thought he was going to volunteer to do the cleaning, but he didn't go that far. As she wiped and squeezed and rinsed and wiped again and Flap forgot his fear, she asked Bobby whether he'd ever had a dog.

'Nah. I don't like 'em. Rats like this one don't matter, but I don't like them big ones. My Dad did.'

Livia asked a string of careful questions and soon heard about the Rottweiler that had lived in the small, gardenless council flat that was already overcrowded with angry humans.

'The dog must have had a terrible temper,' Livia said.

'Well yeah. But m'dad beat it when it barked or bit. It learned its lesson.'

'Didn't he care about it?'

'Yeah. He liked it better'n any of us. Fucking kissed it sometimes, di'n he? Let it lick him, too. His face. Filthy animal. And played games with it.'

Livia concealed her outrage with difficulty, merely saying at the end of Bobby's story that she wasn't surprised he had thought he ought to hit Flap after an experience like that, but that her rather different methods had proved successful in the past and she'd like to go on following them. Then, as she stood up with her knees cracking after their prolonged contact with the cold stone floor, she suggested they go back to Dare.

Bobby carried the bucket back to the kitchen for her, only slopping a little over the side, and returned to the table. He read the whole ten lines they had produced without faltering or abandoning the job. Livia was not sure whether it was a feat of memory or literacy, but she praised him lavishly and invited him to dictate the next instalment of Dare's adventures.

Bobby told her about how Dare was caught by a neighbour as he climbed through the window. Pulling him out, the neighbour managed to break the glass and cut Dare's arms, before handing him over to his father, who beat him hard, in spite of his bleeding wounds.

Intrigued to discover how articulate Bobby could be when he was not trying to establish his independence, Livia wrote the words as he dictated them and then, once he had fallen silent, added some more of her own.

'What's that then?' he asked, watching her hand coming to a stop at the end of the line.

'Dare's dad was wrong to hit him,' she read unemotionally. 'Listen? Is that Colin's car?'

'Yeah. Prob'ly. 'M I going to have to go then?'

'I think so. I doubt if he'll be able to wait. But will you think about what Dare does next so that we can get going quickly in the morning? I really want to know what's going to happen to him.'

He said nothing as he slid off his chair and drained his Coke tin, which he dropped on the floor.

'It would be nice if you could put that in the kitchen bin,' Livia said casually. She watched him struggle with his urge to comply and made no comment when he shook his head and then kicked the can towards the side of the room.

'Ah, Colin,' she said as the front door opened and his sweet, whiskered face looked round. 'How was your morning?'

'Fine. And yours?'

'We had a good time. At least I did. Thank you, Bobby.'

'Yeah. Right.' He looked even more disturbed.

Colin raised his eyebrows so that they disappeared into his curly fringe, silently asking whether Livia wanted him to say something. She shook her head and smiled.

'I'll see you both tomorrow morning.'

When they had gone, Livia went upstairs to make up a bed for her granddaughter, her mind full of the fat, sassy three-year-old she had last seen, characteristically naked and haranguing Ros for trying to stop her turning the garden hose on the vile children next door.

❧❦

Cass lost her way three times after turning off the M6, but once she was on the road that led west from Ambleside towards Wast Water—a road so small that it didn't even have a number—there were hardly any junctions and no excuse for taking the wrong turning. The car coughed and juddered as she nursed it up an almost perpendicular incline towards somewhere called Wrynose Pass.

Sod it. The end of the bloody world. Her mobile probably wouldn't work up here, so if the car died on her, she'd be stuck.

She changed down, feeling the gears slip, then mesh just in time. At the top of the pass, before the road turned down again, the view was huge and exhilarating. She might have stopped for a better look if she hadn't been driving for so long. All she wanted now was to be done with the journey and given an enormous drink.

Plunging to the bottom of the hill, she saw the road rear up again in front of her and made herself concentrate. She timed her gear changes better this time.

Alan's narkiest comments on her driving echoed in her memory. Counting *his* many failings got rid of some of them—and reminded her of why she'd do so much better without him, the lying toerag. Tosser. That was better. She'd be fine on her own now. She didn't really miss him as much as she thought. He'd never loved her. She was fine.

As she drove further west, the country seemed gentler but just as beautiful. Great bare hills rose out of soft green valleys that were crisscrossed with drystone walls, rushing rivers and dark green hedges. There were a few tiny churches and otherwise nothing but small farmhouses, wind-buffeted but stalwart. Some had whitewashed walls, but most were of untouched dark grey stone.

The only moving things in the landscape seemed to be the shuddering trees, the egg-shaped sheep that looked like mobile cotton buds in the distance, and the birds. Cass knew almost no natural history, but they looked like raptors of some kind: buzzards perhaps; bigger anyway than kestrels, which she might have recognized from visits to her wary Scottish relations.

The road seemed to go on and on. Dusk sucked the colours out of the landscape, and the car seemed very cold. Cass turned up the heater, hoping she hadn't got lost again, and saw a signpost looming up out of the greyness. She changed down, slowing to peer at the lettering. One of the three surviving arms pointed to Eskfoot, the village that provided her grandmother's postal address.

From there, so Livia had said on the phone, the house was just over two miles away and easy to find. Cass doubted that. Nothing else about this journey had been easy, and the thought of what she was going to face at the end of it was the hardest part of all.

She had never liked staying with other people in any case and avoided it whenever she could. She'd given up going to her father's relations in Scotland years earlier, bored with the life they lived and hating the way they watched her as though she might do something frightful if she weren't constantly monitored. Now, of course, she knew exactly why they had been so worried. She wished they had told her.

The only house where she ever stayed with any enthusiasm these days was Sophie's parents'. Huge and cold though it was, and furnished only with what hadn't had to be sold to satisfy Lloyds, it was full of paradoxically luxurious ease. It was a house where you could do as you pleased and be liked for whoever you happened to be. No one cherished silent resentments or told polite lies there, and spikiness provoked only laughter or lively argument.

Swerving to avoid a pothole, Cass knew that staying with Livia would be different. After all those years in prison, she was bound to have some pretty crunchy hang-ups. Somehow they would have to get past them and find a way to like each other. Cass had no idea whether she was capable of that.

She had driven through Eskfoot and was now skirting the lake itself, looking for the sign her grandmother had promised. The last of the light had gone. She flicked the headlights on to full beam. Even so she almost overshot the turning.

Three minutes later, driving up a steep narrow road between thickly planted trees, she could see warm, orange light flickering to her left. Moments after that she was outside the house itself, a long, low, grey stone building with tiny windows and a slate roof.

The door opened as soon as she braked, skidding a little on a patch of scree. A slight, white-haired woman in dark-green velvet trousers emerged to stand with firelight behind her, waving or beckoning. She must have been watching for the car.

Cass took her time getting the luggage out of the boot and tidying the old newspapers and plastic bags that lived there from one year to the next. At last she banged the lid shut and straightened up with a firm smile pulling her lips apart.

The dancing light behind Livia made it hard to read her expression. Her soft, straight white hair was pulled back behind her ears, and she wore no make-up or jewellery.

No masks, thought Cass. Good for her.

With the velvet trousers, Livia was wearing a loose pale pink cashmere tunic over a lavender-coloured silk shirt; her flat black leather shoes looked like Kurt Geiger.

So Gordon Bayley's right, thought Cass; she *is* rich.

'Come on in, Cass,' Livia said at last in the hoarse voice that suited her story so much better than her delicate appearance. 'I'd have known you anywhere.'

Just inside the front door Livia turned to face her, wanting something. Cass was not sure whether to shake hands or attempt a kiss. Neither seemed quite right. And she didn't want to touch Livia; not yet anyway.

'I don't remember you,' she said. The words hadn't come out right: more an accusation than an apology. Cass smiled again, hoping she didn't look like a grinning automation. 'I thought I would, even though it's so long ago, and I...But...'

'You were very young then,' said Livia. 'But come right in, Cass, and let me shut the door or you'll let out all the heat.'

So that was all she wanted. That was easy.

'Sorry. It's weird,' Cass said, moving forward and dropping her luggage on the floor, 'I'm not usually this short of words.'

'You can't often have faced a situation quite like this. Shall I show you your room now or would you rather have a drink to oil the cogs a bit?'

Cass laughed breathily and wished the sound had been less childish. 'A drink would be good. My cogs could do with quite a lot of oiling.'

'Mine too: I feel full of all sorts of sand and grit.'

So, she's got a sense of humour, thought Cass. And imagination; perhaps it'll be all right.

'Wine? Or do you drink spirits? It always used to be gin and tonic when I was last offering people drinks, but I gather fashion has changed.'

'It did, but it's changing back again. Gin and tonic is pretty trendy now, like sherry, but...'

'Sherry?' Livia's squawk of surprise made Cass laugh more naturally. 'Only the ancient or the sad drank that in my day. So, what will you have? And do sit down. I've got most things. I was about to open some red wine and have some of that myself.'

'Sounds great.' Cass ignored her baggage and chose the further corner of the huge pale-grey sofa. It took up most of the space in front of the sulky fire. A thick white sheepskin rug covered the flagged floor. She kicked off her shoes and flexed her cold, aching toes against the wool. A small blue-grey and black puppy came bustling over to investigate, sniffing at her shoes and barking.

'He looks fun,' she said, as Livia came back with a bottle and glasses. Then she added doubtfully, squinting at the little creature that was half buried in the long wool of the rug. 'Or she?'

'He. Flap we're calling him. You'll need your shoes whenever you walk about because you may well find yourself treading in a puddle or worse. Flap's still finding it hard to get the hang of either the newspaper or our sessions outside. Are you used to dogs?'

'No. My m—Rosamund didn't approve. Germs and worms, I suppose. She dreaded both.'

Livia was frowning, but that could have been because of the peculiar-looking corkscrew she was trying to insert into the bottle. 'How did you find me?'

'Gordon Bayley gave me your number.'

'Did he now? I didn't realize you knew him.'

'I didn't. But he rang me and we had dinner on Sunday.' Cass watched her grandmother's face in the uncertain light and saw that her composure was only skin-deep, too.

Livia wrestled the cork out of the bottle but couldn't then work out how to clear the corkscrew. Frustrated, she shrugged and dumped the whole lot on the table.

'Here's your wine. I hope you like it. Gordon bought it. He's been a good friend. I owe him a lot. This house for one thing. What d'you think of it?'

Cass grabbed the nice easy subject and ran with it, hoping to keep it off the ground for a good long time. Livia's tense face softened a little as she talked, but her answers grew abrupt again as soon as Cass's questions became laboured.

'You don't have to be polite, Cass,' she said at last. 'You're bursting with curiosity, aren't you?'

'It would be hard not to be.' Cass tried another smile. She didn't get a response. 'I know nothing about you except what I've read in the papers, and I can't believe all that. I have absolutely no idea what your life has been like. I mean, I've never even been inside a prison.'

Livia opened her mouth and then shut it again, as though she didn't know what to say. Cass wondered whether the frankness had been a mistake. She tried a rueful grin: 'Being so ignorant puts me at a shocking disadvantage.'

'Well, we can't have that, can we?' Livia's voice was lightened with laughter now, and had a faint spicing of malice. 'Shall I reassure you? Tell you cosy tales of decent officers who cared and took trouble?'

When Livia paused, Cass nodded to encourage her.

'Describe my friends and the jokes we had together?'

Cass's shoulders relaxed, sending fingers of pain down her back where the clenched muscles were letting go. Her body would soon feel like itself again, strong but loosely jointed, easy. She crossed her legs. Her black Ally Cappelino trousers had survived the long drive with remarkably few creases. She was pleased. They'd been worth the price.

'Or shall I tell you about the first woman I knew who burned herself to death in her cell?'

Looking quickly at Livia in the hope that she was making some kind of black joke, Cass saw nothing so comforting. Livia looked spiteful and as though she were enjoying herself. That was sick.

'The smell hung about for days afterwards, in spite of everything the screws did and made us do: hot and sickly, like pork crackling with extra caramel. You…'

Cass crossed her legs again, saying nothing. Livia leaned back against the sofa, her lips widening into what would have been a smile if there had been any amusement or affection in it. She was obviously expecting a protest or a comment of some kind. Cass did not oblige.

She knew she had to be able to take whatever Livia chose to say and pretend it was no more important than the price of oranges. The streams of smut and racism poured out by Gary and his sidekicks had inured her to most things. She might not have expected tales of burned flesh that smelled like caramel and crackling, but she was tough enough to avoid giving Livia a thrill by any visible reaction.

Livia got up to mend the fire, savagely poking the heavy logs that were still only smouldering. As one began to flare, she turned back, the poker still in her hand.

'That wasn't fair of me,' she said stiffly. 'I'm sorry.'

Cass shook her head. 'No need. As conversational gambits go it was a little startling, but no more than that.' Flames burst up from the rest of the smouldering logs and lit Livia's face. Her eyes were still hard, but her smile was better.

'I must say I like "conversational gambit". But, you know, Cass, it was more than that; one of my friends really did burn herself to death in her cell. I thought you ought to know.'

Cass picked up her glass and drank, hoping that they weren't going to have to play strength-testing games for much longer.

'Did I seem revoltingly smug?' she asked. 'Or were you trying to shock me into showing what I'm made of?'

Livia didn't answer. After a while she shrugged.

'OK. Well, whatever: if you're planning any more shocking, d'you think we could have it all in one go? That way, we could move on to something a bit more civilized.'

Livia's eyes glittered. She abandoned the poker and came back to the sofa. 'I think I could get to like you, Cass.'

'Good.' She wasn't ready to reciprocate quite yet. And besides, Livia owed her one now.

'So, I won't tell you much about the rats that used to come out at night in the old buildings and climb up on to our bunks, or the filthy food we sometimes had to swallow, the beating-up, the noise, the dirt, the cutting...'

'Cutting?' Cass hadn't meant to encourage the list of horrors, but the words were out before she could stop them. She knew her face showed nothing but bland confidence. That was as it should be.

But perhaps the lack of anxiety looked like a challenge to Livia, who said slowly, almost luxuriously, savouring the words: 'Wrist cutting.'

Cass kept her mouth shut.

'We mostly had a go with a smuggled razor blade or a home-made knife once in a while. It's the only thing that gives you any control in a place like that—planning when and how to kill yourself.'

Livia's sleeves were so long that Cass could not see whether there were any scars on her wrists. But she pushed back the cuff of her silk shirt and looked at her watch, murmuring something about cooking dinner. Cass saw what she was presumably intended to see: a three-inch scar running across the inside of Livia's wrist. The thin line was white, so it must have been quite old. But it was there.

Determined not to give the scary old bag any more satisfaction, Cass pretended not to have seen the mark and drank again, commenting politely on the wine's smoothness.

'You always were a formidable little thing.' There was less malice this time and Livia's smile looked more real.

As formidable as you? Cass wondered. She said nothing.

'Yes. Formidable, determined and often very cross. That's one reason I liked you so much. You didn't take crap from anyone, even in your highchair.'

Cass couldn't help smiling. She tried to remember sitting in her highchair, but couldn't. To her, it was no more than an unwanted piece of furniture in the attic, although she had heard a fair bit about the way she'd made Rosamund's life intolerable with her refusal to eat as a baby. 'Not taking any crap from anyone' sounded much better than making her mother's life unbearable.

Livia laughed again. 'I can see you haven't changed. Still as stubborn and tough as old boots, eh, Cass?'

'So they tell me. It's lucky isn't it? As things stand.' As soon as the words were out, Cass wished them unsaid. But she couldn't take them back. The only thing was to offer amends of some kind.

'Of course, you couldn't know,' she said. 'But I've just been dumped by my boyfriend. It's being a bit hard to take.'

Livia's right hand moved. For a moment Cass thought she was going to be touched, and managed not to pull away. But Livia herself stopped her hand in midair and let it drop, to lie on her own thigh, corded and bony like an ancient lizard's claw.

'I'm sorry, Cass. Really. And it must make all this even more difficult for you. I shouldn't have…'

'I've known better times,' Cass said, sounding almost casual. It took an effort. 'But they'll improve.'

'D'you want to talk about him?'

'Not much. But in nutshell: he said his wife had left him; it turned out she hadn't; she found out about me and protested. She took precedence. *Finito!*'

'I'm sorry,' Livia said again. She was frowning. But her eyes were changing, warming.

'I'll get over it.'

'Of course you will, but being told lies—especially that sort—is horrible. He can't have been the man you thought when you fell for him.'

'No,' Cass said drily. 'He can't, can he?'

'Still, I hope you had fun first. Was he good in bed?'

Cass put down her glass with care. She couldn't imagine any other woman of Livia's age asking a question like that.

'Oh, Cass,' said Livia, laughing, and for the first time sounding friendly, 'I'm not your average granny, you know. Where I've been, I've heard more about men and the tactics they use to get their ends away—and what they do to women they despise—than pretty much anything else.'

'I thought it was good at the time, and I hadn't realized he despised me,' said Cass slowly. She was surprised to realize that she wouldn't mind Livia hearing what Alan had said about the 'decent hooker'. One day she might be able to tell this woman the whole story in a way that she wouldn't want even Sophie to hear. How odd!

'At the beginning it was exciting,' she said. 'Different, a bit exotic even. He's good company and he can be very funny, in a rather cruel way. And he can be generous.' She frowned, trying to think of words that would sum him up.

'That all sounds all right. Apart from the cruelty.'

'Yes. Maybe. Now that I'm angry with him, it's difficult to remember quite why he seemed so wonderful.'

'Try,' Livia said.

'OK. He's good-looking; he's got a very quick mind, which I liked because it kept me on my toes; and he could make me feel sexier than anyone else I've ever known.' Cass laughed and didn't like the sound she'd made. 'Maybe it was just that.'

But it wasn't. None of that was enough to explain why she'd loved him, or why she was hurting now. He had made her feel that he saw in her things no one else had ever understood. And he had acted as though she was healing wounds in him that he had never dared let anyone else see. That was why she had trusted him. Fool that she'd been.

Cass glanced back at Livia and was surprised to see sympathy in the hard black eyes.

'Sorry,' Cass said. 'It's harder to talk about than I thought it would be.'

'Don't worry about it. Are you hungry? Gordon's had the kitchen stocked with every possible sort of food. Perhaps we should go and cook something.'

'I wouldn't mind something to eat,' Cass said, getting up, 'but I'm a hopeless cook.'

'Are you? Wonderful. Just like me. Although you've got an excuse, with a successful job like yours.' Livia's face hadn't changed, but Cass could feel that something was wrong.

'Why don't we just have bread and cheese?' she said quickly, wondering whether to ask questions or pretend she hadn't noticed anything. 'Why waste good ingredients if neither of us can cook?'

Livia stood up and put a thin arm lightly around Cass's shoulders for a moment. It was not unpleasant.

# Chapter 8

It was raining again when Livia took Flap out for the last time that night. The darkness was much less inviting than the cosy warmth of the white wool rug in front of the fire, and Flap thought the idea of leaving the house quite mad. Livia felt her small stock of patience dwindling, but she soothed and petted him when she had picked him up. Then she dumped him—quite gently—beside the slippery stone path and kept him there for as long as it took with the toe of her Kurt Geiger shoe.

She sent Cass up to have a bath and unpack while she dried Flap and settled him to sleep in his rug-lined basket beside the hearth. She put the guard in front of the fire in case of sparks and pushed the heavy bolts at the top and bottom of the thick oak front door.

This was home. And there was family in it. Odd how comforting that should seem and yet how difficult, all at the same time. But at least it wasn't quite as difficult as having Gordon here.

When she got into bed, Livia's aching joints spread flat against the firm mattress. It made them hurt more, but it would ease off. Cass was an interesting girl, and brave with it. Not many women of twice her age could have managed their meeting so well.

Livia wished she'd been able to say so or show it in some way. She wished she'd been less tetchy, too, and hoped Cass understood why it had happened. She probably did; there was kindness in her, behind the casual strength and all those throwaway lines that were supposed to show how tough she was.

Picking up her book—one of the modern American novels Gordon obviously thought she ought to read—Livia tried to concentrate. She didn't like the book much, but she was making an effort to read it. The words began to move and merge with each other. The book banged against her chest. She blinked and focused for a few more minutes.

The wind drove splatters of rain against her windows and the few trees around the house began to creak. Livia did not move.

Cass woke briefly to hear the rain and think with astonishing clarity, 'I could like her; I hope she calms down soon,' before falling back into warm black sleep.

Livia dreamed next door and snored once, then woke again, so sharply that she knew she would be unable to sleep again for some time. The storm sounded much more violent. She got up to have a look, wrapping a blanket around her shoulders.

Lightning was ripping through the navy sky as she peered out through the rain-rippled window. The trees were thrashing about in the wind as though they were trying to get rid of a plague of itching insects in their branches. Rain blew in great gusts first this way and then that, drumming on the roof and battering against the windows. It sounded as though there were torrents of water rushing along gutters just above her head.

Livia shuddered and wondered if Cass would wake, too, and whether it would be fair to go in to her room and offer her a hot drink. Some of the rain was sliding in between the edge of the casement and the frame, dripping on to the sill out of time with the steady beat on the roof.

I wish she was awake, Livia thought, but if the storm doesn't do it, I can't.

Peering at her reflection in the dark glass, she thought about everything Cass had told her as they ate, describing her friends and the work she obviously loved. Livia started to count the ways in which they were alike. She had not believed in God for a long time and so she didn't know why she was praying, but the words were urgent: 'Don't let her lose her work; whatever else happens to her, don't take that away. If she can keep that, she'll be all right.'

Shaky, as though the recognition of herself in Cass had taken some of the scaffolding from around her own defences, Livia hated the man who'd made Cass love him and then left her. Someone ought to make him see how cruel he'd been, force him to admit the damage he'd done and apologize.

A particularly loud crash of thunder was followed by a different kind of banging. Livia thought the wind must have forced open one of the outhouse doors. Then the sound came again. Someone was knocking heavily on the front door. She stood up, pulling the ends of the blanket tight and looking around for something she could use as a weapon. Nothing was suitable. Then she remembered the fire irons downstairs.

She was half-way down the stairs, listening to Flap's increasingly hysterical barking, when Cass's bedroom door opened. Livia looked back to smile in reassurance, putting a finger to her lips. Cass nodded and mouthed, 'Wait for me,' as she hurried down. Her bare feet made no sound on the stairs.

Livia collected the poker, murmuring: 'It can't be a journalist. Not in this storm.'

Cass nodded again. Making sure Livia was safely out of range, she pulled back the stiff bolts and hauled the heavy door open.

A man was standing there, dripping and bowed under a huge rucksack. They could not see his face, only the hood of a tightly fastened orange walker's cagoule.

'Yes?' Cass said coldly, just as his knees buckled and he fell forwards, like a giant redwood yielding to foresters' chainsaws. 'Oh, shit,' she added unsympathetically.

'We'll have to take him in,' Livia said, when she peered over his collapsed body and saw that there was no one else there and no vehicles.

Cass was trying to haul the man into the room, but his body was too heavy for her with the bulky rucksack attached. Having wrenched her back trying to unload him from inside the house, she had to step over him, out of the porch. The rain poured down on to her thin nightdress, plastering the cotton against her back. She was wet and freezing—and very cross—by the time she had got his arms out of the straps. With Livia's help, she pushed him over the weather strip into the house, lugged the rucksack in after him, and was able to shut the door on the rain at last.

The strings of his hood were too tightly knotted for Livia's arthritic fingers and Cass's hands were too slippery with wet and cold to be much use either.

'We'll have to cut them,' said Livia, leaving to fetch the kitchen scissors.

'He's boiling hot,' Cass said, feeling his newly exposed forehead and forgetting her own discomfort. 'Even though he's shivering. I think he's really ill.'

The man's big body was wrenched suddenly with a heavy tremor and he groaned but did not regain consciousness. Cass slapped his face experimentally, but his eyelids did not lift.

'I don't think it's just exhaustion; it could be something serious. We're going to have to get him to hospital.'

'How can we?' There was sharp panic in Livia's voice. Cass looked up at her with a quick, reassuring smile.

'Don't worry, Livia. I'll sort it out. You won't have to do anything.'

'It's not that. But I don't see how we could get him out to your car without damaging him. He's far too heavy, even if we both carried him. And I've got no idea where the nearest hospital is. Have you?'

Cass shook her head, remembering her long journey across the empty passes. 'Then we'd better get a doctor to come here. We can't look after him on our own; we might do real damage. He could…' She broke off, looking up.

'Die,' Livia supplied baldly.

Cass nodded. They both knew what that could mean. They'd never be able to keep Livia's identity secret if the man died, and God knew what repercussions there might be and how they would affect her parole conditions. 'Have you got a GP?'

'Gordon's people left a number with all the stuff about taxis and so on. I've put it by the telephone. But will a doctor come out in weather like this, in the middle of the night?'

'They have to if it's an emergency. And this is. I'm sure he's really ill, Livia. Will you ring while I try to get him warm? Or would you like me to do it?'

Livia went straight to the telephone and dialled the number. Cass ran upstairs to fetch towels and the duvet off her bed, catching sight of herself in a long mirror as she went. The rain had turned her white cotton nightdress transparent where it was flattened against her body. She took an extra minute to wrench it off and substitute her thick towelling dressing gown. Then she went back to kneel beside the man on the sheepskin rug.

His limbs felt like sodden sandbags as she pushed and pulled them through his wet clothes, but eventually she had him free and was able to rub his twitching body dry. He must have been quite fit, she decided as she noticed that although he was a big man there was no excess fat over his ribs or around his hips; but he seemed very vulnerable. His penis looked pathetic, shrivelled in the cold and flopping backwards into the coarse curls between his legs, like a broken Slinky.

Full of all the protective instincts she thought had gone with Alan, Cass laid her duvet over the man, tucking the edges between his body and the rug. Then she started to dry his face and hair.

'Has he got any sort of identification?' Livia asked from behind her.

'I haven't looked yet,' said Cass, carefully wiping rain from the dark crescents under his eyes with one finger wrapped in the edge of the towel. She looked away from his rectangular, bony face to say: 'Is the doctor coming?'

'Under protest.'

'Well, sod him! What does he think we pay our taxes for?'

'But when I explained that we've got an enormous unconscious stranger on the floor and that I am seventy-five, alone here with my young granddaughter, he reluctantly said he'd come as soon as he can. But it'll probably take him at least half an hour. He said we were to get the patient dry and as warm as we can. You'll need that duvet later, Cass. I'll get some blankets for him and put the kettle on.'

By the time she came back, Cass had put one of the sofa cushions under the man's head and smoothed the hair away from his eyes. It was drying to a thick blond thatch that lay very flat across his head. She had also sorted through the damp contents of his rucksack and found a wallet.

'I know who he is,' she said, sitting back on her heels as Livia began to substitute blankets for the duvet. 'I can't think why I didn't recognize him.'

'A friend of yours?'

'God no! Nothing like that. But I've heard of him, and seen photographs. He's called Christopher Bromyard. Quite a name in the City. I can't imagine what he's doing up here. I'd have thought a Caribbean beach or a Tuscan villa would have been more his bag than a wet walk through the Lake District. And why didn't he have his mobile phone with him?'

'I can't think,' said Livia with a hint of amusement. The thought of wire-less telephones was still as exotically unreal as the Tardis. 'We've done all we can now until the doctor comes. Would you like a cup of tea? If he comes round, we can give him some, too. Warm him up.'

'I'd love one. Shall I go and make it?'

When the doctor arrived, cold and resentful at being untimely ripped from sleep, he thought they looked ghastly with their thin faces, hard black eyes and wild hair. The elder had some kind of blanket wrapped around her neck and they both had steam emerging from mugs cupped between their hands. It wouldn't surprise him to find they were drinking eyes of toads and legs of newt, or whatever it was.

The doctor sniffed. It must be the sight of the unconscious walker lying at their feet that was sending such uncomfortably fanciful pictures into his mind. But he was a rational man and so he banished them at once.

It was not hard to diagnose exhaustion and pneumonia, and he had to admit that the women had been right to insist he came out, tiresome though it was. He thought of apologizing for his slight rattiness when he had answered the telephone, and even explaining that it was unusual to get that kind of call out of season when most of the irresponsible ramblers were tucked up safely in their horrid little semis in the south, but he did not. He was not a man who liked explaining himself to anyone. Instead he allowed himself a frosty smile for the older woman as he said: 'I'm going to give him a penicillin injection. There is a slight risk that he may be allergic to it, but it's important that we start to fight the infection straight away. If he shows the slightest sign of an adverse reaction, you are to telephone me. Do you understand?'

'What are the signs likely to be?' asked the girl in a voice that was unsuitably sharp for someone so young.

He gave her the necessary details, couched in the simplest possible terms, for which she thanked him briskly, adding: 'And presumably you'll be back some time tomorrow to see how he is?'

It seemed odd that she, so much younger, should have taken the initiative from her grandmother. He looked from one to the other, trying to decide what sort of people they were, and then he addressed the old lady again, partly to show the girl what he thought of her manners. He said he'd be back when he could, but that if they followed his instructions, the patient should do quite well. They could always call the surgery if they were worried in the meantime.

The walker's eyelids were fluttering by then and the doctor knelt down to reassure him as he burst back into consciousness with an expression of absolute terror on his face.

'You're quite safe,' the doctor said at once, in a much kinder voice than the one he'd used for the women. 'I'm a doctor. You were lost. But you've reached a safe haven now. These ladies have taken you in and will be looking after you for the next few days.'

The patient looked past him to the two witches, his eyes still understandably scared.

'What's the matter with me?' he asked. Talking seemed to hurt him.

'You've got pneumonia. It's not dangerous these days; no oxygen tents and crises on the ninth day,' said the doctor with a dry laugh that did not seem to reassure the patient or either of the women. 'I've given you a penicillin injection and left tablets. Do you understand?'

'Yes. I thought it was a cold.'

'Are you allergic to penicillin?'

'No idea.'

'D'you know what your name is?'

'Of course.' The sensitive-looking lips lifted a little. 'Christopher Bromyard. Thank you, Doctor…?'

'Presteigne. Adam Presteigne. You'll do now, Mr Bromyard. I'll be back in a day or two to see how you're getting on, but these ladies have my number in case you need me urgently. I'll say goodnight to you all.'

'I'll see you out, Doctor Presteigne,' said Livia, moving stiffly towards the door.

Christopher looked up at the dark-haired girl, and saw her smile at him. It made her look much less fierce. He smiled back.

'Sorry about this,' he whispered, wishing his chest didn't hurt so much. He felt iller than he knew you could; and the biggest fool in the world. He hoped to God that his name had meant nothing to any of these people. The last thing he needed just now was an account of his self-inflicted collapse in some diary column. Quite apart from the effect on the City, it would give Betka the biggest thrill of her life, and she'd taken more than enough from him already. In a place like this, hundreds of miles away, he was probably safe enough, but you never knew.

'You could hardly help it,' the girl said, laying a cool hand across his forehead, as though she was testing his temperature. She brushed some of the hair out of his eyes, which was nice of her. She had a nice voice, too: quite deep and round at the edges; nothing shrill about it or hectoring. 'We've only got two bedrooms upstairs. Will you be all right if I make you up a bed on the sofa here? It's warm with the fire, and comfortable and quite big enough, I think.'

'Even for me,' he agreed with a sort of laugh that turned into a groan. He pressed his right hand to his chest. 'Sorry to give you so much trouble.'

'Don't keep apologizing,' said the old woman, reappearing in his field of vision. Her voice was a lot raspier than the other's. 'You need help. And we've plenty of room to keep you until you're well enough to travel. Don't worry about it. Now, you probably won't remember, but you ought to know that my name is Livia and this is my granddaughter, Cass Evesham.'

'How d'you do?'

'Cass, get some sheets will you? The airing cupboard's in my bathroom.'

'OK.'

Christopher wished she had not gone. She made him feel safe, and he liked that after all those hours of walking in the storm. He hadn't been able to find a single landmark that coincided with anything on his rain-pulped map; he'd known his torch batteries were about to give out; his blistered feet had burned as though they'd been dipped in acid; and the pain in his chest had made it hard to breathe and impossible to think sensibly. He hadn't felt so helpless since his first night at prep school.

Luckily she came back soon, still smiling at him, with her arms full of linen. He smiled back again, but she didn't see it. She and the old lady put a sheet over the sofa cushions and fiddled about with blankets and pillowcases, and then helped him up, clutching the blankets around him.

God, he felt ill! The old one told him where the loo was and asked if he wanted them to help him get there. But he didn't. He hadn't drunk anything for hours, except the stuff the doctor had made him take. And he didn't want to move. Everything hurt too much and whatever was wrong with his head made him want to keep it as still as he could. He lay against the smooth cool sheets and heard the muffled sounds of the storm outside.

The house must be very solid, he thought, as sleep began to pull his mind even more out of shape. The thunder that followed each lightning crack with hardly a pause sounded much quieter than it had outside. The women were talking to each other about him, but he couldn't understand what they said. He opened his eyes again, wanting to thank them for the rescue, but his voice wouldn't work. He felt himself letting go, and then he couldn't hear anything any more.

# Chapter 9

Cass didn't like the look of Bobby one bit, in spite of his beautiful face and smooth golden hair. He burst into the house without knocking, and started babbling excitedly about someone called Dare before he noticed that the only occupants of the room were Christopher Bromyard, still asleep under his heap of blankets, and Cass herself. The boy stopped dead, his face sharp with suspicion.

'Where's Liv, then?' he demanded, all aggression and quivering resentment.

'She's upstairs. She won't be long. I'm her granddaughter, Cass. And you must be Bobby.'

'Yeah. So?'

Cass didn't smile or answer. She hoped this aggressive child wasn't about to take Livia for a ride. She had said over breakfast that he was more intelligent than either he or anyone else gave him credit for, and was already responding to the novel sensation of being treated with a modicum of respect. But Cass didn't trust him. And she hated to think what he might do to Livia. It might be no bad thing if he saw that his ancient teacher had strong young friends.

As Livia came downstairs, Cass watched a smile dispersing some of Bobby's sulky aggression. But then he turned back to glare at her and started kicking the nearest chair.

'I think we might have our lesson in the kitchen today,' Livia said in a non-committal voice. Bobby, still kicking, shrugged. He didn't look at Cass again, just slouched forwards, scuffing his trainers against the floor and leaving the rugs rucked up wherever he'd been. Cass diagnosed deliberate provocation and said nothing.

'Hello?' said a croaky voice.

She turned to see the patient looking at her in surprise. There was none of the wild terror his eyes had shown last night, but he clearly had no idea where he was or who she might be.

'Hello,' she said, giving him the wide smile she'd withheld from Bobby.

'What am I doing here?'

'You collapsed with maximum drama on the doorstep in the storm last night. Don't you remember?'

'I remember being wet and horrendously cold and stupidly lost,' he said. He swallowed and then rubbed his throat, wincing. 'Who are you?'

'Cass Evesham. You're in my grandmother's house above Wast Water.'

He frowned, shutting his eyes, and she thought she had lost him again. But after a moment the line between his thick fair eyebrows relaxed and his lids lifted.

'You know, I do remember something. Wasn't there a doctor? A thin, sniffy fellow?'

'That's right.' Cass laughed. 'Dr Presteigne. Which reminds me, there's another batch of his pills for you to take. I'll get you some water.'

'I need a pee before I drink anything,' he said. 'But I don't seem to be wearing anything under these blanket things. I'm not sure…'

'No, of course you're not,' said Cass. 'I'd forgotten. Everything from your pack is still sopping, and neither my grandmother nor I have anything anywhere near big enough. Hang on and I'll lend you my dressing gown. That ought to cover the essentials anyway.'

'I'll look a proper Charlie in this,' he said two minutes later, when she handed him the bundle of navy-blue towelling. 'But at least it's not pink or frilly. Are you going to turn your back while I get it on?'

Cass thought of telling him that after last night he didn't need to worry about modesty as far as she was concerned, but she did not. He obviously couldn't remember being stripped and dried like a baby on the hearthrug. She waited until he had levered himself into the dressing gown, then helped him as he got shakily to his feet and showed him to the downstairs loo she had only just discovered herself.

The tiny excursion exhausted him and he slept again as soon as she had persuaded him to swallow his pills. With Livia and Bobby occupied in the kitchen, and Flap as deeply asleep as the patient, there was nothing for her to do. She picked up the book she had taken from the shelf between two of the windows, wishing yet again that Livia had a newspaper delivered. It was not surprising that she preferred to do without, but Cass longed to know what was going on in the world. Once Christopher was properly awake she'd be able to turn on the radio or even the television, but until then she would have to stick with the novel.

After a while she gave up trying to see the point of it and instead started to draft another letter to Rosamund, telling her about Livia. Aware that she would probably never send this one either, Cass looked up, searching for the best words to describe the moment at supper last night when the two of them had broken through the barriers and begun to talk properly. She saw that Christopher was awake again.

'How are you feeling?'

'Vile.' He coughed. 'But I expect I'll live.'

'So the doctor says. I wasn't sure when you got here last night. It was on the alarming side.'

He smiled slightly at her understatement and then looked round, taking in his surroundings for the first time.

'What is this place? It's weird with all these mirrors and things.'

'It's my grandmother's house,' said Cass, 'done up by a sculptor, who seems to be obsessed with light and reflection. Crystal, too. Are you warm enough?'

'Sure. Who is your grandmother?'

'What d'you mean?' If they could get away without direct explanations it would be a lot easier, but she shouldn't have sounded so stiff. That was a dead giveaway. She tried to make her face relax.

'Nothing. Why? I just wondered why she got a sculptor to do up her house. Is she an artist, too?'

'No.' Was it possible that he knew nothing about the Harpy? Or was he still so out of it that he had not noticed Cass's likeness to all the photographs in the papers and made the connection?

'D'you live up here all the time?' He shook his head, wiping his hand over his eyes as though they hurt too. 'No, silly question.'

'Why?'

'You don't have the air of a country girl: too glossy,' he said slowly, examining her face and then her Ally Cappelino trousers and polo-neck before he was shaken with a bout of heavy coughing.

When the spasm was over, Cass took some Kleenex from the box Livia had provided and wiped the sweat off his forehead. His skin was boiling under her fingers. He lay back against the cushions, looking up at her with puzzled but trustful eyes. She smiled as reassuringly as she could and smoothed his hair, which her ministrations had pushed upwards like a cockscomb.

'I'm up here for a few days' holiday. Much more interesting is: what on earth is a man like you doing wandering about in the wilderness without a mobile phone?'

Suspicion chased regret across his face like the shadows that rushed across the lake in the wind.

'A man like me? What d'you mean?'

'I work in the City, too,' she said gently. 'I'm at Stogumber's.'

'Bugger.' His eyes closed again and the line between his eyebrows deepened. He seemed to be getting paler as she watched.

'Don't worry,' said Cass, alarmed by his reaction. 'I won't ask questions and nor will my grandmother. We don't. And neither of us likes gossip.'

'Sorry. I just wanted to be where no one knew anything about me for a bit. Doesn't matter.'

She wanted to know more, but after her assurance that there'd be no questions she could hardly satisfy her curiosity.

'OK. Would you like something to drink? Juice or tea, maybe? Doctor Presteigne said we must keep up your fluids.'

'Juice sounds great. Thanks.' He shut his eyes again.

Cass knocked warily on the kitchen door before opening it, but she had not been circumspect enough. Bobby swore and swept a heap of felt-tips on to the floor, cursing with a violence that made even Gary and the other dealers sound mealy-mouthed.

'I'm sorry to interrupt, Livia,' Cass said. 'Christopher needs some juice. May I?'

Livia nodded and then bent down to collect the pens. Cass left the glass she had just taken from one of the cupboards and went to help, glaring at Bobby.

'It's all right, Cass,' Livia said. 'I can manage. Don't.'

Cass looked at her, surprised by the throttled ferocity of her voice. There was no comfort in her expression, and so Cass did as she'd been told and took the glass and a carton of orange juice out to Christopher's makeshift bed.

Later, once Colin had taken Bobby home, Livia apologized for snapping.

'Don't worry about it. I just thought that lazy child might've given you a hand. Shouldn't…?'

'I know that's what you thought,' Livia said patiently, 'but he's been yelled at and given orders all his life. No one's ever shown any approval of anything he's done, except the other boys he's impressed with his violence and daring. I want to give him a taste of something different. He can't understand why I don't shout and hit him when he drops things or swears. But I hope it'll soon give him enough confidence to let some of his defences down.'

Seeing Cass's surprise, Livia realized she had no idea what it was like to live without approval, endlessly criticized and told how useless you were, and cut off from every source of affection. Lucky Cass.

'Isn't it just going to encourage him to mess you about?' she asked, frowning. 'Won't he see it as weakness and go on pushing and pushing to find out how much more he can get out of you?'

'I've no idea. But it's the only way I know to help him. Now, what d'you suppose your protégé can eat for lunch?'

Not much, turned out to be the answer, but forty-eight hours later Christopher was recovered enough to want to get dressed. His clothes were dry again and he chose navy corduroy trousers, a red-and-blue checked shirt and a navy-blue cable-knit sweater to take into the downstairs loo with his spongebag. He re-emerged, shaven and dressed, looking shaky but more in control, to sit at the table for breakfast. He still could not eat comfortably, but he drank two cups of coffee and roused himself not only to thank Livia for all that she and Cass were doing for him, but also to chat amusingly.

He looked surprised when Livia put one of her thin, bent hands on his wrist.

'It's all right, Christopher. You don't have to sing for your supper. Breakfast, rather.'

'I just feel rather a lout,' he said with an unexpectedly sweet, self-deprecating smile. 'Clogging up your drawing room, eating your food, stranger that I am. I want…'

'I know what you want, but you don't have to. It's a real pleasure to be able to help, isn't it, Cass?'

'Yes. But you look worn out already, Christopher. Why don't you get back to the sofa while I clear up before Bobby comes?'

'Can't I help clear?'

'Certainly not. Go on. Off with you. Do as you're told. I expect it'll be a novel sensation for a man like you.' She grinned at him, enjoying the new light in his grey-green eyes.

Christopher wanted to make her laugh. He liked hearing the throaty gurgle. But he couldn't think of a joke that didn't seem hopelessly feeble. He swallowed his regret and retreated in silence to his sofa.

He left Cass dealing neatly with the breakfast debris. When Livia had gone upstairs, Cass came to ask him if he wanted a newspaper, confessing that she had an itch for news that she had to scratch. He admitted that the novel she'd rejected wasn't doing much more for him than it had done for her and that a newspaper would be great.

'Good. Then I won't feel so guilty,' she said inexplicably, before setting off for the local village.

It was an astonishing relief to be out of the house. Cass wound down the car window, sucking in the air and the glory of the countryside. The village itself was charming, when she reached it, with whitewashed houses and grey stone walls, and no signs of tourist-prettification. She found a parking space in what had once been the market square. There was a small chemist, a climbing equipment shop, and a combined Post Office and general store. She made for that.

Apart from Scotland, where she never went shopping, she had never stayed anywhere so remote, so she had no idea whether the curious but defensive stares of the people she passed in the street were normal. The sudden silence that fell like an absestos blanket over the small crowd in the Post Office when she walked in was clearly not. The customers looked too embarrassed.

Most of them seemed to be waiting for stamps or pensions in the back half of the building, and so she made her way to the newsagent counter and picked up a copy of each of the three main broadsheets. As she moved *The Times*, she saw a copy of the *Post* with yet another photograph of Livia at the time of the trial. Above the photograph, which took up most of the front page, was a headline: 'Have you seen this woman?'

Shaking with rage at the incitement to stalkers and vigilantes, and once more glad of the fringe that disguised the shape of her own face and flying eyebrows, Cass tucked the papers under her arm and fetched a wire basket. She filled it with fresh milk, juice, bread and eggs, and then quietly waited until it was her turn to pay.

The man in front of her was tall and upstanding in his old greeny-brown tweeds. When he had taken his change, he turned to leave and had to face Cass. He looked constrained, perhaps by the heaviness in the atmosphere and the silence of the other customers, but he lifted his ancient hat an inch or two above his bald head, and said pleasantly enough: 'You must be the young lady staying at the Long House.'

'That's right,' said Cass with what she hoped was a friendly smile. 'Mrs Davidson is my grandmother and she wanted me to see the place while she was up here. It's magnificent country, isn't it?'

'We like it. I gather you took in a collapsed walker the other night. Good of you.'

'My grandmother could never leave someone in distress without help,' Cass said firmly. She wondered whether the doctor had been charitably trying to raise Livia's reputation in the village, or gossiping about her and her granddaughter and their likeness to the missing Harpy.

'Good of her, then. Good. Well, good day to you.' He raised his hat again and strode out of the shop, his paper-wrapped loaf of bread tucked under his arm with a copy of the *Daily Telegraph*.

Cass turned back to smile at the thin, grey-haired woman behind the counter and offered the contents of her basket for pricing.

'She's been ill, we were told, your grandmother,' the woman said as she rang up the sums on an old-fashioned till. The sound of subdued chat resumed behind Cass. It seemed that the upstanding man had given the rest of them a signal that she had passed some kind of test. 'When her solicitor made arrangements for her, he told us she was quite fragile still and wouldn't be getting about much. Shall I put these on the account he opened for her?'

'No, thank you. I'll pay this time.' As she handed over the money, Cass noticed that the woman was taking care to avoid touching her fingers.

So, she thought, we're lepers are we? God help Livia if she needs anything from any of these people.

⚘

Christopher's eyes glistened when he saw the papers.

'Wonderful,' he said as Cass gave him his choice. 'Just what I need.'

'If we can finish them before Livia's done with Bobby, that would be good,' she said casually. 'Then I can get rid of them so that she's not bothered.'

The familiar frown pulled down the edges of Christopher's mouth in a way that Cass had come to know over the past two days.

'Don't ask,' she said, and then consumed with a curiosity of her own, added: 'how long is it since you've seen a paper?'

'I'd been walking for nearly eight days before I collapsed on you, so I suppose it must be about eleven in all.'

'Ah, I see.'

'What d'you see?' The frown was still there, and with it a look of fear she had not seen since the beginning.

'Why you're in such dire need of a news fix,' Cass said, laughing. 'I've only been without for three days and I'm like a skin-crawling junkie.' She opened *The Times* and was immediately faced with a paragraph about Livia. Luckily there was no picture.

Cass tried to concentrate on the rest of the news, but she knew that she was only waiting for the question. When it came, it was pretty tactful. All Christopher actually said was: 'Livia? The same Livia?'

'Yes.' Cass put the first part of *The Times* on the floor between her chair and the sofa and slid it towards him. 'But you don't have to be scared of her.'

'Good God!'

'After what she has done for you, I hope you won't burden her with too many comments like that,' she said coldly. 'They're the last thing she needs right now.'

'You misunderstand me.' Christopher's voice was almost as frigid as hers. 'I was surprised that you could even think I might be frightened. She's been astonishingly generous to me, and in any case, I think she's a remarkable woman.'

'Ah.' Cass felt as though a constricting rubber suit had been peeled off her. She apologized and was rewarded with the best of his smiles: trusting and affectionate, but with a speculative glint. She smiled back and knew he had understood.

'We'd better whip through them quickly, then, before the hairy Colin comes back for Bobby,' he said.

There was silence between them after that, an easy, friendly silence, punctuated by the crackling rustle of the large pages as they turned them over, and the spitting of resin in the burning logs.

'Are you done with the *Guardian*?' Cass asked much later. When Christopher nodded, she tore it into four and flung the pieces on the fire. The flames blazed up, lighting the planes of her face and making her skin so hot that she brushed her hair out of the way for safety as she pulled back from the hearth.

'You're very like her, aren't you?' Christopher said quietly. Cass nodded.

'It makes me wonder,' she started before she thought, 'what I...Sorry.'

She turned, ready to talk about the City or his holiday, anything that might persuade him not to ask what she'd meant. He was holding out his left hand.

'I'm sure it must, but it needn't,' he said. 'Cass, come here.'

'It's OK. Here, do you want the *Independent*?'

'You're not very trusting, are you?' he said, allowing his outstretched hand to fall back on to the sofa. Cass resented the comment. He hardly knew her. How could he expect her to trust him?

'It isn't that. More juice?'

'No, thank you. I'm fine. And Livia doesn't like you disturbing Bobby.'

There was a knock at the front door. Cass found the dapper figure of Doctor Presteigne waiting outside, his old-fashioned black bag dangling from one hand.

'Good morning, Miss Evesham,' he said in his pernickety voice. It seemed extraordinary that anyone could load quite so much disapproval into such an ordinary phrase. 'And how is my patient?'

Well, we haven't killed him yet, if that's what you mean, she wanted to say.

'Doing much better, thank you, Doctor Presteigne. Come on in. My grandmother's busy with her teaching. She...'

'Yes, I hear she's taken on young Bobby. It's all over Eskfoot. Everyone's most impressed by her charity.' He looked along the room, saw that there was no sign of Livia, and added in a much lower voice, 'And worried for her. Miss Evesham, you do know the sort of things that young tearaway's capable of, I take it?'

'Oh, yes. The social workers and probation officers who've dealt with him have briefed my grandmother fully. Now, I'll leave you with Mr Bromyard. Christopher, I'll be upstairs if I'm needed. Just shout.'

'Cass?' His voice sounded worried, but she did not answer.

'Now, Mr Bromyard,' said Doctor Presteigne, apparently unaware of the strain between them, 'how are you feeling?'

Cass collected the remaining newspapers so that Livia would not see them if she and Bobby emerged before the doctor had left, and went upstairs to lie on her bed, reading the ones she had not finished.

❧

Doctor Presteigne had taken Christopher's temperature and blood pressure and found both satisfactory.

'Now, are you all right with these rather peculiar women?' he asked as he rewound the rubber tube around the blood pressure monitor.

'They have been extraordinarily kind to me,' Christopher said stiffly. 'Taken me in, nursed me, fed me, and asked no questions.'

'That doesn't surprise me,' said Presteigne, measuring some more pills into a little brown bottle. 'They'd risk having to answer some of yours if they did, and neither of them would want that. I've never met such a secretive pair. You can feel a wall of silence whenever you come into this house. When I first saw them sitting over you, I thought they looked like a couple of witches. I wasn't surprised to see you so frightened when you came round, and I did wonder what they'd been up to. I hope...'

'Don't be ridiculous.'

The doctor looked offended. He fluffed his shoulders. 'I'm relieved that you feel that way, but I should look to your wallet if I were you.'

Christopher's outrage was such that he couldn't get out any words. The doctor must have understood, because he hastily explained that he had been thinking of 'young Bobby', not the women. Christopher was not appeased.

'You've been good coming out to me like this,' he said icily, 'and once the blood test results are through, I don't imagine that I shall need to trouble you again, so I'd better settle up with you now.'

'You're covered here by the National Health Service.' Doctor Presteigne looked as though he had just swallowed a tablespoon of vinegar. 'All I shall need from you is your own doctor's name and address to keep the files and budgets straight.'

'I'd rather pay. You surely have some private patients. Let me be one of those.'

'Well, if you insist. That will mean that the drugs will have to be paid for, as well as the three visits and the tests.' His expression as much as his voice suggested that he had now lumped Christopher in with the two women as deeply undesirable. Christopher felt flattered.

❧

Cass heard unmistakeable sounds of departure and ran down-stairs to catch the doctor before he drove away. As she stood beside his car, while he carefully laid his black bag in the boot, briefly stroking the unscratched leather to make certain that nothing had happened to it, she thought he looked even more disapproving than usual.

'How is he, really?' she asked. 'He won't admit to anything beyond feeling rather sore still in the chest and throat, but I'm worried. He seems so weak and he's worn out by the tiniest exertion.'

'He's doing perfectly well, I can assure you. His temperature is normal again and he's responding to the penicillin. It'll be some time before he's fully fit, but he's in no kind of danger, and provided he rests enough and continues to take the tablets, there should not be any problem. I'm having some tests done at his request and as soon as the results are through he can be on his way.'

'Tests? What tests?'

'Blood tests,' he said repressively. 'To eliminate one or two remote possibilities. But from everything he has told me, it's almost certain that this was a straightforward case of pneumonia, exacerbated because his immune system was weaker than usual from longstanding exhaustion. I estimate that he'd been suffering for at least two days before he reached this house. He admits he had what he thought was a heavy cold and a fever. Well, goodbye, Miss Evesham. Telephone if you need anything. And if those blisters on his feet don't heal soon, let me know and I'll send the district nurse up to put on proper dressings.'

'Fine. Thank you, Doctor Presteigne.' Cass saw that he was not going to tell her what the blood tests were for; she assumed that one, at least, must be for AIDS.

'Cass,' Christopher said as soon as she returned. 'Please don't run away again. We don't have to talk about Livia if you'd rather not, but I got the impression this morning that you might want to. You must know I'd never pass on anything you said. Or don't you?'

She smiled. 'Yes, I do know that. But I can't talk about her. Had you finished with the papers, or do you want another go before I fling them on the fire? She must be about to reappear.'

'I wouldn't mind *The Times* business section if you've finished with it,' he said obediently.

That afternoon, Cass took advantage of the rare sun and went for a run while Livia and Christopher both slept off the lumpy shepherd's pie Livia had produced for lunch. Cass had been missing her regular sessions in the gym and was beginning to feel saggy. There was no evidence of it when she checked her body in the mirror or looked down at it in the bath, but she felt as though dimples were lurking.

The wind was only fitful now, and for once there were no signs of rain. Her knees tightened on the steepest bits of the hill, but by the time she had reached the flatter ground, she felt only pleasantly stretched and speeded up to sprint along the edge of the water.

The movement and the working of her muscles had some of the usual soothing effect, but she missed the pulsing rhythm of Ben's music in the gym and the regular pull of the rowing machine. Running didn't control her thoughts nearly as well as rowing. There was a sudden crack, as though a gust of wind had whipped a springy branch into the main trunk. Cass thought of Alan reeling from her slap and wished she had better control of her memory.

Any reasonable person would have said he deserved it, she told herself, but that didn't let her off. There was still a slight stiffness in her knuckles, where they'd crunched into his cheekbone. She wondered whether his face had healed yet and how he had explained the cut to Melanie. And she wondered what he was thinking about, now that he must know about the Harpy. Even in the Seychelles, they could probably get English newspapers, and even Alan, who never saw anything he didn't want to see, must have noticed the likeness between the killer and Cass.

Was he telling himself that he'd got off lightly with a bruised and cut face? Or congratulating himself on escaping a woman who might have killed him if they hadn't had their row in public?

Reaching the target she'd chosen, Cass stopped and stood for a moment watching the water and listening to the waves lapping against the smooth stones of a little beach. She shook first one foot and then the other to keep the muscles flexible. She hadn't known that inland lakes like this one could have beaches and waves. Close to, the water had none of the gunmetal sheen they could see from the house. From here, it was a clear dark green. There were a few fish nosing about in the weeds.

Trout they must be, Cass thought, since they were speckled along their silver sides like the ones she'd bought in Sainsbury's for the freezer.

What the hell was she going to do when she went back to London? How was she going to answer the questions? It wouldn't only be journalists who'd want to know where she'd been and what she thought about the Harpy. Her friends would be curious, too, even if they didn't ask anything directly, and her enemies would have a field day.

The thought of how Gary would use the story made her sweat. Nothing Michael Betteridge could say would help, even though he'd been more than decent when she'd phoned to warn him of the news that might break about her relationship to the Harpy. He had promised to do everything he could to smooth her path back into the bank, but he had warned her that if the publicity got too bad, he might not be able to do much.

New sounds distracted her, a louder slapping and a mechanical kind of creak. She looked up and saw a wooden rowing boat coming fast towards her. The rower looked over his shoulder towards a small jetty Cass had not noticed before at the far end of the beach, and made a slight adjustment. He had the reddish-tanned skin of someone who spends most of his time out of doors.

'Afternoon,' he said, nodding to her as he climbed up on to the jetty. It was made of wood so weathered that it was silver coloured.

'Hello,' said Cass, waiting for more, but he said nothing else, merely crunching up through the short crisp grass in his gumboots and then away into the sheep-filled field beyond the grey wall. She wasn't sure whether he was taciturn by nature or, having heard about the lepers in the Long House, afraid.

Shivering at the thought of her current and future isolation, she turned to run back up the hill towards light and warmth.

~ 

Livia and Christopher were sitting amicably over a Scrabble board when Cass let herself in to the house, and Flap was playing football with an empty cotton reel that kept getting stuck in the long hairs of the sheepskin. They all looked comfortable.

Cass told herself she'd been a fool to go out in the cold, mooning over Alan, who'd never loved her, and tearing herself to pieces about how to answer questions she might never be asked. All she'd done was make herself glum and scare some innocent Lakelander. She would have been much better off playing board games in the warm and letting the future take care of itself. That's what the old Cass would have done. Lucky her.

'Thank heavens,' said Livia, holding out a hand to her. 'I'm so bad at this, Cass. Will you take over my letters?'

'You can't run away, Livia,' Christopher said, rubbing his hands. 'Not now I've got you at my mercy at last.'

'I must. I'm petrified.' She laughed. 'Besides, I ought to take poor Flap out for a little gentle exercise before tea. He's got to get used to a routine walk every day. Come on, Cass, do me a real granddaughterly favour. It's so long since I've played this wretched game that I'm hopeless, and I hate being beaten, especially by someone young enough to be my grandson.'

Cass peered at the scores Livia had been keeping and joined in the laughter.

'Yes, I see what you mean. OK. I'll take over, but only if we start a new game. I warn you, Christopher. I play to win.'

'I'll bet you do,' he said with the familiar glint in his grey eyes. Then he turned his head away from her. 'Thank you, Livia, I enjoyed that.'

'You're a good boy,' she said, ruffling his hair as Cass looked on in surprise. She had had no idea that they were on such intimate terms. 'I liked it too, but I'm glad to be able to hand over before total annihilation. That's bad for me. Flap! Come on.'

Cass took Livia's place and squared her shoulders, rubbing her cold hands together. It was some time since she, too, had played Scrabble, but she had once been very good.

'Right,' said Christopher. 'The battle's to the strongest.'

'Absolutely. And no prisoners.'

'Certainly not. Pick a letter.'

She rattled the plastic squares in their green bag and pulled out the X, which she always liked, even though it meant her opponent would almost certainly get to start, and have the advantage of a double score.

It took Cass a while to get her brain up to speed, but within a quarter of an hour, she was seeing several moves ahead and collecting some excellent scores. They both played a tactical game, blocking the red squares and making sure that any Us were placed where they could not possibly help the unfortunate who picked up the Q. When Cass found it in her handful of replacement letters towards the end of the game, she did not allow her face to change and waited for three more turns until she was able to lay it on a blue square to make the word 'qadi'.

Christopher instantly challenged her and did not seem impressed with her explanation that it was a variant spelling of 'cadi', meaning a muslim judge. She looked for a dictionary, but there didn't seem to be one in the house.

'OK, Christopher,' she said, returning to the sofa. 'Why don't we make a list of disputed words and check them when we get home? Then we'll each know who really won.'

He pointed out that it would not matter whether 'qadi' appeared in any old dictionary; it was the official Scrabble dictionary that counted. Cass narrowed her eyes at him and hoped she looked as dangerous as a cobra about to strike. It only occurred to her later that snakes probably didn't have eyelids. Either way, Christopher did not look remotely threatened and so she stuck her tongue out at him, which made him laugh.

It was a close fight. Cass emerged the winner by a measly fifteen points, but she had had fun: straightforward, uncomplicated fun of a kind she had not known for a long time. Her skin felt cleaner and tighter and she knew that her eyes must look brighter in the firelight.

'Another bout?' she said before looking up. Then she quickly added: 'No, perhaps tomorrow.'

'Why not now?'

'You look worn out. Your eyes are dragged at the corners and your mouth has gone thin again. Doctor Presteigne said the only important thing now was to make sure you didn't exhaust yourself. I'm sorry. I didn't think. Tea? I wonder where Livia's got to.'

❧

They played again the next morning, three ferocious games in quick succession, while Livia and Bobby were at work in the kitchen. At one point their laughing fury with each other's machinations made them so noisy that Livia had to come out to ask them to keep quiet. Their racket was making it impossible for Bobby to concentrate. Cass apologized at once. The rest of the game was played in silence.

For Cass the wordless struggle was almost more engrossing than the earlier games, when they had been able to puncture tension with teasing chat, and it was surprising how easily she and Christopher could communicate without words. At one moment, when he delicately dropped the J on to a blue triple-letter square to make 'jo' horizontally with the O that was already there, and then added 'inxed' below the J, which included a word-doubling pink square, she lifted her gaze from the board and put all her fury—and a hint of admiration—into her glare. His lips twisted into a smile of sneering triumph before he winked.

She clenched her fists and raised them in a classic boxer's pose. Then she had a small shock. Christopher's smile faded.

Cass froze. She couldn't bear it if he, too, were afraid of her. What had she ever done to him to make him think she might hit him? Was it just because of Livia? Or something he had sensed in Cass herself?

Before she could ask, he bowed his head in what looked like submission. Without meaning to move, she reached across the low table to touch his hair. He held her hand there for a moment with one of his, then shifted his head a little, so that her palm slid down the side of his face until he could kiss the palm.

Surprised, Cass started to calculate his score. He let her have her hand back. She found that the total he'd achieved in that one move came to ninety-nine, and carefully checked her sums before adding it to the paper bag she was using as a score sheet. When she offered it to him for rechecking, she saw the mockingly triumphant smile was back on his face. Reassured, she handed him the green felt bag of tiles and set about beating his score.

Christopher accepted the bag but he didn't take any tiles. He sat watching Cass's bent head and cursing himself for a fool. The last thing either of them needed in this emotionally charged house was any kind of flirtation. But he hadn't been able to help it. He'd had to do something to remove the hurt from her black eyes.

She fascinated him: so tough-minded and competitive and yet so kind to old Livia and so sensitive to all sorts of sub-liminal messages he could only dimly glimpse. He liked her looks, too, with that long, taut figure and the flashing eyes. And the glossiness. She couldn't have been more different from Betka or any of her predecessors.

Betka. He felt suddenly sick. Most of the time he could stop himself thinking about her and the things she had said before she had stormed out, but some of them pulled at his attention whenever he relaxed his vigilance.

Betka had probably been right when she said he'd never taken the trouble to get to know any of the women who'd so briefly enchanted and then so quickly bored him. But she'd been wrong when she yelled that all he'd ever wanted was a blonde, well-mannered but mindless, leggy but voluptuous, to impress his clients and then take home to screw, whether or not she wanted to be screwed.

He'd been so angry by then that he hadn't bothered to answer or point out that neither she nor any of the others had ever tried to find out any more about him than that he could afford to take them to the places they wanted to go and buy the presents they thought were their due. And she'd taken his silence as yet another insult to her dignity, and said…

He cut off the memories. A man could go bonkers if he wallowed too long in that tide of bitterness and resentment.

Focusing on Cass again, he decided that what he liked most was her aura of power. It must come partly from the intense concentration she applied to everything she did. Her fury at his larger scores—when he got them—was only a measure of how much she cared about winning.

He could see exactly why Stogumber's wanted her. That quality of total immersion in the moment, allied to brains and a refusal to be beaten, would propel anyone up the ranks of any dealing room. But it was an odd place for her to have chosen to work. Stogumber's was notoriously the last bank in the City to get to grips with equality, and political correctness was as foreign to them as Sanskrit. Ah, she was moving again. He'd have to concentrate.

She laid her letters down, a smile tweaking at her lips, and then looked at him with a laughing challenge in her black eyes. For nearly thirty seconds he could not look away from her vivid face, but then she tapped the board with her right index finger, mouthing 'look,' at him. He looked and then laughed aloud.

Using the D of his 'jinxed', she had got rid of all her letters. They ran from the left-hand red square to the one in the centre of the board, to make 'adequate' for an astonishing score of three hundred and two points. That was it. There weren't enough letters left for him to have any chance of beating her. He bowed his head again in surrender, hiding his smile.

Cass thought she'd better offer him the chance to retrieve his self-respect with another game, but he said he'd rather talk. He poured the letters back into their green bag and then looked at her.

'Oh, Cass. You look as though you think I'm about to interrogate you.'

'Aren't you?'

'No. I just thought I'd tell you what I was doing out on the bare mountain that night. I think I owe you an explanation.'

'Ah. In that case…' Cass sank back into her chair, ready to listen to anything he wanted to say.

'Just before I came up here something happened that made me take a long hard look at myself. I knew I had to get away, go somewhere no one knew me and work things out for myself.'

'I know I promised not to ask any questions, but I don't understand. What happened?'

'Ah. Well. Someone said something that made me realize how…how narrow my life had got.'

He looked at her, and then tried again, stumbling a bit over the first few words. After a while he began to talk quite fluently as he told her that after fifteen years of solid graft at the bank, he had suddenly been made to see that there was nothing important left in his life except work.

Cass blinked. 'From everything I've heard, you had a pretty whizzy time. A lot of people envy you.'

Christopher shrugged his big shoulders. Her half-intended compliment did not seemed to have registered.

'Client entertaining,' he said and hesitated, looking as though there were more he could have said. After a moment he shrugged again, clearly uncomfortable, and added: 'That's all most of it was, and it gets hard to enjoy after a year or two. Sometimes I think life in hell must consist of sitting through a million operas in expensive seats and drinking pints of champagne (which I hate) and eating tons of ludicrously expensive food in the kind of restaurants where you have to book weeks in advance, and the staff behave as though you've committed a mortal sin if you so much as touch the wine bottle you're paying for.'

Cass thought of the hell Livia had inhabited for so long, and the woman who'd burned herself to death in her cell, and could not feel much sympathy.

'And spending hour after hour dredging up things to say to people I wouldn't mind if I never saw again. Until these three days with you, Cass, I don't think I've had a real uncompetitive conversation with anyone...'

'Uncompetitive?' said Cass lightly, as she thrust all thoughts of prison cells and women with slashed wrists out of her mind. 'Would you say that either you or I could ever be that?'

'I'd have said so, up here.' His voice deepened. 'But it's more than that. I don't feel as though I've ever talked to a real person before, I mean someone I knew and wanted to know better. D'you know what I mean?'

It seemed to matter to him, and so after a moment she said: 'Well, yes. I suppose I do. But, Christopher, was your life really so bad? You must have enjoyed some of it, or you'd never have stuck it so long.'

'Some, yes. Of course I did. I've been very lucky. But the zest had gone. I didn't notice, until one day when I pulled off a mega-deal no one thought would work, and I realized I couldn't give a stuff. That scared the hell out of me.'

Cass sat on her cushion on the floor, watching him and thinking of her last day at work, when the news of the Deutschmark's fall had sent her into a dizzying high more powerful than anything else she'd ever known. To achieve something like that and feel nothing might well leave you wondering what you were doing with your life.

'What are you thinking?' Christopher asked again.

She smiled and told him, adding: 'It was amazing. I'd shown the lot of them—and myself, too. It was the nearest thing to total ecstasy I've ever felt.'

He nodded, as though he knew exactly what she was talking about. Her dark eyes were wide open. The heat of the fire behind her back was powerful and the fibrous springiness of the sheepskin beneath her legs felt odd, intriguing.

The kitchen door opened and Bobby and Livia emerged, both looking as though Dare's adventures had progressed more satisfactorily than usual.

'Colin's late,' said Livia, 'so we thought we'd knock off and have a drink with you.'

Cass saw with a kind of irritated satisfaction that it was Bobby who was carrying the heavy tray, leaving Livia only a dish of crisps. He put the tray down on the slate hearthstone and then turned to Cass.

'You want wine or juice?'

The question seemed unnecessarily aggressive, but it showed some signs of progress. Cass asked for wine and watched him grasp the bottle with both hands and pour the wine shakily into a large rummer. He twisted the bottle carefully as he lifted it, so that the drips wound their way round the lip of glass instead of streaking down the label, and then shot a quick look at Livia, who nodded in approval. Cass watched an extraordinary smile play over his face. For a second he looked young and gentle and eager.

When Cass glanced at Livia, she surprised an expression of such tenderness on her grandmother's face that she had to blink.

'Here,' Bobby said to Cass, thrusting the glass of purple wine at her. His features had resumed their usual truculence.

'Christopher?'

'I'll have juice, please, Bobby. I don't think alcohol will mix with my pills. Thank you. That's very good of you.'

'Liv?'

'Wine, please, Bobby.'

When they were all served, he poured himself some orange juice and sat in the far corner of Christopher's long sofa. Flap tried to leap up to join him, but Bobby's new softness had not gone far enough to allow that. One black trainer kicked out. It did not connect with Flap, but he understood the gesture well enough and whined as he skittered across the stone floor to Livia's chair. She picked him up and petted him without making any comment. His ribs were powering in and out as though driven by a steam pump.

Cass tried to think of something to say to Bobby—or ask him—that would not sound unbearably patronizing and was relieved when Christopher started to talk about football. It turned out that Bobby was a fan of Manchester United and they chatted happily, man to man, until Colin appeared.

Then, while Livia was outside, seeing them into Colin's car and making arrangements for some better books for Bobby's lessons, Christopher said: 'So, what did you do to celebrate your great triumph, Cass?'

Remembering how Bobby had got past his own defences for a moment, and how Christopher had shown himself to be vulnerable, Cass forced herself to say: 'I went out to lunch with someone I thought I was in love with and he told me it was all off.'

'Oh, Cassie, I'm sorry. If it's any help, whoever he is must have been blind, deaf, and completely barking mad.'

# Chapter 10

After lunch on Monday, Livia asked Christopher whether he felt well enough to be left alone in the house with Flap while she and Cass went for a longer walk than the puppy could manage.

'Heavens, yes. I'm fine now. I'll look after things here.'

'We won't be much more than an hour, I don't suppose. And I can't imagine that anyone will come to call. If you feel like answering the phone—if it goes—do; if not, the machine will pick up any messages. We'll see you later.'

They decided to walk up the hill rather than down to the lake because Livia wanted to look over into the next valley. Cass doubted that they would get anywhere near the summit, but she said nothing.

It was a stiffish climb and for a while they did not talk. The short grass crunched underfoot, as though the cropping sheep had made it stronger than any London lawn Cass had seen, but the air was soft on their faces. There was no wind and the clouds were high and pale grey, instead of looming and black with rain.

Cass could feel her lungs working as she strode up the sheep track beside the beck, and blood was soon throbbing in her fingers and ringing in her ears, but she wasn't troubled by any of it. She did not notice Livia's laboured breathing until she suddenly stopped, bent double, holding her ribs.

'Must catch my breath,' she gasped.

'Sit,' Cass ordered, seeing that Livia was scarlet-faced as well as wrestling for breath.

There was a large flat-topped boulder at the edge of the path, and Cass guided her towards it. As Livia's chest heaved with enormous, obviously painful breaths, Cass squatted at her knee, running through all the instructions she'd ever heard about what you were supposed to do if someone had a heart attack.

'I'm so sorry, Livia. I didn't think.'

Livia touched Cass's warm face and smiled as she whooped and hooted. When she could speak more easily, she said: 'Not your responsibility, Cass. I'm grown-up. I choose what I do.'

'I suppose so. But it's hard not to feel in charge.' She smiled. 'I suppose I'm naturally bossy.'

'Or had too much responsibility too young.'

Cass did not know how to answer that one. There had been many times when she had resented Rosamund's insatiable need for reassurance and protection, but it seemed disloyal to admit it.

'Something else that's down to me, I think. I'm so sorry, Cass.'

'Are you ready to go on now?'

'Sure.' Livia needed Cass's arm to pull her up from the low stone, but she set off again up the track at a reasonable pace.

'By the way,' Cass said later, when she was sure that Livia was strong enough to talk as well as walk, 'I thought Bobby was lovely on Friday when he shot that look at you over the wine bottle.'

'Wasn't he? So gentle and funny. I couldn't believe it.'

'A real vindication of your methods. I ought not to have doubted you.'

'Don't be too optimistic, Cass. He was good then, and today, but it won't last. It was only the tiniest of chinks in his defences. Talking of defences, what d'you make of Christopher?'

'I like him.'

'Yes, that's clear enough.' Cass turned in surprise at Livia's tone to see that she was laughing again. 'Oh, Cass, don't look so shocked. Your face is transformed when you're with him. I just wondered how much you know about him.'

'Not a lot,' said Cass. She thought that sounded ungracious and tried to find something to add. 'Except that he's quite successful but seems to be having some kind of crisis at the moment. And he likes you a lot.'

'Nice. How much does he know about me?'

'Only that you're the woman in the papers. You know, I think that could be why I liked him so much so quickly: he hasn't allowed anything he's read to faze him; he's a man who trusts his own judgement.'

'He's a good boy, even if he is a bit in the way. We can't talk about things that matter with him listening.'

'No,' said Cass, aware of how much she would miss him if he weren't there, 'but in some ways perhaps that helps. I mean, we didn't exactly get it right at the beginning.'

'No. Are you still bursting with questions?'

'Only a few,' Cass said quickly.

'You'd better ask them then, before they burn a hole in your brain. That's why I suggested we come out here.'

When Cass did not answer, Livia added a little less harshly: 'What exactly is it that you want to know?'

Where to begin? thought Cass. They had both stopped, as though it was impossible to walk and deal with this at the same time. 'I suppose mostly why you weren't given parole sooner. I'm sure I've read that most women who...whose husbands die like that...'

'Don't pretend to be tactful, Cass. It doesn't suit you. If we're going to talk, let's be honest with each other. There's no point otherwise. Most women who kill their husbands is what you mean.'

'OK. Yes, that is what I mean. Most of them get out after twelve or fifteen years, if not less. Why did you have to do twenty-four?'

'Gordon didn't tell you?'

Cass could not interpret Livia's expression as she looked into the distance, where a kestrel was hovering on the wind. Suddenly it plunged and then powered its way upwards again. They were too far away to see what it had in its talons, but there was something that still moved against the bright sky. Livia watched it disappear, her face harsher than ever.

'No. When I asked him, he said I ought to hear it from you. But I don't want to pry.'

'Let's walk.' Livia set off again up towards the summit. 'There was another death as well. Not Flora. A third person, later. I'm amazed the papers haven't printed anything about it. But then she wasn't as famous as Flora, so perhaps they don't care.'

The shock was almost physically painful. 'Who was she?'

'A prison officer.'

Cass stopped again on the rutted track. She had started to like Livia, and trust her. Had she been suckered yet again?

'Come on, Cass. She was a dreadful woman; not that that makes it any better. I didn't kill her myself, I hardly touched her, but she did die, and it was judged to be my fault.'

There was no one anywhere near. Christopher, in the house, was the only other human being within miles.

'How did it happen?'

'She liked winding up inmates,' said Livia casually, as though Cass ought to understand.

'You talked about winding up once before,' she said, 'but I don't know exactly what you mean.'

'Verbally tormenting you until you lose control. Some screws specialize in it. They do it to make you lose your temper and get yourself into trouble—or do yourself an injury.'

Cass blinked.

'It's usually the stupid ones who do it. They get bored and frustrated and like a bit of drama in their dreary little lives.'

'But why aren't they stopped?' Cass knew she sounded naive, but that was too bad.

'They're in charge, and they have all the power. There's nothing you can do about it. You could make a complaint, but if it wasn't accepted, you'd risk being put on a charge for making a malicious accusation. They have all the power,' Livia said again, her voice raw with frustration. 'The authorities usually choose to believe officers if there are stories that don't match.'

'But what about the other officers, the cleverer ones, the sort you talked about my first night here: the ones you liked?'

Livia shrugged. 'Even the thickest are bright enough to wait until they're on their own with you before they start a wind-up. Of course the decent ones know it goes on, and some of them do their best to stop it, but there isn't a lot they can do, except say what they think. And if the victim's unpopular—a troublemaker, say, or considered too big for her boots—who's going to care anyway?'

Yet again Cass had the impression of standing at the edge of an abyss, looking down at unimaginable people doing unthinkable things to each other.

'This particular officer,' Livia went on as though Cass had never interrupted, 'had an unerring knack of finding the weakest, sorest spots in her victims. This time she went for a girl called Muriel.'

Livia stopped talking as she thought of poor stupid Mu. There were no two ways about it: she was thick, but sweet and very needy. The one source of happiness in her entire life was her three-year-old daughter. Mu adored her. When Mu was sent down for quite a long stretch, her own mother took the child, later writing to say she was finding it hard to cope. Several of the officers read that letter and one of them found the opportunity for a major wind-up irresistible.

Livia tried to explain it all to Cass, but she did not have the words to recreate the thick fug of suspicion and rage that could fill a wing in bad times. They walked on up the track side by side, scattering fat sheep in front of them.

'The officer came up to Mu one day and told her that her mother had had enough and thrown the child out so that she'd had to be taken into care. Mu threw a fit, but even that wasn't enough for the officer, and so she went on and on about what happens to kids in some of those places. You know, all sorts of abuse.'

'That's appalling!' The shock made Cass's voice raw and as she breathed in, cold air poured down her throat: chilling, almost painful.

'Oh, you've no idea. That's only the gist of it. I'd heard her do similar things before to other people. She'd tried to wind me up because they all knew I never got any answers to the letters I sent Ros, but she didn't get any change out of me. I'm tough. Like you.'

Cass looked away.

'Unfortunately, poor Muriel wasn't. She couldn't take it. I saw what was happening—it was association at the time—and so I went over to them and told the screw to stop telling lies.'

Cass wished that Livia would name the officer, but perhaps that would have made it seem too real.

'She wouldn't. And I think I made her even angrier. She had a horrible voice, the worst kind of whiny London twang, and I knew she resented mine. It always did sound much too authoritative for the screws, even when I was trying to soften it, which I wasn't then. I wanted her to do as she was told.'

Livia blinked and muttered something about the wind in her face. Even though there was a breeze now they were nearing the top of the hill, Cass didn't think it was wind that was making tears run out of the corners of Livia's eyes.

'But I couldn't make her stop. She went on and on, until I thought Mu was either going to pass out or top herself. I'd seen enough of that, too. So I slapped the screw across the face.'

'I don't see what else you could've done,' Cass said, trying not to think about what she'd done to Alan.

Livia shrugged. Her voice was hard, distant, when she picked up the story again.

'She retaliated and grabbed me, jamming my arm up behind my back, and tried to call for help. There were other inmates there, who thought I was being assaulted. Since they all hated the screw, they joined in before the heavy mob could get there. It wasn't long before we had a full-scale riot going. The screw was down, on her back on the floor, and the only other one on the threes at the time was neutralized before she could ring the alarm.'

'What happened in the end?' Cass wasn't sure she wanted to hear the details, but she had to ask.

Livia coughed. 'She was kicked.'

'That doesn't sound too bad.'

Livia stared at her. 'They kicked her until she died, Cass.'

Cass stopped and turned away, to stare down at the lake while she thought of something to say.

'But it wasn't you, and you hadn't tried to kill her.' She turned back to face Livia, who was watching her with an expression that looked a bit too like pity for comfort. 'If she was well-known as a wind-up merchant, why didn't anyone speak up for you? They must have known she'd provoked what happened.'

'There'd been a riot and an officer died. They had to make an example of someone. Otherwise they'd never have re-established discipline. I can see that now. It doesn't make me any less angry, but I can see it.'

'What did they do to you?'

'Made sure I didn't get parole,' Livia said brusquely, setting off uphill again.

Even to Cass, she wasn't going to talk about what else they had done to her, about her time in solitary confinement in the new prison. She had been doped for the journey, as they nearly always were when they were to be transferred, the so-called difficult prisoners.

She'd come round in the bleakest punishment cell she had ever seen. There hadn't even been a mattress until the evening, and then it had been taken away again each morning. She hadn't talked to anyone for what felt like months, and they hadn't allowed her any books except the Bible. There had been a few male officers, on duty at weekends, who'd seemed determined to make her understand the full evil of what she'd done. Their only methods had been physical.

In the old days with Henry she had felt helpless, tormented even, but she'd had no idea. No idea at all. She looked at Cass, hoping for comfort. What she saw made her feel as though all her bones were cracking.

Cass was looking at her as Rosamund used to look—and Henry.

Cass staggered as her booted foot crunched into a deep, rain-filled pothole in the path. The water splashed high up her leg. But that shock was as nothing to the rest.

'We ought to turn back,' she said. 'The light's going.'

Without a word, Livia swung round and set off down the path again. Cass followed, not even trying to catch up. She needed time to sort out what she'd learned and work out whether she wanted to know more about Livia's life in prison and what had led to it.

They had to walk the last half-mile in darkness. Luckily Christopher had lit the fire and turned on all the lights, and so they couldn't possibly have got lost. Even so, Cass felt irresponsible and furious with herself. The ground under their feet was uneven and full of rabbit holes they couldn't see any longer. Livia could easily have twisted an ankle, or worse.

'Tea?' Livia said as they reached the house at last. 'Or a whisky?'

'Tea, I think,' said Cass. Her lips felt like cardboard, and she hoped it was the wind that had stiffened them. 'Shall I get it while you have a rest?'

'No, you go and talk to Christopher. I think there are some crumpets in the freezer. I'll heat them up.' Livia pushed open the door. 'Find out if he likes them buttered in advance will you? Some people prefer to keep the butter in chunks instead of melted.'

'Sure.' Cass was glad of something practical to do.

She waited until Livia had removed her boots and parka before taking her place on the old oak bench in the porch and bending to take off her own boots. Her fingers were cold and as clumsy as a five-year-old's.

Padding into the house in her socks, she saw that Christopher was waiting for her, looking worried.

'What happened to Livia?'

'She's gone to make tea and crumpets. She wanted to know whether you like your butter melted in or left off so that you can have it in lumps.'

'No. That's not what I meant. Something happened to her out on your walk.'

'What d'you mean?'

'She looked as though she'd been hurt, Cass.'

*She?* thought Cass. And what about me? Anyway, I didn't do anything to her. I supported her; I said it wasn't her fault the officer died. If she was hurt by anything it was her own memories. It wasn't me.

'I'd better tell her about the butter,' she said aloud. 'How…?'

'Bugger the butter! This is much more important.'

'Not at the moment. Let me deal with first things first. How do you like your crumpet butter?'

'Squashy. Melted. But…'

'I'll be back.'

Livia was standing with her back to the door. The crumpets were laid out on the grill tray, round, pock-marked, rubbery-looking, and the grill itself was already red-hot. Livia's left hand was lying on the kettle's handle. Her veins, thick and very blue, looked like worms about to burst out of the skin, sated on the soft parts she had once had.

'Livia? He says he likes his butter put on the crumpet to melt.'

'Ah, fine.' She didn't turn.

'Shall I put them under the grill? It looks hot.'

'Fine.'

So he was right. I did hurt her. But how? I didn't say anything that wasn't supportive. How else was I supposed to react? Tell her it didn't matter that a woman was kicked to death?

'Cass?'

'Yes?'

Livia still hadn't turned. She seemed to be staring out of the small window at the belt of trees that kept the wind at bay.

'You know, you shouldn't ask questions if you don't want to hear the answers.'

It was too much. First Christopher and now Livia chastising her. With superhuman self-control, Cass said merely: 'I don't think that's quite fair.'

Livia spun round. There was a knife in her hand. Cass felt her eyes widening and she took a step backwards. The aggression in Livia's eyes changed to doubt. She looked down.

Cass saw it was a blunt-ended table knife. It couldn't have done anyone any harm. Livia must have got it out ready to spread the butter. Cass wanted to apologize but didn't know how. Livia's eyes were blank and a bit foggy. She turned away, putting the knife down and leaning on the edge of the worktop, both hands spread flat on the hard surface. Her head was lowered. She said nothing and she didn't even seem to be breathing. Then she coughed. It sounded painful.

'I…'

Livia coughed again and then blew her nose.

'Don't say it, Cass. You'll get it wrong and then I'll get angry and we'll dig ourselves into a pit. Go away. Now. I'll bring the tea in when I can.'

# Chapter 11

Livia stood in her empty kitchen next morning, watching Cass drive away, bitterly envious of her freedom to do whatever she wanted. No one had ever told Cass to pretend to be less than she was, to suppress her talents and deny her identity; and no one had ever cheapened her anger by telling her she was mad. It was probably just as well she'd gone.

Then why are you snivelling? Livia asked herself savagely.

The sound of Colin's wheezy car outside made her rip a sheet of kitchen paper off the roll and clean her face. It wouldn't matter if Christopher saw her with reddened eyes and dripping nose, but Bobby was different. He needed her to be strong.

When she walked out of the kitchen to meet him, she was glad that Christopher had been tactful enough to take himself away upstairs to the bedroom that was now his. At least he hadn't felt the need to escape altogether. There were still some people who didn't find her unendurable.

A car door banged outside and she heard Colin's engine rev. She was smiling as Bobby danced in, full of Dare's latest outburst of rebellion. Flap barked hysterically at the noise and the swagger of Bobby's entrance. Livia watched as he moderated his movements.

Her breath stopped in her throat as she saw him kneel, nearly two feet away from Flap, and mutter something she couldn't hear. His grubby hand moved forwards, palm up, the fingers a little curled. Flap didn't respond, but he didn't retreat either. Bobby's hand did not move. Flap darted forwards and then skipped back again. Still Bobby didn't move.

Livia began to breathe again, as quietly as she could. Flap edged forwards. His thin pink tongue slipped out and touched the boy's fingers as briefly as a floating dandelion seed, and then returned a moment later to try again, and again, until it circled wetly about Bobby's whole hand. His other hand curled over Flap's fragile skull, stroking, as his voice crooned incomprehensible affection.

With an urge to sing pushing away the misery over Cass, Livia moved quietly away towards the table, where she uncapped her felt-tips and spread out the big sheets of paper she'd been using. She was still smiling as she mentally sketched out a few new flourishes for the house she was secretly designing for Dare. Soon she would show Bobby some of the first drawings and see how he reacted to the light and space that would fill the house.

Cass was belting south down the motorway. She had some Gilbert & Sullivan on the CD player, and was singing along in the cracked, tuneless voice she never let anyone else hear. Back in London there might be an empty flat, inhabited only by memories of Alan and the stolen weekends they'd spent there together, but at least it was her own. She was at no one's mercy there, and she couldn't hurt anyone else.

At the turn for Birmingham, the traffic began to thicken. Cass eased off the accelerator a little, only to be flashed in her mirror. A testosterone-maddened idiot was almost sitting on her bumper. There was nowhere for her to go. She was already too close to the car ahead and the middle and inner lanes were chock-a-block. The flashing was dangerously distracting. She put up one finger against her mirror.

Now the lunatic started using his horn as well as his lights. A space appeared on Cass's left as the inner lane's traffic began to spread out, and she put on her indicator. The driver behind ignored her signal and whizzed past her on the inside at nearly ninety, with only about six inches to spare. Swooping back into the outer lane, he started to aggress the car ahead.

'Tosser!' Cass muttered as the automatic changer put a new Gilbert & Sullivan CD into the machine.

'Bow, bow, ye lower middle classes!' trumpeted the singer. 'Bow, bow, ye tradesmen, bow, ye masses! Blow the trumpets, bang the brasses! Tantantara! Tzing! Boom!'

The chorus made her smile, as it always did. It provided wonderful driving music. To Gilbert (or was it Sullivan?) her hard-won career would have made her one of the bowing tradesman. Well, not nowadays, thank God. She was free, powerful, and herself, and she wasn't about to bow to anyone. Not for anything. Tantantara! Tzing! Boom!

That is, she reminded herself more grimly, if I've still got a trade. Michael will have talked to the other directors by now.

By the outskirts of north London she had forgotten even that anxiety, locked into fury, with a pounding headache and a hatred of inconsiderate drivers, the weather, traffic lights, designers of roundabouts, and just about everything and everyone she encountered. It was already rush-hour when she got as far as the City and, picking her way through the few roads that were open through the ring of steel, she longed to be home.

The sight of her not very beautiful building at the end of the undistinguished cul-de-sac south of the river made her feel better than all the ravishing views around the Long House. Cass had never thought of the flat as a refuge, just a place to eat and sleep and from which to sally forth as a conqueror. Now it promised a lot more. And, best of all, there were no journalists or photographers visible. With luck they'd all got bored and gone. Or maybe someone had told them she was in the Seychelles.

There were a few lights in the windows of some of the other five flats, and they decorated the dark, wet street in a throughly satisfactory way. The local council hadn't yet run to more than a couple of dim streetlights, and there was far too much cloud for the moon to do anything to help. A slight movement caught her eye and she glanced to her left to see a cyclist, with no lights, lurch out of the last side street and wobble across the road just in front of her bumper.

She slammed on her brakes, skidding forwards as the figure fell into the gutter leaving the bike to slide under the cars's wheels. She wrenched up the handbrake and smashed open the door to fling herself out into the wet road.

'Are you OK? Where are you?' she called. 'Are you OK?'

A twitching movement in the huddled dark-clothed figure in the gutter allowed her to breathe again. The terror sucked at her as it receded, like the undertow on a steep gravel beach. The figure sat up, revealing itself to be male, white, dressed from balaclava to boots in black.

'What the fuck do you think you're doing?' he yelled, reassuringly vigorous. 'Look at my bike! You could've killed me.'

Cass stood above him in the dark, feeling the rain trickling through her hair and down her scalp, and the anger spreading inside her, pushing against her control until it broke.

'You stupid, *stupid*, little shit,' she yelled with equal force. 'You come silently out of a dark road, utterly invisible, with no right of way and no lights, and bury yourself under my wheels. Are you blind? And deaf? Or just a kamikaze fool?'

Something flashed in her head and she saw her own hands, taut and stretching out towards his throat. She shuddered, pulling them back behind her.

'I'm hurt,' he muttered. 'You hit me.'

Cass made herself concentrate on the rain, cool and dripping, until she had brought the anger back as firmly as her hands. Then she realized that she could be being watched and peered into the unlit side street. There was no one there. And no one behind her either.

'I'm sorry.' She was panting slightly, but her voice was better, softer. 'But it was your own fault. How badly are you damaged?'

'It's my shoulder.'

'Wait. I've got a mobile.' She wasn't going to admit to anyone as potentially dangerous as this man that she lived at the end of the street. Although he probably knew quite well who she was. He'd probably been hanging about in the dark with a photographer waiting for her to come back and tried to set up a scene they could use to show her as a mad violent psychopath like her grandmother.

Oh, come on, Cass, she said to herself. How would he know whose car to fling himself under? You're paranoid.

She rang the police and explained what had happened. The young-sounding officer asked if the cyclist was there.

'Yes. D'you want to talk to him?'

'Yes.'

Cass handed her mobile to the man, who was now sitting on the edge of the curb, massaging his left shoulder and making agonized faces that seemed a bit too good to be true. After all, there wasn't any blood, and she was pretty sure she hadn't actually hit him, whatever he'd said. He'd probably banged his shoulder on the road after he fell off the bike, before her wheels touched it, if he was in fact hurt at all.

His hand shook as he reached up to take the phone. Cass listened to him confirming her story of what had happened.

'And my bike's wrecked.'

There was a pause, as Cass wondered what she would see in the papers tomorrow. She could imagine the headlines: 'Harpy's granddaughter rams innocent cyclist.' 'Hit and run by Harpy Mark II.'

Her victim said goodbye and handed the phone back to her.

'Yes?' Cass said into it.

'You're lucky, miss. He admits it was your right of way and that he hadn't any lights. Is he fit to move?'

Cass watched him for a moment as he hobbled towards his bike and bent to pick it up.

'Yes. The bike's a bit crumpled, though. Oh, not too bad. The wheels are going round. I'll see if he wants me to call him a cab.'

'Right you are. But you are lucky, you know. Even though it was your right of way, if you'd killed him you'd be in bother.'

'I know. Thanks.'

'OK. Mind how you go, now.'

She clicked the phone off and said coldly: 'Shall I call you a cab?'

'No,' he said, looking up. Hunched over the bike as he was, with the rain making his black anorak look slick as a pool of oil, he seemed more like a goblin than anything else. 'I can wheel it. I...'

She just looked at him, and he swallowed. Whatever it was he'd been going to say, more accusation or some kind of apology, she'd managed to choke it off. She waited while he limped theatrically to the far end of the road and then mounted the bike and rode off. So it was serviceable after all. In that case, she'd hardly touched the bike and most certainly had not touched him. Bastard. Sick, sick bastard. So, she might have scared him, but he had sodding well deserved it.

She walked down the side street, checking that there hadn't been anyone else there to see what had happened. Thank God, she'd managed to stop, and thought to phone the police. At least no one would be able to print stories about her callous disregard for her victim, whatever else they might write.

❦

The answering machine tape was full of messages. Cass listened to them as she stripped off her damp clothes and wrapped a towel around herself before heading for the shower. Most were from journalists, including George Jenkins of the *Post*, who said he had been commissioned to write a book about the murders of Henry Claughton and Flora Gainsborough and would appreciate any time Cass could give him, but a few of her friends had checked in. Sophie had called once, breezily, to say wasn't it a weird coincidence the Harpy looking so like Cass? Then, fourteen messages later, came her voice again, much more hesitant: 'Cass, it's Sophie again. I'm not quite sure how...I just wanted to say sorry for that earlier message I left yesterday. I know you won't get either till you come back from the Seychelles, but…Listen, I don't want to be a pain. If she is some kind of relation, I'm really sorry for what I said. Um. I didn't mean to sound so frivolous. Why don't you phone me when you're back. Let's have, you know, supper or something. OK, Cass? I'm really sorry, you know.'

Then came Gordon Bayley's voice, resonant and warm: 'Cass? Gordon here. You must be still up with Livia. I'm so glad. But when you get back, could you give me a ring? I'd love to hear how she's getting on and I don't want to harry her since she clearly doesn't want to talk to me yet.'

Then more journalists, then Amanda Watchman, an old acquaintance, surprisingly inviting Cass to dinner, then Michael Betteridge, asking her to phone him as soon as she could. That reminded her that she need not answer any of the messages until Sunday, when she had expected to be flying back from the Seychelles.

It was a pity that Michael hadn't said anything about his promised discussions with the other directors of Stogumber's. Still, he'd bothered to phone, which was more than she had thought he would do for the Harpy's granddaughter.

The phone rang. Never had she hated the sound so much. She ignored it and went to shower, hoping to wash away the memory of her own fury with the cyclist.

❧

Livia had put the last of the finishing touches to the plans of Dare's house, which she had decided after all not to show Bobby quite yet, and was beginning to think about what she might give Christopher for supper. She didn't mind cooking for him because he was always so nice about what she produced, even when it was a bit odd.

She pushed the top on her Rotring pen and laid it down beside the drawing board. She had forgotten the almost sensual pleasure of the crispness of tracing paper and the smoothness of the black ink that flowed on to it. And she'd forgotten the intellectual satisfaction, too, that could be had from reading those thin lines and seeing in her mind the three-dimensional building they could one day become.

Her head leaned to one side as she squinted down at the row of elevations along the top of the paper. Yes, it would be a good house: small but workable; and fun, too, with those unexpected angles and vistas from room to room. It would be wonderful to build it.

She turned away, blinking. She'd never build anything again. Along with all the rest, Henry had taken that from her for ever. Hatred made her skin shrivel, pulling and wrinkling it all over her body. Surprised, she looked at her hands and saw that they seemed the same as always. The hands were just hands: not claws or bunches of knives. Was she going mad again? Oh, please no. Please.

'Livia?' The quiet male voice made her jump. She'd forgotten Christopher, peacefully reading in front of the fire.

'What's the problem?' she asked without turning. Her voice was rasped with shock and dislike.

'I don't know. It just feels as though something awful's happened to you. I wondered if I could help.'

There was so much kindness in his deep voice that she turned to face him.

'D'you want to talk?' he asked gently.

Her nose wrinkled and she shook her head. 'Not much. It's drinks time. Would you like something? You must be well enough for alcohol by now.'

'Oh, why not? Some wine if you've got any open.' He hesitated as she stood looking at him. 'May I see the drawing?'

'Why?'

'I'm interested.'

Livia was silent. She'd designed the house for Bobby and she didn't want anyone else looking at it. The last things she needed now were crass questions or criticism of her taste or her technique. She was about to say so, when she remembered how she'd driven away first Gordon and now Cass. Somehow she was going to have to find a way to live with other people—other adults—again. If she couldn't, she might just as well have stayed in prison.

Christopher would give her helpful practice. He wasn't expecting any kind of affection from her, and so far she hadn't frightened him. And he appeared to have no need to exercise any kind of power over her. Better him looking at her work, perhaps, than anyone else.

'Suit yourself,' she said gracelessly and went off to the kitchen in search of glasses and ice for her gin and tonic.

When she came back, Christopher was staring at the tracing paper. All her rough sketches were spread out around the drawing board, including the perspective of the tiny boy's figure dwarfed by the hideous, rain-soaked, phallic monstrosities behind him. It was a portrait of a particular kind of modern hell. She'd put a lot of her old furious disgust into the rubbish she'd drawn, the stains on the concrete, the syringes and the used condoms, recreating from memory the descriptions her cellmates had provided over the years.

It had given her an odd unhappy satisfaction to hear from his other victims just how right she'd been about the effect of living in one of Henry's horrible towers. She'd been right about a lot of things, as she'd always thought. Well, not always; if it had been always, she'd never have got herself in such a mess. Oh, God! If only Henry had once been able to admit that she was right—just once—everything could have been different.

She felt someone else's hands on hers and looked down. This time her fingers were curled into the claws she dreaded, and Christopher was slowly straightening them out. She smiled briefly, formally, and made herself relax, moving out of his range.

He pushed aside the sketch of the tower-block slum and picked up one of the other perspectives, a sun-filled watercolour of Dare's house.

Livia's smile became more real and she saw again the plants falling from the balconies, the perfectly pitched flying roof, the windows opening to the sun: all the colour and light and airy freedom she'd put into every building she'd ever been allowed to design.

'You're good,' Christopher said without question or qualification. Livia nodded. That was something she knew. Now. Much, much too late. 'Are you going to practise again?'

'How can I?'

'I don't know. I don't know enough about it.' He smiled at her. 'And you don't need to look like that because I'm not going to ask.'

Livia felt her own lips softening then. How extraordinary that a man like him, young enough to be her grandson, rich and powerful, should understand.

'It's all so long ago,' she said. 'I can't go back. And if I could, I'm not sure I'd want to. There's not much time left and I need to live what there is in the now, not the then.'

He hesitated, clearly about to speak. She thought of freezing him out, but in the end told him to spit it out, whatever it was.

'OK. I was just wondering whether you were planning to tell Cass about the "then".'

'You sound as though you think I should.' Her voice was frosty. She couldn't help it.

'It's not for me to say. Again, I don't know enough.'

She couldn't help smiling. 'For a man of your calling— and standing—you're remarkably humble.'

He watched her in silence for long enough to make her curious about what he could be thinking. At last he said: 'I've learned a lot about myself just recently. Myself and other people. And I'm not half as arrogant as I used to be. But since you've asked my opinion, perhaps it's not fair to pretend. Yes, I do think you ought to tell her the truth, the whole truth.'

Every muscle stiffened again. She couldn't stop them. Coming so soon after his sensitivity, the order was unbearable.

'Livia.' The kindness was back in his voice. 'She needs to know. And I think she has the right.'

She turned away and addressed the wall. That, too, was familiar. She'd talked a lot to the walls in her first months in Holloway.

'Why?'

'Because she's part of you,' he said from behind her, still gentle.

'And so she might have inherited a propensity for violence. Is that what you're saying? That she needs to be given the awful warning?'

'No.' His voice was steady. 'Because, until whatever it was that went wrong yesterday, the two of you were like two halves of the same walnut shell. You fitted together and there was something good—nutritious to you both—between you. I used to watch you both and envy you. It was unmistakeable in spite of the occasional fratching. Don't throw it away. It's rare enough, God knows.'

Livia thought about her granddaughter, who had everything she'd ever wanted.

'I tried and it didn't work,' she said firmly. 'I thought it might. But it didn't. There's too much she couldn't ever understand about what happened. And…' She paused until the pain made her gasp: 'And I can't deal with *her* difficulties about it. I've enough of my own.'

'Perhaps she didn't understand because you haven't told her everything yet.' Christopher said. 'It's hard to see the picture in a jigsaw when you've only got a few of the pieces.'

'What did she tell you?' Livia was frowning as she absorbed the new hurt of Cass's indiscretion.

'She didn't repeat anything you said to her. I've no idea how much she knows about what you did or why. All I do know is that there must have been more to it than I've read in the papers.'

'What do you mean?' The cold that was filling Livia's throat made her voice even more harsh and horrible than usual.

'A woman like you could not have killed a man in a fit of temper because she'd found him sleeping with another woman.'

'No?' The harshness spread until every part of her felt dangerous.

'No. You must have had a much better reason than that.'

'That's what the jury thought,' she said drearily, wondering where his kindness had gone. 'That's why they decided it was murder. If it'd been just a fit of jealous rage, I might have got away with manslaughter and been out after a few years.'

'That's not what I meant. As you must know. Think, Livia…'

There it was again: censoriousness and a command to obey. How she hated it! She felt his hands on her shoulders and resisted their pull. But he was stronger than she, much stronger, and she had no choice but to give in. For a second she was afraid of what he might do to her. They were alone; she knew no more of him than that he played a good game of Scrabble and that Cass had heard him well spoken of in the City. He could be anything, do anything. And he had his hands near her neck. She coughed.

'Livia, listen—'

'I am listening, but I'd be grateful if you'd take away your hands.'

He let her go at once and stood examining his fingers. Long they were, and nicely shaped. Then he looked up at her. His thin face was stern, but not cruel, she thought: so different from that other face, fleshy and contemptuous.

'If you had been capable of killing a man simply because he'd been unfaithful, I couldn't like you as much as I do. I *know* you had another reason. A good reason.'

She felt heat in her eyes and let her head droop. At her age, she couldn't burst into tears and fling herself against a manly chest.

'I can't...' were the only words she managed to say before Christopher took the decision away from her and pulled her against the rough wool of his Guernsey. She felt his hands, one on her back and the other stroking her hair. Over and over again. She couldn't see anything and she didn't have to say anything. Christopher Bromyard, who owed her nothing and expected nothing from her, was offering her the one thing she needed: wordless, unjudging, unqualified physical and emotional comfort.

# Chapter 12

The storage unit was like a cell, long and narrow and lit by a single bare bulb. Down either side were shelves of raw wooden slats, on which stood neat piles of boxes, files and brown portfolios with black corners and spines. There were account books in serried ranks, and below the bottom shelves on each side of the unit were trunks and huge cardboard boxes. At the far end stood four dark-green metal filing cabinets.

Everything had a label in Rosamund's upright black handwriting: letters on Cass's birth; letters from Father; letters from Granny; photographs 1950–1962; Drawing Office 1949–56; Grandfather's medals and citations.

Surrounded by her family's history, Cass stood amazed at the thought that Rosamund could have accumulated so much stuff, arranged it with such obsessive tidiness and yet kept it virtually secret.

The label on the last box intrigued her. She reached for it. Dust rose in a pale, beige-grey cloud, then fell on her face. It looked soft as it came down, but it felt gritty against her skin and got up her nose.

Whose grandfather? she wondered as she sneezed and unfolded a piece of paper that felt as friable as meringue between her damp fingers. It was a citation for gallantry beyond the line of duty at the Somme, in the name of John Antony Tafter, adding a bar to the DSO he had already won at Loos.

Cass looked along the row of photograph boxes for one that covered 1914–1918. Squatting on the floor because there was no chair, she leafed through the small stiff cardboard rectangles, turning them over to read the spidery captions on the back. The answer was quickly clear, but she didn't want to allow herself any false security, so she searched the papers until she was sure.

The eyes should have been enough to tell her, she thought when she was certain who John Antony Tafter had been: the eyes and the cheekbones. Livia's father, her own great-grand-father. A war hero.

Cass sat down on the bare concrete, her legs stuck out uncomfortably in front of her, staring at the biggest of the sepia photographs, allowing herself the thought that even if she had Livia's genes, she also had a hero's. It was weird to feel comforted by that; and even weirder when she remem-bered that the hero must have killed too. That was generally what turned soldiers into heroes.

The rest of the archive could wait. Cass piled together all the boxes of letters and photographs that looked as though they had anything to do with her great-grandfather. Stretch-ing as she stood up, she looked at her mother's neat labels and wished she'd come here sooner.

Rosamund had been so casual about it, on the day, five years earlier, when she had left for her new life, that Cass had never bothered to investigate. Rosamund had handed over a file containing Cass's birth and baptism certificates and other useful documents, along with her new address in the States, the address of the family's lawyers, and this key, saying: 'I've put all the family papers in the Cathedral Self-Storage warehouse in Vauxhall, just in case you should ever need them. I don't suppose you will. Musty old things, most of them, but I can't quite bring myself to throw them out. I've arranged a building society account to pay the annual charge. You won't have to be bothered, Cass. But you ought to have a key. Just in case.'

Cass had taken it without interest and put it away. She couldn't think now why she had had so little curiosity. If she had asked the right questions then, Rosamund would probably have told her about Livia. But she hadn't asked, so she hadn't been told. Heedless, excited by her first job and her new flat, wishing Rosamund well, but relishing the prospect of freedom, Cass had simply taken the key and put it away.

She would come back again, with a deck chair, to learn about the rest of her family. But for the moment, the records of John Antony Tafter's courage would be enough. As she was leaving, with the heavy pile of boxes hugged in her left arm and drawing dust lines against her pale fleece, she noticed another of Rosamund's typically neat labels.

'Cass 0–5', it said, stuck to the spine of a red-leather photograph album. Feeling unusually sentimental, she took down the fat volume and added it to her heap. She had to dump the whole lot on the floor outside, in order to lock the door. The padlock felt heavy and cold as it hung against her palm, like the testicles of some enormous metallic beast.

'What *is* the matter with you?' she asked herself aloud. 'Testicles, indeed.'

'You OK?' called a voice from the far end of the warehouse.

'Fine,' she called back. What must the security guard have thought of her if he'd heard what she'd said? Well, who cared?

❧

There were a couple of people, who could have been journalists, loitering at the front of her building, so she took her usual evasive action. There was no one at the mouth of the alley, or hiding behind the Wheelie bins. She got her loot upstairs unrecorded.

It seemed a good idea to eat something before she plunged back into the past. After her siege preparations, there was more food in the kitchen than she'd ever had before, yet nothing looked particularly alluring. Eventually, she took a loaf of *pain de campagne* and a carton of Tuscan bean soup from the freezer. She peeled the cardboard away from the frozen block, remembering the way her tongue used to stick to orange lollies, and dropped it, clattering, into a pan on a low heat.

There wasn't much point defrosting the whole loaf when she'd eat only a couple of slices, so she plonked the icy bread on the board and started hacking off a slice to put into the toaster. The loaf kept sliding away from the knife, and she put her left hand firmly on the top of it, fingers spread, sawing down through the dense, crunchy substance. A slice fell away with a satisfactory thump. She dropped it in the toaster and, determined not to be beaten, started sawing again, the blade bowing sideways under the pressure.

She didn't see how it happened. The knife hardly moved, but it was enough. One minute she was leaning down, putting all her weight on the handle and the next she was staring at the blade, stuck into the loose flesh between her thumb and fingers. Blood was pouring out, hitting the frozen loaf and sliding down it like ketchup on a child's burger.

It hurt. Sweating, Cass couldn't understand why a little cut should hurt so much. And for a minute she couldn't think what to do. The serrated blade was stuck in her hand, deep enough to stay there unless she did something. She was going to have to pull it out. All it would take was resolution. She wiped the other hand on her jeans.

More blood gushed out as she pulled the knife away and gripped the cut with her other hand, squeezing. Blood oozed around her clenched fingers, thin and surprisingly liquid. It should have been sticky, she thought, pinching the thin, loose bit of flesh that was so like a chicken's wing.

Her mind kept skittering about in a way that worried her. She tried to concentrate. It's only shock, she told herself. Put something on it. Plaster or something. Is there any? There must be.

She found it in the end, a long folded strip of fabric plaster, the colour of stale rhubarb fool, folded up between the empty sugar and flour canisters on one of the open shelves. When she took her fingers away from the wound to pick up the plaster and cut a piece, she saw how small the cut was to have produced so much blood. But it was deep.

The blood still hadn't thickened, but she managed to get a piece of plaster stuck down before her skin became too wet. Even so, the pink fabric was soon saturated. But it held, which was all that mattered.

Cass sat at the kitchen table, nursing her hand and thinking about her grandfather.

How long had it taken him to die? Even if it had been quick, he must have lived long enough to see Livia's knife cutting into his chest, feel it slicing through his skin and the fat below that and then the muscle, probably hitting a rib before it reached his heart, making the warm blood gush out over his skin. And Livia's hand, presumably.

It must have got unbearably sticky, Cass told herself as she felt her own blood gluing her fingers together. She'd wash in a minute. What had Livia thought as she felt that tackiness and looked down at her nails outlined in blood like this? Had she washed it off herself? Or had the police done that once they'd taken their samples? Had she tasted it, like this?

Cass's blood was salty, not unpleasant. But it was her own.

And what had Livia thought as she drove the knife into him? What had made her angry enough to do it?

Cass was shivering. She wanted help, but she didn't know whose or what sort. She didn't even know who she was any longer. She thought of one of the other women who had a flat in her building, a psychotherapist called Annette Sharpe, who had had a drinks party last Christmas. Cass had gone out of neighbourliness and half-listened to her hostess's latest theory, which was something about how you can only be happy while the story you tell yourself about who you are meshes with the way fate and other people treat you.

That's right, Cass thought. She'd said that when your story is a bit askew, you get gloomy. The further apart the two become, the more depressed you are. And when they don't tally in any respect, then you're mad. Or something like that. She probably hadn't actually said 'mad'. Shrinks never do. But that was what she'd meant.

Cass stood up, determined to get her real, tough self back, then had to cling to the edge of the table with her good hand to balance. A smell of burning puzzled her until she remembered the soup. She turned out the gas and, ignoring the acrid blackness in the pan, made herself a cup of tea instead.

Later, with the doors and windows locked, and the tea beside her, she lay against banked-up pillows in bed, ready to get to know her great-grandfather, John Antony Tafter, the hero. That might get her stories back in sync. Her cut hand throbbed still, and felt stiff under the hardened Elastoplast, but it didn't hurt any more. Not much anyway.

John Antony had gone to the war straight from school, she discovered from the captions. There he was at the beginning of the first album, looking far too old to be a schoolboy, and then on the next page he was in uniform, sporting a thick, ugly moustache that made his face glower out of the photograph. Some of the other faces from his school cricket team were there with him.

The pictures didn't tell Cass much in the end, except that John Antony had been wounded—in the head—and married a beautiful blonde woman in 1920. Livia had been born four years later and first appeared in her mother's arms, trailing lace, in the porch of a small country church. There didn't seem to have been any other children, which was a relief to Cass. She didn't need any more surprises.

She knew enough about the war after *Birdsong* and *Testament of Youth*, as well as all the television programmes during the eightieth anniversary of the Armistice, to have some idea of what the medals and the bandages must have meant. In her mind she could see the endless jerky twitching and haunted faces of the men who had returned from the trenches so damaged by four years of fear that they could not speak or walk or relate to anyone who had not been there. How had any of them lived normal lives after that?

Cass hoped her great-grandfather had found some happiness with the beautiful gentle-faced blonde woman who had married him, and she was glad that he must have died long before Livia's trial. Wanting to know more about his wife, Cass looked for letters, taking the lids off all the boxes she had brought away from the archive.

The first box yielded not letters but bound books. Several were covered in rubbed brown leather, one or two in blue cloth, and the last few at the bottom were simple spiral-bound exercise books. Curious, Cass opened the first of the leather ones, at random, to read.

'Mama to visit next week. Thank God. It will be good to have her opinion. I don't know what to do and the doctors are no help any longer. They admit they do not know.'

Cass knew nothing of graphology—and didn't believe in it anyway—but the writing, which must have been her great-grandmother's, was neat, forward-slanting, a little spiky but easy enough to read. She skipped through the pages, most of which contained anxieties of one sort or another, many to do with her husband's health, until she came on one page that contained a single sentence: 'God help me, but now Livia frightens me, too.'

You and me both, thought Cass grimly, nursing her cut hand. But what did she do to you?

She read on until she couldn't keep awake any longer, then slept, not much the wiser, with the photographs and diaries spread out on the duvet all round her and their dusty smell in her nostrils.

❦

Two days later, she was back in the storage room, digging into a past that ought to have been familiar territory. She knew that there must be something about Livia's trial in the more modern files, but she couldn't face them yet.

Reading what was in the old boxes felt like swimming underwater. She could pull herself strongly along, managing well enough and dimly seeing her goal through the foggy water, but then suddenly she'd start to choke and have to come up for air. After one, unusually long breathing pause, she put her head down again and started to read the top letter from a box labelled 'Letters: 1935–47'.

Father,

This is to inform you that the Architectural School is prepared to offer me a scholarship so that you will not have to pay any fees for me. *They* consider my work to be of a high enough standard, and my future promising enough, to be worth their spending money on my training.

There is no point discussing it any further. If you are not prepared to continue to pay my allowance, I shall make other arrangements. I am not prepared to sacrifice the future that I have worked so hard to win in order to satisfy your outdated notions of what it is proper for wives and daughters to do. I shall be staying with Grandmama until the end of the week and so any letter you might wish to send will find me here.

Livia

Cass blinked. She looked at the date and worked out that Livia must have been seventeen when she wrote it. Cass's vertebrae felt as though they were made of fused cast iron, and her knees were beginning to ache even more painfully than after a long session on the rowing machine. She shifted position again, hearing the ligaments crack in her neck, and leaned forwards to shuffle through the letters in the box, hoping to find John Antony's response to his daughter. It seemed odd that anyone should have collected such family letters and bothered to keep them. She assumed it must have been John Antony's wife and wondered why.

Livia,

I do not understand how you can treat your mother and me in this way. How *could* you tell the Architectural School that you would need their charity? Isn't it bad enough that you refuse to behave as your mother wishes and insist on pursuing this absurd selfish desire to have a career? Must you make us look like paupers, too? Have you *no* consideration or sense of what is fitting?

If nothing else will keep you quiet and make you behave, then I shall most reluctantly have to accept that you will be attending the Architectural School for the next few years. The one thing for which I am profoundly thankful is that you will not have time to get into the kind of trouble that girls like you risk when they flout their parents in this way. You will live at home and you will conduct yourself with decency, and then we shall see.

> Your affectionate father,
> John Antony Tafter

Cass folded the letter and put it back in its box, wanting to hit him. Another sheet of paper caught her eye, covered with writing unlike that on any of the other family letters. It was dated 9 September 1943, and began 'My dear Mrs Tafter'. Cass turned it over, but the signature at the end meant nothing to her.

My dear Mrs Tafter,

I promised you a personal note after my examination of your husband, and I wish that I had never undertaken such a commitment. This is such a difficult letter to write.

I have to tell you that he is most unlikely to improve. Our knowledge of the after-effects of head injury develops every year, but our ability to help patients does not keep pace. I regret to have to tell you that your husband's violence may not abate.

I know you are very reluctant to have him committed to a secure nursing home, but I do not think that you can continue to take the risks you are facing now for very much longer. As I have said, his condition cannot improve and it may worsen. You have told me that where he was once merely verbally violent, now he actually strikes you. I have spoken to your general practitioner and we have agreed that if his condition worsens, arrangements will be made to have your husband admitted to the Springfield Hospital in South London. You will, of course, be able to visit him there; and you will be safe.

And now to an even more difficult subject. You have expressed a concern that your husband's difficulties might not be the result of his wounds, but have been caused by some malformation in the brain itself.

On that score, too, I am afraid I cannot reassure you. We simply do not have the facilities to assess the reasons why such men behave as they do. I can, on the other hand, give you the reassurance that you crave as far as your daughter is concerned. I have examined her at length and I can assure you, my dear Mrs Tafter, that Olivia shows no signs of the taint that you so greatly fear.

You have described her as very aggressive, but these are difficult times in which to grow up, and she is working very hard indeed with her studies and her work for the Red Cross. She is also deeply concerned that she may have to give up her architectural course if she is called up. I really do not think that you need to fear that she herself will become violent. I shall see her again in six months or so, but please try not to worry so much about her. She is an entirely normal, highly intelligent young woman, of whom you have every reason to be proud.

Cass swallowed. Her mouth tasted as though she'd just chewed a handful of rancid almonds. Why hadn't Rosamund ever told her any of this? Or her father? He must have known some of it, even if not all the details.

No wonder Rosamund had been so worried every time Cass got into a fight at school, or lost her temper, or broke a piece of china. She had deliberately thrown a cup at the wall once, after one of her friends had annoyed her past bearing. Rosamund had burst into tears and run upstairs, not to reappear for hours. It had all been very embarrassing.

Did I frighten her as much as Livia frightened her mother? Cass wondered.

She thought of the photographs of her childhood that she had looked at in bed when she woke that first morning. Page after page of little grey-and-white rectangles, all of them showing her alone with her father. Rosamund must have been the one with the camera, recording picnics and bathing at the seaside, games, and even some of the arguments that had always worried her so.

There was one photograph in which a fat little Cass, dressed only in ruched bathing pants, was clearly bellowing at her father. There was a flat ribbon of seaweed trailing forgotten from one hand and the other was raised with one finger wagging at him. He was laughing, not in the least frightened. Oh, God how she missed him! It was nearly ten years since he'd died. She needed him.

Suddenly sick of the past and angry with herself for turning into such a quivering wimp, Cass piled the letters back in their box and heaved it up on to the shelf above Rosamund's neat label. It was idiotic to go on asking herself questions she would never be able to answer. The only sensible way of dealing with life was to look forwards. Clearly there had been great unhappiness in her family's past, and cruelty of all sorts, but picking its scabs to see exactly how bad it had been—and who had done what to whom—wasn't going to change anything.

None of it need have anything to do with her unless she chose to let it, and she wasn't going to do that. She had managed perfectly well for years knowing nothing about any of her family: she had constructed a life for herself that worked. She'd go back to that, locking all the hurt and misery behind the splintered door with the testicular padlock.

She folded up her deck chair and switched off the light for the last time. She wouldn't come back. As she turned the heavy key behind her, she thought she might phone Livia. Somehow they would learn to be friends in the present and forget the rest. It needn't affect them if they were careful.

Cass saw a phone box and stopped the car. If she called from home or her mobile, Livia's number would appear on her bill. Cass didn't know how easy it would be for a journalist to get hold of a copy of her phone bills, but it was one risk she wasn't prepared to take.

Livia was in, and they had an amicable if trivial conversation, in which neither mentioned the manner of Cass's leaving the Long House or the possible reasons for her departure. Livia told her that Bobby's reading was improving by leaps and bounds and that Flap's agility was doing much the same. He had already smashed three vases, and Livia had had to move everything breakable to shelves above his reach.

'Oh, and I've lost Christopher. He decided he was well enough to go home. I rather think I may be going to miss him.'

'I'm not surprised,' Cass said, pleased at the ordinariness of the comment. 'He was good company, wasn't he?'

'Very. And a surprisingly good cook. Much better than me. I expect you'll see something of him in London. Cass, I ought to go in a minute, but before I do, might I ask you to do something for me? Do say no, if you want.'

'Of course.' Cass's tongue was as stiff as the sound it produced.

'Do you ever go to the theatre?'

It was such an unexpected question that Cass laughed, then curled her tongue experimentally, pleased to find it flexible and slippery again, rather like Flap's.

'Not often. I'm usually too hung up with work and things. Why?'

'I did just wonder whether you might…I've been reading the papers on the Internet, and…'

'On the Net? But, Livia, I didn't know you had a computer.'

There was a hoarse laugh down the phone. 'I keep it in my bedroom. It's my private toy. But I'll give you my e-mail address in a minute in case you ever feel like writing. Anyway, Cass, I've seen that Julia Gainsborough is starring in Sophocles' *Electra*, which opens on Saturday night in Wandsworth of all unlikely places.'

'Yes, I saw that too.'

'Well, I…I can't get her out of my mind, and obviously I can't go and see her myself. I wondered if you might feel able to be my stand-in, as it were, and then tell me about her. And the play. But not if the idea bothers you, of course.'

'No,' Cass said slowly. 'No, I don't think it does particularly.'

She might have just taken a decision to ignore the past, but Livia had never asked her for anything before. This should be easy enough to do, and it might make up—a bit anyway—for her flight.

'I'll phone up and see if there are any tickets left.'

'Judging by the kind of publicity Julia has been trying to drum up,' said Livia drily, 'I should say it's the kind of play—and theatre—where there are usually plenty of empty seats.'

❧

On Saturday evening, Cass changed into black leather trousers and a favourite grey jacket, and drove to the Old Territorial Hall in Wandsworth. She had no idea what to expect: she never went to the theatre in the normal way and had always thought of it as a grotesquely middle-aged amusement. She didn't think a translation of some classical tragedy was likely to change her mind.

The bar at the Old Territorial Hall was filled with people not much older than she was, most of them dressed in black T-shirts tucked into black jeans. There was a sprinkling of older men and one or two motherly-looking women, but most of the drinkers were as thin and sexy as any of the diners at the Blue Print Café. Cass privately admitted her mistake and bought herself a glass of wine. The edge of the plastic tumbler was uncomfortably sharp against her lips and the wine was vinegar-sour.

Having no one to talk to didn't worry her, but she didn't want to look like a spare part, so she walked across to a large corkboard hung with photographs of all the actors and lists of their past successes.

There was no doubt that Julia Gainsborough was an amazing-looking woman, with her mass of rich blonde hair and broad-boned face. Her c.v. was surprisingly short, or perhaps heavily edited. She had had a season at Stratford, playing minor parts, a role or two at the National, and a few bits in television series. But there had been a gap of nearly five years, during which she had either been unemployed or ashamed of the work she had done.

Cass tried to feel charitable. It was as hard as swallowing the sour wine. She could see that it would have taken a saint to refuse to use Livia's release to kickstart a failing career, but she resented the price Livia was paying.

A bell rang, and the drinkers began to stub out their cigarettes and dump their glasses. Cass abandoned hers on a handy shelf and joined the crowd moving jerkily into the theatre. Her seat was a good one: plumb in the middle of the fifth row, near enough to see the actors' expressions without the risk of being spat on or forced to look up their nostrils. She nodded to a tall, good-looking couple, who thanked her as they edged past to the seats immediately on her left, and settled down to take mental notes for Livia.

The first scene was much as Cass expected, three men dressed in sandals and short tunics standing between pillars that overlooked a bay, yakking on about Agamemnon and Mycenae. Cass's mind wouldn't stick to what she was hearing; it slid about the bay and memories of a holiday she and Sophie had had in Crete one summer.

Bumpy bus rides, plates of honey with a lump of butter in the middle and weak Nescafé for breakfast were pretty much all she remembered, apart from the wild last-night party and the wonderful astringent sea. She ought to ring Sophie now that her notional holiday in the Seychelles was over.

'Aaagh!' A long drawn-out wail of agony from off-stage brought Cass back with a snap. The men on the stage muttered something about servants and walked off. A figure dressed in a torn sacking tunic appeared, furiously sweeping with an unforgiving besom.

Her long blonde hair hung about her anguished face in matted strands. There was ash down the front of her tunic and her bare feet looked raw. A livid bruise on her thigh could be seen easily through a tear in the sacking. Cass's neck tightened and she edged towards the front of her seat and listened to a list of the woman's sufferings. Her mother had killed her father, then turned her into a slave in the house she shared with her new husband. The only thing that kept her alive and relatively sane was her certainty that her exiled brother would return in time to give her the vengeance she needed.

Julia's voice was nothing like her mother's; there was no cream in it or gold. It was more like a Brillo pad, grainy and scouring, except when it sank into painful whispering. At one moment, as she hissed out her hatred of 'all adulterous thieves and murderers', she stopped speaking altogether, her hand pressed against her mouth. Cass became aware of tension in the woman beside her and looked to see that she was biting her lip. As Julia haltingly spoke again, the woman beside Cass relaxed.

Watching Julia, feeling bludgeoned by the intensity of hate and need she was pouring out, Cass lost all sense of the individual words, until she heard: 'the fiend that mercilessly killed and butchered him and wiped her bloody sword upon his hair.'

Oh, God, Cass thought. She kept her eyes open and her back straight. But her mind was churning with sympathy for Julia and for Rosamund. No wonder Rosamund had run away to the States and never said a word about her own murdering mother. Cass tried to concentrate on Sophocles, but couldn't.

❧

'Are you all right?' asked a concerned voice at the end of the play. It had taken less than an hour, but Cass felt like a wrung-out dishcloth. She looked up to see the tall elegant woman waiting to get past her.

'Yes, fine. Fine. Sorry.' Cass struggled to her feet to let the woman and her husband pass. Her hands were clammy and so was the back of her neck. Her teeth ached where she'd been clenching them, and her eyes were burning.

'Are you sure?'

'Yes. Just a bit overwhelmed.'

'I know. Julia was excellent,' said the man with unexpected authority. 'I was quite surprised. And very pleased. Look, we're on our way backstage to see her now. She's an old friend. Why not come with us? I'm sure she'd be delighted to know she'd affected someone so powerfully. You're white as a sheet!'

Cass shook her head and the woman said: 'Oh, do come. Every artist likes to meet people who've been touched by their work. It would be such a kindness. And Julia needs as much of that as she can get right now.'

'All right. Thank you,' Cass said, thinking: She doesn't seem to have recognized me, perhaps Julia won't either, and it'll make for a more interesting report for Livia.

She had never been backstage before, and had no idea whether all theatres consisted of such dark cavernous passages and revolting acrid smells, or whether the Old Territorial Hall was unique in its depressing, dungeon-like atmosphere.

'Here we are,' said the woman, tossing back her black hair. 'By the way, I'm Simone Frankel, and this is my husband, David. As you probably know, he writes theatre criticism for the *Post*.'

'Of course,' she said, holding out her hand to each of them in turn and smiling, even as she thought: Sodding journalists! Do they know who I am or is it a coincidence?

She didn't give them her name and they didn't ask. She decided to call herself Jocasta if anyone did try to get a name out of her, and perhaps award herself the hero's surname. Jocasta Tafter: it sounded all right.

'Great. Come on in and meet the star,' said Simone Frankel.

David grinned at Cass and pushed open the door, revealing a blaze of light that poured out into the concrete corridor, bringing with it a billow of flowers, cigarette smoke and wine, easily strong enough to overcome the mixture of rot, mice and urine that seeped up through the concrete floors outside.

A babble of conversation punctuated with shrieks and laughter made an even greater contrast with the intensity of the bleak little play that had so filled the theatre. Disconcerted by the frivolity and even shakier than she'd realized, Cass hung back while first David and then Simone were hugged by Julia Gainsborough.

She was more beautiful in the flesh than in any of her photographs. Her hair was brushed now into a clean shining cloud and her face, stripped of its make-up, was lit by blazing blue eyes that looked enormous under their smoothly arched brows. To Cass, who knew all about how success felt when you'd won it after ferocious effort, Julia looked almost unconscious with triumph. All the better: she wouldn't be bothering too much about who any stranger might be.

Turning from one admirer to the next, Julia drank in approval and delight. Cass felt a hand on her wrist and was pulled forward to be introduced simply as someone who had been moved by Julia's performance and wanted to meet her. Julia didn't seem to recognize Cass, which allowed her to say with absolute sincerity that she had been bowled over by the play, adding: 'I had no idea before that someone writing two and a half thousand years ago could have anything to say to me, but that speech of yours to Clytemnestra could have come out of any modern adolescent's quarrel with her mother.'

Julia beamed at her and took her hand, while murmuring something to Simone at her side. Then, as though she had only just heard what Cass said, she put her other hand on top of Cass's so that it was imprisoned in a warm soft cocoon of gratitude and pleasure.

'I'm so glad you saw the point.' Her voice, unlike the one she'd used on stage, did now have something of Flora's richness. It made a peculiar, upsetting contrast with the torn sacking she was still wearing.

A camera flash hit her eyes, making Cass flinch. She tried to wrench her hand out of Julia's, turning sharply to see who was taking photographs.

Behind the small instamatic camera was a young woman with a face of innocent, slightly earnest, pleasure. She nodded to Cass and asked if she'd like a drink. Julia, apparently reminded that she was still holding Cass's hand, let it go with another blinding smile. Cass accepted a glass of warm, oily Chardonnay from the young photographer and asked whether she was part of the company.

'No. I belong to the management here. It's been a wonderful success tonight. Much more thrilling than we usually have on first nights. Are you with the press like David Frankel?'

Cass shook her head, trying to look regretful, and watched the woman's face fall. 'I'm afraid I'm just a punter, brought round to meet the star.'

The young woman heroically managed not to look too disappointed and Cass felt even safer.

'But I'm not sure that Julia Gainsborough's noticing who anyone is just at the moment.'

'No,' agreed the photographer, still struggling to be polite, but already looking over Cass's shoulders for someone who might be of more use. 'But she'll remember you in the morning, and be glad you came. It was very good of you. Did you know the play before?'

Cass shook her head, realising that there couldn't be anyone important behind her, and made polite conversation for a moment or two longer, before sliding away unnoticed. Deciding she'd done as much as anyone could have asked, she found her way back down the dank, smelly corridor and through the banked, empty seats.

Next morning Cass made her coffee extra strong and set about returning the few phone calls from friends. The easiest would be Amanda Watchman. They had never known each other that well, so it would be no hardship to decline her invitation. And with luck she would be away for the weekend so that Cass could leave a message on her machine.

Unfortunately she was at home, and sounded quite unable to believe that Cass was not going to come to her dinner party.

'But I've a friend who's positively pining to meet you. I've told him all about you.' There was a short pause, as though she were giving Cass a chance to change her mind, then she added quickly: 'And I'd love to see you myself. It's been ages.'

'Years, in fact,' said Cass coldly. Aware of an impulse to make Amanda pay for her gracelessness, she added: 'What made you think of me?'

'Oh, well, you know. This and that. I don't know really. I just knew I wanted to see you, and so did George.'

'George? George who?'

'Um. Jenkins actually. He's a…a friend of a friend.'

Cass thought of making her squirm even more, but she'd already made her point.

'It was kind of you to think of me,' she said instead, knowing Amanda would know it was a lie. 'Thank you. I hope the dinner goes really well. I'm sure it will. You were always a wonderful cook. I'm sorry I shan't be able to be there.'

'I could always reschedule. When would be better for you?'

'Don't worry about it. I wouldn't dream of letting you go to so much trouble. Goodbye.'

George Jenkins's name was familiar. Cass was almost sure he was the journalist who'd been commissioned to write a book about the murders. She replayed the whole message tape to make sure. Hearing his voice saying that he was from the *Post*, she felt as though she'd been standing on a trap door that had suddenly dropped open. The *Post* was David Frankel's paper, too.

The phone rang. She jumped, hating herself for being so twitchy. Loathing the whole world, suspicious of almost everyone in it, she waited for another bludgeoning. But when a familiar voice came through the speaker, she grabbed the receiver.

'Sophie? Thank God it's you. When can I see you?'

# Chapter 13

Cass was sandwiched between two men in pinstriped suits. Her nose came to just above their shoulders, which meant that she could breathe what passed for air in the Drain between Waterloo and Bank. Lots of passengers had to stand with their faces pressed into other people's backs and armpits. Someone farted. Cass closed her eyes and tried to think of herself as just back from holiday.

When she opened them, she saw the front page of someone's newspaper. There she was, horribly recognizable, holding hands with Julia Gainsborough. Shit, shit, shit, shit, and double shit. The paper was the *Post*, of course. David Frankel must have recognized her and set up the whole thing. No wonder he hadn't asked her name when he took her round to meet Julia. He hadn't needed to ask. He'd known all along who she was. And now the whole world would know.

In about seven minutes she would be walking into the dealing room. Ten and a half minutes, if she stopped off at Costa Coffee to pick up a bracing quadruple espresso on the way. She'd better do that. It might stiffen her sinews, help her decide how to answer the questions she'd have to face. Denial? Fake black humour? Even more fake fragility?

The train slowed as it emerged from the tunnel into Bank station. Cass pushed her way with the rest of the crowd of commuters fighting to get out on to the platform. They were like ants, she thought, trogging on in their predestined routes, never deviating, all part of one horrible, heaving mass with far too many legs and no freedom.

Be dignified, she told herself. Admit that Livia's your grandmother if anyone dares to ask: don't give any clue that you've seen her since she got out; deny all knowledge of her address; point out that you know nothing more than anyone else who's read the paper; and don't retaliate when Gary starts sniping at you. Which he will. And don't volunteer anything. If they don't mention it, you mustn't. You'll only get angry, and then you don't know what you'll say—or do. Stay calm and be polite.

Some hope, she thought grimly.

The air felt dazzlingly cold when she reached street level, and that helped. It was lucky that she was going to be so busy, catching up with the backlog of work, and that Michael Betteridge had already promised his support.

He had been much more encouraging than she'd expected when she'd phoned him on Sunday afternoon. After a lot of discussion, he had told her, the directors had decided that she couldn't be penalized for what her grandmother had done. But they had all agreed that if her clients started dropping away, or there was any seriously bad publicity about Cass herself, the bank would have to come first. Cass would see that.

She did. In fact she thought they'd already gone quite a bit further than most people in their position would have done. But this photograph might change things. How could she have been so stupid?

The great grey doors of Stogumber's loomed ahead of her. She marched in and swiped her card through the security gates, paying no attention to the sly smiles or the whisperings she heard behind her.

⌘

'Why didn't you ever tell us, Cass?' Gary asked as he settled at his desk half an hour later. 'Did you think we wouldn't have sympathized? It must have been awful knowing your grandmother was in prison.'

Cass turned her head to smile meaninglessly in his direction. His own smile was the sickest she'd yet seen. She nearly gagged.

'But it must be great having her out now. Do you get on well? You must; she sounds just like you.'

He waited for a comment, but Cass didn't oblige. She went on smiling.

'It's funny, but I couldn't remember any of the details of what she did, so I dropped into the library on my way in this morning to check. That's why I was late. I found this.'

He pushed a book towards Cass, who looked, saw that it was called *Death of a Star*, and turned back to her screen.

'I was reading it on the tube. Have you seen it? Would you like to borrow it?'

Cass shook her head. She couldn't pretend she hadn't heard him, but she didn't trust her voice. It was a pain that her own local library hadn't had a copy; that way she'd have been better prepared. For a lot of things.

'You know she used a scalpel? It was only a tiny little thing, but she shoved it in with such force that its handle was buried two inches deep in her husband's chest.'

Cass didn't flinch, which took some doing.

'They don't seem sure whether it was that wound that killed him or the one in his throat, but she stabbed him more than twenty times in all, so she certainly made sure he wouldn't be getting up again. Thorough, you see, just like you, Cass.'

'Goodness, Gary, you have been doing your homework.' Cass was pleased with the lightness of her voice. It sounded pretty convincing. 'I had no idea you were so interested in my family.'

She went back to reading the two hundred e-mails that had been waiting for her. Gary's voice went on and on, buzzing like an irritating gnat, but she shut most of it out, and all the sense—or nonsense—of the words.

He really was the most horrible little man. Horrible and little and fat. Horrible and little and fat. She said it over and over again in her head, using it like white noise to block out everything else. And when that didn't work, she imagined herself coated in shellac so that everything he threw at her would just slide off. He'd get bored eventually, and she'd survive.

❧

Livia saw the photograph on the Internet half an hour later and yelped aloud. She couldn't help it. Flap came flying into the room, barking, but she paid no attention. The sight of the two familiar faces on the screen, only inches apart, appalled her. What could Cass have been thinking of to expose herself like that?

All Livia had asked for was a report on the play. The last thing in the world she'd wanted was Cass's face and name all over the papers. And with Julia Gainsborough of all people! Cass had now publicly and irretrievably tied herself into the old scandal. God knew where it would end.

❧

Julia didn't see the photograph until nearly half past eleven. She'd had to take a pill to get any sleep at all and it had laid her out. Someone crashing about in the road outside her windows had vaguely disturbed her at dawn, but it wasn't until her doorbell pealed that she came to real consciousness.

She stumbled as she reached for her dressing gown and trod on the hem. Luckily she didn't do any damage. The dressing gown was pale-grey cashmere and had been a first-night present to herself. It had cost far more than she could afford, but what were credit cards for?

When she opened the door, trying to get the pill's residual fog out of her mind, she saw her agent standing in the lobby with his arms full of flowers and newspapers and his face warm with satisfaction. The Monday reviews must be all right as well, then. Good. She stood aside to let him in.

Anton thrust the papers at her. She stumbled as she took them to the table, stubbing her bare toes. They hurt. Dropping the papers on the table, suddenly too nervous to read any of them, she turned to look at Anton. He was still smiling, but not in an ordinary cheerful way.

'Are they really all right?'

'Amazing. Don't worry, darling: you're going places now. And George Jenkins is doing his stuff for you. Look at the front page of the *Post*.'

Julia pushed away her hair, yawning painfully. It felt as though her jaw might crack. She shook her head to get her mind clear and her thick hair got in the way again. Pushing it aside, she saw a picture of herself bang in the middle of the front page. It was quite good. No wonder Anton was pleased.

'Look closer, my darling.'

She peered at the scrawny dark-haired woman whose hands she seemed to be holding. She really shouldn't have taken that pill: her brain felt like a traffic jam with a queue of thoughts blocked behind the one that had stalled, hooting and jostling and making the sort of row she hated. She put her hand to her forehead and looked again; then she read the caption.

Cass Evesham. Of course. Damn her.

'How dare she worm her way into my dressing room under false pretences and drink *my* drink like that?'

'Just as well, Julia my darling. You'd never have looked so innocent if you'd known who she was.'

'But what was she doing there?'

'David Frankel brought her. Wasn't he brilliant?'

'Frankel? The critic? But why?'

'Julia wake up, for God's sake. I told you George Jenkins was going to make sure Frankel came to the first night, didn't I?'

'So?'

'Well, to make sure he came George really pushed the story about you coming to terms with your mother's murder through getting to grips with Electra. When David showed signs of interest, George told him everything, including what you'd given him about Cass Evesham. So when David saw a woman who looked exactly like the Harpy and who was staring at the stage as though she'd been told she had only a week to live, he guessed who she must be. It was a terrific break.'

Julia wasn't sure. She couldn't get rid of the outrage at Cass's sneaking into her dressing room like that.

'He slid out of the theatre in the interval to warn George. Luckily, George had his mobile switched on at the time and went to work. He got an unthreatening-looking photographer to follow Cass. *Et voilà!* You, on the front page. It's fantastic: the kind of publicity you couldn't buy for the price of this flat.'

'Just as well,' Julia said. 'Nothing else George has tried has got us anywhere.'

'What about that woman he thought would help? Amanda Something.'

'Either she fucked-up or else Cass was a bit too quick on her feet,' George said. 'Anyway, she refused the bait.'

'Pity. But it doesn't matter now. This should be enough.'

Julia looked at the photograph again and felt ill.

'What's up?' Anton asked.

'I look as though she's my long-lost best friend.'

'You know, darling, I've often wondered why you hate her quite so much. After all, *she* didn't kill your mother.'

Julia turned away. She wasn't going to bare her soul to Anton. For one thing, he should've understood; for another she didn't quite trust him.

'Is it because she's been so successful so young? So rich?'

'Don't be ridiculous. I'm not jealous of her, if that's what you think.'

'Oh? Well, don't scowl like that. It makes you look like a hag. Now, I've got a table at the Ivy for lunch, and George will meet us there. He'll make sure there's a photographer ready for when you arrive. So go and get your clothes on, and tart yourself up, darling. You're going to be very very famous and you need to look very very good.'

Cass worked on through lunch, refusing to look as though she were trying to escape, and even hung on after Gary and his closest cronies had slouched off to the local champagne bar at the end of the day. Once she was sure they'd left the building, she gathered her stuff and went home.

She picked up an *Evening Standard* to read on the tube, only to be faced with Julia Gainsborough again, looking ravishing on the doorstep of the Ivy. Cass found she didn't want to read after all, and dumped the whole paper in the first bin she found.

Back in the flat with twenty minutes to spare before Sophie was due to pick her up, Cass listened to another tape full of phone messages, at least a third of them from George Jenkins, and then began to flick through her private e-mails. The only one she spent any time reading was from Livia:

> Cass, my dear, I'm so sorry. I should never have asked you to go to Julia's play: I should never have put you at such risk of discovery. I'm sorry. I'm sorry. I'm sorry.

The triple repetition made Cass type an answer without thinking very much:

> It wasn't your fault, Livia. It was mine. There was no need whatsoever for me to go backstage, and, if I hadn't done that, we'd have got away with it. But I was gobsmacked by the play and I sort of sleepwalked along with some other people from my row. I can't now think why I did, but there it is. Too late to worry now. I can ride it out.
>
> You wanted to know about the play. I don't know whether you've ever seen or read it, but it's a simple enough story: Electra is a semi-slave in the palace belonging to her mother and stepfather. She hates them because they killed her father. Her brother, Orestes, fled after the murder. Their sister, Chrysothemis, has

become a collaborator and has nice clothes and doesn't have to do the cleaning. She tries to make Electra collaborate too, but *she's* too proud. And angry. Orestes comes back in disguise and Electra eggs him on to kill their mother.

Cass stopped typing there, aware that it was not exactly tactful to write to Livia about such things. But then, she had asked for a report on the play. And she needn't read the e-mail if she didn't want.

So far, perhaps, so sympathetic. But then you discover that the reason Clytemnestra killed her husband in the first place was that he'd sacrificed their third daughter, *killing* her, for the sake of his own success in some battle. So even though it's Clytemnestra who comes in for all the flak and is a sort of byword for wickedness, he was much worse.

I found the whole thing stirred me up rather. But funnily enough the trickiest bit was listening to the arguments between Electra and her mother. There was Electra blaming her mother for everything, without even considering what *she* must have felt when she did what she did. It sounds silly, but the two of them really spooked me. Anyway, I'm off to buy a copy of the play, and I'll see if the printed version gets to me as much. You did me a good turn in getting me to go there, Livia. I learned a lot.

And I have to say I was pretty impressed by Julia Gainsborough. It would be plain to a blind cockroach why she chose this particular play, but I have to say she was brilliant.

Anyway, please don't worry too much about that wretched photograph. I came in for a bit of twitting in the office today, but nothing I can't handle. I'll be in touch again soon. Love, Cass

When she'd posted the e-mail, forgetting her original determination never to phone Livia from the flat, she typed another message to her mother, shorter than any of the other versions she'd written and not sent, but saying all that needed to be said.

'Why didn't you warn me? Cass.'

This time, she sent it.

Livia read and reread the e-mail at the desk in her bedroom, with a glass of red wine beside her. Each time she went back to the beginning she found something more.

Had Cass understood how much she had revealed? Probably not. After all, she had no way of knowing what Ros had been like, or what she'd said before the trial. Livia's eyelids closed. She'd had years to get used to Ros's hatred. It shouldn't matter any more. And now she had Cass, who didn't hate her. She'd never have written a letter like that if she did.

❦

Cass had no answer from Rosamund, but Livia sent a chatty e-mail the following Saturday, passing on news of Bobby's progress, of Flap's increasingly entertaining development, of her belated understanding that quite an interesting personality lurked behind Colin's beard and eccentricities, and of the way the winter landscape changed every day. It was getting more and more beautiful apparently, as the frosts turned everything to glitter in the bitter mornings, when the sun was lemon yellow in a pale-pink sky.

Cass answered, just as casually, and, as the weeks passed, began to look forward to what turned into a regular Saturday morning e-mail from Livia. Cass always sent her answers from the local cyber café to avoid betraying Livia's e-mail address to anyone monitoring her phone, and came to enjoy the long-range chat.

Livia sounded fine and insisted that she needed nothing except the occasional bit of news when Cass had time. Gordon had started visiting again, and Livia had spent several perfectly pleasant weekends with him at the Long House. Her cooking was getting slightly better—she was putting on weight—and life was not at all bad.

In return, Cass passed on the few bits of good news from work, telling Livia about Sophie, the films they saw, the restaurants where they ate alone or with other friends. An account of Sophie's parents' annual invitation to spend Christmas in Hampshire pre-empted any suggestion that Cass should go up to Wast Water.

Another bit of good news she could pass on was that Christopher Bromyard had sent her a friendly letter, commiserating on the vile publicity and assuring her that no one would remember it in a year's time. If she needed any help, he had written, Cass was to get in touch with him at once. He owed her and Livia for saving his life, and he would do anything he could.

He had added something vague about hoping she would have dinner with him one evening and promised to phone when 'things at work settle down', but he never did. Cass didn't tell Livia that bit, just as she didn't tell her how it felt to be cold-shouldered by people she'd thought were friends, or what it was like to face down the reporters who wanted comments each time Julia Gainsborough made some new revelation about her tragic life.

The journalists had found their way to the back of Cass's building quite soon, so now she could never be sure of getting in and out unseen. So far she'd managed to keep her temper, whatever they said. She tried to make them laugh, so that they'd see her as a human being rather than a target, and commiserated with them for having to hang about in the cold and wet. Sometimes they even swapped jokes with her. And occasionally they'd leave her alone.

But each time Julia spilled more beans, they were back, determined to needle Cass into talking. She came nearest the edge when they told her that her neighbour, Annette

Sharpe, had an article in the *Post* about the effect of a crime like the Harpy's on a killer's family. That a woman who lived only one floor below her, who'd shared drinks with her, pretended to be friendly, should have taken the *Post's* money made Cass burn with betrayal.

Even then, she managed not to give the hacks any satisfaction. She went on her way, knowing she needn't bother to buy a copy of the paper, since Gary would tell her exactly what was in it.

He did. And she felt as though George Jenkins had wiped his dirty hands all over her life. She wondered how much he'd paid Annette, and who else was going to feed him stories. All the people she'd ever brushed off, or disliked, or argued with, would probably be queuing up to tell him how awful she was, how like the Harpy. At least Gary couldn't; not if he wanted to keep his job.

Cass pretended she didn't care about any of it and forced herself to smile at Annette whenever they passed on the stairs. That didn't happen often. Annette did her best to avoid Cass, which was just as well. But a lot of clients wanted to do the same, which was getting to be a problem.

One Friday, late, after she had learned that she had lost yet another of them, and Gary had been particularly puerile all day, she went to the gym to work off her fury.

It was getting harder and harder to control her temper, and she was scared of what might happen if she lost it. Only when she was working the rowing machine could she be sure of holding all the wrenching, disturbing feelings in check.

Thirty minutes after she'd started, Ben appeared in front of her, mouthing something. Cass pulled off the headphones of her Walkman and waited. Ben ordered her off the rowing machine and sat her down on one of the weights benches, propping his foot beside her and leaning down to stare into her face.

'Look, girl, you got to stop this. I don't know what's got into you lately, but it's doing you no good. You look like shit tonight.'

'Thanks, Ben. That's all I need. And I bet you do know.'

'Maybe. But killing yourself won't help no one. You want to talk about it?'

'No.' She looked into his guileless toffee-coloured eyes and wondered why he'd asked, and how much George Jenkins had offered him.

'You should.'

'Too much of a risk, Ben.'

He looked insulted. She couldn't help that. She'd already discovered that it wasn't safe to trust anyone.

'Have you ever read anything in the papers about coming to my gym and working yourself into a mad sweat because your granny's a murderer?' he asked with considerable dignity behind the anger.

Cass had to admit she never had.

'Well, then.'

'OK. So, I'm sorry, Ben. Is that all right?'

'Right.' He still looked hurt, but ready to be placated. 'You want a drink?'

'I could use one,' she said, trying to make amends. But she didn't want to go out to a pub. Someone would only recognize her and tip off the *Post*. 'Have you got anything here?'

He left her for a minute, returning with two cans of White Diamond, beaded with condensation. He handed one to Cass, who almost dropped it as it slid through her hot hand. They ceremoniously popped the tabs and raised the cans to each other.

'So,' he said, when she'd had a chance to drink. 'What's up?'

'I'm angry.'

'No?' he said, like one utterly amazed. Cass laughed for the first time that day and mimed throwing a punch at him. He looked a lot friendlier.

'And I'm trying to stay angry.'

Ben shook his head, wiped the can on the end of the towel he wore round his thick, corded neck.

'Now you've got me.'

'It's safer. They can't hurt you when you're angry,' she said, surprising herself as much as him.

'That wouldn't work for me,' Ben said. 'But then maybe that's why I'm running a gym and you a bank.'

'I'm not exactly running it yet.' Cass was not sure she liked the gleam that had slid into his eyes.

'Soon will be. Who you angry with then?'

Cass laughed again as she thought of the list, then shrugged. 'Mainly Julia Gainsborough. Sometimes I hate her so much I wish she was dead.'

Now she'd know for certain whether Ben was safe. It would make a good headline, a comment like that. But she couldn't guard her tongue for ever, and she had to know where she was with him. This gym was her last refuge.

There was a long pause. Ben drank, wiped his face on his towel then said casually:

'She the actress right?'

'As if you didn't know.'

'Getting to be a star because your granny killed her mother?'

'Right again,' said Cass. 'That's presumably why she's doing it. And it's working. For her. I'm sick to death of seeing her in print and on the late-night culture programmes and in the papers, and reading about how she's having a telly series written specially for her, and seeing psychological profiles of how she's liberated herself from the constraints that stopped her fulfilling her potential by coming to terms with her tragic past. Faugh!'

'That's a great word, Cass. What's it mean?'

She hardly heard him. She was thinking about today's pictures of Julia, who seemed to get more lavishly beautiful each time she was photographed, and about the other pictures, the ones that must come from somewhere deep in her own psyche. They kept taking her by surprise, blanking out everything else in her brain and making her feel wobbly with disgust—and fear. Shit! It was happening again. All she needed was to concentrate hard, and then she could stop seeing Julia's naked feet treading her face into the gravel.

Cass might have understood what her brain was doing to her if the pictures and their accompanying sensations had been part of a nightmare; she'd always had a lot of those, vivid and memorable, but she'd never been one for day-dreaming, and these were scarily near to hallucinations.

Sometimes Julia's trampling feet would flash between Cass and her screen at work, or the book she was reading before she turned out her light at night. Occasionally, she found herself wiping her face to get the feel of Julia's skin off it before she remembered where she was and what she was supposed to be doing. She was beginning to wonder if there was something seriously wrong with her.

She saw Ben watching her and shook her head. She couldn't explain it all to him. She didn't want him to think she was losing it.

'You have to take care, girl. I'm not having my reputation and my gym destroyed because you kill yourself on my machines so that you don't have to kill someone else. OK?'

She looked at him and saw him blink. It was good that he'd understood, but in a way it was a pity, too.

'Go home, Cass. Eat something, and get some sleep. I'll see you tomorrow.'

'So I'm not barred then?'

He laughed. 'I wouldn't dare.'

She could have hugged him for that.

'Thanks, Ben.'

# Chapter 14

Cass stared at the screen, unable to believe what she read. The last big call option she had written had gone belly-up, just like most of the others since Christmas. This time she had been sure she'd done all the right things: she'd researched every possibility; she'd calculated the risk to the nth degree; she'd consulted Michael Betteridge and even Gary; and she'd listened to everyone who had anything authoritative to say. Now she was stuck with another enormous loss.

Her gut felt as hollow as her head. She was held together only by her skin and her determination never, ever, to show weakness at Stogumber's. Her eyes saw what was happening in front of them and transmitted the news of disaster to her brain, but they could not take in anything else.

They didn't need to; she knew that all round her would be faces full of shock, a little pleasure, and a horrible great heap of sympathy. The phone rang. For the first time since she had joined the bank, she left it unanswered. Any minute now it would divert to one of the others. She was ashamed of that, but it would have been worse to try to speak.

'Lost your sense of humour, Cass? What you need is a good screw.'

Slowly, as though the tendons in her neck had to be twisted by sheer force of will, Cass turned her head to look at Gary. Once she could have stopped him with a laugh or a joking insult of her own, but that was BL, Before Livia. Things were different now.

She pushed back her chair and walked towards him. Gary didn't look up when she reached his chair, pretending he didn't know she was there. Even if he hadn't heard her, he must have smelled her behind him, just as she could smell his sickly aftershave and the washing-powder residues that clung to his limp shirt and fought with his acrid sweat.

Leaning down with one hand on the back of the swivel chair, she spun him round to face her. He laughed uneasily, looking round to collect support. No one joined in. Some of the other dealers pretended they didn't know what was happening and stared at their screens or muttered into their phones, keeping their eyes lowered. Gary began to shift in his seat under her stare and licked his lips.

'Come on, Cass, can't you take a joke?'

She unclamped her teeth to say: 'That was no joke. That was the kind of thing sick, arrogant, self-indulgent wankers like you say to people who won't hit back. But you misjudged it this time. You forgot something important, Gary. You forgot my genes, didn't you? Some women—sometimes— do hit back.'

Gary's pupils dilated. His breathing changed as he took in bigger quantities of air than he could expel in each gasp. She knew he was trying to laugh at her again, so she let him see all her hatred. He wiped his hands on the arms of his chair, his nostrils flexed as his Adam's apple pushed itself forward through his throat. He looked almost like a man on the edge of orgasm.

Suddenly sick at herself, Cass abandoned him, turning her head away so that she didn't have to see the evidence of what she had done.

No one said anything: all the other dealers seemed blind and deaf. Cass returned to her own desk, viciously controlling the tremor in her hands, and grabbed the phone to dial the number of one of her last few faithful clients. Somehow, she had to set up a deal that worked, and quickly. This could not go on. For one thing, it was much too dangerous. She couldn't trust herself anymore.

No one answered the phone. Putting it down without speaking was going to make her look a fool, but could she fake a conversation well enough? She'd never been good at faking anything except indifference.

'Cass!' Michael Betteridge's familiar shout came like an all clear signal. She dumped the receiver back on the phone and picked up the jacket of her suit.

Gary was smirking again by the time she went past the back of his chair. She hadn't done him much harm, then.

As she swung the jacket around her shoulders and walked towards Michael's office, she felt like a plague-carrier. Walking down the long path between the banks of screens, she remembered the day of her great Deutschmark triumph, the day when she was still whole and envied and successful, before Alan had dumped her, before Livia's release, before her madness in letting herself be photographed holding Julia Gainsborough's hands backstage at the Old Territorial Hall.

Echoes of that one stupid misjudgement of the risk she faced were still ringing through her life. She wasn't impregnable any more. She wasn't a winner. Every day she had to fight the belief that taking risks was as dangerous as Rosamund had always claimed.

Somehow she had to get her bottle back and start making money again. Each time Michael summoned her, she had to ride out the fear that he was going to sack her. Today no one commented on her legs or her tits. No one envied her for anything these days, and no one, except perhaps Gary, still hated her. Keeping her chin up and her lips smiling, she sauntered, much more slowly than was necessary, towards Michael Betteridge.

He was waiting for her at the door of his office, leaning against the jamb, one arm raised above his sleek head. He nodded as she reached him and stood aside so that she could go in. She heard the door shut.

'Well done,' he said. 'That took guts. But then you've never been a coward.'

Cass held tightly to her visceral gratitude for the compliment and kept her smile small enough to be dignified.

'Have a seat, Cass.'

'Thanks.' She didn't sigh as she sat down, and her back was straight. Self-respect and the appearance of confidence were just about all she still had going for her, and she was going to hang on to them for as long as she could still breathe.

Michael fiddled with the pens on his desk. Cass had never seen him so twitchy. She'd have to help him start. Whatever it was he had to say, she'd have to know in the end—it might as well be now.

'So, Michael?'

'It can't go on much longer, you know, Cass.'

'Are you telling me that you're going to sack me because of what my grandmother did twenty-five years ago?' she asked politely, concentrating hard on keeping her voice light and her eyes steady.

A distantly recognizable feeling in the back of her eyes, like a half-remembered tune, warned her that if she didn't tighten her grip on herself she might cry. She did what was necessary and the feeling retreated, beaten for the moment. She could still do it, in small ways anyhow. Her smile widened infinitesimally.

'Not for what your grandmother did,' Michael said, 'but because your clients are deserting you. And you've been losing money. We have to do something, Cass. The publicity's been atrocious, and…'

'You're telling me?'

'I'm recapping the situation for us both.'

'Oh, I see.' She was quite pleased with that lightly mocking trio of words. Michael looked as though he appreciated it, too.

'Life is bloody tough for you just now. I know that, and I'm prepared to do everything I can to help. We both know you need a big coup soon, and you need to get some good personal publicity going for you.'

'The Harpy's granddaughter.' The bitterness in her voice nearly lifted the polish from his desk.

'No. Cass Evesham.'

She looked him between the eyes. 'Killer Cass. That's what they used to call me. The greatest compliment Gary ever paid me was that I was "a fucking psychopath". But for some reason it doesn't seem to be a compliment any more. You know, it seems a little unfair that I should be pilloried now just because you're all wondering if I could be both the things you've always said you admired in the past.'

'Don't be stupid.'

She didn't excuse herself. If he wanted to be made to feel better, someone else would have to do it. Cass had enough to do keeping herself together.

'You know perfectly well that any killer instinct you may have inherited has turned into no more than relentless determination to succeed. And that's good, Cass. You don't need to be afraid of it.'

She turned her head away, afraid her face was much too naked.

'It's exactly what we need here. But some people may forget that, if you go on making them feel uncomfortable. That's the only aspect of all this I can criticize you for, Cass. You don't help yourself by forcing everyone to remember all the time who your grandmother is and what she did. That's just stupid. But apart from that uncomfortable habit of yours, you've been bloody dignified, and I'm impressed.'

Tears warmed her eyes again. She smiled and knew that her lips were quivering. Hostility she could take; kindness was much too hard. Perhaps that was why she kept thrusting her potential for violence in their faces. That kept most of the pity at bay.

'But it's not enough,' he said firmly. The quiver and the tears stopped at once. Michael smiled. 'We have to turn things around.'

'We?' she said, trying not to be too touched in case that set it all off again.

'Yes. I've invested a lot of my credibility in you, Cass. I need you to turn yourself back into a winner. And soon.'

'I'm on. It's what I've been trying to do these last few months. But I don't know how to start. I can't disown Livia. She *is* my grandmother, and even though the papers have got bored with her at last, thank God, the taint is still there in everyone's mind.'

What a stupid word, she thought. It was the one that kept cropping up in her great-grandmother's diaries and in *her* mother's letters. Cass continually tried not to succumb to the temptation of the archives, but she couldn't always keep away. At least in that narrow, cell-like room she was at home with people who would have understood her.

Do you think the taint could be there in Livia? Is that why she's always so argumentative, so difficult all the time? Was it always there in John Antony? Or was it the head wound as we thought? Oh, darling, I can't help worrying for you: could he be mad? Could they both be mad?

'Cass!' Michael's voice was sharp, like a slap.

'Yes?'

'I'd lost you. Pay attention.'

'Sorry.' Her black eyebrows twitched.

'You didn't hear a word I'd said, did you? Listen to me now and I'll tell you again. There's an important dinner tonight at Guildhall. I've persuaded my wife to give up her invitation, even though she loves white-tie dinners, and I want you to come with me instead. I'll walk you round, introduce you to everyone, show those of your clients who are there, and there are bound to be some, that Stogumber's is right behind you and that you're worth knowing. OK?'

She frowned again. 'Will it work?'

'God knows, but it's a start, and we've got to try something. Will you come?'

'Of course.'

'Good girl. And no going off into one of these dreams of yours. You know, in the old days I'd have said you were the last woman in the world to fantasize.'

'They're hardly fantasies, Michael.' Julia's foot appeared in front of Cass's eyes and her cheek muscles tightened in anticipation of the sweaty pressure until she forced herself to let them go. 'Sorry. I won't do it tonight.'

'And I'd have thought you were even less likely to apologize. Come on, Cass, you've got to snap out of it. You've got to help me help you. You still look fantastic and you can still do the business, but you've got to put yourself about and show everyone that you're up to it, that you're still the tough risk-taker with the brilliant killer instinct we took on last summer.'

Cass admired the steadiness with which he said it. He had guts, too. But then she'd always known that. He wouldn't be where he was if he hadn't.

'Now, I want you to go on home, have your hair properly done, and buy something spectacular to wear.'

'You mean that if I tart myself up, make myself look seductive, then, if I manage to attract enough people, I may be allowed to keep my job?'

'Broadly.' Michael grinned at her, looking a lot more human than usual. 'I know: it's not fair. And it's demeaning. But it's a way of getting a hearing. You shouldn't knock it. You're bloody attractive when you're not off in a dream somewhere, and to your eternal credit you haven't let your figure go under all this stress…'

'Oh, please.'

'A lot of women would have. Hitting the chocolate for solace and all that. Minnie's always doing it, that's why she has to keep having new clothes, which costs me a fortune. But you haven't. So build on that. Go on now: book an appointment at the hairdresser, buy a dress—full-length and with proper sleeves so you wont't need long gloves—and I'll come by and pick you up at your flat at six-thirty. OK?'

Cass nodded. Hating the thought of being paraded in public, but aware that Michael was making sense, she got to her feet and saw him looking at her legs. Well, at least a long dress would stop that.

'I do appreciate it, Michael. Thank you.'

'She said through gritted teeth,' he added with a friendly grin. 'I know you hate me for it, but one day you'll thank me.'

Cass went through her preparations as though they were any other part of her job. Since she had to do it, she'd better do it as well as it could be done. There wasn't any difficulty choosing what to buy—there were hardly any full-length evening dresses with sleeves to be found, and so she plumped for the first one that fitted. Made of black velvet with a bit of Lycra in it, it clung to her body as far as the top of her hips and then flared out just enough to make walking graceful rather than hobbled.

Her hair was sleek and yet somehow spirited when the stylist finished with it, and she made up her face with great care. Her eyes looked huge and glittery when she'd shaded them with subtly graded greys and khakis, and her mouth seemed more vulnerable than usual. Given how easily she seemed to frighten people these days, she'd decided to ignore vampy purple and try a paler coral.

The evening was going to be hell. Formal City dinners usually were, unless you had the luck to be sitting with people who had something interesting to say and the energy to bother. It wasn't that there was anything wrong with the food or the drink—they were usually on the good side of adequate— it was the deadly hanging about listening to endless, boring speeches, and sitting on your hard chair longing for a pee and having to endure an absurd archaic ceremonial before you were allowed to leave the room. She'd been to one dinner at which a senior judge had been positively sweating with the effort of hanging on to his bladder control, and then when the last of the speeches was over, there had been an unseemly dash to the loos, but luckily no accidents.

Still, this evening was work, and she could put up with most things for that. She'd go through with it, meeting sympathy and prurient excitement with the same incomprehending politeness that she had found to be the only useful defence when she couldn't be openly angry. Dressed and ready at last, she sprayed on Chanel 19, and went to the bookshelves which served as a hiding place for her few pieces of real jewellery.

Picking out the delicate Edwardian diamond pendant that had been her father's last birthday present to her, she let herself remember him. She'd loved him without really noticing it and missed him dreadfully when he died, but it had taken the Livia débâcle to make her admit how much she still needed him.

Come on, Cass, she told herself. Brace up. You were never a wimp BL, and you've never needed anyone before. You can hack this. You can hack anything.

She hung the chain around her neck and settled the jewel just above her shadow of a cleavage. You couldn't have everything. You couldn't have a taut torso and long thin legs as well as breasts like Julia Gainsborough's unless you were going down the silicone route.

The doorbell rang. Michael was standing on the step, resplendent in white tie, his hair even smoother than usual. No decorations, though. He was too young to have been in any wars other than the Falklands, the Gulf or Bosnia, and when they were being fought, he'd already been making money in the City.

But I, Cass reminded herself absurdly, am the great-granddaughter of a First World War hero. She squared her shoulders and lifted her chin, hoping she looked regal.

'You look fantastic, Cass.'

She smiled at Michael and tried to forget the letters and the medals and the long years of fear endured by her great-grandmother, and perhaps by Henry Claughton as well. And Rosamund.

'You've done a terrific job, Cass. Well done. Come on. You'll do it. You'll swing things back your own way. If not tonight, then soon.'

'Thanks, Michael,' she said as she slid into the back seat of one of Stogumber's pool cars, wishing that this wasn't one of the nights when George Jenkins's paparazzi had knocked off early. Presumably Julia didn't feel she needed any publicity. It was typical that it should have been the one time when they could have done Cass some good.

'It's very kind of your wife to give up her ticket like this.'

'She was glad to. She's always liked the sound of you and thinks you're having a perfectly bloody time.'

Oh, help, thought Cass. She wanted to warn Michael not to be too nice to her, but didn't think she could do it convincingly while keeping the shellac in place.

There was all the usual performance of giving their names to the barker at the door and waiting until they could stride fowards to shake hands with total strangers and exchange insincere smiles and banal compliments. A powdered footman in heavily-gilded clothes offered a tray of glasses. Cass took some champagne and felt the prickle of bubbles against her dry tongue. She must be careful. Boredom and anger could easily make her drink too much, and she needed every ounce of self-control tonight.

Michael hailed an acquaintance and, true to his promise, introduced Cass. She watched the flicker of interest in the man's eyes and smiled, opening her mouth to make a well-judged comment on the likely content of the Chancellor's speech in the House of Commons tomorrow, but she wasn't allowed to say anything as the men chatted politely about their families. Cass hovered on the edge of their conversation like a dutiful child, waiting for the moment when she would be allowed to launch herself.

It did not come. But Michael's friend kept looking at her out of the corners of his eyes. He knew who she was and probably understood exactly why she was there. But he wasn't going to help. He seemed to enjoy keeping her hanging at his side, off balance and unhappy. At one moment he turned and asked patronizingly how long she'd worked for Michael. His tone suggested she was a secretary or at the most an analyst. It was a calculated insult. Knowing her identity and her history, he must also know that she'd been the hottest young trader of her intake, BL.

Cass hated him. If it had not been for Michael, she might have said what she thought of his show of petty malice. But face was involved, Michael's as well as her own, so she merely smiled submissively and waited for better things.

A familiar voice reached her across the babbling crowd and her head jerked round. Taller than most of the others, surrounded by a group of sycophantically laughing acolytes, stood Christopher Bromyard, looking the picture of health and vigour.

Cass felt her coral-painted lips parting in a smile she hadn't planned. She thought about the letter he had written when the press coverage was at its worst. And she thought about his idle suggestion of having dinner with her some time when he wasn't too busy.

He must have seen her movement or felt the strength of her interest because he looked straight at her, his eyes widening just before he smiled and raised his hand in recognition.

Cass moved a little way back from Michael and his friend and didn't notice their surprise or the way Michael looked over his shoulder to see what had attracted her attention. Christopher was moving deliberately towards her through the crowd. Several people tried to talk to him, some even tugging at his sleeve, but he ignored the lot of them and came straight towards her.

'Cass!' he called from at least fifteen feet away so that everyone between them could hear. All of them turned like chickens at feeding time to stare. 'How wonderful! How are you?'

'I didn't know you knew Christopher Bromyard,' hissed Michael from behind her.

Christopher reached her side and put his hands on her shoulders, leaning down to kiss her first on one cheek, then the other.

'You look spectacular,' he said. 'How've you been? How was Christmas?'

'Fine. Fine. I had a really good time with friends in Hampshire. And you? How are you? You look well.'

'I am. Hell! I wish I'd known you were going to be here— I'd have had us put together for dinner. Come on, let's get out of the crush for a minute so that we can talk.'

He propelled her to the side of the room, grabbing two more glasses of champagne from a footman, who took away Cass's half-empty glass.

'Thank you for your letter,' she said, forgetting that she'd already written to tell him how much it had meant. 'How have you been? Really? Are you properly fit again now?'

'Oh, sure. But it was tough getting up to speed at work. It was weeks before the doctors would let me do full days again. It is *really* good to see you, you know, Cass.'

'You sound surprised.'

'I am a bit.'

'Because I'm such an old bag?' she said, laughing at him.

'No,' he said at once. 'Not like that. Don't be silly.'

Cass raised her eyebrows.

'How's Livia?' he said, not answering her unspoken question.

'OK, so she says whenever she e-mails me, but in fact I don't think she is. I think she's lonely and depressed, but I don't know how to help. I can't exactly move up there, and even if I did that wouldn't solve her problems.' Cass hesitated and then, remembering the way they'd talked to each other after the Scrabble match, added more frankly: 'And anyway I haven't got much to spare for anyone else just now.'

Christopher looked as though he understood. 'Have you been back to see her?'

'A couple of times since Christmas and before the snow got so bad up there. But e-mail's easier. We tend not to wind each other up on screen. And I'm happier for being certain that I haven't led any bastard journalists to her house.'

'I can understand that. Is the fiendish Bobby still behaving himself?'

'Apparently. She seems to like him. And Flap, of course. She swears he's fully house-trained now, if a bit destructive. Gordon goes up to stay quite a lot. Even in the snow. So she hasn't been abandoned. He was with her over Christmas.'

'Gordon?' Christopher was watching her over the edge of his glass.

Cass wondered whether she had sounded as guilty to him as she had to herself. It didn't seem fair: Livia was the source of most of her difficulties, and couldn't possibly be her responsibility. She explained about Gordon.

'That must help. Coming out after so long must be bloody hard, and without close friends—unthinkable!'

Cass snatched another quick smile at him and almost stopped breathing at the sight of his face. You can't really read messages in people's expressions, she told herself. Just because he has a kind, warm, sexy smile, that doesn't mean he's any of those things. And there's no way he could understand everything you haven't told him and forgive you for it. Anyway, you don't need forgiving. Much.

'I think it does help, but they find it tricky, too. Both of them. Gordon once told me it had been easier to talk in visitors' rooms with a prison officer watching them.'

'Sad.'

'Yup. And talking of sadness: how's the mid-life crisis?'

He put a big hand lightly over her mouth. His eyes were dancing. She laughed. 'Don't breathe a word about that, Cass. You're the only City bod who knows anything about it.'

'I won't tell. In fact I…Oh, shit! That sounds like dinner.'

'Shit indeed,' he said, making her laugh again. 'How are you getting home when all this is over?'

'I expect Michael Betteridge will drop me off. He brought me—to boost my image in public and try to get some of my clients back before Stogumber's have to sack me.'

Christopher nodded, no longer looking even the slightest bit amused. 'It must have been a bugger for you, Cass. I wish I'd…I could've…Look here, why don't you dump him after dinner and let me give you a lift? We've a lot more to talk about.'

Michael was coming towards them, approval flashing out of his face like a disco strobe. Cass thought that if Christopher had ever owed her anything for the little she had done to help him after his collapse at Wast Water, he had just repaid it a hundredfold.

'That would be great, Christopher. Thank you.'

❧

The speeches were quite as boring as Cass had expected, but she put up with them. With Michael so openly pleased with her, and three particularly entertaining judges sitting around her, she enjoyed the banquet a lot more than she had expected. One of the judges seemed positively anarchic and made her laugh so much she nearly forgot the formality surrounding them. And with the possibility of being driven home by Christopher, she felt almost perky.

She hadn't said anything to Michael about taking a lift from someone else because she wasn't certain Christopher would remember, but as the diners were at last released from formality, stretching their backs and waving to old friends, he materialized at her side.

'Michael, do you know Christopher Bromyard?' she said, turning from one to the other. 'Christopher, this is my boss and great support, Michael Betteridge of Stogumber's.'

'We have met,' Michael said, holding out his hand. His smile was eager and quite unlike anything Cass had seen him show before. He shifted a little from one foot to the other, like a child hoping for a present. 'At dinner a couple of years ago in Greenwich.'

'Oh, I remember,' said Christopher. Cass wasn't sure whether he was just a good liar. He certainly showed no signs of wanting to hang about and reminisce about their meeting. 'Good to see you again. May I remove your protégé, or is she still on parade?'

'No. Goodness. Whatever.' Michael clearly itched with curiosity. Cass was enjoying herself.

'Thank you for bringing me tonight, Michael,' she said blandly. 'Christopher, I'll just get my coat. Meet you on the steps?'

'Inside in the warm's more sensible. I'll get them to give my driver a call straight away, but it may be a bit of a scrum and there's no need to get cold if we don't have to.'

She nodded, not sure that she liked the idea of the chauffeur much, but when she was sitting in the back seat of a luxuriously large Mercedes, with a thick glass screen between them and the driver, she decided she could just about put up with it.

'Would you like another drink, Cass? A bit more relaxed than in all that gilt and flummery?'

'Well, it would be nice. Yes. Thank you.'

'D'you mind my house? It's probably the quietest and most comfortable place at this time of night. I hate clubs, and all the decent wine bars will be shut.'

'Me, too. No, your house would be fine.' It would be good to find out how he lived, and with whom.

He called instructions through to the driver and then sat back to entertain her with stories of Flap's antics in the days after she had left the Long House.

'Gordon gave him to her,' Cass told him after a while. 'It was such an imaginative present; made a real difference. I haven't done nearly so well with any of the things I've sent or taken her. Just books and bath smellies.'

'But then you haven't known her nearly so long. It must have been tough for you when she was released. Had you had much warning?'

'I never knew anything about her,' Cass said, slowly realising that there weren't many things she couldn't say to Christopher. It seemed odd, considering how many of the great and the good at dinner had behaved like sycophantic ten-year-olds as they tried to impress him. But then, when you've played Scrabble with a clever man and beaten him hollow, you do know him pretty well. And when you've stripped him naked and dried him like a baby.

'What's amusing you?' he asked.

'I just remembered our Scrabble and "adequate".'

'Aha! So it was satisfaction, not amusement. I see. I'll get my revenge one day. Here we are,' he said as the car drew up outside a charming Queen Anne house with a pristine white-painted door and a bright brass knocker. 'It was offices when I bought it, and I'm never here enough to turn it into the kind of house I want. So it's a bit magaziney inside, I'm afraid.'

'D'you share it with anyone?' Cass asked, deciding that frankness was better than trying to weasel it out of him. Christopher didn't look as though he minded, and the driver, who was holding open the door for her, didn't even turn his head.

'Not any more.' Christopher led the way up the steps and unlocked the door, dealing clumsily with the burglar-alarm keypad. 'Wretched thing, as Livia would say! I hate it. Come in. What would you like to drink? Wine, champagne, brandy?'

Cass shivered, understanding what he meant about the house as soon as she walked into his drawing room. It wasn't physically cold, quite the opposite in fact, but everything in the room was amazingly clean, and it all fitted, as though it had been made or bought for the exact position it occupied. The furniture was beautiful and perfectly in keeping with the age of the house, but there were no books piled on the little tables, or newspapers heaped in front of the fireplace, as there would have been in any house of hers. There wasn't even any traffic noise. The whole place was filled with warm, soundless, mildly flower-scented air, like an undertaker's chapel.

'Or a cup of tea?' Christopher asked, laughing at the distaste in her face as she looked around at his perfect possessions.

'Great. Tea-bag tea, in a cloddy mug, if you've got anything so basic in this museum.'

'Come into the kitchen while I make it. It's better in there.'

Cass stood in the doorway, breathing more easily. She pushed some of her hair behind her ears and kicked off her new—very uncomfortable—shoes. Here were all the books and newspapers she could want, piled up with letters and bills on the central table. There was a saggy old sofa in one corner and a basket chair with a rubbed patchwork cushion in it. There were even a few jars and pots and pans piled on the worktops.

'Yes. *Much* better. I like this room.'

'Have the chair,' he said, smiling at her over his shoulder as he filled the kettle. 'Bernie will wait and drive you home whenever you want, so relax. You don't have to worry about anything for once.'

Does he have to take me home? she thought and hastily suppressed the silent question in case Christopher picked it out of the air.

He doesn't fancy you, she told herself, trying to feel stern enough to control the prickles that were teasing her. If he did, he'd have phoned long ago instead of writing that letter. Just because you feel weak at the knees at the sound of his voice and ready to collapse at the sight of his smile, that doesn't mean anything.

With all the rebuffs she'd been having at the office, she wasn't going to invite another by pouncing on him. Or not yet anyway.

'Here,' he said, handing her a large, white bone-china mug. 'Biscuit with it?'

She shook her head. 'No, thanks. I ate too much at dinner. You know, Christopher, I'm not sure I'd realized quite how important you are.'

He raised his eyebrows.

'All those people hanging around, thinking that everything you said was a masterpiece of wit. And Michael Betteridge wagging his tail and begging for a chew like a little puppy. Does it ever turn you up?'

'Frequently,' he said, plumping down on the sofa, wrenching off his white tie and removing the top stud. The rigidly starched fronts of his shirt sprang out from his chest and sat stiffly there like half-dismantled armour. 'Ah, that's better. This kit is bloody uncomfortable, you know. You're lucky to be able to wear dresses.'

'Careful, Christopher! If anyone heard that, it would be worse than talking about mid-life crises. Bromyard the Transvestite!'

His eyes crinkled at the corners again. 'You do me good, Cass. As I said, I can't think why I've waited so long to get you here.'

'You must know some other irreverent women,' she said, bending her head to sip some of the boiling tea so that she didn't have to look at him.

'I'm not sure I do,' he said, so slowly that it sounded as though each word had to be assayed before he could certify it as genuine. She knew he was watching her. 'And you, Cass?'

'Me what?'

'Who are you living with at the moment?'

'No one.'

'Oh, come on. You can't expect me to believe that.' His smile tightened, but his voice softened as he added: 'Are you still involved with the shit you told me about who dumped you on your way to the airport? Or are you not prepared to risk it again?'

She took a moment to think. 'Neither really. I haven't thought about him much since I got back from Livia's that first time. I...I...'

'He really hurt you, didn't he?'

'At the time.' She turned and smiled. 'But compared with all the rest it's as nothing. Not important.'

He reached across the space between them to tuck a strand of hair behind her ear. The sensation of his finger touching the top of her ear set off a chain reaction she wasn't sure she could hide. 'Would you like to stay, Cass? I mean, shall I tell Bernie he can go?'

She shook her head, while all her instincts screamed at her: Say yes, say yes, say yes; you deserve a treat; go on, go on. You could have responsibility-free fun for once. It's your turn. Enjoy it. Go on.

'I don't think I could take the look in Michael Betteridge's face tomorrow morning if I'd stayed with you now,' she said. 'And he'd know, even if I were back at my desk at dawn in the severest of all my suits.'

'Especially if you were in your severest suit, I imagine.' Christopher did not look particularly disappointed. 'OK, Cass. Whatever you want.'

So, she told her instincts crossly. You see. He was only being polite. So shut up and stop tingling. Damn you. She finished her tea and said she thought she ought to be getting back south of the river now.

'OK, Cass, whatever you want,' Christopher said again. He put his own mug down and led the way to the hall. There, he draped her coat around her shoulders. Gripping the two edges of the collar, just below her neck, he looked down into her face. The sides of his stiff shirt rubbed against her coat with a sound like fine sandpaper.

'Will I see you again?' he asked.

She thought he sounded almost as though he minded.

'Why not?' she asked lightly.

'Good.' He bent and she felt his lips on her forehead.

Don't stop there, shrieked the instincts. She wanted to push herself forward and slide her hands between the armour that kept his skin away from hers, but his hands on her coat kept her safely in her place. She felt his lips on her nose, which was still cold in spite of the steam from the tea. He laughed.

'A cold nose means something, but I can never remember what.'

'A warm heart, I expect.' She was breathless and wished she'd hidden it better. He looked surprised, as well he might. And then he did kiss her, just for a moment, and she almost turned into pancake batter.

'Goodnight,' she said brightly as he straightened up. 'I enjoyed this evening much more than I expected—because you were there. Thank you, Christopher.'

'Cass,' he said, much more urgently than he'd spoken all evening. 'Cass, don't go.'

'I must.'

Sitting in the back of the car, glad that she didn't have to direct Bernie as she always had to direct taxi drivers, Cass longed to find herself back in Christopher's house, going upstairs to his bedroom, standing perhaps in front of an open fire, as he…

Oh, stop it, she thought, recognizing old fantasies that had never served her well. The reverse, in fact. Stop it and grow up. If he phones, all well and good: if he doesn't, you haven't lost anything and you would have if you'd stayed and then been dumped. And he would've dumped you. You know what they say about him: he's never stuck with anyone for more than three months. You probably wouldn't have lasted even that long. Grit your teeth, Cass.

# Chapter 15

Colin put down the phone just in time to pick up a handful of tissues to catch the sneeze. Never had he regretted his beard so much. Recovering from the paroxysm, wiping his face, he tried Meg's office number yet again. This time she did answer, her voice scratchy with impatience.

'I'm stuck at home with the flu, Meg,' he said as quickly as he could. He had to make her stop long enough to listen. 'And I haven't got my address book here. Can you get it from my desk and give me Livia Davidson's number? I must warn her I won't be able to pick up Bobby this morning.'

'Colin, for Christ's sake! I'm deluged. It'll have to wait.'

'Please.'

'I'll do it when I can, but it's not a priority. I've got files four deep on my desk, clients coming out my ears, and three quarters of the office away with this bug. Goodbye.'

'Meg, wait. I...'

'God give me strength.'

'Wait. Please. Meg, it was you who said we'd have to be careful because Livia's a serious suicide risk, and...'

'She's hardly going to kill herself because your unspeakable protégé doesn't turn up for his lesson. Goodbye.'

This time she got her phone down before he could stop her. He lay, his eyes and nose burning, hardly able to breathe, clinging to the receiver in the hope that she would relent.

When he'd got some strength back, he tried Directory Enquiries, but they told him Livia's number was ex-directory and they wouldn't even phone to ask her to ring him back.

Later, when he'd thought to ask and tried them again, they did give him the number for Bobby's foster mother. He phoned her and was able to explain to her what had happened. That was something. At least Bobby wouldn't decide he'd been deserted and go on the rampage. But Colin was too worried about Livia to lie in bed, however daunting the alternative.

He got out from under the mess of duvet, books, used tissues and empty Lemsip packets, determined to let her know what was happening. Before he'd even started to dress he knew he wasn't safe to drive. Too dizzy. There was a thermometer somewhere in his bathroom if he could stagger that far.

It took time, but eventually he found the black plastic tube, lying on the floor under a heap of dirty clothes, and took his temperature. Squinting at the mercury, he saw it had shot up the old-fashioned Fahrenheit scale to a hundred and four. No wonder he felt ill. He reeled back against the cold, tiled wall and slid down to a sitting position, holding his head between his hands.

He couldn't go out in the car like this. He'd only crash and kill someone. Livia would understand. At least he hoped she would. And Meg would phone her eventually. He supposed he ought to do something about a doctor, or a hot drink, but he hadn't the energy. He let his head tip back against the cold tiles and for a moment that felt better.

Back in bed and breathless, ten minutes later, he shut his eyes in relief. Despite the thundering in his head, it hurt less lying down.

❧

Livia was standing by her bedroom window, looking at the road up which the car should be coming. The three hills at the head of the lake looked very black today. Threatening. Almost like Appeal Court judges watching and waiting for evidence. Colin had never been this late before. Everything was ready for Bobby, and Dare's house was now finished. Livia had woken alight with excitement at the thought of showing it to Bobby.

He wouldn't be able to read the working drawings, she knew, so she had painted watercolour perspectives of every room. They looked ravishing. It was a house she'd love to live in herself, quite different from this chilly grey and silver cave under the looming hills. She couldn't remember why isolation in a beautiful landscape had once seemed so desirable. Now she needed warmth and people.

She shivered, knowing that if she had them she wouldn't want them. And she'd only hurt the people, whoever they might be, just as she'd hurt Gordon and Cass. And perhaps Bobby, too. Perhaps that was why he hadn't come yet. He'd seemed perfectly happy yesterday, but something she'd said could have stuck in his mind and upset him.

Voices started echoing in her head again, making it ache.

'You're so destructive, Livia. Why can't you be *nicer* to people? Why must you always argue? You hurt me when you shout like that. And your father needs peace so much. Why can't you let us be?'

'The law allows me no discretion in sentencing you to life imprisonment, but even if it did, I should have no hesitation. You are a vicious woman and a serious danger to the public.'

'Really, Mother, why must you be so violent when you disagree with Dad? Can't you just accept things that can't be changed? You'd be so much happier. And he'd like you better. We all would.'

'Livia, for God's sake, have you gone mad? You must get a grip on that temper of yours and stop insulting clients. And while we're on the subject, you upset Annie Prestwich very badly yesterday and for no good reason. If you can't control that vicious tongue of yours, you'll have to work at home in future. I can't have you causing trouble in the drawing office. D'you understand?'

Vicious, vicious, vicious. Livia opened the window and felt the damp icy cold on her forehead, cooling the memories. She stayed there, breathing in the clean air, until she had scoured out enough space to think about Dare's house again.

She had considered making a model as well as the drawings, but there were too many bits and pieces of equipment she didn't have. So far Gordon had been very good about providing her with anything she wanted, but she wasn't sure he'd send everything on this list. And if he didn't, they...

She cut off the thought. It was better not to know what he would have done if she asked him for a scalpel.

The road was still empty. Nothing was moving anywhere. There wasn't even any wind to disturb the trees today. And the hills still loomed at the head of the lake, black under the grey clouds.

It was silly to read disaster into the empty stillness. There was no more reason to imagine a car crash than a puncture. And Bobby had been fine yesterday: funny and full of the kind of affectionate impudence that couldn't have been more different from his first sullen obstinacy. There was no reason for him to have turned against her.

The telephone rang. Livia tripped on one of the cream wool rugs as she ran to answer and fell prone on her bed.

'Hello?' she said, breathless with the shock of her fall. Her heart was banging so hard that she rolled over on her back and put her hand against her ribs. 'Colin? Is that you?'

'No, Mrs Davidson,' said a cool female voice, which sounded disapproving but excruciatingly kind. 'This is Meg Heaton. I'm a colleague of Colin's. He's phoned in sick this morning, and so he won't be able to bring your pupil for his lesson. Colin asked me to be sure and tell you.'

Some of the knots in Livia's intestines unravelled and her heart began to quieten. She felt a fool and melodramatic, too: Henry's second favourite insult after mad, until he came up with vicious. She pushed herself up against the headboard and moved the telephone to her other ear so that the flex wasn't stretched tight across her throat.

'So how will Bobby get up here?'

'I'm afraid we've rather too many more urgent matters to worry about this morning. Bobby will have to do without his lesson today. It's not that important, and it won't do him any harm to miss one.'

'I'm not so sure.' Livia wasn't going to be told what did or didn't matter, even by this unknown woman, but she hadn't meant her voice to come out so sharp. She wasn't in a position to go annoying anyone in the probation service. They could probably recommend the withdrawal of her licence and have her sent back.

'I'm sorry. I've been so worried this morning. I wonder, could you give me Bobby's telephone number? If I could just talk to him, he'd know…'

'I'm afraid I can't do that, Mrs Davidson.'

'Please. It's important. You must admit that he hasn't been in any trouble since he's been coming for lessons with me.' There was a pause as Livia waited for the acknowledgement that must have been her due. It didn't come. 'I don't want to spoil that record. Please let me have the number and then I can talk to him at least and make sure he's all right.'

Eventually Meg Heaton gave up the number with the worst possible grace. Livia only just kept her temper, and the fake sweetness of her own voice made her gag. Her hands were shaking when she made the call to Bobby's foster home.

It was lucky that telephones had buttons now, she thought, and not the old type of dial that could be so stiff and took ages to click back into place before you could turn it again for the next digit. A woman answered.

'Hello,' said Livia, trying to make herself sound unthreatening. 'This is Mrs Davidson here. I wonder if I could speak to Bobby?'

'No.'

'Oh. Has he gone out? What a pity! He was due to have a lesson with me this morning, but his probation officer's ill, which is why he hasn't been to collect Bobby.'

'He's phoned to tell us. You didn't have to. Bobby's fine here, this morning. With me.'

'I think it's important that he does have his lesson,' Livia said mildly. 'He's doing so well.'

'He's not here.'

'Do you know when he'll be back?'

Unmistakably in the background, mixed in with the sound of an engine and various odd bangs and swooshing noises, Livia heard his voice.

'Ah, good, so he's back already,' she said, letting Mrs Gaddon off the hook as neatly as she could. 'Please let me speak to him.'

Mrs Gaddon didn't answer, but a moment later Livia heard Bobby say: 'Liv? Is that you?'

'Yes, Bobby. I've just heard from Colin's office about what's happened to him, and I don't want to miss our lesson. I thought the best thing would be for me to order a taxi to pick you up and bring you here. Would that suit you?'

'OK. Yeah. Cool.'

'Good. Stay by the telephone then. I'll ring back when I know what time the taxi will come for you.'

It took longer than Livia expected to persuade the local taxi driver's wife to accept the booking. When Livia protested at her first refusal, the woman gave her a list of everything Bobby had done in the past to houses, cars, the village phone box, and to several small wild animals. Apparently there had been mutilated corpses left on the doorsteps of several houses in the village, as well as the charred remains of others in some of the fires he was thought to have lit.

And Colin never told me, Livia thought as she listened. She glanced at Flap, who was apparently trying to work out how to get all four legs over his head at the same time. He collapsed on to his back, panting heavily.

Livia's shoulders softened. Perhaps Colin had been right not to tell her. If she had known about the animals, she might not have taken Bobby on, and she would have missed a lot. And he hadn't misbehaved with her; not once. After the first attempt to kick Flap into submission, he had never shown the slightest threat of violence; he'd never set fire to anything in her house, even when she'd asked him to put a match to the logs in the grate one morning; and he'd never stolen anything from her.

She needed to see him today. If only she'd learned to drive again as soon as she got out, she wouldn't have been dependent on the taxi driver's wife. There were too many people in her life with the power to dispense or withhold favours. From the probation service she could just about accept it, from a taxi company it was too much.

'Will you accept my booking or not?' she asked, surprised to find it easy to slip back into the old *grande dame* role, even after so many years and so many prison officers determined to teach her better ways. 'I have an account. I'm a good customer. If you prefer not to accept my business in future, tell me so that I can make other arrangements.'

There was a pause, then an almost audible shrug as the order was accepted.

'I'll tell my husband. He'll do the pick-up in five minutes. But I wouldn't have that child in *my* house.'

❧

Bobby's eyes widened as he saw the ten-pound note Livia handed through the window to John, the taxi driver. He gave her back two pound coins and a fifty pence piece. The usual fare from the village was three pounds fifty, but even so, Livia gave him one of the pound coins as a tip.

'You're ripping her off,' Bobby said viciously as he poked his head under the arm Livia was holding through the car window. He spat.

Livia looked at the bubbling heap of sticky grey-white liquid on John's trousers. Their eyes met.

'I'm sorry, John.'

'I'm not having him in my car again, Mrs Davidson. Not even for you.'

'Perhaps this will help pay for cleaning,' she said, handing him back the rest of the change.

He shook his head and put the car in gear again. 'He's a filthy little beast, and the oughtn't to be living with decent people. You want to watch yourself.'

'Don't worry, Bobby,' Livia said quickly, feeling the quivering tension in the slight body beside her. From the corner of her eye she could see him open his mouth, whether to spit again or say something, she didn't know; but she wasn't prepared to risk it. She thanked the driver, then turned her back on him as he moved off, standing between him and Bobby.

His face made her ache to comfort him. She rarely touched him, aware of how he must feel about all the other adults who had laid hands on him, but this time she couldn't help it. As the car drove away, she put one arm round his shoulders.

It was a mistake. He stiffened and his face hardened, like setting concrete. Without a word she let him go.

Leaving him to settle himself in his usual chair in front of the growing pile of pages filled with the details of Dare's life, she fetched her coffee and his Coke from the kitchen. Then she went back for a plate of biscuits.

'What's these, then?' He pointed to the drawings. His voice had all the old aggressive hoarseness she hadn't heard for weeks.

'I've been designing a house for Dare to live in when he leaves his family,' Livia said casually, hating herself for having transgressed the boundaries he'd set, and John for having hurt him, and Colin for having been so stupid as to catch the flu.

'Why?'

'I used to be an architect a long time ago and so I thought I'd work out the best kind of house for a boy like Dare. Would you like to see it?'

Bobby kicked the table leg. Livia thought of the early morning's happy excitement, spoiled now.

'OK,' he said at last. He sounded worn out, as though he'd been through some kind of battle.

Taking care not to lean over him or stand where he could not see what she was doing, Livia pulled the pile of drawings towards him. The perspective of the outside of Dare's house lay on top. After a while, she slid the sheet away and led Bobby, drawing by drawing, through the house to the garden beyond. He was still silent. She took her coffee cup and went to sit down opposite him.

He didn't know what to do, and she wasn't sure how to help him.

'You done a lot of work,' he muttered at last, not looking at her.

'Yes.' It wasn't the moment to correct his English. 'But I liked doing it. We've talked a lot, you see, about how Dare feels and what he does and why he does it. And I've become so very fond of him. I wanted to do something for him, and all I know is how to design houses. So I thought: why not?'

'He's only a story.'

'I know.' This was not the moment to point out the similarities between Dare and his creator, or to explain why she longed to do something—anything—to help change Bobby's life. 'And the house isn't real either, although it could be.'

''S stupid then. Waste of time. Crap.'

'No. It wasn't a waste of time,' Livia said steadily, wishing that the easy physical communication they could have had was not barred to them. 'It gave me real pleasure to design the house and make the drawings, and I hoped it would give you pleasure to see them.'

He shrugged and kicked the floor, hard. She tried again.

'And it isn't unreal in the sense of fake. This could be a real house. All new buildings start like this, with an architect like me making the drawings. They're like a recipe for cooking.'

Bobby looked blank: perhaps he'd never seen anyone cook from a recipe.

'There's everything here to tell a builder how to make a house exactly like the one in this picture.'

'If you paid him.'

'Yes.' Livia smiled. 'If there was a client to pay.'

'How much?'

'I don't know exactly,' she said, becoming aware of where this conversation might go, and wishing she'd thought of the danger in time.

'Why not?'

'Because I haven't done any work, any architectural work, for a long time, so I'm out of touch.' He looked so contemptuous that she thought she'd better rescue the conversation with some real information. 'But I expect it would cost something over a hundred and fifty thousand pounds.'

There was a pause before he looked at her, and an even longer pause before she realized that his expression was one of puzzled admiration.

'You rich, then?'

Livia laughed, remembering Gordon's endless warnings about Bobby's lightfingered tendencies and the danger of letting him know just how much she was worth. 'I'm a pensioner, Bobby. Too old to work. Pensioners aren't rich.'

His eyes narrowed as he looked around the room. He could have been assessing either her worth or her reliability. She wasn't sure which.

'When d'you stop working?'

What a weird question, she thought. Well, I can't lie to him.

'More than twenty years ago. Twenty-five.'

He looked at her, his clenched eyes so penetrating and yet so cold that she wondered who had been talking to him and what they'd said, whether they'd asked him to cross-question her about her past. She quickly thought of a diversion.

'Would you like something hot to drink instead of the rest of that Coke? It's so cold out today. Why don't we have some hot chocolate? I've got enough milk for once.'

''F you want.' He shrugged. 'I don't care.'

You did that, she told herself as she went to find a pan and chocolate powder and clean mugs. Bobby's been able to ask for what he wants and decline anything he doesn't for weeks. Now he's back to putting all the onus on you. It's your fault he's regressed. Why the hell didn't you leave well alone this morning and wait for Colin to get better?

'Why'd you stop working then?' Bobby asked as soon as she appeared in the kitchen doorway with the two mugs of foaming chocolate.

Livia looked at his bent head and wished she knew what was going on in his brain, and whether he was someone else's mouthpiece. Should she lie? No. She'd already done him enough harm this morning.

'Because I went to prison, Bobby.'

His head snapped up then. His eyes looked amazed and—to her shame—excited.

'What you done, then, Liv?' he asked. His lips were twitching into a mischievous smile.

Now what? she asked herself. Lie and risk one sort of damage, or tell the truth and face the other?

'I killed my husband,' she said at last, turning to look out of the window to give him time to absorb the news unwatched.

There was silence. She couldn't feel anything in it and so after a while she turned back.

Bobby's face was completely blank. There was no mischief, or malice: nothing.

'It was a long time ago, Bobby, and I've served my sentence. I've paid for what I did.' God, how I've paid, she thought as the memories crowded in on her. She tried to push them down and failed.

The old panic was making her pant. She could feel the sweat crawling down her spine at the smallness of the cell as the heavy steel door thudded between her and the outside world for the first time.

'How d'you do it, then?'

The sharp voice brought her back out of the choking past.
'Bobby, I...'

'You scared?' He laughed, a shrill sound that held no
amusement. It was more like a taunt, or a dare. 'Go on. Tell
me how you done it.'

'No, I'm not afraid of you, Bobby.' He flashed her a quick
look then, acknowledging their connection for an instant before
the blankness wiped it out again. She smiled, a little encouraged,
but he didn't see it. He was back to kicking the table leg.

'But it was all so long ago, and I don't want it to be
something between you and me. It's over. In the past. It isn't
real any more. It was, but it isn't now.'

'Did he beat you up?'

'No. He never did that.'

'Then why d'you kill him?'

How to explain to this damaged child, whose experience
had been so limited, so different in nearly every way from
hers, how she and Henry had lived and what he had done to
her? She hadn't ever tried to tell anyone. She didn't know if
she could do it without breaking down. It would be easier to
describe her father and his rages. Bobby would have understood those.

'Well?'

The single demanding word was so full of aggression that
she had to answer it. She tried to smile and to choose words
he might understand.

'I was very angry with him for something he'd done that I
couldn't forgive, as I usually had had to forgive him. I tried
to talk to him about it, but he wouldn't listen. He told me I
was mad. And he told everyone else too, so they'd believe
him not me.'

How feeble it sounded! No wonder she had never tried to
explain it to anyone else. No one else who hadn't been there
could have understood.

Bobby was frowning. He sounded puzzled as he said: 'You
mean he'd been dissing you?'

'Yes.' Livia couldn't help a tiny smile at the thought of standing in the witness box to explain to her 1970s judge and jury that Henry had been dissing her.

'Why di'n' you just kick him out then?'

Why indeed? 'I don't know.'

'Why d'you have to kill him?' Bobby's voice had wobbled. Livia tried to focus on his face, but she couldn't see properly. She shook her head. That made his face clearer. At once she knew she had to say something to take the bruised look out of his eyes.

'I don't know, Bobby. *Now* I can see that I could have walked away. Should have walked away. But at the time I didn't know I could.'

'But why d'you have to kill him?'

Livia had to find a way to make him understand. She was thinking out the words as she leaned towards him. He pressed himself back in the chair, flinging up one of his arms against his head. She wanted to lay her face on the table and howl. She muttered something about the bathroom and tried to get upstairs. Her knees locked and her back shrieked in protest. Somehow she made herself move.

She didn't know how long to give him, or what he'd say to her when she went down again. There were no sounds coming up the stairs. She wondered what he could be doing. Then there was a sharp bark. She was back at the top of the stairs before she could put words to her terror.

Flap came bustling along the corridor from the bathroom, barking and bouncing up and down, his ears flapping away with the most insouciant cheerfulness. Reaching her ankles he leaped upwards. She caught him and held his squirming, furry, trusting body to her face. His wet tongue lapped about her cheek.

'What about my lesson then?' Bobby's shout made her stiffen. Flap barked in protest. She put him on the floor at once and followed him more slowly downstairs.

'What'll Colin say when I tell him we didn't do any reading today? You're supposed to be learning me to read,' Bobby said. He had a red felt-tip in his hand.

With superhuman self-control, Livia refrained from looking around the room to see if he had scrawled graffiti over her landlord's walls and furniture.

'You're right. And I'm a fool. I always did talk too much. I'm sorry, Bobby.'

''S all right.'

She smiled into his tight face. 'OK. Let's get started. Here's what we wrote yesterday. Will you read it through for me?'

The inner corners of his eyes looked as though they were tied together with strings tightly knotted somewhere at the back of his head. But he seemed to be doing his best to get their dealings back to normal. The least she could do was copy him.

As he stumbled over the words she had written to his dictation yesterday, making mistakes he had overcome weeks earlier, she had to work to keep her hands in her lap. She longed to stroke his hair, to hug him, but she couldn't. The only thing was steadiness and as much normality as possible. If he could do it, so could she.

Slowly, his face began to unclench and he began to read more fluently.

'So,' said Livia, smiling at him as he finished the last sentence they had written. He didn't respond.

Give it time, she thought. 'That got much better, Bobby. Thank you. And now, on the next chapter: where does Dare go next?'

'Prison,' he said shortly. So she had not been forgiven.

'Why?' she asked calmly, uncapping a felt-tip and taking control of the half-empty page.

'Because he burns the house down, and everyone in it dies. Crackling like.'

'Oh, Bobby,' she said before she could stop herself. 'I'm so sorry.'

He shrugged and kicked the table leg. The tray with the drinks slid on the polished surface and her coffee cup rattled in its saucer.

'Listen, Bobby. I know what I told you today has shocked you, hurt you…'

'I don' want to talk about it.'

'All right.' She didn't let the sigh escape. She would do her best to play the game his way. 'Then tell me about the fire so I can write it down. Did Dare do it on his own?'

'No. He has mates. You don' know anything about them. But *they* like him.'

'What are their names?'

But that was all he was going to tell her. He sat, apparently not even listening, as she sketched out possible other ways for Dare's story to go. Bobby drank his cooling chocolate, but he didn't say another word. Eventually, more exhausted than she had thought possible, she put down her pen.

'How'm I going to get home then?' Bobby asked, satisfaction at his victory glistening in his eyes.

'We could walk.'

'It's fucking miles.'

'Not that far. And you might enjoy it. Even though it's cold out, it's a lovely day. Look at that sky. It's only ever like that—clear and blue and thin—in winter. And we'd soon warm up once we were walking.'

'You oughtta have a car. Or don't they let you when you're a killer?'

'I haven't tried to drive recently.' Steady, Livia. Keep steady. He'll work it out in the end and stop taunting you. Just put up with it while it lasts. You can do it. 'But I might get myself a bike.'

She noticed a flicker of interest in his face and gave in to the temptation before she had realized what it was: 'Can you ride one, Bobby?'

'Yeah. But I never had none after my Chopper got nicked.'

'I think a friend of mine might have a spare mountain bike for someone of about your size. If you had one, d'you think you might ride it up here without having to wait for Colin?'

'Dunno.' But there was a glint in his eyes. Acquisitive? Or friendly? Livia couldn't tell.

'Well, I think I might give him a ring tonight anyway and see if he still has it. If he has and is prepared to send it, you could see how you feel when it arrives. In the meantime, I'll walk you back to the village.'

❧

Bobby was still protesting as they reached the lake. Livia couldn't believe he was as oblivious to the glory around them as he pretended, but he scuffed along the road, looking at his feet and complaining.

With the woods at their back, the lake on their left, unruffled again and looking almost blue with the newly revealed sunlight and the bright sky reflected in it, and the open country ahead of them, Livia longed to stride out, using every muscle and breathing in the still-freezing air. As it was, she had to use all her spare breath to urge Bobby on: Look, there's the signpost. Eskfoot's only another three-quarters of a mile. See, there's a heron! Those clouds over there look as though it might rain again later. Only another half mile now.

''S all up hill. I'm tired. My legs hurt.'

'Come on, Bobby, it's not far. You can do it. What are you likely to get for lunch, do you know?'

'Beans. She's a crap cook.'

'What food do you like best?'

'Dunno. My legs hurt.'

'What kind of hurt?' Livia asked, thinking that she might as well turn the walk into a vocabulary lesson if nothing else was going to get through to him.

'What d'you mean?'

'Is it a dull ache, as if you've bruised them? Or sharp, as if you've cut them; or torn, as though you've pulled a muscle?'

He danced around in front of her, putting out both arms like someone stopping the traffic. If it hadn't been for the calculation in his eyes, Livia might have thought it part of an ordinary childish game. She stopped, about a foot away from him. He looked up into her face.

'They feel like you've stuck a knife into them,' he said and then turned and ran laughing towards the village. Livia suppressed every emotion and tried to catch up with him.

Like a child playing tag, Bobby would slow down and allow her almost to reach him and then start running again. She didn't protest or run, but she did her best to keep him in view. Her relief at the sight of the first grey stone cottages made her aware of all her aching muscles and clattering lungs. Her old fear of the people she might meet was overtaken by her physical sensations and her irritation with Bobby.

That's all it is, she kept telling herself: any adult in charge of a child like this one would be angry; it's normal; I'm not a danger to him; irritation's not so bad. It's no different from being angry with Flap.

Her kneecaps felt as though they might crack open if she didn't rest soon. She passed a small shop with a Post Office sign hanging above the door, then a plate-glass window full of ropes and brightly coloured cagoules and waterproof trousers. Bobby was loitering on the edge of the pavement.

He looked back, doubtful. She must be showing more signs of decrepitude than she'd realized if she had actually worried him. She straightened her back and made sure that she was smiling as she caught up with him.

'You're as bad as Flap,' she said, the panting breaths rasping in her cold throat. 'Much too exuberant and fast for me at my age.'

He smiled a little sickly.

'Now, Bobby, which is your house?'

'There.' He jerked his chin in the direction of a small pub. Outside it were a group of youths in anoraks and woolly hats. They mostly looked a year or two older than Bobby, but not much more than that. 'Past them.'

'Well, that's OK. Come on.'

'I…They don' like me, Liv.' He looked up from under his lashes. She watched him, her heart banging less and less hard. So, it seemed that he needed her now. At least he had the grace to admit it. In many ways he was a more admirable person than she was. She didn't have the grace to admit anything very much.

'Don't worry. Stand up straight and we'll get past them together. Brace yourself, Bobby. We can do it.'

She stepped out, as though to swinging martial music. Bobby fell in at her side and they strode forth. The gaggle of youths, among whom she noticed with relief were a few girls, parted without trouble.

'There, you see. They're like dogs: don't let them see you're afraid and you won't panic or challenge them into attacking you.'

'Yeah. Right.'

But when she and Bobby reached the edge of the small crowd, someone shouted: 'Fucking animal.'

Livia wasn't sure whether it was she or Bobby who was the target, but she said nothing. Bobby swivelled his head, ready, she knew, to return the insult. She ignored her self-imposed rule about not touching him and plonked a heavy hand on his shoulder.

'Come on. You'll be late for lunch otherwise.'

There were other shouts, but she refused to let their sense reach her brain. She was fairly sure no one was going to throw anything at either of them. Not in the middle of the village anyway. Most of the inhabitants must be indoors eating lunch, but they would almost certainly respond to shouts for help.

At last they were well away from the young louts and Bobby was banging on a green-painted wooden door. It soon opened and a plump, motherly-looking woman stood there, wiping her hands on her apron.

'So, you've seen fit to come back, have you?' she said. 'Get in and wash your filthy hands.'

Bobby sidled past her, turning to look briefly at Livia from the end of the passage. She thought there might be apology in his eyes, but there wasn't enough light to be sure.

'It's Mrs Davidson, is it?'

'That's right,' said Livia, holding out her hand. 'And you're Mrs Gaddon. It was good of you to let him come to me this morning.'

'I hear he spat at John.'

'It was a bit of a misunderstanding.'

'That's not what I hear. He's not teachable, you know, Mrs Davidson. If Mr Whyle told you otherwise, he was lying. He's beyond help, that boy. I'll not be keeping him much longer myself, but I can't throw him out until they've found someone else to take him. They're trying now, but there's not many will take a lad with his record.'

'He's learned a lot with me so far,' Livia said as calmly as she could. 'And until the spitting episode today he's never done anything in my presence that could be construed as more than ordinary small-boy naughtiness. I consider myself very lucky to be allowed to teach him.'

'It's easy to see you don't know much about boys like him. You've been giving him things, haven't you? Like the roller blades at Christmas. And buying Coke for him and sweets, he tells me—letting him draw and never making him do any lessons at all if he doesn't want.'

Livia raised her eyebrows. She wasn't sure whether this was guesswork, or Colin trying to explain her methods to a sceptic.

'Oh, he tells me all about it, whenever I try to make him do what he doesn't want. It's Livia this and Livia that till I could have brained the pair of you. It won't work for ever, you know. He knows which side his bread's buttered, but as soon as you cross him, he'll turn on you: and then you'll see what your precious pupil's capable of.'

She turned her head, listening, and then shouted: 'Will you stop doing that, Bobby. I've told you before.' Looking back at Livia, with triumph in her smile. 'What did I tell you? He's at my biscuits again. Spoiling his dinner. I'll sort him out. Don't you worry.'

The door banged shut in Livia's face. She could hear the giggling shouts of the youths outside the pub. Reminding herself of her own advice, she turned and faced them. She refused to cross the road and forced herself to walk up to the group.

Three of the biggest boys stood across the narrow pavement outside the pub, blocking her way. One had bad acne. All of them had nearly identical expressions, challenging, closed and mean, a lot worse than Bobby at his most truculent.

Livia smiled and asked them to move.

'You going to make us?' asked one in a high nasal voice.

Livia put a hand on his chest. He was far stronger than she was, and she knew she could never push him if he didn't want to move.

'Say "please",' he said, crowing with laughter.

'Please,' said Livia, hating what felt like the hundredth act of submission she'd made in the day. The boy moved aside and she had time to take two uninterrupted paces before another group took his place. The first trio had moved in behind her and there were others between her and the road. Now she couldn't get round them, even if she wanted to. The only way was forward. She moved on, asking, pushing, thrusting her way through, pursued by jeers and laughter. But none of them actually touched her. There was no reason to find them so frightening.

Now I know how witches felt, she thought, when the whole village was determined to burn them for being weird or poor or single in a married world.

She still had two and a quarter miles to go before she was back in her sanctuary. With her back as straight as she could make it, she walked away from the childish mob. The Salem witches were hanged on the accusations of children no older than these, she thought, hoping they wouldn't follow. It seemed unlikely. Despite their cagoules and walking boots, they didn't look like happy walkers. She wondered who was in charge of them and what on earth they were doing in Eskfoot.

Only when she was well out of sight of anyone peering from the last of the straggling cottages, did she find a tree stump and allow herself to sit down and catch her breath. She bent double over her knees, dizzy and aching. Soon she'd have to find enough strength for the climb up to the Long House, but she could give herself a minute or two to rest.

As the pain in her legs and chest receded, the thoughts flooded in, bringing the knowledge that by getting out of prison, she had lost the one thing that had kept her going. Inside, she'd still had dreams of freedom. Now she knew what it was like, she wasn't sure she wanted it. She'd alienated everyone, except Flap. He at least was uncomplaining, unable to hurt her, unable to be hurt by her—except in the most unimportant of physical ways. She loved him nearly as much as she had loved Val.

Feeling a tickle against her hand, Livia looked down and saw a woodlouse crawling laboriously up over her knuckles. Shuddering, she shook her hand and the little greyish-black armadillo-like thing flew off. She didn't see where it landed, but it was probably dead.

# Chapter 16

'What in God's name does Livia think she's doing now?'

Cass held the receiver away from her ear as Gordon Bayley's voice shook with outrage.

'I'm to buy her a mountain bike, if you please, for this unsavoury child she's taken on. Has she gone mad?'

Cass propped herself up on one elbow. Her eyes were gummy. She wished Gordon had remembered that it was Saturday, and anyone who worked her hours deserved a lie-in at the weekend. She pushed the hair out of her eyes and excavated some of the goo from her tearducts. It was nine-thirty. Could have been worse. At least she'd had nearly three hours' extra sleep.

'Presumably she wants to give him a present. Why shouldn't she, Gordon? It's her money.'

'That may well be true, but she's not thinking straight. She seems to have no idea of the risk she's taking.'

'I don't understand. It's only a bike.'

'To you, perhaps. But to a child like this, there'll be no "only" about it. He'll get greedy. That sort always do. He'll start working out what else he can get out of her with the right sort of pressure.'

'So? Livia's quite tough enough to resist the blandishments of an eleven-year-old.'

'Wake up, Cass. I'm not talking about blandishments. Haven't you thought of blackmail?'

Cass paused. Maybe he had a point.

'But she's known as Mrs Davidson up there. How…?'

'Oh, come on, Cass! Don't be naive. Even if he didn't recognize Livia herself, he saw you, didn't he? Only a week before you were all over the papers with Julia Gainsborough. You and Livia keep telling me how bright he is. Don't you think he will have done the arithmetic?'

Oh, God, I hope not, Cass thought. And not only Bobby, but all those people in the village shop.

It was a miracle that none of them had found their way to George Jenkins yet. He seemed to have spoken to almost everyone else she had ever known, leaving his slimy slug's trail over her entire life. Luckily she had enough real friends like Sophie to put up such effective resistance that he'd run out of things to print about her. There hadn't been anything in the *Post* or anywhere else for weeks, and the loitering hacks had gone from outside the building, too. Cass pushed herself up on one elbow to check the street. Yes, it was still empty.

'Even if he did work out who I was,' she said firmly, 'that was months ago. If he was going to use it, he'd have done it by now.'

'But…'

'Come on, Gordon. Livia adores Bobby. Let her give him the bike. And try not to worry too much. When are you next going up there?'

'The weekend after next. A fortnight. I wish…But I can't. She won't let me see her more than once a month—says she can't bear feeling I'm monitoring her. She gets enough of it from her probation officer and the social workers.' The outrage was beginning to soften and he sounded more like himself. 'But I will telephone her now. I'm sorry to have disturbed you, Cass.'

'Not at all, Gordon. Give her my love.'

Cass put down the phone and lay back under the blue-and-white checked duvet, closing her eyes, willing sleep to come back and banish the anxieties he had dribbled into her mind. But he'd done too good a job. She got up.

The day was not inviting. She had no urgent work to do, and Sophie was away for the weekend with her parents. They had invited Cass, too, but it was a bit soon after Christmas to go again. The gym would take care of the morning, and then she could see a film, or take in an exhibition. Or she could go back to the storage cell and read about Livia's trial. In a way she was almost ready for that. But breakfast first.

The kettle was beginning to boil as the phone rang again. There didn't seem much point answering, so she made coffee instead, stirring the granules until a smile-inducing voice echoed from the answering machine.

'Cass, Christopher Bromyard here. I wanted to thank you for Thursday night. You made a dull working evening into something extra. And I…'

'Christopher? Sorry. I was making coffee. I didn't hear the phone ring. How are you?'

'I'm fine. Glad I haven't woken you. I wondered, Cass, are you very busy or would you like some lunch?'

'What, today?'

'Mmm. Any good?'

'Well, yes. That would be great. I'm due at the gym later this morning, but I'll be out by one. Where shall we meet?'

'How about Tentazione? Do you know it?'

'Yes. I like it. And it's dead convenient for me. Quarter past one?'

'Terrific. I'll see you then. Thanks, Cass.'

There was no sign of Cass in the small, plain brick restaurant when Christopher arrived five minutes late, which was a relief. He wasn't sure how she would take to being left to sit alone in public. It was bound to happen at some stage if they saw much of each other, but he didn't want to set too many tests too soon.

He wasn't at all sure about her. Up in the Lake District, well away from real life when he'd been feeling so unlike himself, she'd seemed everything anyone could want: intriguing, funny, fantastic to look at, and powerful. He'd liked that then. But he had been ill.

After she'd gone, he found himself missing her—a lot— and planning to see her as soon as he got back to London. Then, when he did get back, he slotted straight into his own life, and there didn't seem any room in it for her.

He'd almost forgotten her by the time he saw her in Guildhall. She'd looked like a bullrush there, emerging from the self-satisfied swamp that filled it, and something had clicked in his brain. He'd known he had to see her again.

It was partly her courage, he thought as he waved away the waiter, who wanted him to order a drink. She must have needed a hell of a lot to go to a dinner like that, when the whole City had been gossiping about her and her murderous grand-mother.

Maybe that was what had got to him, her courage. And her loyalty, of course. There had been several days during the autumn when he'd braced himself to expect gossip-column titbits about his midlife crisis. Most women would have offered whatever they had to buy off the journalists who were giving Cass such a hard time. But she had kept her mouth shut. It must have cost her.

He should have rung her then. He probably would have if he hadn't still been smarting from Betka's last savaging. But he hadn't needed any more aggro, so he'd just written the letter, hoping it would be enough to keep her on side.

He was rather ashamed of that now, but he'd make it up to her somehow. This lunch would be a start.

❧

Cass felt wonderful. The morning's rowing session was still with her in the pleasantly stretched muscles of her back and shoulders. The subsequent shower had left her feeling sleek, and she was moving with real pleasure in her skin. She saw

Christopher the moment she came into the restaurant, and she liked the way his eyes widened for a second before he smiled and raised his hand.

It could have been just a reflection of the white tablecloth adding light to his face, but it looked more alive than anyone else's. Cass handed her coat to the waiter and walked into the room without waiting to be shown to his table.

As she reached it, Christopher stood up. Hardly any of the men she knew did that. She put her hand on his shoulder and he leaned down to kiss her cheek. It wasn't an air kiss; she felt his lips on the top of her ear and the slight roughness of his chin against her skin.

'This is…' she began as he was saying, 'Cass, you…' He laughed. 'You first.'

'I was just going to say that this was such a good idea of yours. You?'

He was still laughing as he pulled her chair back for her. 'Good. No, I was just going to say you look terrific. You are lucky to have the kind of body that looks as though it's graciously allowed the clothes to rest against it.'

One of Cass's hands was in the air, where Christopher's shoulder had been. Realizing that it must look like a weird Fascist salute, she let it drop.

'Haven't you ever noticed?' he said, still holding the back of her chair. 'Some women—men too probably—look as though they've poured or squeezed themselves into their clothes. You're not like that. I spotted it as soon as I was in a fit state to spot anything in the Long House.'

Cass sat down, thinking that there was no luck about it; just hard work. 'I must say it's a novel chat-up line, Christopher.'

He grimaced, which surprised her. Perhaps he hadn't intended a compliment. Then the laughter returned to his face. 'Good; perhaps it'll single me out among the many.'

'You know, I don't understand any of this,' she said. If she were going to take a gamble on him, she would need to know the odds. 'If you wanted to see me, why…?

'…didn't I phone you sooner?'

She nodded.

'Lots of reasons.'

'Like my grandmother being a murderer?'

His face twisted again. This time it made him look angry. The waiter brought a basket of various kinds of Italian bread and a dish of green oil to dip them in.

'Thank you,' Christopher said in the tone that means, And now get the hell out of here.

'I'm sorry if I've embarrassed you,' Cass went on, picking up a piece of bread and making an elaborate business of dipping it and shaking off the excess oil. She didn't do a good enough job and a greenish-gold drop fell on her chin. She put up one long finger and scooped up the oil, looked at it, sitting like a bead on her fingertip, and then licked it off. 'Mmm. That's good.'

'Cass,' he said slowly, 'I'm beginning to think you could be a bit of a monster.'

She looked at him, her black eyes laughing. 'Too right. It's just as well you picked it up straight away. D'you mind?'

'I don't know. And, by the way, you haven't embarrassed me. But I'm not sure I understand quite what you're up to. D'you want to tell me, or is it a guessing game?'

Suddenly sobered, she wiped her finger on her napkin. 'No. I hate those. And I didn't mean to tease. It's just that I want to clear all this…this stuff out of the way before I let myself like you too much.'

'Ah. Could you do that?'

The waiter was back with menus before Cass had a chance to answer. She accepted the maroon folder and opened it, saying casually: 'Yes, I think so.' The waiter looked puzzled.

'It'll take us a minute or two to choose. Cass, would you like a drink?'

'No, but perhaps some wine later.'

'Fine. Thank you.' The waiter obediently disappeared. 'Did you mean that?'

She looked at him, and decided against pretending to misunderstand. 'Yes.'

He nodded, breathing carefully. 'Good. Now, what will you eat?'

Oh, you are my kind of man, she thought as she read the list of ingredients in each dish. No romantic protestations. I'm glad I changed the sheets. Should I have Hoovered the bedroom? Do I want to go to bed with you as much as I think I do?

'I think I'll have the monkfish, with perhaps the scallops to start.'

'Perhaps? Is that *politesse* or doubt?'

She laughed. 'Actually it was *politesse*. I know that's what I want.'

'Good. White wine, then. OK with you?'

She watched him choose and order the wine without any more reference to her, the archetypal Alpha male, certain of his place in the tribe, his resources, his taste, and accustomed to deference. As the waiter left, Christopher glanced up and caught her watching him. His lean cheeks creased and his eyes narrowed as he grinned.

'Humour me, Cass.'

'I'm not sure that it's good for men like you to be humoured *all* the time.'

'It's a harmless enough amusement, isn't it?'

'Maybe.'

'Oh, you're a hard woman.'

'Yes, you can be sure of that.'

He was dipping a piece of ciabatta in the oil as she spoke, and he left it soaking there as he looked carefully at her.

'Actually, I don't think I can. I don't think there's anything hard about you, Cass, except the carapace.'

'It's a pretty tough and all-embracing one,' she said, thanking God for the extra layer she'd grown since Alan. She wasn't going through anything like that again. Not ever.

'But one that could be shed?'

She took another piece of bread and tore it open, picking off the crust. Her eyebrows were tight against each other. The squashy bread from the middle of the slice was pulpy and unattractive. No bite to it. She dropped it on the table-cloth.

'Couldn't it, Cass? It struck me the other night that it might.' Christopher sounded serious. He was still watching her, apparently well aware of her distaste. At last she put the crust on the table and dusted her fingers on her napkin.

'Probably. But I don't know how or when or what losing it might do.'

'Then perhaps we'd better just let rip and see what happens.'

Her eyes lit in response. She remembered him lying naked and unconscious on Livia's sheepskin rug, infinitely vulnerable. The contrast between that and this powerful, confident man made her feel as though she had twice the usual oxygen coursing through her. Her finger ends tingled.

'Are you prepared to risk it, Cass?'

She felt her eyebrows twitch again.

'I've always enjoyed risk,' she said, and wondered if there was still the remotest truth in that. It seemed unlikely. 'But what about you?'

He laughed. His teeth were quite remarkably even and white. She wondered if they'd been capped and hoped not. She wanted him to be real; she'd had enough of hidden damage, hidden shame, hidden violence. Whatever Christopher was and whatever he wanted from her ought to be on the table for honest negotiation. This deal mattered. She wanted to make sure there could be no unexpected debts or recriminations to come. She'd had enough of those, too.

By the time the waiter tried to interest them in pudding, Cass knew that Christopher's plans for the afternoon were not much different from her own, whatever he might be thinking about a longer term investment.

'Coffee then?' he asked with a smile that said something quite different.

'Why don't you come and have some with me?' she answered casually, not caring that the waiter was probably quite as well aware of their intentions as both of them. 'My flat's only just round the corner. And the press have got bored with me, thank God. There hasn't been anyone on the doorstep for weeks. It should be safe to be seen with me.'

'Great.' Christopher's eyes would have reassured her if she'd been in any more doubt about what he wanted. 'Just the bill please.'

Cass thought about offering to pay half, then decided to let him have his fun.

It was raining and neither of them had an umbrella. But it wasn't cold. The wet found its way through their hair and slithered down their necks. Cass was interested to see that her fingers were shaking as she disentangled her keys from her bag and tried to unlock the door.

'Sorry,' she muttered as she dropped the bunch. 'Perhaps it's the wine.'

Christopher didn't laugh. He put his hand on the back of her neck, trapping some of the rainwater between his skin and hers. It warmed immediately. She felt steadied. The key slid easily into the lock and turned without snagging. She pushed open the door and stood aside so that he could go in first. He looked around and said something. She couldn't hear the words for the drumming in her ears. She said his name and then told him to take off his wet coat. With a bundle of damp cloth in her arms, smelling of what must be wet sheep, she went through to the bathroom and draped both coats over the rack she used for her tights.

He hadn't followed her. She went back, aware of threats and dangers from her own past and his. He was standing by the front door. He'd shut it, but he hadn't assumed anything else. His eyes made him seem nearly as vulnerable as he'd been when she had undressed him on Livia's rug. He'd been wet then, too, and shuddering with fever.

'Will you come to bed?' Her voice croaked.

He smiled and put out his hand. Cass took it between both of hers and then, not quite sure what to do with it, lifted it. She saw that there was a tiny fresh cut, probably a paper cut, across the base of one finger. She licked the fine red line and then let her tongue push between that finger and the next. He tasted a little salty, and very slightly of the olive oil in which he'd dipped his bread. She heard him breathing hard, as though controlling pain, and looked up quickly.

He was biting his lip, staring over her head. She put her right hand against his lips and felt his tongue, first soft, slippery, as hers had been and then insistent. There was a slight roughness about it as the muscles hardened. He looked down at her. Her fingers spread.

Later, as she slept with the back of her head pressed against his shoulder, Christopher tried to make sense of what had happened. She'd come. He knew with a certainty that was rare for him that she hadn't been faking. And he felt as though she'd shed the carapace for the moment at least. He wasn't sure how she'd react once she was awake again. He hoped she wouldn't regret it.

It had been extraordinary to watch her hover on the brink, then suddenly choose to let go, to feel everything he was trying to give her. Her eyes had been open all along, the pupils dilating as he watched. He hadn't expected that. He'd assumed she'd be a secret hoarder of sensation.

A phone was ringing. Christopher slid sideways out of bed to silence it, furious with the caller. He'd wanted Cass to sleep on, untroubled. She deserved that. He reached his mobile before she moved, only to find it quiet. Someone must be after her. Unaware of his fury, she began to smile before her eyelids lifted. She licked her lips.

'Sorry,' she said, voice as slurred as her eyes were sleepy. 'The answering service will cut in any minute. Did it wake you?'

She stretched, her whole long, magnificently smooth body arching sideways against the sheets, as her hips shifted. She blinked and her eyes focused. 'Tea, Christopher? Or a drink?'

He wanted to say the right thing, but he didn't know what it was. She was so different from any of the others. He'd always known what to say to them, whether he was going or staying. Her face was changing as he watched, the sleek sleepy delight sharpening into doubt.

'What is it?'

'I…Cass…'

'What?' She looked really worried now. He had a moment's scary pleasure that he instantly suppressed. The fixed phone by her bed started to ring.

'Christopher, what's the matter?'

'I…You…'

The mobile was ringing again, too, whoever was trying to get her wasn't going to give up. She ignored the mobile and grabbed the receiver of the fixed phone.

'Yes?'

Christopher watched her. Her face grew tighter and tighter as she listened. When her voice came it was like coarse sandpaper against his belly.

'You are the most arrogant man I've ever known. And selfish and despicable with it. A self-satisfied little prick with no conscience and no spark of generosity. I wouldn't have you back if you crawled on your hands and knees, *begging*.' She crashed the receiver back, saying shortly, without looking at him: 'Sorry about that, Christopher. I'll go and put the kettle on.'

As Cass turned away from the phone, she caught sight of Christopher's expression. It changed in a micro-second from shock into a guarded smile. A few months ago, she wouldn't have understood the constituents of the shock. Now she did. And one of them was fear. With her back to him, she grabbed the counterpane and wound its brilliant patchwork around herself, tucking the edges into her tiny cleavage.

She wanted to explain the call, which had been from Alan, but she had to get hold of her temper first.

Alan had said he'd been thinking about coming back to her for months, but that it had taken him until now to get to grips with who she was and what she'd done to him. Now that he was confident of being able to handle her, he would be over in five minutes with champagne and roses. Arrogant prick.

In the kitchen she leaned her forehead against the cupboard door with her hand on the kettle's handle. It began to quiver as the water boiled, but she didn't do anything about it. The automatic switch cut out. She remembered what had happened just before Alan had phoned and she'd lost her temper: Christopher had been trying to tell her something, something difficult that had been making him look ashamed.

It seemed impossible that what they'd just given each other could have made him look like that. But maybe it hadn't meant so much to him. To her, it had been so important that she'd hardly been able to bear to let go because that meant ending it. But she hadn't had time to tell him. All she'd done was screech like a fishwife down the phone, making herself sound like someone who'd sleep with any man who offered and then dump him as soon as a better prospect came along.

If she took long enough making the tea, Christopher could always dress and go without having to say whatever it was that had been so difficult. Hearing his footsteps, she pulled herself away from the cupboard door. If he was on his way, she hoped he wasn't going to come into the kitchen to say goodbye. It would be so much more civilized if he just left. But if he did come in, she didn't want to look weedy and needy.

She felt his hands on her back and put the kettle down. She was in such a state that she might start flinging hot water about.

His hands slid round her waist. She felt his chin on her head.

'Cass, I don't know how to say this.'

She tightened her muscles so that she was standing a little away from him. He pulled her back, but she resisted.

'And I don't want to say the wrong thing and put you off. But you've done something for me today that I...I don't have the language for this. You've given me something I didn't... Oh, hell! It all sounds like such an idiotic cliché.' She felt his lips on the back of her neck and began to understand. She raised her right hand and laid it on the top of his head.

His hair felt much more fibrous than she'd expected: she felt each separate strand against the skin of her palm.

'I'm very bad at this,' he said more calmly. 'I don't know how to tell you clearly that I loved the way you looked at me, the way you touched me, the way you moved as I touched you. I felt as though something momentous was happening.'

She turned. Her back pressed hard against the worktop. Heat from the kettle reached through the counterpane to her skin. She was laughing, perhaps from relief, or from pleasure, receding shock, anything. Hysteria even. She didn't know. He kissed her. His hands held her head and his tongue was gentle.

'We have to make this ordinary soon,' she said as he drew away at last. 'Or we'll both blow up.'

# Chapter 17

Cass pushed aside the pile of Sunday papers and stuck her long legs out from under the blue-and-white checked duvet. Christopher put his hand on her shoulder, pressing her back.

'Don't get up,' he said. 'Let me remember you like this. It'll sustain me through the meeting.'

She relaxed against the pillows and felt a shaft of sun drive warmth across her left cheek.

'It does seem unfair that you've got to go in on a Sunday,' she said, ignoring everything she knew about life in corporate finance. She felt gentle and confiding: she wanted him to stay.

'I know, but it's a deal, and it's the life I chose to come back to.' His voice was brisk and his hand was tight as he ruffled her hair. He seemed distracted. In spite of the narrow stripe of sunlight, Cass was chilled.

'Will you be here later, if I can manage to phone?'

'Yes,' she said simply.

He kissed her quickly and left without looking back. She waited until she heard her front door click behind him, then got out of bed for one last sight of him, winding the counterpane around her body in case there was anyone else in the street.

'There she is!'

Cass pulled back from the window immediately, swearing, and ran for the front door to warn Christopher. But he had already reached the ground floor.

She heard the shouts as soon as he emerged into the sunny street: 'What happened? Are you OK? Aren't you scared to get too close to the Harpy's granddaughter?'

'Is it true she's got a terrible temper?'

'How long have you been having an affair? Did you know what you were taking on?'

'Has she hit you yet?'

Cass leaned against the doorjamb, tears of rage heating her eyes. Bastards, she thought. Oh, the bastards. And why now?

She heard Christopher's imperturbable voice telling the hacks that he didn't know what they were talking about, then she heard a car door bang and the engine start up. The voices didn't stop until the car had driven away. Then she heard a yell: 'Cass? Come back to the window. Cass. We know you're there. Cass!'

Keeping her back pressed against the wall so she could be sure they couldn't see her, she slid into the bathroom to check the back of the building. They were there too. There was no way out.

Her only consolation was that they had no proof that Christopher had been with her. He could have emerged from any of the other seven flats in the building, even Annette Sharpe's. And he hadn't answered any questions. There was no proof. They might still get away with it.

If only she hadn't looked out of the window! That's what sentimentality does for you, she thought, as the last of the tenderness was forced out of her.

Her mobile rang. She hoped it was Christopher, taking advantage of the first empty road to stop and make sure she was all right.

'I hope he's worth it, Cass, whoever he is,' said Alan's voice.

She didn't have time to count to ten, but she managed two, and hoped that would be enough.

'What are you talking about?'

'I knew you had someone with you when I phoned yesterday. You only ever talk in that throttled voice when you're being overheard.' Alan laughed. 'It's a dead giveaway, Cass. Besides I know you: you wouldn't have turned me down if you hadn't found someone else.'

He left a gap for her to comment. She did not bother to fill it, still concentrating on keeping calm.

'In any case, I heard him breathing. So I tipped off one or two press contacts. I was sure it would be worth their while to doorstep you again. And I hear it has been. How about that, then?'

'What exactly did you hope to gain?' Cass said, while her mind produced a string of boiling insults as gross as anything she'd heard from Bobby.

'I could call them off, you know. If you made it worth my while.'

'So it's blackmail now, is it?' It was hard to keep her voice light with pretend amusement. 'Isn't that a bit grubby for a respectable solicitor?'

'It's nothing of the kind.' He laughed again. 'I was just trying to be friendly. You might as well let me help, you know. He won't be back, not now he knows he'll be photographed every time he comes round to screw you.'

The vindictiveness felt like a physical assault. Once, in bed, Alan had told her she had transformed his life, made it worth living. Now this. How could he?

Cass tried to remember what she'd heard about using noise to burst the eardrums of phone pests. She would have liked to burst his eardrums, the bastard.

'Or I could give them something extra to think about, by telling them what you did to me in the restaurant that day. It would be fun to see what else they can dredge up about your violent past. I can't have been the first man you slugged. You were too damned good at it.'

'And *I* could tell your wife all about your nasty black-mailing habits, and the rest of the Law Society, too,' Cass said, impressed by her self-control. She felt as though worms of hatred were eating their way up her body from the soles of her feet, like bilharzia. 'You have a lot more to lose than I have. Stay out of my life, Alan, and don't phone again. I'm not coming back to you, and your threats don't impress me. OK? Goodbye.'

She put down the phone with the force she usually reserved for double-glazing salesmen. It rang again at once.

'I told you to keep out of my life. Leave me alone.'

'Hello?' said an entirely strange woman's voice, with a smoky drawl. 'Hello? Could I possibly speak to Cass Evesham? Hello?'

'Who is it?' The question came out very aggressively, but Cass couldn't help that.

'My name's Annie Prestwich. I used to work with her grandparents.'

A thick cloud had covered the sun. Cass felt very cold. She took the phone back to bed, pulling the duvet up round her bare shoulders.

'As an architect,' the woman went on. 'I worked for Henry Claughton and Associates for nearly ten years.'

'And who do you work for now?'

'Myself,' she said, affronted.

The bed suddenly seemed very frowsty with the papers all over it and a large greasemark where one of last night's bacon sandwiches had oozed. Cass looked away.

'This is Cass Evesham.'

'Oh, good. I hoped it was. I've been meaning...wanting to call you since I first read about you in the papers after Livia...I wonder: could we meet?'

'I am not going to answer any questions about my grand-mother.'

'You don't think I'm a journalist, do you?' There was surprise in the question, and some anxiety.

'How would I know?' said Cass. 'But whoever you are, I'm not answering any questions.'

'No. That's not what I want. I don't want to ask you anything. There are things I have to tell you.'

'Oh? About what?'

There was a sigh down the phone, then the voice again: 'I was very fond of Livia at one time, and there are things I haven't been able to say to anyone else. I…There's something you need to know.'

Cass held the receiver away from her, frowning at it. She heard the tinny sound of the woman's voice going on and on and put it back against her ear.

'…if we met somewhere in public in, say, a couple of hours. That way you could check me out, make sure I am who I say I am. Would that do?'

Cass knew she couldn't stay in the flat all day with the ravening journalists outside and the grubbiness pushing away more and more of her once-glorious memories of last night.

Forcing a way through the hacks and photographers would be unpleasant, but it would have to be done. Go out with all guns blazing, she told herself, and grit your teeth. Dare them to write unsupported crap in their filthy rags. That was better. She could still be tough, even though she'd slipped out of her armour last night.

The fixed phone rang as she was making the arrangements with Annie Prestwich. She left it until she heard Christopher's voice through the answering machine, then she grabbed the receiver, silently cheering the discovery that Alan was wrong again.

'You OK, Cass?'

'Angry. And very apologetic that you should've got involved.'

'It's not your fault. But we will need to make plans. Neither of us can afford to go on like this.'

No, she thought, we can't. So is this going to be it?

'I can't talk much now,' he went on. 'This place is pullulating. But when I'm done with the meeting, I'll phone you and we can talk properly. Will you be all right till then?'

'Sure. But ring my mobile. I'm not letting them imprison me in here all day.'

'Take care when you go out, Cass.' He sounded urgent. 'Don't let them see you riled, and smile whenever there are any cameras around. They could damage you if they catch you looking…'

'Like a harpy?' she said bitterly. She couldn't help it.

'Just that. I'll phone you later. Got to go now. 'Bye.'

Cass turned to look at the dent in the sheets where he'd slept beside her all night.

❧

'Julia? George Jenkins, here. How are you?'

'Fine,' she said, rolling over and squinting at the clock. It wasn't ten yet, and on a Sunday, too. This had better be good.

The whole campaign was dying on its feet, and George hadn't done anything for ages. No one was writing about her brilliant future any more. The television proposal had come to nothing. Audiences in Wandsworth were beginning to dwindle, and the rest of the company was becoming tetchy. They'd had to put on *Electra* again when *The Revenger's Tragedy* had flopped, but even that wasn't doing enough for ticket sales. It was beginning to look as though she'd had her fifteen minutes of fame.

The bank clearly thought so, because they were talking about raising the interest on her loan for the Big Deal Theatre Company. A sure sign they thought it was on the skids. Destitution loomed, and the old contempt, and the loneliness. Julia shuddered.

'What's up, George?'

'Good news. We've had a sniff of something interesting about Cass Evesham at last.'

Julia sat up, bursting out of the clouds of anxiety. 'Why? What's happened?'

'A bloke, disaffected boyfriend I imagine, tipped us off last night that it could be worth sending someone round to her flat.'

'And?'

'She's got a new man, and we caught him on camera leaving less than an hour ago.'

Julia looked down over the end of her bed to the mirror and slid the sheet a little lower. She ought to be the one with the new man, not scrawny, ugly Cass. It was her turn. She was owed.

'How's that going to help?' she asked sourly.

'He hasn't been identified yet, but according to my boys, he's a good six-feet-four, late thirties, drives a Merc.'

'Rich, you mean?' Her throat felt sore, as though she'd swallowed undiluted loo cleaner.

'Looks like it. Which should help. If he's a success somewhere, he isn't going to want this sort of publicity. The boys are showing his pic to the City desk in case. And if he's one of her clients, which he looks as if he could be, things could really roll for us.'

'How?'

'We can needle her about him and get her angry again. With luck, this time she might hit one of the boys in front of a camera. Then we'll have all we need to run stories about inherited violence.'

'And you'll have the climax of your book. But, George, she's never hit any of the others, and you were sure she would. Just like you were sure her friends would give you juicy titbits, but they didn't. Nothing you've done has got us anywhere.' Julia hated sounding so petulant.

'If at first you don't succeed, try, try, and try again. I've never not got a story I was after. If there is one here, I'll have it in the end.'

'Oh, don't be so cocky.' The words were out before Julia could stop them, but they were a mistake. If you alienate this creep, she told herself, you won't have anyone on your side.

'Temper, temper.' He was laughing, which made it worse. 'You ought to thank me, Julia. I've been working my socks off for you. Now, how about coming to have some lunch with me?'

Do I want to go out with a sleazy tabloid hack? No I don't. But I need him. I'll have to. Ugh.

She licked her lips and smiled seductively at her reflection, putting herself into the role so that her voice would sound right.

'That would be heaven, George. How sweet of you!'

❧

There was no sign of Annie Prestwich in the dark wine bar under the old railway arches when Cass got there. It seemed an odd place to have chosen: dank and furnished only with tatty chairs and old barrels, with rainwater dripping through the vaulted ceiling and collecting in pools on the uneven stone floor.

Cass chose a barrel with two reasonably level chairs and no rainwater, and sat there, waiting. She picked some of the grimy soft wax dribbles off the candle on the barrel and rolled it between her thumb and finger, flattening and then balling it again, as it cooled. The wine list lay open in front of her.

'I always have the house claret,' said a smoke-scratched voice. Cass looked up.

Annie Prestwich had a small cat-like face, covered in a network of fine lines, as though a sieve had been pressed into her thin, dry skin. Her hair was the dark orangey-red that only henna gives, cut short and wildly untidy. The lines around her puckered mouth and a heaviness about her eyes suggested she must be nearing sixty, but she was dressed in tight faded jeans and a multicoloured South American sweater, which had slipped off one shoulder, revealing a tightly shrunk lavender-blue T-shirt.

'Christ! You look like Livia.'

'So everyone says. I'll order some claret.'

'It's all right. It's coming. And I've told them to bring us some Stilton. That's what Livia and I always had.'

Cass thought she could see tears oozing out from beneath Annie Prestwich's darkened lashes. They reassured her. No journalist was going to be able to cry to order.

Annie lit a cigarette with a battered gold lighter, dumping it on top of the packet as she sniffed and wiped her nose on the back of the hand that held the cigarette. 'You don't mind, do you?'

Cass shook her head, waiting.

'Have you seen Livia since she got out?'

'I told you, I'm not answering any questions. You said you had something to tell me.'

'I know.' Annie scratched her head. Cigarette ash dropped into her hair. 'But it's hard to begin. Do you know anything at all about her career?'

Cass was surprised by the question, but it was one she could answer without trouble.

'Virtually nothing except that "she never fulfilled her potential", as they say. And that her father never wanted her to be an architect in the first place.'

'He was mad, you know. Her father. Stark staring bonkers and dangerous with it. He was committed in the end. Sectioned it would be called now.'

Cass hid her lurching doubts behind a bland, confident smile. Annie's hands were shaking and she was smoking as though the nicotine was more important than oxygen.

'He died before she qualified, which is a pity because she did staggeringly well. Came top most years and won the Wren prize for the best domestic building in her last year. Did you know that?'

Cass shook her head and noticed a flash of contempt on Annie's face, which seemed a bit unfair.

'She got it for a tiny house, a two-person house, that aroused a lot of interest at the end of the war. A man who owned a small bomb site in Oxford was so impressed he commissioned her to build it. That's how she got her job with Henry, bringing him a client and a well-known project.'

'Good start to any career,' Cass said, interested, but wanting to get the revelations over as soon as possible. Christopher might phone at any moment and she couldn't have an audience then.

'Absolutely. They called it the Wren House when it was built, and it won a whole lot more prizes. International ones.'

'Does it still exist?'

'God yes! Didn't you know? Architecture students make pilgrimages there from all over the world. I can't understand why none of the papers has mentioned it.'

'Presumably because it wouldn't fit with the picture they want of a mad, murdering Harpy.'

Annie met Cass's eyes for a second and then she looked away, searching the packet for another cigarette she could smoke. There didn't seem anything wrong with the one she'd just stubbed out, or all the others she'd already rejected, half-smoked.

'Or perhaps because no one else remembers now that it was Livia's project. It's always referred to in terms of the practice: Henry Claughton and Associates.'

Annie put the cigarette between her lips again and used both hands to make the lighter work. It looked quite extraordinarily heavy. She gave up the effort and put it down, the unlit cigarette still stuck between her lips.

'I think that's why…'

'Why what?' Irritation was beginning to roughen Cass's voice. Either the woman wanted to tell her something or she didn't. This neurotic fiddle-faddle was wasting time.

The waiter brought their bottle, two glasses and an enormous plateful of Stilton with a pile of biscuits. Annie poured out the wine and mashed her unlit cigarette in the ashtray.

'She sort of fizzled out, career-wise, after that, even though she was probably the most original mind who ever worked for the practice. You see, something went terribly wrong.'

'She had a baby.' Cass picked up her glass. 'My mother. Wasn't it quite tricky for a woman to have a professional career and children in the fifties?'

Tasting the wine made her think of last night. She had opened a bottle of extra-special Burgundy for Christopher, and they'd drunk it in bed as they ate their bacon sandwiches.

'I won't take much longer,' Annie said with a hint of petulance. 'This is important, Cass. Try to listen to me. Please.'

'I am listening.' She tried to remember what Annie had been talking about. 'So, Livia had great talent as a young architect and was then sidelined into being a child-carer. Is that right?'

'Yes. She did come back to the practice after Ros was in full-time school, but she'd lost her touch. Henry started her off again assisting with some of his less important projects, to kind of ease her back in gently.'

'I don't suppose she liked that much,' Cass said, remembering the confident, flowing lines of the sketches Livia had made whenever she was doodling in the Long House.

'No. It made her livid. That's how we became such muckers in the first place. I was a bit bolshie, too, you see. And we used to come here after work and drink claret and eat Stilton as we moaned about Henry.'

'So you liked her?'

'I did.' Annie's twitching lips and wary eyes softened for a second. 'I thought she was great, and much more interesting than Henry. He could be pretty earthbound, you see, as well as earthy. Livia was different. When she was perky, she kind of flew. But he could bring her down to earth so easily.

Sometimes she was absolutely shrivelled by the things he said to her. For someone who seemed so hard, she could be amazingly sensitive to criticism.'

Annie propped both thin elbows on the rickety table and rested her young-old face in her hands, chewing her lower lip. 'I've often thought she must have found prison absolutely terrifying.'

Cass thought of her first encounter with Livia in the Long House and said drily, 'I think maybe she was a tad tougher than you realized.'

Annie glanced up quickly, looking hopeful, almost as though she'd been given a reprieve.

'So you *have* seen her?'

Cass nodded. Annie broke off a corner of Stilton and ate it, still chewing as she lit the next cigarette. Cass waited. Annie slopped more wine into her glass and sucked at it as eagerly as a hungry baby with a bottle. When she put down the glass, she braced herself. 'What did she say about me?'

'You? Nothing. She never mentioned your name. Should she have?'

There was silence.

'Oh, come on,' Cass said. 'You got me here because you wanted to tell me something. I haven't got that much more time.'

'I feel so guilty.'

Cass stiffened, wondering if she were about to hear that Livia hadn't killed anyone after all, that she'd taken the rap for this woman.

'Henry told me he'd fallen for me, you see.' Annie stared at the sweating stone floor. She began to scratch both forearms through her sweater. 'And he made me believe it. I didn't realize quite what…'

'Are you telling me you had an affair with my grandfather?' Is that all?

'We mostly did.' Annie lifted her thin shoulders, making the bright knobbly sweater slip a little further off one, revealing big bleached splodges on the T-shirt beneath. 'But I didn't know that then. I thought it was just me.'

'Well, Livia's hardly going to worry about that now.' Cass thought of everything Livia did have to worry about and was amazed at Annie's self-absorption.

'I've wondered since if it was just a way of getting us to work like slaves for peanuts. Which we did. Or perhaps give him the credit for all our best work.'

So, thought Cass, self-absorbed but not vain. That's something. But poor Livia.

'Look, have you had enough to drink?' Annie said, pushing back her chair so hard that it rocked as she stood up. 'D'you mind if we get out into the fresh air?'

'Not at all,' Cass said, thinking it was a waste of wine, but quite liking the idea of being back above ground.

Outside the sky was a peculiarly bright, clear blue. When they reached Trafalgar Square, the white spire of St Martin's in the Fields looked like a jewel. There were very few people in the square itself, and the grubby pigeons were disconsolately trampling over each other, scrabbling for what little food there was.

Cass led the way to a bench from which she could see the clock on St Martin's spire. Annie found yet another cigarette to light.

'So, you started sleeping with Henry and presumably stopped having bonding drinks with Livia in basement wine bars. Is that it, or is there more guilt you want to shed?'

Annie shook her head. Her eyes were wet. 'You're hard like her, aren't you?'

'Oh yes, I'm a dead ringer for my murderous grandmother,' Cass said bitterly, 'and her mad father, too, no doubt. If you want absolution for bonking my grandfather, you've come to the wrong place.'

Annie turned away. In the bright sun, her face looked even more crumpled than it had in the candlelight. Ill, too. Cass shifted along the bench.

'I don't want to be unsympathetic, but I really am going to have to go soon. Is there more?'

'Only about the Southampton Opera House,' Annie said, looking away from Cass, down towards Admiralty Arch. Her voice was wobbly with tears.

Cass's conscience pricked, but she wasn't going to apologize; in this, as in so much else, she was on Livia's side. Annie seemed paralysed. Cass tried to prompt her.

'My grandfather won the competition to design it, but then it was never built because of the scandal. Isn't that right?'

'Yes. It was a stunning building. Amazing. Quite different from everything he'd done before.' Annie wiped her nose again, sniffing. 'At the time it made me feel a bit better about being dumped for Flora. I told myself that if loving her had opened him up to this incredible creativity, it was worth it.'

Cass tried to think of something sympathetic to say.

'And I knew she wouldn't stay with him for long, so I thought if I hung on and didn't make a fuss he'd come back to me.'

'What was so special about the building?' Cass looked at the clock. The hands were crawling towards three. Christopher might be out of his meeting at any moment and then she'd hear whether she was going to lose him because she was the Harpy's granddaughter. She didn't want to get all dramatic about it, but it did seem rather more important than Annie's stories of the dead past.

'I'm not making much sense, I know,' Annie said. 'But you see, it was a staggering building. I'd never have believed Henry capable of it, if I'd been thinking straight.'

'So?'

Once again Annie's crumpled face aged in front of Cass. It was like watching Dorian Gray's portrait, she thought. Annie shivered, and suddenly hitched up her sagging sweater, wrapping her arms around her waist.

'He'd produce all the ideas in funny little sketches of a kind I'd never seen him do before, then hand them over to me to get the technical details sorted and the working drawings made. It was bloody hard work, but I felt…oh, transfigured. He might be in love with Flora, but he still trusted me enough to make his masterpiece work technically. I'd have done anything for him.'

A particularly greedy pigeon waddled up to them, crooing and ducking its head. Perhaps it thought the cigarette butts were some delicious kind of food. Annie kicked out and it flapped resentfully away.

'It was all terribly secret. No one except my tiny team was allowed to know what we were doing. That made it exciting too. We all worked ludicrous hours and felt like "we few, we band of brothers".'

Annie's gaze was fixed on Admiralty Arch. Cass was beginning to see where the confession might be going. She wondered why it had never occurred to her as she'd watched Livia doodling.

'And when the judges came to me saying Livia claimed that he'd stolen the whole thing from her, I thought he'd been right all along and she'd been mad for years.' A mouthful of smoke gushed out with the words. 'It's that I can't bear: that I joined in with Henry and said she was mad.'

'She wasn't.' There was no upward intonation in Cass's voice, no hint of a question. It was a flat statement. She was glad to be able to make it with absolute certainty.

Annie pushed her hands through her mop of hair, releasing a new shower of cigarette ash and dandruff. 'No, she wasn't.'

'What did you do about it?'

'Cass, be fair.' Annie swivelled on the bench and put one skinny, shaking hand on Cass's knee. Cass pulled away. It was the least she could do for Livia.

'What could I do? By the time I realized what must have happened, Henry and Flora were dead and Livia was in prison. They weren't going to let her out just because I told them she had an even bigger reason to be angry with her husband than the one they already had. It wouldn't have made any difference. I was so worried that I checked with a lawyer.'

'I bet it would have made a difference to Livia. Couldn't you have told her?'

Annie sniffed and, holding the cuff of her sweater in her clasped paw, wiped the tears off her face.

'I didn't know how. The longer I waited, the worse it got. I hoped…I sort of hoped you might tell her for me.'

'Me?' Cass was on her feet. 'Why does everyone dump their consciences about Livia on *me*? You tell her.'

'But she won't listen to me.'

'How do you know? Have you ever even tried?'

Annie shook her head. 'I don't know where she is.'

Cass ripped a page out of her diary and wrote on it. 'Here's her e-mail address. Write whatever you want. She can read it or not, answer or not, as she chooses. I've got to go.'

'Please help me.'

Cass wheeled round to stare at her. 'There's nothing I can do for you. Livia might, if she chose. But it's up to her.'

She walked away, fury at what Livia had had to put up with blinding her. A lamppost loomed up ahead of her and she swerved just in time to avoid banging her head against it. At the traffic lights she turned back to look at Annie.

The pigeons were chuckling and strutting around her ankles. Suddenly she shuddered and picked up her feet, to sit hunched with her arms around her knees. Her tousled red head sank down on to them.

She must be very cold, thought Cass, shivering herself. But it's her problem. Her fault. Nothing to do with me. She deserves anything she gets. What she did was appalling.

The lights changed and Cass set off across the road to her car. The mobile cheeped in her pocket. It was Christopher calling to say it looked as though he was going to be embroiled for the rest of the day and would she be OK?

Cass tried to laugh. It didn't work, but at least she didn't sniff as she said: 'I think I can probably survive. In fact, I've been thinking of going to Oxford to look at something. I might go this afternoon if you're not going to be free. It won't take long.'

The thought of not seeing him again stopped her breathing for a second. She coughed.

'D'you think you'd have time for a late supper somewhere? We could talk then. We need to talk, Christopher.'

'Yes, I know. I'll do my best. I'll phone when I can. Drive carefully.'

Carefully? Cass thought later as she roared through the almost empty streets towards the M40. Me? Now? What would be the point of that?

# Chapter 18

Colin was well enough on Tuesday to bring Bobby to the Long House as usual. When they arrived, Livia saw that something was wrong. Colin's hedgehog face was screwed up into a tight defensive mask and Bobby was sulking. What could they have been saying to each other?

'Will you stay and have some hot chocolate with us?' she asked Colin, hoping for a clue.

'I think I'd better get on—there's quite a backlog in the office—but thanks all the same, Livia. I'll be back by about twelve thirty if that's all right.'

'Fine. Can I ask you something before you go?'

'Of course. Fire away.'

'Bobby and I had a nasty experience down in the village while you were ill. Did you tell him, Bobby?'

There was no answer from Bobby, who was ignoring Flap's overtures as deliberately as Livia's. He kicked the leg of the nearest chair. Livia turned back to Colin, who was looking surprised.

'We were harassed by a group of yobs: young, but still yobs. I can't believe they're from around here.'

'They're from Manchester,' Bobby said, still kicking. 'They're s'posed to be learning to climb.'

'They must have some adults with them,' she said. Bobby shrugged.

'I'll see what I can find out, Livia,' Colin said. 'But I must dash now.'

When she had seen him out, Livia went to make the hot chocolate. With the two mugs steaming on the table, she turned to the last page of Dare's story.

'Here we are, Bobby: all the people in the house were burned to death,' she said casually, not looking at him. 'What happened to Dare himself? Did he get burned, too?'

Bobby was silent for so long that she eventually raised her eyes from the page. She couldn't help laughing at his mixture of surprise and resentment.

'Oh, Bobby, it's your story. I told you that at the beginning. Whatever you want to have in it goes in it.'

'Anything?'

'Yes,' she said with a moment's doubt about the night-marish horrors he might produce. But then if he had nightmares to share, they were probably better out than in. She could take it. At least she already knew about people burning to death; probably rather more than he did.

'OK. Yeah. His left hand's burned.'

'Badly enough to go to hospital?' Livia was writing busily, keeping the letters round and smooth and very clear.

'Yeah. A & E they call it, like on the telly. He has to wait with his skin still burning off of him.'

'Who else is there?'

A little interest was showing in his eyes again. Livia waited before asking any more questions. Soon he was off, weaving a wild digression about an old man Dare met, who'd had one of his legs bitten off by a dog.

Livia did little to restrain the fantasy, only occasionally pointing out where a touch of realism might be included, and wrote to Bobby's dictation.

Once he became involved in the story, Bobby's vocabulary increased, as it usually did when he forgot to pretend to be stupid. His description of the ragged wound left by the dog's teeth at the top of the thigh was graphic enough to make her feel sick. But she was proud of him, too.

They were both deeply into a discussion of whether even a Rottweiler could bite through a grown man's main leg bones when they heard an engine outside the house. Flap had been yapping for some minutes, but they'd ignored him because he'd already been let out twice in the space of an hour and they thought he should learn to be quiet when they were busy.

'Sh'll I go?' Bobby asked, already off his chair. Livia was so encouraged that he had bothered to ask that she nodded. Then, thinking of the various problems he might cause, she followed him at a careful distance.

There was a red Datapost van parked on the little plateau. The uniformed driver had the two back doors open and emerged with a large brown parcel in his hands.

'Mrs Davidson?'

Livia nodded. It must be Bobby's mountain bike. Gordon had done well to get it here so soon. There was a white envelope attached to the box with her name on it.

In a frenzy of yapping excitement, Flap leaped on to the box when she heaved it into the drawing room. Bobby was trying to look as though he didn't care what was in it. Livia opened the envelope and started to read Gordon's letter. After the first sentence, she looked up, smiling.

'The parcel's for you, Bobby.'

'Me?'

'Yes. D'you want to open it, or shall I?'

'Who's it from?'

'A friend of mine. I asked him to get it for you.'

She put the letter in her trouser pocket to read later, and settled herself on Christopher's sofa to watch. The brown-paper covering was easy to rip, but some of the enormous staples beneath almost defeated Bobby, and the cardboard around them was too thick to tear. He fetched a short thick knife from the kitchen and, sweating and cursing, got them out in the end.

Livia watched the knife slipping and jerking between his hands. She knew better than to interfere, but she was reviewing her first-aid supplies and hoping that if he did damage himself he wouldn't hit an artery.

Tourniquet, she muttered to herself, hoping that if it did happen her mind wouldn't betray her. Blood: there would be pints and pints of blood that spattered up into her face and…With a huge effort, she blanked the pictures in her mind.

Unaware, Bobby piled the staples neatly on the far side of the package and spoke sternly about their dangers to Flap, who danced over to investigate them. Livia watched Bobby's face as he pulled the first thick cardboard flap away from the contents. She could see only the glint of light on the spokes of a wheel, but from where he was kneeling, he must have seen exactly what it was.

He stared down at the contents, then up at her, looking almost ill. His eyes were huge and his mouth was tightly shut.

''S mine?' he whispered eventually.

'Yes. We'll put it together if you like. There must be some instructions and some nuts and bolts somewhere. You look for them while I get the tools.'

'You bought it for me?'

'Yes.' She wasn't going to touch him and make another mistake, so she just smiled.

'Why?'

'Because I thought you'd like it, and because I'd like it if you could get up here easily and not have to wait for Colin or the taxi.'

'You mean it's only for when I come here?' Suspicion and relief fought in his sharp eyes.

'No. It's for whatever you want it for. But if you want to come up here, it'll help.'

He turned away, rubbing his nose. She waited, trying not to be disappointed at the lack of visible pleasure. She saw him grab Flap and sat forward in case she had to intervene.

But he held the puppy quite gently, rubbing his face on Flap's fur. Flap licked his nose.

'Oh, you filthy thing,' Bobby said. But he was laughing. Livia tried to pretend that she didn't know he was crying too.

'I'll go and get the tools. Then we can put the wheels on.' She took her time fetching the spanners that Gordon had, of course, supplied, along with every possible hammer, screw and wire-stripper. There was even a weird-looking polystyrene helmet. When she came back, Flap was investigating the sparkling wheels, which were lying ready on the sheepskin rug, beside the instructions and the frame.

It wasn't hard to put the bike together, but Livia was breathless by the time she was sure they'd got the last nut tightened safely.

'There. Are you going to try it out?' she said, standing with one hand on the saddle and the other on the handlebars.

Bobby grabbed it from her then, as though he still couldn't believe she wouldn't take it back. Livia followed him slowly to the door, where she stood in the cold, watching him leap on the saddle and pound up the hill. He stood up on the pedals to get more power out of his stick-like legs, then turned and freewheeled down again, legs stuck out almost horizontally. She'd once ridden her own bike like that.

When the cold began to seep through her clothes, she hugged herself, rubbing her hands up and down her sides, and eventually retreated to the house with Flap. In spite of the central heating, she lit the fire, kneeling to watch the flames and hoping she had done the right thing.

At the most obvious level she had. For the moment Bobby was happy. And that was worth anything. Nearly anything. But Gordon had been so sure it would be dangerous. He might not know Bobby as she did, but he wasn't stupid, and he'd had a lot more experience than she had.

Colin came back at twelve thirty, obviously expecting to find them both hunched over Dare's story. Instead, Livia was still sitting in front of the fire with Flap in her arms, surrounded by a sea of torn cardboard and brown paper.

'What's up?' he said, charging through the door, looking as though he was ready to do battle or mend broken bones.

Livia scrambled to her feet, dislodging Flap, who clearly couldn't believe the indignity and set about Colin's shoe laces in revenge.

'Oh, I am glad you're here. Although it's too late to change anything now even if you disapprove,' she said, before explaining what she'd done, adding at the end: 'But I couldn't possibly take it back now. He loves it.'

'I think you've probably done rather a good thing,' Colin said judiciously. 'And it'll certainly be a relief to me if Bobby can ride to and from his lessons. The extra driving's been eating into my other clients' time.'

'I'm sorry. It's been good of you to do so much for us. I should have thought.'

Colin's little eyes shone out from the tangle of hair with such penetrating clarity that she was taken aback.

'Judging by the number of people who thought I was mad to put the two of you together, it was self-preservation.'

'Did they think I'd damage him?' she asked after an uncomfortable pause. 'A child like Bobby?'

'Either that or he would damage you. But you've vindicated me, Livia. I've been very impressed by the way you've handled him.'

'I haven't always got it right,' she said, uncomfortable with praise. 'I put my foot in it the other day, when you were ill. I think that's why he was a bit odd this morning when you brought him here.'

'What did you do?'

'I told him about my past.' Livia still found it hard to tie Colin's innocent, slightly weird appearance with the dispassionate intelligence that shone out of his eyes. 'And he didn't...didn't respond well.'

'Ah.' Colin squeezed his pudgy hands together between his thighs. 'Now that could have been a mistake, Livia.'

'I know. The bike's distracted him today, but it can't have changed anything.'

Colin was looking so disappointed that she burst out: 'I had to tell him. I couldn't lie to him once he started asking questions. No one's told him the truth or been straight with him since he was born. I had to change that.'

'Maybe, but it's a pity. Anyway, it's too late to change now. We can't put the milk back in the bottle. I'll see if I can find a way to talk to him about it in the car going back.'

'But don't...' Livia stopped. She knew she had no idea how Colin would approach the subject, or what could possibly make it any better for Bobby, or herself. 'Please be careful. Of him, I mean.'

'I'll do my best.' He didn't sound confident. Livia thought of all the damage she'd done in her life. She looked out of the window. Bobby was pedalling up the track, shrieking some incomprehensible war cry. He was happy. She wanted him to have that for a bit longer.

'Have you got time for some coffee, Colin?'

'Why not? Thank you.'

She could still see Bobby from the kitchen window. He waved to her, his face alight. She waved back.

'By the way,' Colin called after her as the kettle boiled. She put her head round the kitchen door to encourage him. 'Those boys who bothered you in Eskfoot. I've been making some enquiries. They're on a kind of character-building holiday with a couple of social workers. They're all difficult kids, though not in Bobby's league. His old league. But I'm sorry they annoyed you.'

'It wasn't so much annoyance.' Livia brought the coffee tray and laid it on the hearth. 'They frightened me. And I think Bobby's encountered them before. He was very reluctant to walk through the crowd.'

'They've been there since the middle of last week. I can't think why no one warned me.' Colin said, just as they both heard Bobby from outside the house.

'Liv, Liv.' She stood up and opened one of the windows. 'Watch me.'

'I'm watching.'

He made the bike leap over tussocks, riding high on the back wheel alone and then letting the front wheel crash down again. She smiled at his easy mastery.

After a while, when Colin had finished his coffee, she called out: 'You'd better come in now, Bobby. Colin's here.'

'But we don't need him no more. I c'n ride back, can't I?'

'Any more,' said Livia before she'd thought. Bobby glared at her for a second and then he laughed.

'Yeah. We don't need him *any* more.'

'Is that all right, Colin?' she asked, pulling her head back into the room.

'I think I ought to take him back today at least and explain to Mrs Gaddon that he's been given the bike. Otherwise, knowing her, she'll be convinced he's stolen it and call the police. Then we'll all be in deep doo-doo.'

Surprised by yet another of his eccentric expressions, Livia didn't comment, but she went out to explain to Bobby in a way she hoped wouldn't upset him.

When they had gone, talking cheerfully enough to each other, she made herself an omelette for lunch and ate it with broccoli, buttered brown toast and a glass of red wine as she read the rest of Gordon's letter.

She would see him again in less than a fortnight. And this time, they might get it right. The last few visits had been bearable, sometimes quite a lot better than bearable. But she wanted more. She wanted the kind of affection he poured into these letters but couldn't express when they were face to face. She wanted him to hug her as easily as Christopher Bromyard had done in that never-to-be-forgotten moment of unmatched comfort. She needed to be touched. But not grabbed by someone who felt he had a right to imprison her.

Still, she was too old to be mooning like a teenager. There was washing up to be done and the house to be tidied, and e-mails to be sent.

'You have mail,' she read when she had switched on her computer. She frowned. It couldn't be from Cass, who never wrote more than once a week. Gordon was infuriatingly Luddite when it came to new technology. There wasn't anyone else.

Curious but wary, Livia clicked to receive the message. Words scrolled up on the screen:

Dear Livia,
    Breaking this silence is harder than anything I've ever done. You must hate me.

Her finger bent under the pressure she was putting on the cursor key to bring up the name of the writer. The sender had been listed only as a number. Annie Prestwich.

Livia thought affectionately of the funny little skinned rabbit of a girl she'd known. Henry had valued her for her dedication to work and despised her for her lack of feminine allure and the inkstains round her mouth whenever she'd been sucking her pen. But he'd had no idea what she was like. He'd known nothing of her unexpectedly dry humour and huge capacity for wine. Or that her friendship had brightened some of Livia's bleakest days.

How can she possibly think I hate her? Livia wondered. Then she remembered that Henry had somehow found enough allure in Annie to take her to bed. Well, that was hardly Annie's fault. But perhaps she still didn't know how many other girls had been there before her.

Livia had known at the time that she ought to tell Annie, warn her that it would be over soon and she'd be left in bewildered misery as soon as Henry found someone better, but she hadn't been able to think of a way of doing it that wouldn't sound like spite. She hoped Annie hadn't suffered too much.

She scrolled back to the beginning of the letter and concentrated:

> Breaking this silence is the hardest thing I've ever done. You must hate me. If it hadn't been for Cass I might never have dared, but she's made me see that I have to do it. She's very forceful, isn't she?

Is she? thought Livia. I suppose she could be.

> And looks just exactly like you as I remember you. Perhaps it was that more than any of the things she actually said to me. I've thought of writing this letter for more than twenty years. Here goes: it was you, wasn't it, Livia, who designed the Opera House for the Southampton competition?'

Livia swung away from the screen, spinning the swivel chair so fast that her head got left behind and she ricked her neck bringing it back into line. She wished she smoked. She needed something in her mouth. Walking down to the kitchen was more difficult than she'd expected. She kept staggering and having to hold on to the wall.

Once there, she'd forgotten what she wanted and filled a glass with water from the tap. Even that was too much. She choked as soon as she tried to swallow, and covered her mouth with both hands. Her swollen knuckles shrieked as she tightened her fingers over her lips. But she couldn't let go. She didn't want to be sick.

Annie's letter had dug up everything Livia had struggled to bury. All the little devils were crawling out of the pit again, just like the woodlice in the tree stump. She could see them in exact and horrible detail: half-rat, half-baby; naked but with tails; tumbling over each other and clawing at each other's eyes. She'd never get them all safely under their lid before they dragged her back down into the hot dark past.

The knowledge that the shortlisted architects would all have been contacted, when she herself had heard nothing, did not surprise Livia. But it hurt. She sat on with the wreckage of Henry's breakfast all round her, telling herself that it didn't matter. Not really. She might have had plenty of fantasies about a repetition of the Wren Prize, but she'd always known that they were only dreams.

She should count herself lucky that she'd once had a moment when she'd known for certain that she had a right to a place on the earth and a talent that mattered. A lot of people never had that much.

And the months spent on the Opera House competition weren't wasted just because she hadn't been shortlisted. She had enjoyed herself sketching, planning, measuring, calculating and preparing pristine drawings; working in her own way at her own pace, without anyone telling her she was an extravagant fool or a hopeless designer.

The work had fed something in her that had been starving for a long, long time. It wasn't spoiled now, just because someone else had produced something better. The judges were all architects she respected: they'd have chosen a worthy winner.

Livia pulled herself up from the table, moving as though she were about a hundred and ten, and set about clearing up the eggshells and the toast crumbs Henry had left. The newspaper was lying in a crumpled heap beside his plate. It was like his bedclothes: Henry had only to get into a bed or pick up a paper for the whole thing to look as though it had been tossed about in a hurricane for a week.

She tried to concentrate on what she was supposed to be doing today as she tidied up. There was something for Ros. What was it? Babysitting Cass, probably. That's what it usually was. Yes, that was it. And it would be fun—being with Cass always was, responsive and original as she was. Life wasn't all bad while it had Cass in it.

Livia picked up the now-tidy paper, folded it shut and shook it to get rid of the crumbs. She saw at the foot of the page an announcement about the shortlist for the Opera House competition. Squinting, groping for her glasses, she saw Henry's name.

She found her glasses and sat down to read the whole piece, searching for explanations. There were none. But at the bottom of the column was a short announcement that models of the three shortlisted entries could be seen at an address in Piccadilly.

When she had put on her one good black suit, she did her hair and face properly. She didn't often bother these days: Henry always found something to dislike, whether she took trouble or not, so what was the point? But today it mattered.

The doorway in Piccadilly seemed portentous when she got there, heavily grey and forbidding. The kind of building Henry liked. Livia shuddered as she went in. There were a few people standing with devotedly bent heads as they circled a series of large Perspex cases. Livia waited, hanging back, until all but one had gone.

It was just as well. Only the one man heard the stream of whispered invective that poured out of her mouth.

'Are you all right?' he asked tentatively as she was muttering to herself. With a supreme effort, she took hold of herself and produced a smile of a sort. It must have been more like a glare because the man fell back, saying: 'Sorry.'

'I'm fine. Thank you for asking.'

'Fine. Right. Sorry.' He was backing away as he spoke.

Livia leaned forwards to see more clearly through the Perspex, as though that might change the floating structure she'd laboured over for so many months. Henry couldn't even steal properly, the fool. He'd completely misunderstood the point of the winged towers. Her hands curled into claws. Her toes shrieked with pain from the way they were clenched inside her shoes.

Livia found herself standing on the pavement hailing a taxi, unaware of having left the building, or even of having planned what she was going to do. But she was there, and she knew exactly what was going to happen and the effect it would have on him.

The taxi driver got her to the office in record time. Unfortunately there was no sign of the Saab in Henry's parking space, typically labelled in bigger type than anyone else's.

Inside the building, Klara, the receptionist who had always loathed Livia, was painting her nails. She'd never have dared do any such thing if Henry could have caught her at it. She looked up, saw Livia, and dipped her brush carefully in the bottle to paint the next nail. She made no attempt to stop or hide what she was doing.

'Mr Claughton's at a site meeting,' she said, examining the nail she had just painted. 'He said he'd go straight home when it was finished. So you'll see him before I do. But d'you want to leave a message in case he rings in?'

The youngest of the assistants passed on the other side of the glass wall and waved cheerily.

'Which site?' Livia knew her voice was sharp enough to rip through anyone's discretion, but Klara would have told her anyway. She looked as though she was enjoying herself.

'Gladstone Gardens.'

'Flora Gainsborough's house?'

Klara nodded, watching her boss's wife with satisfaction. A large gob of vermilion varnish was hanging off the end of her forgotten brush. It dropped on to her typewriter. Livia thought with primitive satisfaction of the trouble she'd be in when Henry saw the mess on the keys.

'Is Annie in?'

Klara languidly dialled the number of Annie's extension with one long, unpainted fingernail. There was no answer. Klara started wiping excess varnish from around the coloured nails. After a while she glanced up.

'She's not there. Is there anything else you want, Mrs Claughton?'

Not from you, Livia thought, wondering if Henry's catholic taste had ever been wide enough to include his receptionist. Probably. Otherwise there was no reason for her to be displaying quite so much contempt. Perhaps she was a stand-in for the days when Flora was too busy or disinclined for his attentions.

Livia knew she had to do something quickly, so she borrowed Annie's desk to write to the competition judges, explaining exactly what Henry had done. Then she forced Klara to give her a stamp, and got herself out of the office before she said anything she might regret.

She banged impatiently at the lift button. Nothing happened. Swearing, she abandoned the lift and ran down the stairs. There was a draughtsman's supply shop just round the corner. She'd be able to get what she needed there.

'A whole scalpel, madam? Or just replacement blades?' The elderly salesman wore a brown linen coat over his suit, like an old-fashioned grocer.

'The whole thing, please, and a packet of replacement blades. I left my last one with one of the associates in the drawing office, and he's gone away with it. Such a bore.' Too many words, Livia, she told herself, too many excuses. Don't explain yourself.

'Yes, indeed, madam.'

She exchanged the little package for what seemed a tiny amount of money and then took another taxi to Gladstone Gardens, where Henry was building one of his dreary, feature-less houses for Flora Gainsborough.

Livia had been sorry when she'd first seen the plans because she liked Flora and thought she deserved a lot better. Later, when they had got to know each other really quite well and Flora had been so enthusiastic about the tentative sketches for the Opera House, and full of helpful information about what singers need and who the best acoustics experts were, Livia had told her about the Wren House and shown her pictures of it.

Flora had begun to look at her very oddly soon after that, and after another week or two she stopped dropping in for tea and chats.

It hadn't taken Livia long to work out what was happening. She wasn't surprised that Henry had had a crack at Flora, but it did seem odd that she could be bothered with a man like him. The only consolation was that Ros loathed this affair too. For once Ros didn't start patronizingly explaining to her mother that a man as creative as Henry needed more emotional sustenance than she could possibly provide. Creative indeed! Damn Ros for her mindless, blinkered, partisan stupidity.

And damn Flora for telling Henry about Livia's Opera House. It must have been her. No one else knew anything about it until she submitted her entry to the judges. Especially not Henry. Between them he and Flora must have found her plans and stolen them.

Livia carefully attached one of the blades to the scalpel she had just bought, fashioning a protective envelope from the cardboard of a matchbook she happened to have, and put the whole lot in her jacket pocket.

The first thing she saw when her taxi turned into Gladstone Gardens was Flora's E-type. That wasn't exactly surprising. The only odd thing was that they hadn't asked her to babysit Julia. They usually did when they had an assignation. Maybe they'd known Livia was supposed to be with Cass and hadn't wanted to upset Ros any more.

Remembering her obligations, Livia looked at her watch. Damn. She should have been at Ros's house by now. Too bad. Ros could look after Cass herself for once. This was more important.

She paid off the taxi and waited until it had disappeared at the end of the road. Henry's bulbous Saab was sitting self-satisfiedly behind Flora's E-type. Livia took the scalpel out of her pocket, sliding it carefully out of the cardboard sleeve. She'd do the tyres first and then attend to the paintwork.

Should she just scratch it in abstract patterns? Or write huge great insults all over the bonnet? 'Henry Claughton is a thief.' A bit long. 'Wanker' might be better. She'd heard someone call him that when they'd nearly collided at a roundabout. It suited him. Wanker.

She bent down to stick the point in the first tyre, then straightened up again. There'd be only half the satisfaction if Henry didn't know who had done it. She wanted him to watch it happening, hear the screech of the blade, feel it slicing through bits of the car he loved better than anyone, even Flora. Livia yelled up at the lighted window of the main bedroom, hoping to see the curtains parting and his jowly face staring down at her.

'Henry! Come down here. Henry!'

There was no response. Livia slipped the blade in its cardboard sleeve and into her pocket as she walked towards the door. When no one answered her knock. She yelled, 'I know you're in there,' and crashed the knocker against the door again and again.

❧

Livia gagged again and poured the water back into the sink. She rinsed the glass very carefully, as though she might have infected it. There was a bottle of very dry manzanilla in the fridge because Gordon liked to drink it sometimes before lunch. Livia had had a taste during one of his weekends and now thought its astringent salty chill might help deal with her nausea.

It did help. Steadier, she went back to the screen to read the rest of Annie's e-mail.

# Chapter 19

Cass was in the loo at Stogumber's the first time she heard her new nickname. Two of the secretaries had come in and were repairing their make-up at the basins.

Cass heard one of them, whose voice she couldn't identify, saying to the other: 'Why are they calling Cass Evesham "BLT" these days?'

'You mean you don't know?' The second voice was easily recognizable. It belonged to Marietta, Michael Betteridge's beautiful American secretary, whose legs were even longer than Cass's.

'No. I can't see anything sandwich-like about her.'

'It's got nothing to do with bacon, lettuce and tomato, Dumbo. Honestly, Steph, sometimes I worry about you.'

Steph, thought Cass. Steph? Oh, that must be the new temp. If she really is a temp.

'So what *does* BLT stand for, Marietta?'

'"Bromyard's Leggy Totty". It's how someone who saw them together in a restaurant described her when he was trying to find out who she was.'

'But what's Bromyards?'

'Oh, Steph, really! Don't you even read the paper? Christopher Bromyard. You must have heard of him. Even you.'

Yes, thought Cass, keeping very quiet behind her door. Even Stephanie-the-temp would know that. No one who worked in the City could be that ignorant. So do you belong to George Jenkins of the pestilential *Post*? Or to someone else? Shit. When am I going to be able to stop watching my back?

'You mean she's having a bonk with *him*? God, she's lucky! It's not fair. I saw a photo of him only the other day. D'you suppose he knows who she is? You know, about her grandmother and what she did?'

'He must do. It's been all over the papers.'

Come on, Marietta, wake up, Cass thought. You know no one could be that naive. Think what she's trying to do and keep your wretched mouth shut. I've always been nice to you. You've got no reason to dump me in it.

'Perhaps it gives him a thrill,' Marietta went on blithely. 'I mean, it's only a bonk for him, isn't it? Whatever it is for her. He's never lasted more than three months with any woman, and most of them have been a lot more gorgeous than poor Cass will ever be. Someone ought to warn her.'

'What d'you think he sees in her? I mean all his others have been blonde, haven't they? And much sexier.' Stephanie's voice was hopeful, and betrayed a lot more knowledge than she'd pretended.

Wake up, Marietta!

'Whatever it is, she'd better make the most of it. She won't have him for long. I just hope it'll be long enough to save her career here. I quite like her.'

'What d'you mean, "save her career"?'

'Haven't you noticed? They're already looking at her differently, and one or two of her clients are showing signs of coming back. Being known as Christopher Bromyard's girlfriend won't do her any harm. But I wonder if he's told her the rules yet. If I know Cass she won't like them.'

What's coming now? Cass asked silently from behind the door, forgetting the threat of more revelations in tomorrow's *Post*.

'What d'you mean?' asked Steph again.

'It's a long list. Goes something like this: you have to adore him and do whatever he wants, even if it bores you; you have to be ready to go out with him whenever he's gotten time, but you mustn't object if he has to take a rain check at the last moment. You mustn't be too clever; you mustn't cry; you mustn't complain or phone him at work; you mustn't embarrass him in public. And you mustn't talk about him. To anyone. Ever. That's the most important one of all.'

'How on earth do you know all that?'

'I had a friend who went out with him. He was great and she was happier than she'd ever been. Then she phoned him at work one day to ask why he'd stood her up the night before, and he dropped her. Just like that. He refused to take any more of her calls and he never called her again.'

Cass pulled up her knickers and pulled the chain. As she was unlocking the door, wondering what they'd say when they knew she'd heard them, Marietta added: 'We'd better hurry. Michael will be screaming for me.'

The door banged behind them. Cass emerged to wash her hands, hating everyone at Stogumber's.

As soon as she was back at her desk, Gary lounged up towards her with a sickly smirk on his fat face.

'Cass, I was wondering if you'd introduce me to your new friend.'

She sat with her back to him, watching his leering reflection in her screen, well aware that he was winding her up. Should she take the request at face value and blast him for asking for favours after treating her like shit for months? Or should she show she knew he was still treating her like shit with his insinuations about sleeping her way back into her job?

'What friend is that?' Her voice was cool enough to freeze a polar bear, she thought. But it didn't seem to have much effect on Gary.

'Why, Christopher Bromyard, of course. I'd really like to meet him. You could ask me to dinner, couldn't you?'

'And what makes you think I know him well enough to have him to dinner?'

'Everyone knows. You were seen in Tentazione last Saturday, Cass.' Gary's laugh, knowing and suggestive, rang out across the banked computers. A lot of faces turned their way, the smiles just as knowing as his laugh. 'Suitable name for a restaurant in the circumstances. From what I heard you were practically fucking him under the table. Is he going to give you a job over there, or are you intending to stick it out with us?'

Cass turned her head, slowly, enjoying the sensation of anger well under control.

'Grow up, Gary.'

She picked up the phone and rang her best client's number. As his secretary answered, sounding reasonably cooperative, Cass began to plan her approach, ignoring Gary's almost tangible frustration. After a while he slunk back to his chair, pursued by catcalls from his fickle friends. Those, too, she blocked out as she persuaded the client that it must be in his interest to take a good big punt in Euros before the next G8 summit meeting.

When at last the markets closed for the day, she totted up her wins and losses as she always did, needing to know exactly where she stood, and discovered the total wasn't too bad. If it went on like this, she might meet her targets for the week, which would be great, even if she did owe some of it to her new status as Christopher Bromyard's leggy totty.

He hadn't been able to get out of his Sunday meeting in time to see her, and he'd been too busy to do more than phone on Monday. But tonight they were due to have a quiet drink in his house before going out to dinner to talk about what they were going to do. At least, that was the plan.

❧

The lights were on as she walked towards his house. Smiling, she speeded up, ready to grin at any hovering hacks. But she was lucky. There wasn't anyone waiting for her. Perhaps it hadn't occurred to people like George Jenkins that Christopher would let her anywhere near his own territory.

He opened the door, wearing a butcher's apron and carrying a pair of dripping wooden spoons.

'Cass, darling. You got here. Good. Come on in, quick.' He kissed her as soon as he'd shut the door and said: 'Good day?'

'Not bad.'

In the kitchen piles of fresh vegetables and fruit spread colour all over the worktop. Something was bubbling on the hob. The pungent scents of cumin and crushed chilli caught in her throat.

'You're cooking.'

'Don't sound so appalled, Cass. Why shouldn't I?'

Thinking of his Alpha-male performance in the restaurant, and everything the secretaries had said in the loo, she nodded and then shook her head.

'*Can* you cook?'

'Unlike you, Cass, yes.' He sniffed and then turned to stir and lower the heat under one of the pans before looking back to say: 'You don't mind, do you? The deal went quiet today, so I had time. I know I said I'd take you out, but this seemed better.'

'It's great. And no one can spy on us.'

'Yes. But I wasn't thinking like that. It was supposed to be a kind of present, you know, to have your supper hot and bubbling when you came home from the office. And your slippers warmed. Was it presumptuous?'

She let her bag and briefcase drop to the floor and walked forwards to lay her head against his chest, her arms clasped around his broad back. She, too, sniffed. Remembering the rules, she quickly said: 'It smells delicious. No. Not at all presumptuous. Just surprising. Do you often do this kind of thing?'

'No. Not often. But I like cooking. It's kind of therapy after a rough day. We're having Moroccan chicken and couscous. But you've plenty of time for a drink first. It won't be ready till after eight. Or you could have a bath. You said you like doing that after work. How about it?'

'Great,' she said, a bit surprised, but assuming he wanted her out of the way while he completed his mysteries. And he was right: she had told him she liked sinking into hot water at the end of the day.

He showed her the bathroom, provided a whole heap of clean green towels, and left her. It was surprisingly luxurious to wallow in his bath while he cooked for her downstairs, and even better when he reappeared in the doorway with two glasses of wine in his hands. He sat with his back to the warm towel rail and sighed in pleasure as he swallowed a mouthful of wine.

Cass listened to stories of his day, carefully edited, she noticed, to avoid any mention of the names of his clients, and then reciprocated equally carefully. She thought of making a funny story out of his effect on her standing in the office and then thought better of it. Christopher might not find it as funny as she was still hoping she could.

'Damn,' he said, interrupting her, 'there's my phone. I'd better answer in case it's the deal.'

'It's not yours. Unless you brought it up with you. Listen: it's coming from over there, with my clothes.'

'D'you want it?'

'No. I'll wait and see if whoever it is leaves a message.'

But the mood had been broken. Cass hauled herself out of the bath. Christopher wrapped the biggest emerald-green towel round her and went back to his pots and pans.

Cass found the phone, pressed in her PIN and collected the message.

'George Jenkins from the *Post*, Cass.'

Shit, she screamed in her head. Can't you ever bloody leave me alone?

'I thought you might like to give us a comment on this business of your grandmother teaching the Hell Brat up on…' There was a pause and a rustling of paper, 'Wast Water.'

She switched off the phone, yelling curses that would have made even Gary blush. Christopher came thundering up the stairs to ask whether there was anything the matter.

'Those bastards have found Livia. And now they know about Bobby, too.' She sighed and leaned her head against the tiled wall. 'Haven't we had enough yet? What the hell do we do now?'

'Ring Livia and offer her support, I should think,' Christopher said mildly. Cass blinked.

He was right, of course. And she should have thought of it herself. She would have in a minute or two. At least she hoped she would. But it didn't help because when she dialled Livia's number, it was engaged. She had probably taken the phone off the hook. Or she could be on line, waiting.

Gordon Bayley was answering his, though, and almost gibbering with rage. It took a while before Cass could hear him properly.

'I knew it was a mistake to give that appalling child such an expensive present. I told you, didn't I, Cass? He must have tried to blackmail her and, when she refused to give him money, gone to the press. But she wouldn't listen, would she? It's always the same. I try to help her, but she complains whatever I do. Now, look what's happened. I can't take it any more.'

Well that's wonderful, Cass thought, just what we need. But she produced a soothing, wordless murmur of comfort for him.

'I haven't the strength to go on with it,' he said. 'If she needs legal advice, or an injunction, James can deal with it; otherwise, she's going to have to cope on her own, or depend on you, Cass. I'm very sorry for you, but I'm afraid I've shot my bolt.'

Poor Livia. Someone was going to have to help her. Cass got Gordon off the line and called downstairs: 'Christopher, are you on e-mail here?'

'Sure. D'you want to use it?'

'If I may. Livia's phone is off the hook and you're right: she needs to know she hasn't been abandoned. Will supper wait a couple more minutes?'

'As long as you like.'

Christopher waited while she dressed, then took her to his study and logged her on to his computer. She didn't plan what she was going to type, just let the words come off the ends of her fingers:

> Livia,
>
> I'm so sorry they've found you. D'you know how? Is there anything I can do? I've just spoken to Gordon, who says that his son James should be able to get an injunction if the press are bothering you.
>
> But would you like me to come up and stay? I'm sure I could take time off, if you think it would help. Or I could come on Saturday morning. Just ask for whatever you want, and I'll do it if I possibly can.
>
> I'm with you all the way, you know. You could come and stay here in London if you'd prefer. Or I can find some out-of-the-way hotel somewhere else. Whatever.
>
> Love, Cass

She clicked twice to send the message and waited for a moment to see if there might be an immediate answer. There wasn't, which presumably meant that Livia hadn't been gazing at her screen hoping for comfort. She was pretty tough after all. There was nothing more Cass could do tonight. She shut down the system and went to eat Christopher's food.

❧

Christopher was up before six. Cass's mind was sluggish when she woke and saw him standing fully dressed at her side of his bed. He bent down to kiss her tangled hair. She automatically put up her hands to smooth it, while levering herself into a sitting position.

'Where are you off to so early?'

'Paris. I've got a meeting this morning. I'm catching the six thirty shuttle. Here are the keys, Cass, and the code for the burglar alarm. Will you set it and double lock the front door when you go?'

'Yes.' She rubbed her eyes to try to sharpen her brain. 'Don't you mind leaving me here? It won't take me long to get dressed.'

'Take as long as you like. And there's lots of hot water. But don't forget the alarm or the locks.'

'I won't. Thank you.'

'Take care of yourself today, Cass.'

'I always do.'

He nodded. 'Good. May I ring you when I get back?'

'Of course.'

He was gone. Cass felt a bit bleak. Making love last night hadn't been as cosmically wonderful as it had been on Saturday. They had been clumsy, both of them, getting their arms tangled and their legs in the way. Sometimes she'd feel herself beginning to relax, but then she'd hear Marietta's voice again and think of all the other women who'd been in the bed before her.

She got out of it and put on his dressing gown. It smelled faintly of his almond-oil soap, and of him, which she liked. Wrapped in it, she went into his study. If he'd been happy to give her the burglar alarm code and leave his keys with her, he couldn't mind her using his computer to check her e-mail.

There was a letter from Livia, dated that morning and timed at five thirty.

> Dear Cass,
>
>    I can't tell you what it's done for me to read your e-mail this morning. It means more than you could ever imagine. Thank you. I don't think there's anything practical you can do. I've e-mailed James to ask him to get any kind of injunction he can, to move the journalists away. They're already here.
>
> Bless you for writing, Cass, Livia

Christopher's burglar alarm was different from Cass's and it took her a few minutes to work out which buttons to press, but she got the confirming signal on the LCD in the end. It was only as she was bending down to put the key into the bottom deadlock in the front door that she knew she was being watched. She felt the bolt clunk home, then turned to face whoever it was.

A camera flashed, and then another one. Remembering what Christopher had said about dealing with the press, she smiled, keeping her lips together to hide her gritted teeth, and walked down the shallow steps towards them. There were only two photographers and one other man.

But they'd be enough to do all the damage she dreaded. She was standing on Christopher's doorstep, alone, with his keys in her hand, having just set his burglar alarm. No one in the world could have any doubt about what she was doing there.

'Hi, Cass,' said the hack. 'You look surprised. You didn't really think we wouldn't find you, did you?'

She said nothing, walking on. One of the photographers shifted so that he was in her way. She kept smiling as she stepped round him.

'I'd never have said you were well matched, Cass, you and Christopher Bromyard. We're taking bets on how long it lasts. He's never been a stayer, but he's never gone out with a woman like you before. Does he know what you did in the Blue Print Café?'

Cass flinched, but she kept on walking. He matched her stride.

'We've been building a nice little dossier of your past, and we're wondering just why you're here. Does Christopher Bromyard like it rough, Cass? Is that it?'

Walk away, she said to herself. They can't do anything if you just walk away. Don't say a word.

'That's what we're going to print anyway. That we've heard he likes it rough and you're happy to oblige. We'll ask ourselves in print if you're maybe going in for a bit of a sideline in S & M now your career's hit the buffers.'

'No one would believe anything so ludicrous.' She shouldn't have said it, but she couldn't help it.

'We've got a pic of you in Greece from years back,' he went on, licking his lips in a way that made her want to strangle him. She looked away.

'D'you remember it, Cass? It looks like you and some friends were having a barbecue. You're in a bikini, nice and revealing, with your foot on a bloke who's lying on the floor with his jeans half torn off. You look pretty violent in that. So obviously nothing's changed.'

A small crowd of people had gathered to watch. Cass did remember the photograph. It had been staged at the end of the Greek holiday she'd had with Sophie. They'd met up with some other university friends and had a riotous time on the last night, playing charades after an evening barbecue on the beach.

It had been very silly, but none of them had been older than twenty, and they'd had a great time, high as kites on the boatman's wine-and-Metaxa punch. No one had had his jeans torn off—one of the boys had half undone his for the photograph. And the stiletto-heeled sandals hadn't even been hers. One of the other girls had thought they'd look good and swapped.

'If you print anything so stupid, I'll sue,' she said, as she walked away. The hack's voice rang out after her, probably thrilling the little crowd: 'You wouldn't win, Cass. You've no reputation to lose. And Bromyard won't help you. He's never liked women who've embarrassed him.'

Cass knew that. She'd heard the rules.

❧

Livia was sitting on the closed lid of the lavatory, hugging Flap and waiting for half-past nine when she thought it would be fair to ring Gordon.

She didn't know how many journalists were outside, but it was enough. More than enough. Every time her head rose above one of the windowsills they all started yelling at her: questions, insults, anything they thought would make her come out to talk to them. They wanted to know about Bobby, but they kept asking about Julia, too. And Cass.

At intervals, when they hadn't seen anything for too long, they'd start banging on the door and knocking on the glass of the downstairs windows, calling her name over and over again. Livia! Livia! Harpy! Mrs Claughton! Livia!

The banging and the shouting brought back all the sounds and feelings she'd tried so hard to keep out of her mind: her own fists crashing on the door of Flora's new house and her voice, hoarse and hectoring, calling Henry to come down and face her.

❧

There was no answer, so Livia hit the door again, a long, banging demand to be let in. After a few moments she heard the sound of bare feet on plain wooden stairs.

So, she thought, they haven't had the carpets laid yet.

Later, she'd been surprised to remember the thought, but it was clearer than almost anything else except the white-hot righteous fury that was driving her on.

The door opened and Flora stood there, glowing and luscious with her long blonde hair falling down her back and her body wrapped in an old-gold brocade bedspread. She'd tucked it around her breasts like a bath towel. When Livia did that her breasts were squashed into nothingness. Not Flora. Of course.

'Oh, go away, Livia,' she said, her voice as clear as ever. 'For God's sake find a little dignity.'

There was so much dismissive contempt in the voice that Livia simply put her hands on Flora's shoulders and pushed her out of the way, slamming her against the wall. It was already hung with the most expensive grasscloth available.

Later, they said they'd found the imprint of the fibres on her back, and even one or two actually dug into her skin. They also found a bruise on her hip, where Livia's shoulder-bag, heavy with a purse full of coins and a book, had swung into her. And finger-shaped bruises, which matched Livia's fingers, on her shoulders.

Livia charged on past her, clattering up the uncarpeted stairs. The main bedroom door was open, flooding the bare dark staircase with golden light. Even from the outside, Livia could see Henry lying in bed like a pasha. The thick hairs on his fleshy chest caught the light. He turned his head lazily as she came through the door, his eyes half-shut, his face full of satisfied desire.

Livia knew she looked tight and tidy and intense in her good black suit with the gleaming black patent-leather pumps. She had no place in this generous, warm, fat, happy room.

The bedclothes were tousled, the room smelled of scent and sex. There was even a still gleaming puddle in the dip where Flora had lain. Livia was staring at it when Flora came running back into the room, breathless.

'She hit me, Henry. She hit me,' she whispered from the doorway. Her hands were busy tidying her hair so that her elbows were in the air, making her look even more beautiful, more abandoned, more free.

Henry flung back the duvet and stood up. Livia gagged at the sight of his big, hairy body with its spent genitals hanging limply between his legs. As he came towards her, he said, still lazy, still happy, still utterly in command: 'You're insane, Livia. Why can't you behave?'

The question locked on to all the others from the past. He sounded exactly like her father. For a second she couldn't remember which of them it was in front of her. Then her vision cleared and she knew it was Henry and she knew what he'd done to her. She told him why she'd come.

He laughed. He looked really amused, and turned to collect Flora and make her join in. Her laugh provided a descant to his bass. The two of them together, laughing.

Livia staggered on, telling him that he had to write to the judges to confess what he'd done, to support the letter she'd already posted.

'Stop it, Livia. You'll only embarrass yourself if you go on with this idiotic story,' he said, still laughing. 'Everyone knows you're completely mad. And I've already written to the judges, warning them about you.' He was coming nearer all the time; he'd almost reached her. 'Do you think anyone would believe any of your ridiculous fantasies? They all know you've been seeing shrinks for years.'

'You're evil,' she said, backing away. He came on, taunting, hairy, horrible, utterly dismissive. Laughing. 'Don't. Come. Near. Me.'

He didn't listen. He never listened. He came on, his bare feet thudding on the rough boards. Then he wasn't laughing any more, and she saw what he really felt about her. All that anger, even worse than hers.

She put her hand into her pocket, where the scalpel was resting in its makeshift cardboard holder. It slid into her hand as though it was meant. It helped her to know it was there. He took another step. She moved backwards again. She could smell the wine he'd drunk at lunch time, and the raw, warm smell of sex.

He stretched out his hands for her. Her back was against the wall. She couldn't go any further. She got the scalpel out of her pocket. When he saw it, he laughed again, and again he told her she was a mad embarrassment to him.

'I mean it, Henry. Don't touch me.'

Flora was watching them, breathing fast. 'Henry! Don't. She's dangerous.'

'Don't be ridiculous. Come on, Livia, give it here, and we'll get you some proper help. Flora and I. There are plenty of doctors who know how to treat people like you. Hand the scalpel over before you hurt yourself.'

Livia shut her eyes and pushed. She knew the tiny blade wouldn't be enough to stop him, and it didn't. He was shouting something at her, but she didn't listen. She knew it would be more contempt, more laughter, and so she just went on digging, slashing, pushing, hitting, keeping him off her in any way she could.

Someone was screaming. Someone else was swearing. And she was screaming, too. Blood was spurting in her face, pouring over her hand, too, and over the horrible fat, hairy body in front of her. It was on the floor now, but it was still moving and so she went on stabbing at it, to make it stop.

Then it did stop moving, and everything was all right. Livia looked round. There was something sticky holding her fingers together and she wasn't breathing properly. A band was tightening around her head and her eyes didn't really work. Her left hand seemed to be free and she brushed it against her eyes.

That helped her see again. There was a golden bundle in a heap by the fireplace with the telephone beside it. A voice was coming through the receiver, which was lying away from the rest of the telephone.

Livia moved forward, between one still bundle and the other, and picked up the receiver. A man's voice quacked, demanding the address. Livia obediently gave it and then very carefully put the receiver back on the cradle and picked up the whole ivory-white telephone and put it back on the bedside table, where it should have been all along.

The room was very untidy and the embarrassing marks were still there for anyone to see on the sheets. Livia put down the sticky scalpel beside the telephone and started stripping the bed. She was making the sheets even messier with the blood from her hands, but if she was very careful, she wouldn't get any on the mattress. She was still folding sheets into flat, neat piles when the police arrived.

❧

'Livia! Hey, Harpy! Come and talk to us. You'll have to in the end.'

Livia put her hands over her ears. She was hungry and she was angry. She hoped to heaven that Colin would have the sense to keep Bobby at home.

'Hey, Harpy! Give us a good quote and we'll leave you in peace.'

How had they found her? Someone must have told them, but who? Bobby? Cass? No, not Cass. Never Cass.

'Come on, Livia. It won't cost you anything to talk to us and give us a few photos. Come on! How was it having a tearaway like that in your house? Weren't you frightened? Aren't you angry with your social worker for exposing you to all that?'

'You'll have to come out some time. You'll need food. You can't stay in there for ever. They're not going to help you in the village, you know. They're furious you've brought such notoriety down on them. I talked to lots of them. They hate you. And they're planning to send up a deputation to ask you to move out before you cause any more trouble and embarrassment here.'

She stuck her fingers right into her ears. She'd hardly slept, listening for their footsteps inside the house.

'Livia! Come on out and stop being such a coward. All you've got to do is talk. If you don't talk to us, we'll have to use what we've been told in the village. You know that. Come on out.'

She got up, catching the loo seat in a loose fold of her jersey. It dropped down again with a crash they must have heard. Still hugging Flap, she pressed herself against the cold tiled wall. They couldn't see her. She must remember that. She was safe here in this one room with its frosted glass in the window. She started pacing it out, only to sit hurriedly back on the lavatory. The room was almost the identical size of her first cell in Holloway.

Thank God: half-past nine. She put Flap down and crawled into the bedroom, which didn't have any proper curtains, keeping well below window level, and sat on the floor with her back against the side of the bed. She pulled the telephone on to the floor beside her and tapped in the number. Gordon answered within two rings and Livia felt a little blood warming her face at the sound of his voice.

A knock on the window shocked her into looking up. A camera flashed and a triumphant face grinned at her, waving a camera.

'They've got ladders now,' she whispered at Gordon. 'Oh, God almighty, what am I going to do?'

'I don't know, Livia. I've spoken to James and he's confident of getting an injunction. Luckily the land all round the house belongs to you—at least as the lessee—so James will get them on trespass, if nothing else. They'll have to withdraw pretty much out of sight.'

'You mean you can't get rid of them altogether?'

'Probably not.' He sounded stiff and unfriendly. 'But James will do his best. You might pray for rain.'

'It's belting down now,' she said, looking at the streaming glass. 'But it's not stopping them. They must have underwater cameras. D'you know who told them where I am?'

'No. But I imagine it was your ghastly protégé.'

Livia felt as though someone was driving a knife under her fingernails.

'I don't believe it,' she said. 'You don't know him, Gordon, and you've always been prejudiced. He wouldn't. I believe in him.'

'That's your privilege.'

What a put-down! she thought.

'Ring James if you need him, Livia. He'll do anything he can. And there are always the police if you get frightened. I have to go now. I'm sorry. Goodbye.'

She was left with a buzzing receiver in her thin distorted hand.

# Chapter 20

At first all Julia could see was how smug Cass looked on the front page of the *Post*. It could have been a fashion shot. The steps on which she was standing were black-and-white checked stone, the railings on either side were black, and framed in the fluted architrave of a white door was Cass, wearing a fantastic black suit—Armani, probably—and grinning like a Lottery winner.

Julia's skin felt like wet clay. The caption helped a bit: 'Is there a gene for violence?' She started to read the column below it.

> 'No comment,' says Cass Evesham. And who can blame her? She won't talk about her grandmother or her own past (*see picture, right*), but they must keep her awake at night.

Julia looked at the smaller, fuzzy photograph and smiled. That was much better. George had done his stuff after all.

The dancing figure in the picture was unmistakably Cass, looking like a maenad as she drove her spiked heel into the ribs of a half-naked, beautiful, but obviously dissolute, young man. Most of the buttons of his Levis were undone. His face looked pulled apart by a rictus of agony, and the tendons in his neck stood out like tree roots. Cass looked drunk. And cruel.

The phone rang as Julia was taking in the full glory of the scene. She reached out for the receiver without looking away from the *Post*.

'Julia? George here.'

'George. Hello. You are brilliant. It's a fantastic picture. How did you find it?'

'Not bad, is it? We got it from one of the other girls on the holiday. Had to pay through the nose for it.'

'Whatever it was, it was worth it. But what went wrong yesterday morning? She looks utterly in control.'

'Doesn't she? Amazing.' George sounded almost warm, and definitely admiring.

Julia couldn't understand it. He should have been popping with frustration like her.

'She's got real guts, that girl,' he went on. 'It looks to me like she's been taking lessons in media management from someone.'

'Christopher Bromyard, no doubt.' Julia had to wipe a tiny blob of spit off the phone.

It was typical of Cass to have picked up a millionaire along with all the rest. No wonder she looked as though she'd won the Lottery. Cow.

'The boys couldn't shake her, not even when they told her we'd got the Greek picture and would be running it today. She knew what they were talking about all right—they're sure of that—but she didn't give an inch. Still, Julia, Cass isn't really the point. We don't need her any more.'

'Why not?'

'We've found the Harpy,' he said as though he was talking to a child. 'And the story of the Hell Brat is terrific bunce. We'll be majoring on them from now on.'

'George, you can't. You promised.'

'The Harpy's the real story, Julia. You know that.'

'Only for the paper. Not for you and the book.' She had a sudden sickening doubt. It felt like the time a year ago when she'd suddenly realized she must be pregnant.

'George, you're not going to let Cass off the hook, are you? The book *is* going to be all about her, isn't it?'

'What makes you think that?'

From anyone else the words would have sounded contemptuous. But not from George. Surely. Not after everything she'd given him. They had a deal. He couldn't renege now.

'It's what you said, George.'

'No. What I said is that the book is going to be about the long-term effects of violent crime, and that I'd be using your mother's murder as the prime case study.'

Julia wished he was in the flat with her so that she could see him. The sense of the words he was using wasn't enough. She needed a face to read.

'And I'm very grateful to you,' he went on, sounding friendlier but still with that puzzling edge. 'You've been giving me great stuff. You still are.'

She sighed and wiped her forehead on the back of her wrist. Two fat tears of relief oozed down her cheek.

'But what I still haven't worked out is why you hate Cass so much. Rather than the Harpy herself, I mean. And I can't get any further till I've got to the bottom of that.'

The sickness was back, and the cold hard lump of dread under her diaphragm. She tried the simplest of her breathing exercises. That made it worse.

'But you're not writing about me, George.' She hadn't meant to produce such a trembly whisper. 'George? George, are you still there?'

There was silence, brooding, hateful.

'George?'

'Tell me, Julia. Make me understand. What has Cass Evesham ever done to you?'

'Isn't it enough that she's had a mother all her life?' Julia was finding it hard to breathe through the hurt. 'And everything else I should have had?'

How could he not understand? She'd let him right into her life and all her secrets. He'd been to see *Electra*. That should have shown him. He'd heard the words she'd flung at Chrysothemis, just like everyone else.

'But Cass didn't take any of it from you. She's as much of a victim as you are.'

Julia put down the phone, dropping it back into its cradle. Her fingers felt sticky, disgusting. She wiped them down her dressing gown. The phone was ringing again. Hating the nagging sound, she tried to ignore it and got back into bed, hauling the duvet up over her filthy dressing gown. She wanted to go back to sleep, to shut out everything, but she knew she couldn't close her eyes.

If she did she'd see that horrible ugly little goblin of a child who was always in the way and took everything that should have been Julia's. Too young to deal with the pans of boiling fudge Mrs Claughton helped Julia make and too naggy and silly for them to ignore, the child caused all sorts of trouble.

She'd open Julia's satchel and put her horrid grubby little fingers all over the books inside, taking them out and pretending to read them, and asking what they were for and what they meant. She never let up, how ever often Julia told her they were too difficult for her to understand and too important for her to mess up. Mrs Claughton sometimes had to leave off what they were doing to make the horrible little goblin-child behave properly. Once they'd even burned a whole pan of fudge because Cass wouldn't stop tanking on about what she wanted. It had to be thrown away and the pan was spoiled for ever. But even then Mrs Claughton hadn't tried to punish Cass.

She'd always wanted everything, and done everything she could to stop Julia having anything at all. She'd earwigged all the time, too. Once, she'd overheard the blissful invitation: 'Julia, we've become much too friendly for you to go on calling me Mrs Claughton. Why don't you call me Aunt Livia?'.

Right on cue, the goblin-child had piped up: 'She can't call you Aunt Livia, Granny. You're not her aunt. You're my granny. She doesn't belong to us.'

Stuck-up, selfish little goblin-cow, with a mother and a grandmother, and a father, and friends and a home and people who cared enough about her to spend time with her and stay with her and look after her. All Julia had ever had that was safe was Aunt Livia, and then suddenly she wasn't safe either. Or there. One day she was there just like always, the next, gone for good, along with the unreachable, yearned-for, unknown woman who called herself Mama and never had any time at all.

Julia turned over and pushed her wet face into the pillow.

❧

Cass was on the phone to Sophie. The *Post* was lying on the floor in front of her with its appalling caption and worse picture.

'I'm so sorry, Sophie. Did you have a hellish time at work today?'

'No. No one recognized me. I knew they wouldn't. I've got far too fat since then. But what about you?'

'Your parents must be furious with me.'

'Don't be a clot, Cass. They know perfectly well the photograph was part of that last-night party's charade. They wouldn't care anyway. They know you and like you. And they don't read the *Post*, nor do any of their friends. Not the ones that matter. Much more important, how are you?'

'I'll survive.' Cass thought of Christopher and wondered whether he'd been shown the paper yet. Probably. From where she was sitting, with the phone tucked between her ear and shoulder, she could see his keys in her open bag.

'You must feel a bit like in one of those dreams when you wake up in the middle of the street without any clothes on,' said Sophie.

'Exactly like that. Christopher once said that in a year's time no one would remember any of this, but I'm not so sure. Oh, Soph, I'm not sure what I'd do if I didn't have you.'

'Well, you have got me,' she said briskly, 'so you needn't worry about that. Now, my mother wants you to come and stay this weekend. She said they'd love to have you. I'm going, so I could give you a lift.'

Cass let herself lean back against the sofa. The temptation of taking refuge with Sophie's parents was almost irresistible. She had to resist it, but the generosity of the offer was almost enough to make the rest bearable.

'I wish I could, but I'm going up to Wast Water.'

'Must you?'

'I think so. I've arranged to take tomorrow off, and I'll stay there till Sunday anyway. Maybe longer. Livia needs help.'

'But not because of anything you've done, Cass. It's only because of what she did that you're in this mess at all.'

Cass looked at Christopher's keys again.

'I know. But I have to go.'

'Is Christopher going with you, or would you like me to come? I could easily do that instead of going home. I've got bags of holiday left. I could take a day without any problem.'

Cass had to wait a moment before she spoke, afraid she'd pour out much too much.

'You are such a friend, Sophie. But it's fine; honestly. I don't want you splattered all over the *Post*. I'll be OK, and I'll come back and take refuge with you when it's over. If you'll still have me then.'

'Of course we will. But ring me if you need me before then. OK, Cass? Promise?'

'I promise.'

Cass put down the receiver, wishing she could believe that Christopher would phone. She knew she shouldn't even think about it. She'd only be disappointed.

The front door bell rang. She didn't bother to answer. There was no point. It rang again, just as her mobile started up. Then the fixed phone chimed in.

'Will you all bloody well shut up?' she shrieked.

Someone had his finger on the front door bell. She put her hands over her ears and thought about hiding in the shower. The noise of the water on her head ought to drown out all the other sounds.

Instead she poured herself a huge slug of gin and added a little tonic and got some ice. She turned on the television, loud, switching channels until she found some news.

They were showing a peculiarly unfortunate photograph of Colin Whyle, looking as shifty as the defendant in a serious trial. He had been standing half in and half out of his front door when he was caught on camera and had turned, presumably in answer to his name. His beard was even wilder than usual and his collar rucked up, hiding half his face. Above the collar, his eyes looked frightened. The voice-over explained who he was and then the picture changed to one of Julia Gainsborough, looking radiant on the studio sofa, smiling straight into the camera.

'Livia Claughton is the last person who should have charge of a damaged child,' she said, her voice creamier than ever.

God, I hate her! Cass thought.

'I feel very sorry for this boy, whose life has already been destroyed by violent and unreliable adults. Now he's been betrayed again by the very people who were supposed to keep him safe. They should have known better than to put him in the charge of a woman as evil as Livia Claughton.'

Cass aimed the remote control at the screen, as though it was a gun, and hit the 'off' button. There was a knock at the flat door. Some idiot must have let the press in through the main door of the building. Some idiot, or else a malicious pig like Annette Sharpe.

'Cass?' It was Dan's voice, the man who owned the other flat on her floor. He had never been quoted in the *Post* and, as far as she knew, he had played no part in its hate campaign. But he might just have been cleverer about it than Annette.

'Cass, It's Dan. I've got a friend of yours here. Can I let him in?'

He'd always had her keys, in case of fire or flood when she was away, and he'd never misused them so far. It might be safe.

'Cass?'

She carried her drink to the front door and peered through the spy hole. Dan's face was there all right. She squinted sideways to see who he had with him and nearly dropped her glass.

The door chain snagged as she tried to wrench it out of its socket, but she got the door open a minute later. Her thanks to Dan were muffled in Christopher's chest. She heard Christopher thanking him, too, and then the door shut. One of Christopher's hands was on her back, the other on her head, stroking her hair. She had never wanted to cling to anyone in her life. Now she clung.

'Are you OK?' he asked when her heart began to slow down again.

She found a way to wipe her eyes on her sleeve, checked that she hadn't left any marks on his shirt, and pulled back to put down her glass and admit that she was fine.

'Have you seen the *Post*?' She had to ask.

'Sure. I thought you looked great. In *both* pictures.' He smiled as he wiped her cheeks with his thumbs. 'Don't worry so, Cass. As I said once before, in a year's time no one is going to remember any of this.'

'They were at your house, Christopher. I'm so sorry. I know they haven't printed anything about you yet, but it'll come. We haven't a hope of getting away with it much longer. You'd better…'

'Cass, stop it. It doesn't matter.'

'But you hate being embarrassed by the women in your life.'

He took a step back, his face changing, hardening. 'What do you mean?'

'I heard it in the office on Tuesday. I meant to say something that evening. But then we were overtaken by the news.'

'The office? Just what are you talking about?'

'Two of the secretaries. In the loo. They didn't know I was there. One of them was talking about your past. Your girlfriends.'

He turned away. Cass sniffed. She'd never been such a fool before. This was the last moment to have started such a stupid conversation.

'My past is something about which I feel most uncomfortable,' he said clearly, icily. 'But it has nothing to do with you...'

'I know, and I'm not asking about it, believe me. It was silly of me to bring it up. Let me get you a drink.'

'Cass, will you stop and listen to me for a minute, please? Without interrupting?'

She nodded, feeling as pathetic as her mother, and hoping it didn't show. At least her back was straight. And she wasn't looking at him, so he wouldn't see anything in her eyes.

'My past has nothing to do with you and me. I did some stupid things—very stupid—and caused a lot of misery. It wasn't all my fault. But a fair amount of it was.'

She couldn't think what to say.

'I cocked up, Cass, over and over again. Because I didn't realize what I was doing. Or what I wanted. D'you understand?'

He seemed to be asking her for something, which seemed very odd.

'No. I don't think so.'

'When I met you, I'd been taking a long hard look at myself after someone had told me exactly what she thought of the way I'd used her. I hadn't realized I had been. But she made me think. I hated her for it then. But now I think maybe I owe her.'

'You mean your mid-life crisis was about a woman, not about work after all?' Cass said, trying to sound as cheerfully irreverent as she would have been in the past.

'Both. But Betka's home truths started the process. And there I was, peeled in every sense of the word, face to face with you. It was the biggest shock of my life.'

'But…'

'But I was still reeling from what she'd said, and I couldn't face any more trouble. Complications. So I didn't do anything about you. And I let you go through all that hell in the autumn without any help.'

'Christopher, I…'

'I'm sorry, Cass.'

'You did help, Christopher,' she said, grabbing his hand, and not thinking too much about what else he'd said. 'You wrote that letter and it meant a lot.'

'Then there you were at Guildhall, looking even more spectacular than I'd remembered, and brave. So brave, Cass. I wanted to grab you there and then, trouble or not. I think I knew straight away that I needed you, whatever happened. But even then it took me a day or two to admit it.'

His eyes looked as naked, stripped and vulnerable as he'd been on the night of the storm. Cass let her hand loosen around his wrist, then slide up his arm. Before it had reached his shoulder, he had both arms around her and was almost carrying her to the sofa.

❧

Later, as they ate the spinach and cheese omelettes he'd cooked, they discussed the best way of helping Livia now. Christopher agreed that Cass ought to go up to Wast Water, but he said he wasn't letting her go alone.

'Letting?' she repeated, raising her eyebrows.

Christopher nodded casually. 'Yup. I'll come with you tomorrow. I can drive you.'

'But tomorrow's Friday. What about work?'

He shrugged. 'There isn't anything I can't shift. If we set off early, really early, we'll miss the traffic. I can ring the office from half-way, sort out what I have to, and we can be with Livia well before twelve. How about it, Cass?'

She knew she ought to refuse, for all sorts of reasons.

'It would be great.'

'Good. Then you can do the washing up, while I ring my secretary at home to warn her I won't be in. Then we'll have an early night and get going by six.'

And don't forget your frilly apron, Cass said silently to herself. Talk about the Alpha male.

Then she caught his smile and her own lips softened. He wasn't entirely joking, she thought, but he knew enough about himself to make the arrogance bearable. And, after all, she could always disobey whatever orders he chose to give her.

She stopped by her laptop on the way to the sink and switched it on in case Livia had sent another message. She hadn't, but there was a letter from Rosamund, the first since her uncommunicative Christmas circular. This one began 'Dearest Cass'. That was rare enough to make her sit down and concentrate.

Dearest Cass,

I should have answered your October e-mail before but I didn't know how. You asked why I'd never told you about my mother.

I know I should have; I always meant to. I very nearly did just before I left England, that day when I gave you the key to the storage unit. But somehow when it came to it I couldn't. There are lots of reasons, too many to list, but here's a start:

1. She causes trouble wherever she goes and I didn't want her to cause any more between you and me. We had enough as it was.

2. I hoped you would never need to know anything about her. I hadn't realized that there would be this much publicity when they let her out.

3. Knowing you, I thought if I ever told you she existed, you would insist on seeing her.

4. She ruined my life. She killed my father. That wiped out any obligations. I never wanted to see her again. And I didn't want you contaminated. You're too like her as it is.

I think I'd better stop there.

I hope all this fuss isn't being too difficult for you.
If it is, would you like to come out here to stay for a
week? Or two. Roberto sends his regards.

Rosamund

Cass shivered and turned off the computer. It took a very
long shower to get warm again. Christopher asked no questions, but he hugged her until she slept.

Nearly half an hour later she was driving up a perpendicular hill, only to find the car slipping backwards. She
pulled on the brake, changed down and revved the engine.
Nothing worked. The car went on sliding back and back,
driving over Bobby's legs as he lay pinned down in the road.
The crack of his bones woke her.

She pulled herself up out of sleep, gasping and sweaty, to
see that it was still only eleven o'clock. Christopher was asleep
on his back beside her, looking as if he'd always been there.

# Chapter 21

Livia was pottering in the kitchen, happier than she'd expected. James had got her an injunction, and the journalists had slunk out of sight. She could move freely about the house again, knowing she didn't have to worry about strange faces peering in through the windows. And Christopher was bringing Cass back at last.

There was enough there to celebrate. The rest needn't matter for the moment. She had been trying to think of something she could cook to mark the occasion. The lemon grass had long since withered in the fridge and been thrown out, but most of the dried exotica were still in the cupboards. Lacking Christopher's unexpected skill, she had leafed through some of the recipe books Gordon had provided to find a dish that would use some of them, but nothing appealed to her.

As daunted, though nothing like as angry, as she had been when she first saw the truffle oil and the tins of caviare, Livia eventually decided to ignore them and go for a plain roast chicken. Even she ought to be able to cook that decently. The bird had been defrosted in the microwave and was now roasting on its side under buttered greaseproof paper, just as Elizabeth David had recommended.

An onion was slowly infusing its taste into warming milk for the bread sauce, and the kitchen had begun to smell faintly but deliciously. White wine was chilling in the fridge, and an apple pie with reasonably unfingered pastry waited to be baked. It looked a little grey, but nothing too frightful.

'Egg wash,' Livia said aloud as a memory of her mother's fat cook painting pies in the huge, dark basement kitchen made her smile. She moved more lightly than usual to fetch an egg and milk and find the pastry brush.

When she'd done, the pie looked much better, glossy and pale yellow with a sprinkling of sugar, almost professional. She was still looking at it and admiring herself when she heard the sound of voices, children's voices, outside the window. She recognized Bobby's among the babble and went straight to the front door, which was still bolted against the journalists.

'Bobby,' she said as she opened it.

He pushed past her, leaving her face to face with five or six others. Livia didn't recognize any of them, but she knew who they were. The aggression in their eyes was the same as she'd seen down in Eskfoot.

Propelled back into the room, she looked quickly over her shoulder, but Bobby had his back to her. One of the boys banged the door shut.

Livia felt as though someone had his hands in her innards and was squeezing tighter and tighter.

'OK. So, where's the money, then?' The biggest of the boys, who already had the splitting spots of adolescence mixed in with badly shaven black stubble, was squaring up to her.

'Money?' she said, her voice unnaturally high. She breathed carefully and then said it again, adding: 'What money? Bobby, what is this?'

'You talk to me, bitch,' said the bigger boy, pulling her chin round so that she couldn't look at Bobby. 'Come on. Where is it?'

Livia took another step back, then made herself stop. Think of them as untrained dogs, she reminded herself. Look them in the eye and don't give ground.

'Come on. Hand it over.'

'I don't know what you think you're doing here,' she began, just as Flap came bounding down the stairs, his ears flying, barking his head off.

As she turned to hush him, the boy put his hand flat on her chest and pushed. Livia staggered backwards and struck out, feeling for a handhold. Her hand met something soft and there was a cry. She looked quickly sideways and saw that she'd hit one of the smallest children in the face.

Not again, she thought. Don't let me get angry again. Don't let one of these children get hurt. Please.

'Keep your hands to yourself, bitch,' said the biggest boy, pushing her again.

Livia fell backwards, only to be caught by the rocking chair, which careered madly across the stone floor, squeaking in all its joints. Flap, picking up every bit of her fear, began to squeal hysterically.

'Bobby,' Livia said quietly, trying to take control of them all. At last he turned to face her. She looked directly at him. 'Bobby, what is this?'

He kicked the sofa, then looked up to stare at her. His beautiful mouth was twisted and sneering. But his eyes were blank. She didn't know what they'd done to him to make him come, but she knew she couldn't reach him in this mood.

'Give us the money. It's all we want. Then we'll go,' said the leader. 'We know you've got it here.'

'I am afraid you have been misinformed,' she said with laborious formality, forcing herself to look at him and ignore Bobby. It was all she could think of, to bring them down with quasi-official language. 'I have very little cash in the house. There might be as much as eight pounds in coins in my handbag, but no more. It is over there. You are welcome to anything you can find. But I have nothing else.'

'Cut the crap.' The boy slapped her face, hard, making her head jerk back and her mind acknowledge the incredible fact that she was in real physical danger. The gripping hands in her gut twisted tighter.

'You've got more. And credit cards. You bought him a bike. They cost hundreds.'

Livia tried to laugh, prodding the raw place where her teeth had cut into her tongue as her head had snapped back. The boy hit her again, harder. When she could talk again, she said: 'Where I've been these last few years, you don't have credit cards.'

One of the smaller boys was turning her bag upside down. Everything in it clattered down on to the flags. There was the big bunch of keys, to both doors of the house and each of the outbuildings; there was her wallet with the promised eight pounds, and there was a cheque book. And then he found the cheque card that her bank had sent and she hadn't yet used.

'Look, Darren. Here's a card.'

'I knew it. What's your PIN number?' asked Darren.

Livia said nothing. Knowing his name gave her the first small hint of hope. He nodded to two of his lieutenants and said: 'Hold her arms.'

I don't believe it, she thought. They're going to try to torture it out of me. These children. She tried to keep her face calm.

Flap was still barking. They paid no attention. But they didn't know what to do next. Livia kept herself smiling quietly, watching them.

Darren had his hand in his pocket. When he withdrew it, Livia's muscles contracted in a spasm she couldn't hide. The blade of a Stanley knife was pointing straight at her face. Darren was grinning. Her heart thumped. She swallowed and her dry throat felt as though it was filled with barbed wire.

'See this?'

She couldn't move.

'You know what I c'n do with it, don't you? So, what's your PIN number, bitch?'

'Darren,' said Bobby, coming away from the window at last. 'Don't. You can't.'

'Shut up. The old bitch has money, Bobby. You said so.'

Livia looked through a gap between their tousled heads straight at Bobby. This time he caught her eye and held it. His own looked desperate. She tried to will confidence into him.

'Not like this,' he said after a moment. 'Darren, you can't.'

'I'll do it any way I like,' said the leader, flexing his muscles. The knife blade was almost touching her skin. 'And you can fuck off if you don't like it.'

'Liv, give it him,' Bobby said, his voice shriller than usual. 'He's not going to stop. Give him what you've got. Then we'll go. You'll be OK then. Liv, please. Please.'

The growing panic in his voice scared her more than anything else. She shook her head.

'Bobby, I can't. You must see that.'

'Darren. Leave her alone.'

'Why do you care? Come on, bitch. You're wasting time. D'you *want* me to cut you? What's your fucking PIN number?'

Livia would not speak. The squat triangular blade hovered under her left eye. The boy said something, she couldn't hear what. She was concentrating on the blade. Staring at it made her squint, pushing her eyeballs painfully towards each other. The point touched her skin. He said something else. She didn't take it in, but that didn't matter. She wasn't going to answer, whatever he said. She'd learned to withdraw herself from the unbearable long ago. She could do it again. She brought the knife into focus, concentrating on the ache in her eyes.

The blade pricked her. She could feel blood, a tiny amount, trickling down her cheek like warm tears. She heard Bobby's voice again and Flap's frenzied barking. But she kept staring at the knife. Suddenly, jerkily, it withdrew. Livia looked up.

'Fucking animal!' said the boy, looking down as he hopped on one leg.

Livia's muscles let go for a second. Her arms were still dragged behind her by two of the smaller boys, and her shoulder sockets felt as though they were being torn apart. But the knife had gone. The boy bent down and grabbed Flap by the neck. 'Fucking animal's bitten me. Oh, shit! Now it's crapped all over my trainers.'

Good for Flap, Livia thought and then she screamed: 'No. Flap. No. Bobby. Oh, for Christ's sake. Help!'

Screaming was the worst thing she could have done. She knew that. But she couldn't stop it. The boy, who was holding Flap by the throat, grabbed a chunk of silvery-grey polished granite from the table beside her and smashed it down. Flap hung limply from his hand as blood and brains spurted out of his broken head.

Someone was being sick behind her. Flap's pale-grey jelly-like brains were all over her legs. Bobby was yelling something inarticulate and backing towards the door. His face was very white and his eyes looked enormous. The bigger boy dropped Flap's body at Livia's feet and put the knife back under her eye.

'Now, bitch.' He laughed. 'Did you think I'd forgotten you? I c'n do it to you, too. An' I will. So what's your fucking PIN number?'

Bobby was slinking away out of her sight. She wasn't sure if he was escaping or going for help.

'It won't do you any good even if I give you the number,' she said, wishing her voice was not so shaky.

'That's what you think. Come on. You don't want to lose an eye, do you? Feels different doesn't it when you're on the wrong end of the knife? Harpy.' He laughed. 'Harpy.'

One of the others, perhaps the one who'd been sick, was sitting on the floor by the fire with his head in his hands. He was crying, but the rest were still on their feet, supporting their leader—more—egging him on.

He knocked the big glass and silver vase off the table on to the floor. As the glittering pieces spread all over the stone, he laughed again. Livia could see the excitement growing.

His eyes shone and his lips curled as his tongue flickered, making them glisten too.

A movement caught her eye and she glanced quickly sideways.

'Let's go,' said the sniffing child. 'Come on, Darren: the old woman's not going to give us nothing. Let's go before the filth get here.'

There was a general movement towards the door. Darren didn't move, still smiling down into Livia's face, willing her to challenge him or squirm, anything to give him the trigger he needed to push him into hurting her. She looked down and felt the tip of the knife dig a little further into her skin. More blood tears seeped out over her face, tickling. She couldn't brush them away because her arms were still dragged behind her back.

❧

Cass cursed as she saw a flock of sheep filling the narrow road ahead. The scenery as they drove over Wrynose Pass was magnificent in the clear weather, but she wanted to get on. Christopher didn't seem to feel any urgency—or irritation with the sheep.

He changed down, creeping along behind the lumbering ewes at about four miles an hour. The man in charge of the flock turned with a cheery smile of apology and waved towards a gate about half a mile further up the road.

'Don't fret so, Cass.'

'I'm worried about Livia. She sent me an e-mail overnight. I read it while you were in the bath. It was the full story of what happened the day she killed them. I'll show you one day. She had a hellish time. I need to see her. Sodding sheep. Why won't he move them and let us get past?'

'We're not in that much hurry. Give her a ring, if you're bothered.'

'I can't. It's a mobile black spot up here. I tried last time.'

Most of the sheep reached the gate and obediently shambled through, chased by the black-and-white collie, but three lurched away further up the road. Cass thought Christopher could get past them if only he'd try, but he wouldn't.

The dog patiently galloped after the leading animal and rounded it up. It trotted towards the car, which was now stationary. Then, at last, the ewe veered into the field.

'Go on. Now, Christopher. As fast as you can.'

'All right, Cass. All right. Don't worry.'

They reached the lake at last, which looked nearly silver with the bright white sky above it, and drove on to the turn up to the Long House. Small stones spat out from under the tyres. Cass saw a child flying towards them on a bicycle.

'It's Bobby,' she said, winding down her window and calling to him. 'Stop for a minute, Christopher.'

Bobby skidded to a stop beside the car. His voice was so hoarse and scrambled that it took her a moment to understand what he was saying.

'They've got Liv. And there's a knife. You've got to help her. They've killed Flap. Go, go, go!'

Christopher was forcing the car up the slope, revving the engine hard, but his deep voice was slow as he said: 'Try your mobile again. Ring the police.'

She knew it wouldn't be any good, but she tried. He put the heel of his hand on the horn, blaring out a warning to whoever 'they' were and, Cass hoped, encouragement to Livia.

'There's still no service,' she said in despair. She was wrenching the door open even before the car had stopped.

'Cass,' he shouted as she flung herself out. 'Wait.'

She tripped over her feet and took an extra second to disentangle one leg from the other. 'Come *on*, Christopher.'

Three small boys with terror in their faces were running out of the door as she reached it but she didn't waste anytime on them. All she could think about was getting to Livia.

Cass could hear Christopher yelling something, and then the sound of a hand smacking against flesh. She didn't stop.

Livia was trapped in the rocking chair, two figures behind her and one in front. There was a knife at her face. Cass launched herself at her attacker.

He crashed face down on the floor and she straddled his back, reaching to pin down the wrist of his knife-hand. She could hear panting, crying and running feet. And Christopher bellowing at her to wait for him.

'Cass,' said Livia's voice, gasping. 'Cass.'

'Lemme go,' screamed the boy under her.

Cass saw he was a child, a shaven-headed child. Still holding his wrist, she got off his back and saw how small it was. Icy trickles of shock made her heart thump. She'd been exerting all her strength on someone she could have broken with one hand. Crouched near his head, still holding his right wrist, she tried to prize the knife from his hand without hurting him.

One of her fingers slid along the blade, and an inch of flesh opened. Blood poured out of it. She held on to his wrist.

The boy yelled at her, scrambling to his feet. He still didn't let go. Cass saw snot under his nose and tears on his spotty cheeks.

'Let go,' she said, pulling at his fingers, scared of breaking one if she tried too hard.

'Lemme go. You're breaking my fucking arm.'

I could have, she thought. I could have broken it across my knee, as easily as a dry branch.

She looked up for a second and saw Livia's battered face. There was a big, spreading bruise on one of her cheeks and a rusty line of blood down the other. On the floor near her was a puddle of sick.

Hating the boy, disgusted at what he'd done and terrified of what she could have done to him, Cass told him again to drop the knife. With her free hand, dropping blood all over the boy, she worked his fingers away from the fat metal handle.

Christopher appeared behind him, huge and far more powerful, and took the boy away from her, removing the knife without any difficulty. Cass began to breathe again.

'I've got him, Cass. And the others are locked in the car. It's OK now. I checked them for knives. They can't do any more harm.'

'Will you phone the police while I see to Livia?' Cass went to help Livia and almost tripped over something soft on the floor. Looking down, she saw Flap and bent at once to find out if he was hurt. Then she remembered what Bobby had said.

'Flap's dead,' said Livia.

There was no emotion in her voice, but when Cass glanced at her, she saw the most bitter misery in Livia's eyes. Cass didn't bother to listen to the boy's furious muttering or Christopher's answers.

'Are you sure?' She picked Flap up and shivered at the sight of his head, with a huge gash in the top. She carried his body to the basket Livia had lined with blankets for him and laid him down, straightening his ears. It didn't help Flap, but it did help Cass, a little, and she hoped it would do something for Livia. Cass's finger was still bleeding and dropping gouts of wet blood wherever she went. She remembered the Kleenex in her pocket and used it to wrap round the cut.

'Thank you,' Livia was saying. 'Now, Christopher, let that boy go.'

'What?' he and Cass said in unison. 'He's…'

'She broke my fucking arm,' yelled the boy.

'No, she didn't,' Christopher said. 'Or you couldn't wave it around like that. Keep still. Livia…'

'Let him go.' Livia's voice was astonishingly strong.

Cass, who was kneeling at her feet, put a hand on her shoulder and tried to press her back into the rocking chair. The blood had soaked through the tissue and was leaving marks on Livia's sweater.

'Christopher, let go of that boy and unlock the others from your car. Now.'

'Livia, he can't,' Cass said urgently. 'Not after what they've done to you.'

'Let him go. Now. And, Cass, get some plaster on that cut. You're making a mess.' Livia put back her head, her eyes narrowing. 'Listen.'

They all heard it then, a siren in the distance, then an engine.

'Christopher, let him go at once.' Livia's voice was harsher, but still full of authority.

Christopher hesitated, then did as she said. The boy rushed for the door, looking from one to the next, as though he expected to be jumped.

'And the ones from the car. Quickly.'

'Livia, why?' Cass demanded, as Christopher went to obey.

'They're children, Cass.'

'Lethal children.' Cass felt as though she'd been stopped half-way through a bungy jump and was hanging at someone else's mercy, bouncing in the air. 'It's irresponsible not to…'

'Cass, you don't know what you're talking about.' Livia smiled faintly. 'So don't say it. Go and get some plaster. It's in the kitchen.'

In spite of the blood still oozing down her face, the big bruise blackening at the side and the fact that her lip was split in two places, Livia looked more dignified and in control than Cass had ever known her.

'You don't know what it's like to be taken to a police station and questioned and locked in, and hauled into court. I do. And I do not want it done to Bobby.'

'But…'

'Cass, listen to me. Bobby tried to stop them. He obviously had no idea they had a knife. But with his record, he wouldn't have a chance. Now go and deal with that cut.' In a much rougher voice, she added: 'I can't bear watching you bleed.'

With a strange feeling of *déjà vu*, Cass washed her finger at the kitchen sink and stuck plaster on it. When she came back, Livia was still sitting in the rocking chair, apparently unmoved by the blood and sick and the corpse of her dog.

Christopher came back, looking grim, as the sound of the siren shrieked into full volume just outside the house, and tyres squealed before the engine stopped.

A very young police officer in uniform appeared behind him.

'What's been going on here?' he demanded in a soft local voice that did nothing to disguise the threat.

'As you see,' Christopher said firmly before either of the women could speak. 'Ms. Evesham and I arrived about ten minutes ago to find some children assaulting her grandmother. Look at what they've done to her. There's the knife they used.'

The young officer looked at the Stanley knife, then bent to peer at Livia's injuries. Cass was holding her hand, which was absurd. Livia didn't need either comfort or reassurance. The young officer put gentle fingers under Livia's chin to turn her face to the light.

'I'm all right,' Livia said. 'It's all quite superficial. There's no need to make such a fuss. It's not important.'

'I don't think you need an ambulance. But you do need a cup of tea, don't you?' He looked towards Cass, who stumbled to her feet.

'Yes, of course. We could all do with that. Sugar, Livia?'

'For shock?' she asked drily. 'Well, why not? Who called you, Constable?'

'A man called Bernard Goodwood. Luckily we were in the area or we'd never have got here so soon.'

'Who?'

'He said he's a photographer. He saw the kids come to your door, but he didn't realize anything was wrong until some of them started running out, crying.'

'He's got a telephoto lens, then. We had an injunction to move them all off.'

Cass couldn't understand how Livia could sound so calm. She knew exactly what the photographer would have said when he called the police. His camera and his imagination would have shown him terrified children fleeing the Harpy's lair. Cass glanced at Christopher, whose face gave nothing away. There was nothing for it but to make the tea.

When she came back with a tray full of mugs, there was another constable, a young blonde woman, who had obviously been running. Her face was tomato-coloured and beaded with sweat. She was still panting.

'I'd have caught that last one if I hadn't tripped in a sodding rabbit hole,' she said. 'I need his name.'

'I don't know it.' Livia's voice was firm. 'And there's nothing for you to do. I'm sorry you were bothered. It was just a game—a boy's game—that went wrong.'

'You must persuade her, sir,' the other officer was saying quietly to Christopher as Cass came to offer them tea. She felt as though she were in a madhouse. A game? What could Livia be thinking of?

'It's her business,' Christopher said equally quietly. 'Her choice. I'd hang them up by their thumbs if it were left to me. But it's not.'

'Is she afraid of them? Intimidated?'

'Does she seem intimidated?'

Cass and the constable both turned to look at Livia. If it had not been for the mess the boys had made of her face, Cass wouldn't have believed that she'd had anything but the most peaceful of mornings. Hoping Livia's self-control wouldn't make the police believe she'd played a part in what had been done to her, Cass gave her a cup of tea.

'You're shocked and frightened,' the woman officer was saying. Her colour was nearly normal again, but impatience was roughening her voice and making her placatory words sound like a threat. 'I quite understand that. I can see why you don't want to give us a statement now. We'll leave you with your granddaughter to rest, and come back tomorrow. You'll have had time to sleep on it then.'

'It would be perfectly delightful to see you tomorrow,' Livia said in the voice of a vicar's wife opening the local fête, 'but I shan't change my mind. Ah, Cass, this is good tea. Thank you.'

They stood absurdly drinking tea and making polite conversation around Livia's chair. When she had finished hers, she put the cup on the floor and started to push herself to her feet. Cass put a hand under her elbow to steady her.

'Thank you both so much for coming to my rescue,' she said, still gracious and in charge. 'I won't trouble you any more now. My granddaughter and Mr Bromyard will look after me.'

She stood erect, smiling and nodding gravely until the police officers obediently got rid of their teacups and left the house. The others heard the engine start and the car crunch over the stones.

Cass felt the brittle arm she was holding tremble, then shake. She was only just in time to catch Livia as she sagged.

'Christopher!' she called as he ran to help.

Between them they lowered Livia on to the sofa. Tears were pouring out of her eyes, diluting the rusty bloodstains. She was sobbing so hard that her whole body was wrenched with each gasp. Cass thought she would choke or be sick any minute. She crouched beside Livia, stroking her head as gently as possible, trying to think of the right thing to do. Or say.

Christopher waited until Livia's worst paroxysms were over, then he said her name. She looked up and tried to smile.

'Sorry,' she gasped. 'Just reaction. I'll be fine in a moment.'

'I don't want to interfere, Livia, but would you like me to get hold of Doctor Presteigne?'

She shook her head. 'No fuss, Christopher. It's all over after all. I'll be all right in a minute.'

There were still tears in her eyes, and her lips were mumbling against each other. Shaken, Cass still did not know what to do to help. As Christopher spoke again, she realized she didn't have to do anything. For the first time since childhood she was not solely responsible.

'I know you don't, Livia,' Christopher said. 'And I understand. But shouldn't the cuts at least be checked out? You might be risking infection of some sort.'

'They're not big enough to need stitches. The policewoman told me that, and the blood will have washed away most of the germs.'

Livia's voice was more controlled, but she looked dreadful. And every so often the rhythm of her breathing would change, hang for a moment, before it got going again. Her eyes were still so hurt that Cass's teeth ached.

A knock at the door startled them all. Livia grabbed the back of the sofa as though she were afraid she might fall off.

'Don't worry,' Christopher said, striding towards the door. 'I'll see to it.'

His bulk blocked Cass's view as he opened the door. Livia swung her legs off the sofa, ready to face whatever happened.

'What do you want?' Christopher's voice was stern enough to make the women look at each other in surprise. There was no answer. Cass leaned sideways so that she could just see round him. Bobby was standing in the doorway, holding out a bedraggled bunch of daffodils.

'You'd better come in.'

'No. She won't want…I've wrote a letter.'

'Bobby? Is that you?' Livia's voice was impressively firm. 'Please come in. Please.'

Christopher stepped aside. Cass saw Bobby's face, dirty and swollen with tears. He came crabwise through the doorway and towards the sofa, holding out his ragged bouquet like an anti-vampire charm.

'They're lovely,' Livia said. He came a little closer.

Cass saw huge straggling letters on a piece of paper wrapped round them flowers. The only word she could make out seemed to be 'sory'.

'I've wrote you a note.'

Cass backed silently away, gesturing to Christopher. Together they went outside.

# Epilogue

### HARPY INTO HEROINE

'Only a game that went too far,' says Livia Claughton.

Police hopes of charging the gang of boys who broke into her Lake District hideaway and viciously assaulted her were dashed when she stuck by her story that they didn't mean any harm. Parents of likely local suspects think she's wonderful, but police are furious. Without identification of the boys, they've nothing to go on.

Her granddaughter, Cass Evesham, who saved her life, says, 'I'll do whatever Livia wants'. (*For Julia Gainsborough's reaction, see page 3*).

There was a three-column-wide photograph of the Harpy, bruised and cut and looking like a sweet old lady who wouldn't hurt a fly, and beside her, Cass, dressed in sagging khaki combat trousers and a short, tight black sweater. She looked amazing.

Gary pushed his copy of the *Post* over the top of his screen towards Sam, who raised his eyebrows as he talked into the phone that was clamped between his shoulder and his chin. Sam reached for the paper and glanced at the pictures while still talking. His eyes popped and he looked up, suddenly focusing on someone behind Gary.

Turning to see who Sam was waving at, Gary saw Cass. She swung her jacket off her shoulders and round the back of her chair in one flamboyant movement. She looked even better than in the photograph. Her shirt was the colour of ripe raspberries, which added a glow to her cheeks, and she had new, socking great pearl earrings gleaming under the ragged edge of her short dark hair. They looked real. Presumably a present from Christopher Bromyard.

For once Gary couldn't think of anything to say. Cass laughed at him.

'It's a great photo, Cass,' Sam said, putting down his phone. 'Much better than the Greek one, and that was pretty special.'

Cass made a face.

'Don't worry about it,' Sam said. 'It made us all laugh. And this one'll have your clients flocking back, if I know them. How about coming to celebrate in Corney & Barrow tonight?'

'Great, Sam. I'd like that.' She looked at Gary's fat face. 'Oh, come on. Stop pouting, Gary. You can't have wanted me and my grandmother starring as tabloid villains for ever, can you?'

He stared at her, his little piggy eyes hard.

'Cass!' Michael Betteridge's familiar shout distracted her for a second.

'Coming, Michael!' She lowered her voice. 'Come on, Gary: isn't there the slightest speck of generosity in you anywhere? Be pleased for me. Just this once. Then I'll let you off the rest.'

His eyes narrowed even more as the flesh around them was squeezed tight. It was so unexpected, that Cass didn't realize the expression was a smile for a good five seconds.

'Only if I don't have to congratulate you on your sodding bonus,' he said. 'They seem to believe you've earned one. Can't think why.'

'Cass! Get your arse in gear.'

'Sorry Michael. Gary, I'd forgotten it was bonus day.'

'Go and get it. Then you can pay for the champagne tonight.'

As she passed the back of his chair, she dropped a kiss on the top of his head, raising a cheer from the whole trading floor. She lifted her right hand high above her head and waggled her fingers at them as she walked towards Michael's expectant face.

# FLASH FLOOD
## THE FIRST DAN MAHONEY MYSTERY
### by Susan Slater

ISBN: 0-7434-7959-9

Dan Mahoney, insurance investigator, lands in Tatum, New Mexico, where several prize cattle on the famed Double Horeshoe Ranch have mysteriously died. The claims put a lot of money at stake for Dan's company, but that just scratches the surface of the hijinks—and high stakes—afoot in Tatum. And Dan hadn't counted on witnessing a murder, falling in love, or becoming a pawn of federal agents.

It's the flash flood that changes everything, as Dan stumbles across secrets that implicate his employer, his sister, and what seems like half of southern New Mexico. Sucked into small town duplicity, he struggles with truth and learns that dead men can come back to haunt.

To receive a catalog of other Poisoned Pen Press titles,
please contact us in one of the following ways:

Phone: 1-800-421-3976
Facsimile: 1-480-949-1707
Email: info@poisonedpenpress.com
Website: www.poisonedpenpress.com

Poisoned Pen Press
6962 E. First Ave. Ste. 103
Scottsdale, AZ 85251